# Serial

## by

## N.E. Castle

PublishAmerica
Baltimore

First printing

PublishAmerica has allowed this work to remain exactly as the author intended, verbatim, without editorial input.

All characters in this book are fictitious, and any resemblance to real persons, living or dead, is coincidental.

Hardcover 978-1-4489-2981-8
Softcover 1-60474-119-8
PAperback 978-1-4512-4257-7
PUBLISHED BY PUBLISHAMERICA, LLLP
www.publishamerica.com
Baltimore

Printed in the United States of America

In memory of my mother, Shirley, who always
inspired the impossible.

# Acknowledgments

Thank you to my friends and family who encouraged me by sharing their enjoyment in reading my first drafts of *Serial*. Many thanks to my best friend, Edward, for pushing me to finish this book and for having faith to take it to market; Edward's love of this book and his dedication to marketing it have made it possible for you to read and enjoy *Serial*.

# Chapter 1

Laurie Sharpe downshifted her Chevy Camero, encouraging it up the long steep ramp from Plantation Street onto the busy Route 290 expressway—headed home! She merged into traffic as the setting sun glared in her eyes, blinding her. A deafening horn startled her as a tractor pulling two full size trailers scraped by, bullying its way up the long steep incline with speed borrowed from the trip down the previous hill. Laurie swallowed her stomach and applied the brake generously to avoid plowing into the side of the second trailer.

She shot a glance over her shoulder and sized up a space barely large enough for her car to squeeze into between the tail end of the trailer and a heating oil delivery truck surging up the hill in its wake. She carefully angled the Camero into the narrow gap as the oil truck grudgingly granted her space rather than sandwich her into the tractor-trailer.

Bumper-to-bumper traffic with the blinding sun in her eyes—joy! Fourteen miles and a half-hour to go, Laurie affectionately patted the dash of the 1978 convertible that she and her father had worked to restore after she'd bought it for $300 from a farmer who had it rusting in a field of tall grass and nettles.

She popped a CD into the stereo and the sounds of George Winston's piano echoed through the car as she strummed her fingers in time on the steering wheel. She loved George. With the modern stereo she'd added to the dash the notes were so clear and crisp, she felt like she was curled up inside the piano itself, feeling the wires vibrate against her heart.

This was Laurie's ideal for winding down after ten hours of investigating crime and dealing with the dregs of Worcester, not to think of the stacks of paperwork that accompanied all the fun.

She moved into a snug position behind another tractor-trailer to shield out the bright sun and settled into the slow highway crawl of traffic moving along in stops and starts—an inch here, a foot there—until Route 290 took its sharp turn to the left, putting the bright sun to the right of the traffic instead of into the drivers' eyes.

With the solar glare gone, the distance between the cars lengthened and their speed increased as Laurie glanced left in time to see a long stretch of empty asphalt. She adroitly pulled the wheel sharply to the left, sliding out from behind the truck, and stepped heavily on the gas pedal to force her Camero to match speed with the other cars in the left lane that were rushing to close the gap.

Finally, she settled back in her seat and began to whistle along with Winston's music as the stark buildings of downtown Worcester drifted by on her right. The old Union Station, now restored to its former glory after years of abandonment, glowed a brilliant orange in the rays of the setting sun. Laurie marveled at its beauty as she always did. City officials had made a tremendous effort to improve Worcester's dilapidated appearance—adding cobblestones where they had long since disappeared; tearing down vacant buildings that had been vandalized into skeletons and repairing those that were worth saving.

The blue Camero skirted a familiar pothole as she guided it into the first turn of the S-curve by the College of the Holy Cross. The perilous design of the highway here had contributed to many accidents, but Laurie thought little of those tragedies as she casually sped along at an overzealous speed of sixty-five, the car lurching as it struck each seam in the bridgework.

A middle-aged woman in a classy black Cadillac cast her an angry look as the Camero struck a pothole and careened in her direction, but Laurie took it in stride. She knew this road with her eyes closed, knew just how much each seam and each pothole would throw her off course. Smiling at the woman in the Cadillac, she gently guided the car away from her as she rounded the far side of the S-curve and turned into the final stretch toward home.

The driving was easier now that she was on the outskirts of the city. Laurie took a moment to adjust the volume on the stereo until the dashboard reverberated with sound.

Hunter pulled the steering wheel hard to the right to make the last opening into the parking lot in front of the Men's Warehouse. He was eager for an evening out, an evening of satisfying his taste for fear and death.

He usually dressed casually for his game, but the thought of wearing dress clothes for play this evening appealed to him. Perhaps he could be an attorney tonight. And what type of girl did he fancy? Should he choose a casual woman or a businesswoman? Older or younger?

He pulled the car into a parking spot right in front of the door and hopped out eagerly. Visions of bright blood on pale skin flickered brilliantly in his thoughts. Maybe Boston wasn't the right place for him tonight as he'd originally thought. Maybe instead he'd turn around and go back to Worcester or maybe Springfield. Worcester, he decided. He had a good feel for playing in Worcester, even if it was a little close to home. Just this once he would play in his own backyard. It would be so exciting! He hit the remote lock for the car and headed into the store, smiling happily to himself.

Laurie left the highway as she entered Auburn and at last pulled into the driveway of her Cape Cod style house. The blue paint had begun to peel this year, but she was still as proud of it as the day she bought the little house. It was all hers and no one else's, and she would paint it herself as soon as her schedule was clear. She parked in the driveway—the garage was reserved for yard equipment and clutter that had overflowed from the house—and gathered up the stack of papers, reports, and evidence she had planned to review over the weekend.

Clutching her homework to her chest, she fumbled with the key and almost lost the stack onto the floor of the front entry when the door flew open, slamming against the wall. She kicked it shut behind her, worked her shoes off with a toe to each heel, and stumbled to the couch where she unloaded her arms into one big, jumbled heap.

"So good to be home!" she sighed and padded toward the kitchen in her socks. She took the water filter from the refrigerator and poured herself a glass, refilling the reservoir so it could seep down through the carbon filter. After watching it drip a moment, she returned the pitcher to the refrigerator.

Sipping at the water, she pulled a clip from her hair and tossed it onto the counter. She ran her hand through the thick blonde curls that fell to her shoulders as she glanced toward the answering machine with its red message indicator flashing rhythmically.

"Who might you be? Jeff?" She checked the caller ID and then pushed the button to retrieve messages.

Jeff's voice filled the small kitchen. "Hello, love. I've missed you today. Work was hell. Call me. Maybe I could take you to dinner?"

Laurie smiled warmly. "Of course you can," she breathed before punching the erase button.

She and Jeff had been dating six months and every minute with him was wonderful. Did that mean she loved him? Occasionally, they had discussed their feelings for each other. Jeff was not afraid of commitment, so gradually she was learning to trust him, but somewhere deep inside her, experience warned to keep at least one toe on solid ground so she could easily find it if she had to, though she didn't think she would.

Jeff was a hopeless romantic who was falling in love and was trying to pull her in with him. And maybe she *was* falling in love with him. Not only was he sexy, Jeff was funny, full of energy, and had an endless supply of ideas on where to go and what to do and managed to talk her into doing all of them. He'd even talked her into hiking, something she otherwise hated, on Wachusett Mountain. They had ridden the chairlift afterwards, cuddling up together thirty feet in the air to watch the view. It was well worth the hike. He promised to take her skiing there in the winter or maybe up to New Hampshire where, after skiing, they could rent a condo and snuggle by a warm, cozy fire. "…If we're still together," she mumbled aloud—always wary. But she looked forward to this weekend when they planned to take a ferry out to Provincetown at the tip of Cape Cod. She loved the ocean but never seemed to see enough of it. Jeff had remedied that with countless trips to the water.

She sipped languidly at her water, pulled the cordless phone off the wall and strolled back toward the living room where she plopped herself onto the overstuffed couch.

The line rang twice. "Hello?" Jeff's low soft voice flowed soothingly over the phone. Of course, he knew it would be Laurie calling. Caller ID took the surprise out of answering the phone. He waited expectantly for her voice from the other end of the line.

"I missed you," she said softly. "Work was crazy today."

"I've missed you, too," he said tentatively.

"Is everything alright?" She asked sympathetically. Work generally wore him out.

"Oh. I'm fine, just had a long, stressful day. I'll tell you about it over dinner tonight. I'll pick you up around seven?"

Jeff was doing his residency at the University of Massachusetts emergency room, where they met while she was questioning one of his trauma patients. It was a busy ER and he frequently brought stress home with him. Laurie tried to lend her support and listen, but often, he refused to discuss his work, saying he'd been there ten hours too long and didn't need to relive any of them. She wondered if he would still want to be a doctor at the end of his residency.

"Sounds good. I'll see you later, love." Laurie hung up the phone and looked at her watch. Quarter past five.

Laurie smiled as she considered moving up the time of their date. Jeff needed stress relief and she would surprise him with just that. She stripped out of her work clothes, showered, donned a lacy teddy under slinky black dress and was out the door in less than fifteen minutes.

Nicely supplied with a not-too-expensive pair of gray slacks, and a designer shirt and tie that were likewise on sale—there was no sense paying a fortune for clothing he would wear only once and discard—the hunter headed west on Route 9 toward Worcester singing along to a 60's tune on the radio, adding lyrics to fit his mood.

*It's been a hard day, yeah and now I'm looking for a fight.*

*It's been a hard day, yeah; and I'll be hunting in the night.*
*And when I go out tonight I'll cut her throat with my knife*
*And then I'll feel all right. And she'll be dead, oh yeah.*

He had his usual preparations to do at home: showering, brushing and plucking away any loose hairs, and making sure he was free of anything that he might leave behind that could be connected to him later. It was a whole ritual that he enjoyed nearly as much as the hunt, itself, right down to covering the pads of his fingertips with an invisible layer of silicon gel to hide his fingerprints.

The phone rang and he turned down the volume on the radio before he answered the call.

"Hello?"

The voice on the other end of the phone was familiar and Hunter spoke for a while, dodging in and out of traffic, eager to be home preparing for his evening tonight. But gradually, he slowed, and then pulled to the right lane behind a long line of steadily moving traffic as he disconnected the call. Play would have to wait; he had work to do. But he would play soon. He'd already decided, was excited about the prospect, and would save it for the very next available night when his time was not otherwise occupied.

Laurie took the last empty parking space at the liquor store. She hopped out of the car, was into the store and checking back out with a bottle of very fine Chianti, Jeff's favorite wine, in less than five minutes. He lived in a duplex on the far side of town and she made the trip in record time. But as she drove down his street, she began to feel uneasy. *I don't usually drop in on him like this.* She drove ahead hesitantly and pulled into the narrow driveway.

Suddenly, Laurie's hands froze to the wheel and her body went numb. A woman emerged from the front door, stepping backwards with her lips still clinging to Jeff's mouth. Laurie recognized the married mother of two who lived two doors down the street. Jeff pulled his face away from hers and met Laurie's horrified look with a dry smile. He patted his secret lover's generous rump and sent her skipping giddily back home; her long, wavy chestnut hair messed and matted from their afternoon activities.

Laurie sat for a moment, holding Jeff's stare. Then she silently heaved the bottle of wine as hard as she could, smashing it on the black asphalt of the driveway. She did not look back as her foot pressed heavily on the gas and brought her halfway across town before she cooled enough to slow down.

Her hands trembled and she gripped the wheel tightly to steady herself. "Goddammit!" she yelled aloud. "Fucking asshole!" She fought the burning in her eyes and the threat of tears. She would not cry for that son of a bitch. How could he make her think he was so in love and so infatuated with her, and then turn to some trampy housewife from down the street? And how long had he been seeing the tramp? Was he with her before every date they had? After all, he was with her today and planned to see Laurie tonight. Laurie shuddered and bit into her lower lip; the pain drove the tears back and she breathed a little easier, while her mind raced with a history of failed relationships and a hundred questions tormented her.

Are all men like Jeff? Are they really all the same as every woman insisted? She knew of women who had found love or seemed to find it. Were their men really faithful or just better at concealment? She had to believe love was real or she wouldn't stand a chance. Dwelling on Jeff's bullshit wouldn't help either. Just move on and maybe the next man will prove every woman wrong. *Dream the impossible, but seek the support of friends until you achieve it.*

She picked up the cell phone hanging from a clip on the dashboard and activated the speed dial. After three rings, she heard the click as the line opened at the other end.

"Hello?"

"Jessie! How are you, girlfriend?" There was a brief silence in response.

"Okay, what's wrong?" Jessie had been like a sister since high school. She could always tell from Laurie's tone of voice exactly why she was calling. She knew before she was told that the relationship with Jeff was over, but she silently listened to her friend's brief accounting of the events that had just transpired.

"Sounds like you need a drink," she offered. "I could meet you at Pete's in about twenty minutes."

"You read my mind, as always. I'll see you there." Laurie replaced the phone on its clip and turned a sharp right onto the Route 290 onramp, headed east.

She cranked up the volume on the radio and sang along with *Queen*, but even music from her favorite rock band couldn't stop her punishing herself. Laurie's mind turned over and over with memories of times she and Jeff had shared. His emotions had seemed so real! *How in hell could a woman even begin to believe what any man might say when they all seemed to walk the same path?* She had been certain Jeff was sincere with his feelings, yet he cozies up with that pathetic slut!

*Enough! He's not worth another thought.*

Laurie suddenly swerved left into the empty outer lane, narrowly avoiding a tractor-trailer that slid into her lane without warning. *Too bad I'm not a traffic cop anymore.* She brushed off the chill from the narrow miss and settled into the outer lane, cruising along undisturbed for the remainder of the trip until she reached her exit.

Jessie was already sitting comfortably at the bar. Laurie recognized the tight curls of chestnut hair that fell to her shoulders and the way the bartender focused his attention upon her, flirting shamelessly. All men flirted with Jessie, it seemed. She was a magnet that pulled them to her, willing or not.

A glass of Captain Morgan's Parrot Bay rum was already on the bar for Laurie. It was her "had a bad day" drink and always made her think of a poolside bar across from the most beautiful white sandy beach she could imagine.

"Sweetie, how 'bout you leave my friend and I for some girl talk, OK?" Jessie smiled at the bartender and waved him away as Laurie threw her pocketbook on the counter and slid onto the stool beside her.

"Sure thing, babe." The flirtatious bartender gave Laurie a dead smile, accompanied by a once-over, then moved away with a sullen expression. His eyes kept darting back to Jessie from the far end of the bar, but he left the women to themselves.

"So, what happened? I thought he was prince charming on a white horse." Jessie held a Manhattan to her artistically applied plum-colored mouth.

Laurie rolled her eyes to the ceiling. "Everything was going so well, too. I mean last we were together, this past Saturday, he was just wonderful. I was actually a little nervous because I thought he wanted us to move in together. He took me shopping for a dining room table for his place at Jordan's in Framingham. We had a great time, too, I might add. He was pretty romantic—kept grabbing me for a kiss. He kept asking my opinion on whatever he looked at—said he wanted to be sure I could live with it if we were to have a place together. I mean, that sounds pretty serious, doesn't it?"

"Yeah, that's serious for a guy. What did you say to him?" Jessie angled her body away from the bartender who was still trying to flirt from the far end of the bar.

"I was sort of shocked when he said that. I don't think I really responded at first. Then I told him I would like anything he chose." She paused. "Shit! I guess maybe I could have shown a little more interest, maybe a little more commitment."

"Maybe a little. Even if it was just to call his bluff. I mean, that wasn't the first time he hinted at sharing a place, was it?"

"I guess not. Funny, he's actually been saying stuff like that right from the beginning, but he never really comes right out and discusses us getting a place together. He just throws out these subtle hints. You think he's just been teasing me—looking for a reaction?"

Jessie thought a moment. "You know, it's bullshit, but I think some guys actually do that. My friend, Cyndi, went through the same thing with a guy she dated for a year. It's like a game to them. They just want to see your expression, I think. Maybe just to see if you're still interested. Or maybe they think they'll get better sex if they dangle a carrot."

Laurie chuckled sadly. "Maybe it really is just about sex. I mean sex is good, but it's not everything."

Jessie nodded. "Half the time they're not even that good. I can get more satisfaction from toys."

"Jeff wasn't all that great," Laurie snickered. "He wasn't a hands-on man, I guess you could say.

"Oh girl, the guy's got to have good hands. Otherwise, you really might as well just go out and buy a dildo. If they can't touch you in all the right places, just dump them. Was he at least a good kisser?"

Laurie's cheeks flushed, and she nervously sipped her drink. "You really are obnoxious, you know."

"Just looking out for my friend's best interest. There are a million choices out there. You're beautiful so you have your choice of at least three quarters of them. Why would you waste your time with bad sex and head games?

"In my defense, I didn't know about the head games until now."

"Bad sex is a good indicator. Just remember that. If there's no magic in their touch, there's no magic in their heart.

"What're you the old wise woman of Worcester now?"

"Yep. And I'm keeping your sexual interests at heart. You should be glad you're still single. Here's to freedom!" She held up her glass, showed a full set of perfect pearly teeth in a glowing smile and winked.

Laurie hesitated a moment, then smiled hopefully. "To hell with Jeff," she said softly.

"What was that? I didn't hear you."

Laurie grinned. "To hell with Jeff!" she asserted.

"Much better. Now go out and find good sex." She touched her drink to Laurie's and drank the rest.

The bartender eagerly rushed over when he saw Jessie's empty glass. Jessie smiled and ordered them another round. Then their conversation moved on to Jessie's life, which had its own set of bumps and scrapes.

"You think you find the worst. Last week I was at a bar at the golf course after nine holes and this guy, not great-looking, but not homely either, slides up after sending me a drink. He started feeding me this story line about his new company, telling me how fast it's growing and how it would be nice if he had someone to share it with. Then, just when I'm thinking he's a little more attractive than not, his wife walks up and taps him on the shoulder."

Laurie's mouth dropped open and she laughed.

"Yep. This guy actually has the gall to introduce me to his wife like we're old friends and he hadn't just been trying to pick me up. She was not impressed, but I just played up the old friend thing with the 'Wow Frank, you didn't tell me you'd gotten married!' I shook the wife's hand and gave her a wink. She got the hint and for the next hour we shared drinks and I made up stories of when Frank and I used to know each other and she told all sorts of embarrassing stories about him. You should have seen him squirm—every man's worst nightmare."

"You're too funny," Laurie giggled as she sipped her drink. "And the wife knew that you and her husband didn't really know each other?"

"Oh, she knew. We left him at the bar to pay the check. I suggested she keep a sharp eye on him and of course thanked her for her sense of humor and for understanding that I had no idea he was attached. She said it wasn't the first time he'd done that, but that she'd not ever known him to actually succeed at picking up another woman. She thought it was just a game he played. She was way too nice and way too trusting. He definitely didn't deserve her."

Laurie shook her head slowly. "What a bastard! I don't know why some men are so ridiculously sleazy."

"I swear, I think they like the risk. They always do it where they know they might get caught—like this guy flirting with me while he's waiting for his wife. I think the chance of being caught is half the thrill for them. Maybe it makes for better sex for them later. Me, I just want a little sanity from a guy." Jessie grabbed a bowl full of peanuts and began pulling the shells off, throwing them onto the already shell-covered floor.

"And good sex."

Jessie grinned. "Yes. And good sex."

Let's be fair, though. There are plenty of horrible women out there too. Too bad men like Frank can't just get together with them and leave us good girls for the good guys. But it doesn't work that way."

"Yeah. What do they say? Opposites attract? So we sane women get the nutty men and the sane men get all the nutty women." Jessie glanced at her watch. "Actually, I'm supposed to meet a guy for dinner. Are you all right? Or should I just blow him off? I mean he could turn out to be a loser. I don't really know him and I wouldn't want to leave you on your own tonight for some loser."

"No." Laurie laughed. "I have some work to do at home. I'll be fine. You go ahead." She started to pull out her wallet to pay the bartender.

"Don't be silly," Jessie protested. You can buy drinks next time I get dumped. I got this one." She threw twenty bucks onto the bar. "Ready?"

"Yeah, thanks and I'll buy next time, whether or not you get dumped." Laurie gathered her things and joined Jessie heading out then paused, ready to push the door open, and smiled at her.

"For the record, I officially dumped him."

# Chapter 2

Neighbors Bank was empty at one-thirty; its lunch crowd of merchants with their bags of earnings from the morning's business had been and gone. As the only bank in Tatnuck Square, it attracted most of the local business owners and bank management prided themselves on providing a relaxed and friendly atmosphere for its clientele, including open counters that lacked the usual bulletproof barriers and young, attractive tellers in their twenties with no shortage of smiles and friendly remarks for the clients. The sunshine that the girls were urged to exude even brought some of the local merchants in several times a day.

Sharon smiled broadly at the proprietor of the gas station down on the corner. This was his third time in today and, as always, he had come to her window so he could flirt. The man was hideous, with a pockmarked face and too many pounds on his too-short frame, but she acted her most charming like she was expected to do. She really just wanted to tell him where to go.

She took the bag that he tossed up onto the counter and said a quick prayer before opening it that she wouldn't catch anything deadly by touching it.

"So, how's it going, Sharon?" Lenny, that was his name, reached his hand across the counter in the not-so-secret hope that she might touch him, even if by accident. Though he'd been married three years, he liked this girl. His wife never looked this fresh and sexy, even when they'd first met, but she was the best he had thought he would ever get for his looks, even with all his money.

"Hi Lenny, how are you this hour?" Sharon gushed between clenched teeth, trying to ignore the greasy hand on her counter, which would have to be wiped down with a strong cleaner after he'd gone. She counted the bands of bills as quickly as she could, careful not to look up, even as she spoke to him.

"You know, I could take you someplace really nice with all that dough."

"That's awful sweet of you, but I'm engaged." She never would have believed that Lenny was actually married even if he did wear his ring. How any woman would consider touching this man simply appalled her.

"We wouldn't have to tell him. Maybe you'd rather be with me anyway. Does this guy have money like this?" He reached his hand further toward her, almost grabbing the other side of the counter as he pointed a chubby finger at the bills she was counting.

Sharon cringed inwardly—almost done, just one more band. She wet her finger on the sponge and quickly flipped through the band, then punched the total into her system. Three thousand, six hundred dollars only four hours after his last visit. But not enough to make him attractive.

"All set, Lenny! See you next time!" She quickly handed him a deposit slip and waved him away. Then, before he could object, she turned and headed into the backroom to hide and to wash her hands, of course, until he had left. Sharon had a hand on the bathroom door when a crescendo of screams and shouts brought her running back to the front of the bank in time to see two men dressed all in black, with nylons over their faces, waving handguns at the tellers while they barked orders.

Sharon gasped and ducked back behind the wall, but one of the robbers had already seen her.

"You! Blondie in the back there! Get out here now!" He was well over six feet and his voice boomed like thunder when he bellowed at her.

Sharon hesitated a moment, her legs shaking uncontrollably. Finally, she started to move out from behind the wall, but not before a shot rang out and a bullet struck the corner of the wall over her head. She threw her hands up as plaster showered down on her. Then, ducking low, she cautiously stepped out and stumbled toward her station.

The tall man in black threw a bag up on the counter in front of her. "No dye packs. I want to see you fan each handful of bands you put into the bag, but you better do it fast. You got fifteen seconds. Now!" He shouted, and threatened again with the gun when she didn't move immediately.

Five thousand dollars just in her drawer alone. She wasn't supposed to keep that much money, but she had just taken it in from Lenny the creep. Sharon quickly fanned the bills before throwing them into the bag, carefully avoiding the dye pack that was at the bottom of the drawer beneath the twenties.

The robber stopped her with several hundred still left in the drawer. He wasn't taking any chances. Almost two minutes had elapsed since they had walked into the bank and it was time to run before the cops arrived. They turned and fled to a black sedan parked at the front door, then disappeared up the street a whole three minutes before the first police cruiser arrived with its sirens blaring.

Fear had subsided and the people in the bank were milling about in little pockets of gossip when Laurie Sharpe arrived with Gunnar Hincks, her partner of two years. The bank doors had been locked and a handwritten sign was taped to the door that stated simply, "Closed." The eight police cruisers packed into the tiny parking lot would have told anyone passing by that there had been a robbery.

Gunnar strode toward the group of tellers talking loudly against the back wall, taking particular interest in the leggy blonde wearing a short skirt, while Laurie approached the manager, an average height, scrawny, balding man with a sweaty brow who looked like he might break into tears at any moment.

"Couldn't you send away some of these cars?" the bank manager whimpered. "It's bad for business. People like to feel that their bank is a hundred percent secure. They don't really want to think what would have happened if they had been here." He ran a shaky hand through hair that was wet with nervous sweat. He'd never been through a robbery before and worried that it would affect his career.

"I can do that in just a moment, but first could you give me a description of the robbers? Did you see them?" Laurie pulled out a notebook and waited for his response, pencil poised expectantly. The manager's worries about a few extra police cars in the lot didn't concern her—she was all business.

But the manager, though shaken, was not daunted. "No...." he said slowly, deliberately in a voice that threatened to crack. "First, get rid of some of these police officers. They don't all need to be here now. We could have used them before, but now they just make us look bad. Once they're gone, I'll talk to you." He folded his arms emphatically across his concave chest.

Laurie hesitated, measuring his defiance, but decided that giving the mousy little man this small victory would get her more information. "Fair enough," she said and turned toward the captain, ranking uniform on the scene, to relay the manager's request. The captain nodded and began herding the officers out the door. Once the cars were pulling out of the lot, the bank manager nodded stiffly and motioned Laurie to his desk where they sat on opposite sides.

He took a deep breath and some color seemed to return to his face. When he spoke, his voice was parched. "There's not really a whole lot I can tell you about these guys. They wore black nylon over their faces, long sleeves, pants, gloves. I couldn't really even be sure of the color of their skin, since they didn't leave anything uncovered. Both looked like they were in great shape— no extra weight at all. The tall one was about six-four, based on those measurements they post next to the door," he pointed toward the entrance of the bank, "medium build, I guess. The other one was my height, about five-eight, also medium built. They put us all through these trainings on how to handle a robbery and what to remember about the robbers. I never thought I'd ever really have to use what I learned." He ran a hand through his hair as his eyes shifted between Laurie and his desk.

Laurie nodded as she quickly jotted notes. "You're doing fine. What else can you tell me?"

"I can get you the film from the security cameras. That'll only take a minute and you can see the details for yourself, but there's not really much to see. The shorter one stopped at my desk when they came in, but he never said anything. Only the tall guy spoke and, this may sound politically incorrect, but even though they were fully covered so I couldn't see their skin, the tall guy sounded white when he spoke. At least, that's my impression."

Laurie smiled reassuringly. "I understand your concern, but no detail is overlooked here, even an impression. I'll just state it that way in my notes."

The bank manager nodded and relaxed a little.

"So, what else? Did you see what kind of guns they carried?"

"Oh God, I don't really know much about guns, I wouldn't know."

Laurie pulled her gun, a nine-millimeter, from its holster and showed it the manager. "Were they like this? Or were they more like what you see in westerns—like a revolver?"

"The one the short guy carried was a revolver, I guess. I didn't see what the other guy had, but the girls might have."

The manager put his head in his hands and shook it side to side. "I really wish I had more to tell you, but they were pretty well covered in black. Even their shoes were black. They looked like a couple of those ninjas you see on TV."

"Any bit of information is important," Laurie prodded. "Did you notice if their clothes were distinctive in any way? You said they had black shoes, were they dress shoes, boots?"

The manager shook his head. "They were more like sneakers or running shoes." He pointed to Laurie's shoes. "Sort of like what you have on. That's really all I saw though. Sorry."

"Don't worry about it. You've been a big help," Laurie lied. Guys with no faces wearing gloves gave them very little to go on and even the supposition that one was white might hurt rather than help them. This wouldn't be an easy case.

She talked to the three customers who were in the bank at the time of the robbery, but none of them saw any more than the bank manager. In fact, they were even less help.

Gunnar strutted over to her after talking with the group of tellers.

"Anything interesting?" he asked. He stood tall, hands on his hips looking every bit the ex-marine that he was. His military-style haircut gave him a threatening, warlike appearance and he liked it like that. Intimidation.

"Not a lot," Laurie replied. "These guys were dressed head-to-toe in black. Nothing really stood out, except maybe their shoes."

Gunnar folded his arms across his chest and waited for the explanation.

Laurie smiled subtly—she had something Gunnar didn't, even though it might be nothing. "The manager said they both had black sneakers like mine. Nobody really wears all-black sneakers except with a uniform. Security guys usually, or cops. They're comfortable but can still pass as professional shoes because they're all black, while most of your every day sneakers have at least some white trim on them.

Gunnar nodded and motioned to his feet, "I've got my own pair for that reason."

"Exactly," she replied. "Also, one of our boys had a revolver. That's about all I got from this guy, that and the security tapes that we'll take with us when we leave.

"What did the tellers have to say?" she asked.

"Well, the blonde over there got shot at." Gunnar enjoyed another look at those stylish legs as he pointed from Sharon to the broken gypsum board.

"She said she had just gone into the back room to wash her hands when she heard them come in. They shot at her because she didn't move fast enough. I dug the bullet out of the plaster." He rolled the bit of lead around in his palm to show her.

"Well, maybe if we're lucky we can get something from that. Anything else?"

Gunnar shook his head. "They couldn't tell me much about the men themselves. They were too scared after the gunshot."

"That and these guys didn't leave much to see of themselves," Laurie added.

When the two detectives had finished interviewing the witnesses, they bid goodbye to the manager and left with the security tapes.

"Well, that gave us a whole lot of nothing to start with," Gunnar mused. "I hope the tapes can give us more."

"Maybe the security tape from the camera outside will have something," Laurie suggested. "I pulled that one from him also. If they put their masks on in the car, we might see a face. Or we could get a plate number."

"Right. If we did get a plate, the car would probably turn up stolen," Gunnar grumbled as he peeled out of the parking lot into traffic.

"But maybe they won't be so smart about prints on the car or fibers. They're probably only concerned with the witnesses in the bank. Maybe they won't think about the car." Laurie said hopefully. "Anyway, we'll get them one way or another. If not this time, they'll probably do another job if they think they got away with this one."

"You're hoping for this?" Gunnar asked.

"No. But they're never smart enough to quit while they're ahead."

"True."

"So, how's Jeff these days?" Gunnar asked as he turned out of the bank. He cast a glance at his partner and noticed her face tense. He shook his head and sighed.

"What's wrong? I thought you two were sweatin' it up," he grinned.

"Nice words from a man's man," Laurie scolded. "I'm done with that asshole. I caught him with some tramp that lives up the street from him."

"Ouch! That's a hell of a turn-around. I thought he was really into you. That's what he told me anyway. Not that long ago, either. Guys don't usually play that up to other guys. You know, we usually talk about whether or not the woman's good in bed, is a great cook, shit like that. We never fess up to loving someone unless it's true. This guy's a jackass if he's cheating on you when he thinks he's in love with you."

"He said that to you? I didn't know you guys got together without me."

"Just once. Bumped into him at a dive down on Shrewsbury Street. So he either meant that shit or he played me too, making me think my friend and partner was safe with him. Shit, that's just low." Gunnar shook his head. "Chin up, though. You're definitely better off without a fuckup like that." Gunnar flashed his toothy smile and jabbed her gently in the arm.

"Right. Thanks. I'll get over him soon enough. The bigger problem is trying to shake that fear of trusting the next man that comes along. What is it with men, anyway? Aren't you ever honest with women? I know, for instance, that you'll say anything to have sex with a woman and do anything to avoid a relationship. Are you all like that and love's really just a pipedream or what?" Laurie looked back to the road in time to see a Dunkin' Donuts approaching.

"Let's grab a coffee," she urged.

Gunnar slowed and turned into the drive-through lane of the donut shop and stopped to place an order.

"Don't think that way, Laur. Not all guys are like me. There's plenty of them out there that really do want kids, and love, and all that crap. Even those that aren't looking for love change their tune when they find that magic woman." He turned and ordered two medium-sized coffees with cream in response to a static request for his order, then pulled forward to the service window.

Laurie giggled. "Sorry, but I can't see you finding that magic woman and having kids."

"Not right now, that's for sure. I like 'em once and if they're really good, twice. I haven't been in bed with a woman who's worth a third go 'round."

"Any other man talked like that, I'd smack them. But from you it just fits."

Gunnar took the coffees from the girl at the window. Seeing his badge, she waved him off when he tried to hand her money. He handed a coffee to Laurie who immediately pulled the top open to sip from it.

"Anyway, there are plenty of guys out there who want to be married, so don't give up looking. Just stop and have a little fun here and there. Good sex is important.

"Now you're starting to sound like Jessie."

"No shit. I knew there was a reason I liked that girl, besides the fact she's got a nice ass."

"Outstanding! I'll be sure to tell her you said so."

Gunnar grinned.

"Thanks for the pep talk, anyway. I'm still facing the gauntlet but thanks for at least trying to get the real deal out of Jeff, even if it was just bullshit."

"Hey, anytime. I'll expect you to interrogate the girl I fall in love with, if that could ever happen." He grinned, and pulled forward into traffic.

The black and white video from the bank's drive-through window showed two black-clad figures climb out of the front and rear passenger seats of a dark-colored Ford Taurus outside the bank. The license plate was mostly obscured by mud, and the two men were covered completely in black as the witnesses had described. The taller man appeared to be in charge and issued orders to the man beside him and to the driver, a black woman with long hair who remained in the car. They played the security tapes taken from the cameras behind the teller's station and watched as the two men stormed through the glass doors into the bank. The tall robber shouted silently at the patrons and swung his handgun in the direction of the tellers. He tossed a bag onto the counter of the first teller, waited for her to fill it and passed on to the next teller. Suddenly, he shouted, looking at an area beneath the camera. Then he aimed and let go a round in that direction. He shouted again and soon the blonde teller appeared and walked toward him slowly, hands held out from her sides. The thief tossed the half-full bag onto her counter.

"That bank manager was right. These guys didn't leave anything showing. We can't tell from these tapes what kind of shoes they're wearing either. The tall guy looks like he's got a nine millimeter and that revolver is definitely a .38."

"What do you think about the way the short one stands?" Laurie mused. "Keeps going back to a two-hand hold, almost like he feels uncomfortable with only one hand on the gun. Think he spends a lot of time at the shooting range?"

"That's a thought. Most guys at the range do their shooting practice two-handed." Gunnar rubbed his chin absent-mindedly, rewound the tape, then took a sip of coffee while he watched the tall thief fire off a shot toward the rear of the bank, then motion with his free hand for the teller to come toward him.

"The tall guy seems pretty comfortable one-handed," he observed.

"I wonder if we'd turn anything up at the shooting ranges. Can't be too many guys six foot four at a shooting range. But does he go as often as his average-height, average-build buddy?" Laurie sipped her coffee as she looked up at Gunnar.

"We can check it out, there are only a couple indoor ranges, but I'm thinking maybe this guy could have picked up his gun habits from TV cops. Maybe he's never really done much shooting. He's only really *holding* the gun here; he doesn't ever use it and wouldn't ever have to unless he actually intends to shoot someone, which he most likely doesn't want to do. He just wants the money."

"Yeah, but that's a proper two-hand hold. Perfect, even if it is a little stiff. He's just not as comfortable with a piece as his buddy is."

Laurie pulled out a report form and started writing. "Let's get this written up and head out to the ranges."

"Sure thing." Gunnar grabbed his own report and began transcribing his notes from the bank. "If you're not doing anything after work tonight, how about I buy you a drink."

"Would that be the 'pity you got dumped' drink or are you trying to pick me up?" Laurie challenged.

"Just trying to score with you now that you're single. If I get you drunk, I can take advantage of you." He grinned and laughed.

"Come on, we've been partners for two years, I think it's okay if I buy you a drink as a friend."

"Well, I *was* just gonna go home and pour myself a bowl of Cheerios for dinner and mope, but I think I can handle a drink."

"Cheerios for dinner?" Gunnar shook his head. "Only if you're pouring beer on 'em instead of milk."

Only a couple shooting ranges existed in Worcester. There were others out in the suburbs, but Laurie and Gunnar headed to the local ones first. The parking lot at the first range was nearly empty, but it was an indoor range and charged a fee for use, so there would be someone who might be able to offer information.

Laurie entered the building first and was immediately greeted by a middle-aged man who leered at her as though she were an exotic dancer on stage. Laurie set her jaw and shoved her badge in his face as Gunnar took a stance beside her.

The man ignored her badge and looked at Gunnar when he spoke. "What do you want here?" he drawled. "I ain't done nuthin' wrong."

"Didn't say you did," Laurie stated. "We just want information on your clientele."

The man leered at her again, then responded to Gunnar. "Ain't nobody here right now. Range is empty."

"And unless you want it to stay empty, you can help us with some info," Gunnar replied.

Laurie remained silent and let Gunnar take the floor with this man. She knew the type and knew that no woman would ever get any help from him, even with force.

"Whattaya need?" he barked back.

"We're looking for a couple guys who might use your range. One's pretty tall about six and a half feet."

"Hmmm. Yeah, we got a tall guy comes in here. Kinda heavy." The man turned leering eyes upon Laurie again, but Gunnar reached out and grabbed his shoulder in a vice-like grip to redirect his attention.

"Thanks, but the one we're looking for is a bit lighter. He's got a medium build, probably like mine."

The man held Gunnar's eye as he fought to hide the discomfort that Gunnar's grip on his shoulder was causing him.

"I don't remember anyone else that tall," he stated evenly after a moment.

"Anybody else work here who might remember?"

The man shook his head. "I'm the one here when we're open."

Gunnar released his grip and patted the man's shoulder. "Thanks. I'm sure you'll call us if you do see anyone like that in here?" He handed the man a business card.

He took it and nodded, grateful for the relief in his shoulder.

"How do you deal with that BS?" Gunnar asked as they left the building.

"What? The look?" Laurie asked. "Usually I ignore it, but this guy would never have given me anything."

Gunnar shook his head. "I can't believe there's still guys out there like that who won't respect a woman cop."

"Yeah, but it's people like him that keep us employed. With an attitude like that, he's probably got a sheet."

"True."

They checked out six other firing ranges and gun clubs in Worcester and surrounding towns but no one knew of anyone fitting the description they had of the bank robbers.

Laurie looked at her watch as they headed back toward the station. "Five o'clock," she announced.

"Beer's calling," Gunnar replied.

"I hear it, too."

The Ground Round in Shrewsbury was nearly empty but for a couple sharing a drink in a corner booth and three girls laughing loudly at the far end of the bar. Laurie and Gunnar chose two corner stools at the bar and ordered beers on tap from the bar maid when she sauntered up, wiping her hands on a towel that was wet from use.

"So, you think these bank guys are security guards?" Gunnar asked as the bar maid placed a glass of foaming beer on the counter in front of him.

"I think they could be. Their body language and movements on those tapes, the shoes; you know how gung ho rent-a-cops are—it just seems to fit."

"The shooting ranges turned up nothing. Tomorrow we call around to the security companies for starters. Look for a six-foot-four guard." Gunnar's gaze shifted toward the other side of the bar and quickly returned. "You don't think they're cops, huh?"

"Maybe, but I think cops would be a little more comfortable about procedure, don't you think? These guys seemed more like wannabes."

Laurie followed Gunnar's gaze and saw an attractive brunette, part of the group of laughing girls at the far side of the bar, looking over at Gunnar. She saw Laurie looking at her and quickly turned back to her friends.

"I agree." Gunnar took a thoughtful draw on his beer as his eyes again shifted in the direction of the brunette.

"Don't tell me you're checking out that girl over there." Laurie grinned at him.

"Well, you know it's you I want, but you haven't been checking me out the way she has. You're still thinking about that jackass Jeff."

"Hardly. He's not worth the energy it takes to fire a synapse. But I appreciate your taking me out for consolation, even if you are flirting with another woman while you're supposed to be consoling me." She sipped her drink and turned her eyes on him, teasing.

"Well, what can I say—I'm a man. You know we only want one thing."

"Yeah, that's what worries me. I haven't yet found a guy who wants more."

"Don't worry, beautiful. That guy will come along before you know it." Gunnar placed a comforting hand on her shoulder. "In the meantime, though, you should have a little fun. Get out there and meet some guys. Quit worrying about whether every guy you meet is going to enter a relationship. Dating is supposed to be fun."

"Okay, Dad." Laurie rolled her eyes to the ceiling for effect, and then noticed Gunnar's gaze was back on the brunette. "Why don't you go talk to her?"

"But I'm here with you, babe. I don't want to be insensitive."

"Oh, but flirting shamelessly is alright." Laurie grinned. "I need a bathroom break. Order me another beer?" Laurie slid off the stool and headed for the restroom in the direction of the women at the other end of the bar. She saw the brunette turn away from her, embarrassed, so she stopped beside her.

"My friend has been checking you out, not that you haven't noticed. He's definitely interested. Why don't you go talk to him a minute while I'm in the bathroom?" The brunette hesitated a moment, shocked that Laurie wasn't angry with her.

"You two aren't together?" She brushed some wandering strands of black hair out of her eyes.

"We're sitting together, yeah but we're just friends. We work together. I'm Laurie." She held out her hand and the brunette took it hesitantly.

"Katie." She smiled.

"And that's Gunnar." Laurie motioned toward him and noticed him shaking his head, grinning. "You've got about five minutes." Laurie headed into the restroom around the corner.

Katie smiled at Gunnar and held up her hand in a tentative wave, waggling her fingers. Gunnar slid off his stool and sauntered over.

"Hi. Gunnar." He announced and held out his hand to her. She took it gingerly.

"Katie." She smiled. The two girls with her fought back smiles and turned away from them.

"I hope my friend didn't embarrass you. She can be a little forward."

"That's alright. I'm glad she is, otherwise we wouldn't get to actually meet. But we've both got other plans at the moment. You want to call me and we can get together?" She handed him a business card.

"Yeah. I'll give you a call later. Maybe we can make a plan for the end of the week." Gunnar pulled out his wallet and put the card safely inside. He smiled one last time and headed back toward his seat as Laurie returned from the restroom. Laurie smiled at the girl as she passed then rejoined Gunnar.

"So, did you two get to talk while I was away?"

"You are amazing. Any other woman would be insulted that I looked at that girl, but you go and set me up."

"Any other woman with you would probably have a right to be insulted. But you and I are just friends and I look out for my friends." Laurie popped him gently in the shoulder.

"So, you got a date?"

"I got her number. Told her I'd call for a date the end of the week."

# Chapter 3

Evening encroached upon Worcester and with it, heavy clouds rolled in, led by a massive thunderhead that hosted a stunning light show of pink and blue flashing deep in its crown like a giant cauldron cooking up black magic.

Abra watched the show from the third-floor porch of a three-decker in Greendale. She sipped listlessly from a cup of freshly brewed coffee while the wind whistled through the old eaves and swirled her long black hair around her face. She brushed it back gently, tucking a few strands behind her ear. Friday evening after a long workweek had Abra wanting to go dancing at her favorite clubs. Her usual Friday night friends had dates so she had no one to go with and although clubbing alone usually meant a better chance to meet someone new, she really hated to face the scene alone. But it had been over a month since Jerry, the mechanic, had dumped her for some slutty blonde and she was tired of lonely weekends. If she were alone, men would be more inclined to talk to her and there might be someone interesting out tonight. She smiled at the thought, quickly finished her coffee, and left the porch to dress for the night just as the thunderhead stabbed at the ground with brilliant wands of lightning and released its brew, dumping torrents of rain outside Abra's door — a loud, clear omen that went unheeded.

The rain drenched the city in an instant, turning the streets into rivers that rushed loudly to the storm drains and disappeared below. But, like typical summer storms, the rain did not last. It ceased as quickly as it had started and the sun came out immediately to chase the chill from the air. It felt like a perfect evening to go out.

Nine o'clock found Abra perched on a stool at the end of a crowded bar where she sat with legs crossed, sipping a Fuzzy Naval through a cocktail straw. Her eyes searched the crowded, smoky room for likely prospects, settling on a group of men in suits hanging in the far corner. One man in particular caught her attention and she studied him in every detail until light glinted off a ring on his left hand as he raised his drink. Oh well, she thought, and returned her attention to the peach and orange cocktail. She made a conscious effort to drink slowly, but soon she was pulling up air in a loud slurping sound.

"Sounds like you need another," said an unfamiliar voice behind her. She turned and found herself face-to-face with the most attractive man she thought she had ever laid eyes on. She considered that her third drink in less than an hour might possibly have tainted her perception, but perhaps he was buying her next one and since she had only a few dollars left in her wallet....

"Are you offering to refill it for me?" She asked, a flirtatious note in her voice. Don't want to appear too eager, she thought. *Damn, but he's gorgeous!* She gave him an inviting smile and told him her name.

"If you will allow me, I will gladly do that for you, Abra. My name is Hunter." He pronounced each word crisply and returned a smile with what seemed a poor attempt at pompousness.

"That's an unusual name. I like it." Oh God, she thought; I hope he's not one of those geeks who tries to pull off the rich boy routine. This is hardly the place that anyone with anything better to do would hang out. But the drink was free and lately her pocketbook had been a bit light, so she didn't chase him away.

Her cocktail arrived and again she worked at drinking slowly, sipping daintily between idle chatter.

"I haven't been around here before; is this the hot spot in Worchester?" Hunter asked.

She giggled a little at the common mispronunciation of her hometown. "It's Worcester and actually, around here, it's pronounced Woosta," she corrected, putting emphasis on the local pronunciation, and smiled as he blushed a faint red. Maybe he's not a geek, she thought. Any man that blushes is enticing.

"I'd offer you a seat," she said, "but it's kinda crowded here. Would you maybe like to dance?"

"Oh dear, no. If you don't mind too terribly, I'd prefer to chat a bit if that's alright." That pompous bit again.

"Sure, that's fine. Where are you from? Not from Worcester, I take it. " Abra straightened up on her stool and leaned toward him, savoring the scent of his cologne.

"Oh, do you mean the accent? My parents were British so they left me the accent, but I'm from California. I've only just recently moved to Massachusetts." He gazed at her with piercing blue eyes behind gold frames and she was immediately uncomfortable. He's just too attractive, she thought. What on earth was he doing talking to her? She was no beauty—a little too short and a bit too wide in the bottom. Not unattractive, but her face was too round to be considered beautiful, even if she was great at applying makeup.

Abra sized the man up—lean, muscular, and over six feet tall with perfect, wavy blonde hair. She really liked the hair and his neatly trimmed mustache gave him a look of sophistication. Of course every detail that Abra noticed was fake, but the lights were too dim for her to see that. Her drink came and she watched with interest as he pulled money from what looked like a woman's purse.

"My travel bag," he said in response to her giggle. "I know, men don't carry these things around here, but I don't think I could live without it. I don't know who decided that men only needed to carry money, cards and little bits of stuff that fit into a wallet." He flashed her a brilliant smile and edged a bit closer.

She laughed, a giggly laugh. This guy could be fun. She could certainly get used to that sparkling white smile. He looked like a movie star. They continued to talk on about nothing and she giggled and blushed at all his silly compliments—her eyes, her hair. He even made a bold comment about the cleavage that showed in the deeply scooped neckline of her blouse.

Abra finished her drink and he bought another for her, which she attacked with nervous thirst, but after four drinks, she could feel pressure building in her bladder so she excused herself as politely as she could. "I will be right back," she said, struggling to form each word to hide her drunkenness. She failed, tripping horribly over the word, "will". She slid off the barstool, careful that her loose skirt did not reveal more than it should, and pushed her way through the overcrowded club toward the restroom at the back.

Hunter watched her disappear into the crowd and turned casually to her drink, half-finished, still sitting on the bar. He glanced around at the other patrons, noting that no one was paying him any attention, then quickly, as if the bartender was about to take it because Abra had left, he grabbed the glass at the top of the rim with his hand over the drink, and pulled it back a few inches. What no one, not even those immediately beside him, saw was the thin stream of white powder that fell from his pinky and ring finger as he uncurled them over the glass. He swirled the drink gently before he set it down and watched with satisfaction as the white powder disappeared. He settled back and patiently awaited the return of the silly girl with the annoying giggle.

The man turned his back on the bar and the tainted drink and leaned casually against Abra's empty chair. He watched the female singer whose sparse clothing did little to cover her plump figure. Her bare midsection jiggled and vibrated as her body gyrated to the music that blared too loudly from over-sized speakers and deafened the drunken couples while they danced on the small wooden floor. The singer's voice was a strong soprano that held high notes in a clear trill, but fell badly flat when she hit the lower ones. If the patrons were not already well under the influence when the band had begun to play, they might have booed her off the stage. But they danced wildly around with companions they had met that evening, hoping to cast a sexual spell that would carry them through the next morning or at least to a secluded spot where they could explore their desires.

The man hated this scene; hated all of the feigned sincerity between people who had only just met. He loathed playing the interesting, intelligent, attractive, and available man to get what he wanted. Besides an unnatural personality, he wore a wig that made his scalp sweat, a mustache that felt like a giant scab on his lip, and colored contact lenses that made his eyes water. He failed to understand how anyone could put plastic in their eyes every day. He much preferred the glasses he wore to help disguise his eyes. He needed neither since his vision was perfect, but these discomforts were all necessary for him to play safely, and he had become an expert at his little serial game.

Picking up women in bars was a favorite pastime for Hunter. He had never met anyone he truly liked—they were just toys. He never intended the relationships he promised while filling them full of alcohol. Women wanted tenderness, while he quite simply wanted sex. But a simple fuck was never enough to satisfy his desire. He liked to take by force and loved the fear that it produced. He craved the look when they realized he intended harm and the panic in their eyes when they felt their lives slipping away. Fear excited him like nothing else. He waited patiently for it like the hunter he called himself and would soon get what he craved. This girl, though not beautiful, reminded him of the sitter who had tormented him. He would think of her as he tore Abra apart.

A tall, emaciated woman swing dancing with a man twice her age crashed into Hunter as her partner spun her out from a cuddle hold. She was too drunk to apologize or even realize the collision before he pulled her back, grabbing her free hand on the return and swinging both hands up into the air while they spun around back-to-back. Hunter flashed a glaring look, which he quickly banished when he saw Abra emerge from the restroom. Better not to give her any worries until her ability to worry was properly dampened. He welcomed her back with a glowing smile, which she returned with a blush as he pulled out the stool for her to sit.

"Bit crowded in there," she apologized. "I hoped you hadn't given up on me. Feels like I've been gone forever." She climbed clumsily onto the stool and carefully crossed her legs, keeping the heel of the supporting leg hooked onto the rung of the stool.

"Thanks for watching my drink while I was away. You never know what weirdoes might do these days." The man smiled at the irony of her comment and Abra smiled back.

She took a long drink. "You know, we've been talking all this time and you haven't told me what you do for a living. You look like a lawyer." She felt a flush of heat across her face. She'd always had a mild allergy to alcohol and ignored the burn in her cheeks, though they seemed hotter than usual.

"I *am* a lawyer. You're very perceptive," he lied. "I'm in from Boston for a deposition today and I'm very pleased that I stayed late and got the chance to meet you. You're very attractive, you realize." Abra blushed at the phony compliment.

Hunter took her hand by the fingers and held it up, palm down as though he might kiss it, but instead, his eyes met hers and held a moment. He sized her up then—how intoxicated she was and how soon the drug would take effect once she'd finished drinking it. Not long, he realized.

Abra reddened further at the depth of his stare. That look! His eyes—attractive and icily blue—felt as though they bored into her soul, searching for who she really was. She wanted to know him; to tell him every little detail of her life that she could remember. He was just so beautiful!

She took up her drink in a sudden fit of embarrassment and took a long pull on the straw, drawing up the rest of the liquid in two large swallows. The straw slurped loudly at the bottom.

"That went down quickly," he smiled. "Your face seems a bit flushed, are you as warm as I am?"

"Yeah! It is hot in here! Would you like to go outside to cool off? Maybe we'll be able to hear each another, too. It's really loud in here."

"Certainly," he smiled. "Would you like to take your things with you?" She shook her head.

"No, I'll leave them here. They'll hold my seat open for when we come back. Abra slid off the stool, leaving behind a sweater and her purse. She pushed through the crowd toward the door, feeling the noise and the heavy air close in around her. There seemed a thousand people between her and the door. Her head felt numb. Abra could usually hold her liquor pretty well and didn't think she'd had that much to drink. Maybe she was just tired or had caught a virus. She thought of her sweater back on her stool.

"Maybe I *should* get my sweater," she reasoned. "I feel like I might be coming down with something."

"Don't worry, I'll keep you warm. You just need to get outside into some fresh air. It's stuffy in here, feels like the oxygen is low—probably from poor air circulation." She was fading fast, he thought.

He had to get her out of sight before she collapsed or someone might call an ambulance.

At the door, she held up her hand to the doorman who pressed a rubber stamp to it, leaving a smudged black logo on her skin that would allow her re-entry to the club. The hunter quickly offered his own hand for the mark, and then pushed his conquest gently through the door into the cool night air.

He drew in a long, deep breath, emphasizing the sound through his nose. "Much better!" He exclaimed. "I can finally breathe again. Take a deep breath," he encouraged her. "It will clear your head."

Abra did as she was told, pulling the cool, fresh air into her lungs. She felt a spark of awareness, but still her head was in a fog.

"Maybe a little walk would help," he suggested. He grabbed her firmly around the waist and guided her toward the corner. They rounded it and she staggered slightly. "Maybe you should sit for a moment," he soothed as he led her toward a small copse of shrubs beside a hotel, out of sight of the empty sidewalk, and leaned her against the wall. He studied her a moment, watching her head loll listlessly to the side as he considered his attack. Then he thrust both hands against her shoulders and pinned her tightly against the cold bricks.

"Ow," she mumbled. "You're hurting me."

"Good," he smiled wickedly. "For a moment, I thought you might be falling asleep on me. You drank a lot more than I anticipated." His phony accent was gone.

She struggled halfheartedly against his grip, but gave up as the bricks dug into her shoulders.

"Wake up, slut," he said cheerfully. We're going to have some fun." He pushed his foot between hers and roughly forced one leg aside, putting her in a wide stance, then slid his hands down her arms and squeezed hard, digging his fingers into her to bring her back to alertness.

"Wh-what are you doing? You're hurting my arms," she whimpered. She lifted her face to him and her eyes went wide as he sneered and slammed her back against the wall. She opened her mouth to scream, but he covered her lips with his, muffling any sound she could make. He forced her jaw apart and kissed her harshly, driving his tongue in too far and too deep until she was unable to breathe. Her head swam from the effects of the drug and her body slumped.

Feeling her resistance fade, Hunter leaned in and stared into her eyes, holding her awareness. "You drunken bitch, don't you fall asleep on me," he growled in a whisper.

"Y-y-you d-d-rugged me," she moaned.

"Oh, poor darling," he sneered. "I only gave you a little something to help break down your inhibitions so you can do what you really want to."

"I don't want you, asshole!" she spat and her head lolled back uncontrollably against the bricks.

"Ah, but you will have me," he said smugly as he pulled her slack arms above her head where he held them with one hand while he pulled the tie from around his neck with the other to tie her wrists.

Creases of drunken fear deepened in her brow as she felt herself helplessly bound while he kicked her legs farther apart. He held her up with one hand on her wrists, grinding them against the bricks, while his free hand ran under her blouse to her breast and kneaded it painfully before grabbing the silk blouse and brassiere and tearing them from her body with one effort. Her breasts jiggled free and she felt the cold of the night as her heart pounded against her ribs.

Abra tried again to fight as his lips caressed her nipple, but her body would no longer obey her commands, then she felt his teeth cut into her and the warmth of her own blood. She opened her mouth to scream, but only a pitiful hiss escaped. Abra swam down a deep dark ravine and as she approached the bottom, she felt her attacker tear off her skirt. She whimpered feebly, feeling close to tears, then darkness closed in and she wilted.

"Damn drunken bitch!" he cursed as her body fell heavily to the ground. He pulled her up by her hair and backhanded her across the face with all his strength. She moaned unconsciously, but did not move.

"Stupid cunt!" he cursed and grabbed Abra's limp body under her armpits and dragged her to a large boulder near the wall where he hoisted her up and laid her out on her back, her arms and legs dangling over the sides. He removed his shirt while admiring the way the silver light danced upon her breasts before he retrieved his travel bag and withdrew a small pocket camera. "I guess you're a picture-worthy bitch," he grumbled as he snapped a photo. Then he glanced around and located a nesting place in the nearest shrub where he could prop the camera to aim it at her. As he adjusted the camera's angle, he listened for sounds from the street, but heard only the music and distant voices of the club.

The hunter pulled a condom from its designated pocket in his travel bag, placed the bag on the ground away from Abra, and set the timer on the camera to automatically take a picture. Then quickly and systematically, he undid his belt and slid his pants to the ground, leaving them around his ankles. Applying the condom, he tossed the wrapper aside to be retrieved when he'd finished, grabbed Abra's thighs and heaved her to him, thrusting himself roughly inside. He hoisted her midsection, arching her back as the camera flashed before he slowed and relished the experience, pushing himself deeper and surging forward again and again until his body stiffened and a groan of pleasure escaped his lips. Then he pushed himself away.

Carefully, he removed the condom, pocketed it and dressed, then took the tie from her wrists and retied it around his neck. He placed the camera in his travel bag and withdrew, instead, a hunting knife with a sharp, curved blade and dragged it across her throat, slicing cleanly through the carotid arteries and severing the windpipe. Abra's last breath rattled noisily through the exposed pipe as blood spurted. Her killer stepped back and retrieved her torn blouse from the ground to wipe the blood from his knife. He admired his work, then he stepped cautiously from behind the bushes and walked casually to his car.

# Chapter 4

The early birds were just beginning to land at Dunkin Donuts. Mostly construction workers, these men were no strangers to the sunrise. They sauntered toward the door with grins and waves for friends they passed each morning at the same time.

Laurie rolled into the parking lot, her eyes straining to stay open. She preferred to sleep until the sun was high in the sky before crawling out of bed, but not today. Jarred from her slumber by a call from the police dispatcher, she desperately needed a cup of coffee to get her revved and operating at full capacity. She waited patiently, sleepily, for an oversized pickup to pull out before turning in to park.

A group of men, freshly showered in stained and torn jeans, walked out of the donut shop, laughing loudly amongst themselves. They saw Laurie and immediately began making catcalls and sexual remarks, leering at her lustfully.

Laurie chuckled to herself, though being careful not to let the corners of her mouth turn up lest they think she actually appreciated their abrasive display. Instead, she gave them a stone face as she casually reached into her jacket and pulled out the gold emblem hanging from her neck, holding it up for them to see. "I sure wouldn't want to remember you boys as being this crude and impolite if I ever had to pull you over for speeding." She smiled at their shocked expressions, a serious but warm smile. "I'd much rather remember you as the gentlemen I'm certain you are."

It had been a long time since Laurie had worked traffic, but the simple threat was effective. The catcalls quieted instantly and they quickly turned toward a beaten and battered pickup.

"Niko," she greeted the clerk behind the counter. "Staying out of trouble lately, Niko?"

"Yes ma'am," he responded with confidence. "School's good, too." He gave her a broad smile, showing a perfect set of thick, white teeth.

"Glad to hear it," she smiled back.

Niko was a good boy who had been born into a bad neighborhood. His mother was a single parent as many mothers were in Great Brook Valley, known in Worcester as "the valley" or "the project". She had struggled daily to keep her boy from joining the local gangs or turning to drugs.

One night, Niko had called police while he watched three boys beat up on a homeless man. He stayed on the phone through the incident, terrified for the old man and for himself if the boys discovered he had made the call. He begged the dispatcher at the other end of the line not to send a car to his apartment and create trouble for him and his mother, who was badly handicapped and could not afford to move them out of the valley and away from the gangs.

The following morning, Niko had taken a bus to the police station and met Laurie and a detective. They placed him in front of a lineup and he identified two of the boys who had attacked the old man, boys he knew lived just up the street from him and went to his school. Niko was certain they would come for him, but Laurie saw to it that his name was not released and neither he nor his mother ever suffered for being good citizens.

A month later, a friend mentioned to Laurie that they had a tiny house to rent which needed some work to it to update it. Laurie thought of Niko. She helped work out a deal for Niko's mother to pay the same rent she was used to if he would help work on the house. So, just before his twelfth birthday, Niko moved out of the Valley to a dead-end street near Coe's Pond at the far side of Worcester.

Laurie felt a rush of pride for him now as she watched him work. Then Niko handed her the coffee and bagel she requested. "No charge for you of course." He smiled broadly. "Me and Momma will pray for you like always." He told her this frequently and Laurie wondered if it weren't these prayers that were to thank for some of her narrow escapes from serious trouble.

After taking her complimentary java, Laurie flew down Park Avenue without catching a single red traffic light Although with the blue light flashing on her roof, she would have gone through them anyhow, slowing only enough to avoid traffic, if needed.

She pulled in beside the route car which had responded to a hysterical call from a bellhop who made the gruesome discovery while looking for a spot to have a cigarette. He now stood far back from the scene, one burning cigarette hanging from his mouth and a half empty pack to be smoked clutched tightly in his grip. The ground around his feet was already littered with spent smokes.

Abra's naked body, stiff with rigormortis, sprawled across the boulder where the hunter had left her, throat cut ear to ear so deeply that it appeared her head would simply roll off if she were bumped accidentally. The hunter's knife had severed her windpipe and it jutted from the open wound like an old hose. Blood from the wound had sprayed across her chest before her heart stopped beating, leaving the rest of her blood to flow lazily down the sides of the rock and coagulate in a thick dark pool at its base.

Laurie winced at the sight of the bloodied corpse. She'd been a detective for two years now, had seen all sorts of death and gore, yet still she was unable to desensitize herself. The guys claimed it was because she was a woman, but she knew they were just as squeamish, though better at concealing it.

She stepped carefully around the corpse, watching where she placed her feet. There were no footprints in the bark mulch that covered the floor of the planting bed; the material was laid thick and the chunks of bark were too coarse to make a footprint possible. She looked around the ground and at the base of the shrubs that surrounded the alter where the corpse sprawled, but she could see nothing except the girl's clothing, which had been torn and left at the base of the wall. She noted that the blouse had a stain of blood on it.

She pushed one of the folds aside, revealing the smear of blood where the hunter had cleaned his blade.

"Bag these up separately," she instructed one of the officers nearby. "Impressions in the blood might give us a better idea of what sort of knife was used. Not to mention, we could match it to the weapon later if we find it." She meticulously studied Abra's skin, looking for hair or fibers that might belong to her killer, but she saw nothing apparent. She did note bruising around her wrists and arms and scribbled in a notebook to have the medical examiner check for DNA.

The hunter admired his work, watching smugly as the police held the curious back. Only a few spectators had turned out this early to see what had transpired steps from their homes and businesses; too bad there weren't more around to appreciate the fun he'd had. He loved a good crowd!

He focused on the woman exploring the bloody wreckage of naked flesh, pleased with the horror in her eyes. He knew she had seen blood before, but not like *his* work. He smiled as he remembered the satisfaction of watching the blade cut through Abra's flesh and hearing the gurgle of her breath as she struggled to live even through unconsciousness. He loved how they always struggled.

The woman looked up from her work and studied the crowd. She was looking for someone. Was she looking for him? Her face flooded the hunter's thoughts with memories of his first love. Strange that he should see his Karen picking through this scene. Strange that the way they had parted was now what brought them together again. The hunter smiled to himself and reached for the car door.

Laurie felt an acute awareness. Someone was watching her. Several rubberneckers had gathered, anxious to get an entertaining look at real gore, and she looked around from one to the next, searching the crowd with her eyes. She spotted Gunnar's Monte Carlo as he climbed out of the vehicle and the feeling of being watched dissipated through the relief of seeing her partner. Maybe she'd only imagined it, but still, she raised her camera and snapped off a few shots of the gathered crowd as Gunnar walked toward her.

He eyed her suspiciously as he saw the tensed look on her face. "You gonna lose it this time, Sharpe?" he joked.

"Not before you do," she replied with a sickly smile as she once again became aware of the nausea this bloody scene had caused her. What were partners for if not to encourage you to puke at a crime scene?

"Whoever did this really put some muscle into it. Looks more like he ripped her throat out with his bare hands rather than cutting it," She mused. "Someone likes to play with very big knives."

"Looks like human sacrifice the way he's got her laid out on the boulder like that." Gunnar added.

"That would be something for a secluded hilltop," Laurie responded. "This poor girl is probably here because it was convenient."

"Any ID on her?" Gunnar asked as he looked around at the ground.

"No. No purse, nothing. The killer must have taken it." Laurie paused as she looked down at the dead girl's hand.

"Or she left it at the bar. Look. She's got a stamp on her hand." Laurie fought the rigor to turn the girl's wrist and display a black mark on the back of her hand. "Did she forget to take it with her when she left?" she mused. Laurie straightened and propped her hands on her hips while she pondered the dead girl's last moments. "Or did she step outside for some fresh air—maybe with someone she knew or hooked up with?" She cocked her head in Gunnar's direction. He met her look inquisitively.

"Why wouldn't she take her purse with her if she was leaving the bar?" he asked.

"Well, nothing I would ever do, but a lot of girls think nothing of leaving their purse on the bar when they're only getting up from their chair for a minute." She pulled out a pocket notebook. "I'll make a note to check out the local bars for the purse and anyone who might recognize her from last night. Most likely, she was raped, considering the body's position, but we'll check the pathologist's report to be sure."

Jimmy got in late for his three o'clock shift. He had gone out the night before after he finished cleaning up the bar and didn't get to bed until after five that morning. Now he was both tired and hung over, a hell of a way to start an eight-hour shift. Fortunately, he thought, I won't be staying for the really late shift, with all the heavy drunks. He sluggishly wiped down the bar and checked stock to be sure that he had a replacement for any bottles that were almost empty. The bottles of Absolute Vodka and Jack Daniels whiskey were the only ones running dry so he ran quickly to the back room to get new ones. When he returned, Laurie and Gunnar greeted him, holding up their identification.

It was the third bar they had been to within a block of the murder scene—no luck. They hoped that would change here. Laurie kept a watchful eye on the bartender's reaction while Gunnar asked if he had worked the previous night. When he admitted that he had, Gunnar let him know of the girl who'd been killed and gave the shocked boy a description of her. Had she possibly left her purse there?

Jimmy thought hard for a moment, trying to clear the cobwebs from his head. "I think I remember a girl who might fit that description, yeah. And actually, I think I saw a handbag in the office this morning. Maybe it's hers. Can you hang on a minute?"

Gunnar nodded and Jimmy momentarily returned with a small shiny black purse.

"I don't know where this came from, but I don't remember seeing it here yesterday." He handed it to Laurie who opened and flipped quickly through it until she came across a driver's license. She showed it to Gunnar.

"Looks like our girl. Abra Wilson's her name. She was only twenty-two. What a waste," Laurie sighed.

She held up the photo for the bartender to see. He studied it closely a moment. "Yes, she was a regular here at the club. Nice girl; liked to drink though."

"You remember anyone she might have met up with last night?" Laurie asked.

"She was with some guy, not a regular here that I know of. I don't remember ever seeing him before, and I'm not sure I could really give you much of a description. I only got one look at him when he bought a drink for her. He was pretty tall, built pretty solid. He looked like the average, professional type with a suit and tie, ya know."

"Hair color, facial features?" Laurie prompted.

"Blonde and I think he wore glasses. Oh, and a moustache! He had a pretty heavy moustache; I remember that. That's about it, though. He was pretty much your average guy. I think he only just met this girl at the bar that night."

"Would you be able to talk to a sketch artist?" Laurie asked.

"I could, but I don't think I'd help much. I really don't think I'd recognize him if I saw him again, so I don't think I could help with a picture much. Sorry. It just gets too busy around here at night." He backed away a few paces, ready to return to his work.

"Thanks." Laurie clapped a hand on the bar and turned toward the door. Gunnar followed.

"Think he'll do it again?" Laurie asked her partner.

"Maybe, if he's stupid. Chances are if he does do something else like this, he'll be less brazen about it. He must know we'll be looking for him. Could also be he did know her or did a friend a favor by getting rid of her."

"All stuff we'll figure out," Laurie mused.

"Listen, now that we know who she is, we gotta go tell her family. Let's flip for it—loser gets to do the talking," Gunnar said as he pulled a quarter from his pocket, tossed it in the air and caught it, pausing for Laurie's call.

"Tails," she announced. Gunnar slapped the coin onto the back of his hand and uncovered it, revealing the dead president's portrait.

"Fine. I always get the touchy/feely shit jobs," she complained halfheartedly.

Gunnar laughed. "Right then. Let's get to it." He hated to tell the family that their loved one had died and never felt comfortable consoling strangers—it was too personal. He felt women were just better at that sort of thing, but Laurie would disagree.

At her address in Greendale, Abra's roommate answered the door with puffy eyes and matted hair.

Laurie did the talking as promised. "Is this Abra Wilson's residence?"

The girl nodded sleepily.

"Are you related to her?"

The girl shook her head and yawned. "Roommate."

"Where can we reach her family?"

She yawned again. "West Boylston, I think. Why?" She finally noticed the badge hanging from Laurie's neck and some of the sleep faded from her eyes.

"We need to talk to them about Abra. Were you out with her last night?"

"Uh-uh." She shook her head. "I worked. Waitressing."

"Where's Abra? She alright?"

"She was murdered last night."

The girl's eyes went wide and she was instantly awake.

"Murdered? Where?"

"I can't get into too much detail, but it seems she met up with someone at a club downtown. Do you know if she was planning to meet someone?"

"I don't think so, but I don't really know. I haven't really seen much of her this week because I've been working a lot of shifts. So, do you know who killed her?"

"That's what we're trying to find out," Laurie replied. "We need to get in touch with her parents to let them know. Do you maybe have a number or address for them?"

She thought a moment. "I think she has an address book in her room. They might be in there. You want to come in?" She motioned them in and closed the door.

In the bedroom, she found a well-worn notebook with a faded floral cover. She handed it to Laurie who leafed through it.

"Mum and Dad," Laurie declared. "835 phone exchange. That's West Boylston."

"May we take this?" she asked.

The girl nodded

The ride to West Boylston was only 20 minutes. Abra Wilson's mother answered the door of her tiny green cape house in West Boylston. She sobbed when Laurie broke the news and Laurie caught her in a hug to keep her from falling to the ground in her grief. Abra was her only daughter.

The day had ended, and still a murderer remained free and unknown. Laurie walked out to her car, waving at a couple officers who were arriving for duty. Images of the dead girl with her open throat gaping at the sky flashed repeatedly through her mind. How could anyone do that to another person? The girl must have suffered horribly.

Laurie shook her head sadly as she opened the door of the Camero and slid into the driver's seat. She started the engine and sat with her hands on the wheel, her mind wandering to that bar to meet with a stranger who had evil plans for her demise. How many times had she and Jessie been out and met strangers who appeared charming and innocuous?

Had this man simply talked her into taking a walk? Or had he drugged her? The examiner's report would reveal the truth. Laurie shuddered to think that this might not be the first of a number of young women that this beast would destroy in her town.

The ringing of her cell phone brought her back to the moment and she dug into her bag to retrieve it.

"Laurie Sharpe," she answered.

"Hey girl," came Jessie's voice, directed in from the nearest cell tower. "I'm thinking, it's Saturday night, and there'll be gorgeous men out for the picking. Whattaya say? Want to join me in the orchard?"

Laurie again envisioned Abra Wilson's mutilated body before she responded. "I have a better idea. How about we grab a couple of good movies and stay in with some really buttery popcorn and maybe some Chinese food?"

"Stay in? Something wrong? It's a beautiful night to go out. Can't I convince you?

"No," Laurie replied sadly. "And you're not going out either. You'll probably see it on the news later, but we had a girl murdered last night. Picked up at a night club."

There was silence for a moment.

"But you and I are always careful. We'll be fine," Jessie persuaded.

"We are careful, sure, but I'm not so sure this girl wasn't careful herself. We don't have the ME's report yet, but she could have been drugged. I mean, she left her purse at the club. Who does that?"

"Maybe she just wasn't too bright," Jessie replied.

"I just don't feel up to going out into the lion pit tonight after seeing that and I really would feel better if you would stay in with me," Laurie pleaded.

Jessie breathed a heavy sigh of resignation. "What time do you want me over, Mom? Seven o'clock sound good?"

"Seven would be great." Laurie smiled with relief. "And don't call me Mom. I'm just looking out for your sorry butt."

"Who was it by the way? No one we knew, I hope."

"No one I knew, but I'll tell you more later. You want me to go ahead and grab some movies?"

"Sure. Get at least one sappy chick flick, though," Jessie said. "I know how much you like the action movies, but I need to at least see some romance if I'm not getting any for myself."

"Alright. I think I can handle that," Laurie giggled. "I'll see you at seven." She hit the button to end the call and smiled to herself, happy that for at least one night, she could keep herself and her friend safe from danger.

Laurie stopped at the liquor store to replenish her supply of Manhattan ingredients and picked up *Sleepless in Seattle*, Jessie's favorite 'chick flick', along with *Gladiator*, which she knew neither of them had seen yet. Tonight would be a good night to spend three hours on a movie and she could handle the violence of a world she had never known, but she couldn't handle seeing violence from her own time. Not tonight. Not after seeing Abra Wilson's cold body, with her throat open and bloody, staring vacantly at nothing through dead eyes.

# Chapter 5

Laurie was huddled over her desk engrossed in a case file when Gunnar slapped the pathologist's report onto an already cluttered corner of her desk. She finished the last words of the page she was reading and slowly looked up at her partner.

"You'll like this one." He folded his arms across his chest as he prepared to tell her what he'd learned.

"What?" Laurie turned her attention away from the file on the Neighbors Bank robbery. She leaned back in her chair, toying with the badge around her neck.

"Our Wilson girl killer is a bit more thorough than most." He unfolded his arms and began waving and gesturing in rhythm to his report. "This guy drugs our girl to keep her from fighting, rapes her and kills her." He paused for effect. "And somewhere in the middle of all this, he takes the time to slip on a condom and then dispose of it after the fact, probably down a storm drain."

"A rapist who practices safe sex?" Laurie made a face. Gunnar seemed amused.

"Better than me, even. The pathologist didn't find a thing. No hairs, no skin under her nails, no fibers. Nothing! Like this guy never touched her. So we have no DNA on him. Did the fingerprint guys find anything?"

"No. There weren't too many good surfaces around there. "

"I spoke to the family," she continued. "They never saw much of her since she moved out on her own. She lived with her roommate and rarely stopped by to visit, so they didn't have much to offer."

Gunnar pulled up a chair from a neighboring desk, sat backwards on it, and gripped the backrest. "Did they know if she had any friends?"

Laurie shook her head in response.

"Maybe we should head to the club Friday and see if anyone there knows her or has hung out with her, maybe even picked her up at some point. Her roommate said Friday was her night of choice for clubbing."

Gunnar agreed. "I finally get a date with the sexy Laurie Sharpe! Are we going dancing?"

Laurie raised an eyebrow. "And here all this time I thought you didn't want me."

"Oh baby, if only you knew," he joked. He did want her, but he had never sensed from her that she might want him too, so he had never asked. He could get sex anywhere, but Laurie's friendship meant a lot to him and he did not want to lose that. Gunnar knew many people but he didn't have a lot of true friends and Laurie was one of the few.

"What, I don't hafta wait for you to finish a two hour beauty marathon?" Gunnar teased as Laurie appeared in a modest skirt with jacket in-hand when he rang her doorbell.

"Sorry. That would make this a real date," Laurie grinned as she slipped on her jacket. "It might have been less weird if we'd met at the station."

"Relax. You know this wasn't out of my way." Gunnar opened the passenger door of his Monte Carlo and stood by as Laurie slid gracefully into the seat, silently appreciating the delicate bend of her silky legs as she drew them up into the car after her. If only she wasn't his partner! But she was and expressing his desire for her would only complicate that. He climbed in behind the wheel next to Laurie, holding his gaze forward as he felt her eyes turn in his direction. She had no feelings for him, he knew. He was merely Laurie's partner—

needed only for backup or to save her life when their job got dangerous. Not for love.

"So did you ever get together with that girl from the Ground Round?" Laurie asked while she studied Gunnar's profile.

"Yeah we got together for a couple drinks last Saturday. She's not my type though. Seems a little uptight." Gunnar kept his eyes forward, not just watching the road, but avoiding Laurie's gaze.

"Hmmmm…. Considering the source, that means either she didn't put out or she did, but didn't give it much effort."

"Well, a man does have to have priorities." Gunnar grinned, making light of Laurie's comment while he fumed silently that this was how Laurie thought of him. Sure he liked sex. What man didn't? But he wasn't as shallow as Laurie thought. He just didn't see the point in leading a woman on if he really didn't enjoy her company. If he got a little sex out of the deal before he decided not to see her again, well then that was a bonus.

"You need to have a relationship with a woman that's based on more than just sex, Gunnar. Don't you ever think about settling down with someone?" Laurie sometimes wondered at Gunnar's expression when she caught his eyes upon her. She knew she was attractive, but certainly Gunnar had respect for her as his partner. She couldn't imagine that he would ever really try to hit on her.

"Come on. Let's not go there," Gunnar protested. "You know I'm not ready to settle. I'm too young with too much life ahead of me."

"Don't kid yourself, Gunnar. It'll happen when you meet the right woman. The question is, will you open your eyes when she comes along or will you let her slip away?" Gunnar looked in her direction for a moment, then smiled and turned his attention back to the road. Was Laurie trying to drop him a hint? He knew she wasn't like other women he'd met—they were all superficial, as was he. But Laurie was deeper. She was comfortable with herself and with being tougher than most women. He'd never known Laurie to back down from a challenge or from any of the dangerous situations they'd encountered in the two years they'd worked together. He wondered how she would be in bed. Did she scream during sex?

"Maybe if she comes along after I'm done having fun. You know, when I'm about forty-five or fifty. I'm just out for fun until then." Gunnar kept his eyes straight ahead. He knew Laurie hated this sort

SERIAL

of talk, but he hated how she was always trying to push him to settle. Even if Laurie were trying to hit on him, though he didn't think so, he wouldn't want to commit to her now. He wasn't ready for anything serious. Maybe in a few years he would be ready, but he'd only turned thirty last month. Way too young!

Laurie said nothing else as she felt Gunnar's thoughts turning around her. She would never fall victim to one of Gunnar's advances or his sour attitude toward women. Too much testosterone! He's a great guy, a great partner, but not someone any reasonable woman would try to get serious with. Gunnar was just too much work and headache to try a relationship with. Laurie chuckled silently to herself, wondering what would Gunnar's reaction be when he really did find the right woman.

But Gunnar already had, even if he could never tell her.

The club was already filled with hungry singles when Laurie and Gunnar arrived. They sought out Jimmy behind the bar and waved him over. "Any chance you see that guy here tonight that was with our girl last Friday night?" Laurie leaned across the bar and yelled to be heard above the music.

The bartender shook his head. "I've been watching for him. Can I get you anything?"

"Two cokes." Laurie held up two fingers to support her request. The bartender nodded and returned with the drinks, waving Gunnar off as he tried to hand him payment. "You guys are working. Drinks are on me. I'll let you know if I see that guy, OK?"

Laurie nodded her thanks.

Gunnar tentatively pushed his hand against the small of Laurie's back, urging her into the crowd.

"We might as well get at this." Laurie pulled two identical 8 x 10 photos from her pocketbook that Abra's parents had provided, handed one to Gunnar, and displayed the other to the nearest group of women.

"Have you ever seen this girl in here?" The three women studied the photo a moment and shook their heads dubiously. Laurie and Gunnar headed in separate directions, showing the photos to each group, couple, and individual in the bar.

A group of girls in short skirts huddled in the back corner, chatting, giggling, and pointing around at various people, making

55

comments about each patron that were apparently very funny. Laurie walked toward them and presented the photo.

One of the girls, waiflike with large doe-eyes, studied the photo, glancing at Laurie suspiciously and trying to assess Laurie's reason for asking about the girl in the photo before she offered any information.

"You know her?" Laurie asked, seeing recognition in the girl's eyes.

"Abra. What do you want with her? She's not the type to do anything wrong that cops would care about."

"No? Then it's even more tragic that she was murdered Friday night," Laurie replied solemnly.

Six hands flew to three astonished faces in unison. The timing could not have been more precise.

"The girl outside the hotel? The one that was on the news last week? That was Abra?" The doe-eyed girl's hands fell to her sides as she withered where she stood.

"There was no name on the news. Abra and I were supposed to go clubbing together that night, but I got a call from a guy I see sometimes, so I went out with him instead." She buried her face in her hands again. "If I had gone out with her like we'd planned, she'd still be alive, wouldn't she?" The girl sobbed uncontrollably.

"You don't know that for sure. You might have been hurt or killed also." Laurie tried to comfort the girl, but she knew she was right. Abra was attacked because she was alone. If she'd had company, another girl's body would've been found behind the hotel, but still, someone would have died and Laurie would still be here, only the photo would be different.

"Did either of you know her and were you here that night?" Laurie turned her attention to the other two girls, but they shook their heads silently.

"Carm and Lydia are in from Springfield for the night," the doe-eyed girl replied for them. "Abra didn't have a lot of friends that she went clubbing with. Just me, Marilyn, and Amy. But I've already spoken to them today—they both went on dates Friday night for dinner." Again she broke into sobbing, shaking her head. "When we couldn't reach her, we joked that she'd met someone and that we weren't important enough to call because she was out with him. We had no idea…," the girl's voice faltered.

"I'm really very sorry," Laurie consoled. "Have you spoken with her parents?"

The girl shook her head. "I don't know them and wouldn't know how to get in touch with them."

"I have their number here." Laurie fumbled around in her pocketbook and came out with a notebook and pen. She copied a number from a card onto a sheet in the notebook, ripped it out, and handed it to the girl.

"Thank you. I'll call them. Maybe they need help with arrangements." The girl sobbed again.

"Could I just get your name and the names of Abra's other friends?" The doe-eyed girl recited the information as Laurie scribbled, then as politely as she could, Laurie said goodbye and slipped back into the crowd in search of Gunnar. It seemed this lead had dried up, bringing them no closer to the killer.

# Chapter 6

Johnny Bryant was an awesome hacker. And why shouldn't he be? He practiced at it every day after school. He could get into just about anywhere, whether or not they thought they were protected by a firewall. Even the best firewalls were nothing to him—just a few extra keystrokes. He was good at covering his tracks, though. He never left a trail that they could follow. In fact, rarely did he leave anything that would let anyone know that he'd been in at all. But just in case, he liked to set blame for some sorry sap in whatever company he breached. No one in particular, maybe someone whose name he didn't like or maybe he'd just pick someone at random. He liked to lay out tracks that made it look like his scapegoat had broken into the system from the inside. That way, if he slipped up and left a trace that he'd breached security, they would blame that dumb asshole and not come looking for him. Piece of cake! He never got caught. The stupid ass on the inside never knew what hit him—if anyone even knew of the breach. But sometimes they did and once he read about one of these poor guys in the paper after he broke into an airport system.

He even used his talents on his parents. They were jerks who never let him do anything fun! All they ever talked about was money. When it was tax time this year, they complained that they wouldn't be able to get him anything for graduation—he would be going to high school in the fall—because Uncle Sam was taking everything. They were loaded, he knew. They went out everywhere; his mother wore expensive jewelry; they took trips without him. They had money, he knew, but they never had anything for him. He wondered if he would even get to college; they would probably leave him high and dry. The only time they were glad to have him was when they spoke of tax deductions. He was worth a pretty penny then, but he never saw any of it.

So he got even with them. He broke into the IRS. Yes, he, Johnny Bryant, broke into a government system, undetected! He found his parents' information—they had foolishly filed online—and he doctored it. He created children they never had; wrote off huge stock market losses they had never experienced. His parents never lost when it came to stocks. And then, the biggest red flag of all, he changed the amount of his father's earnings to half what was on his W2 from Medisoft. There were no tracks that time. He made sure there was no evidence of a breach. The IRS came calling within the month and he relished the expression on his father's face when he heard the word "audit". He wanted to thank the IRS personally for dropping by during dinner so that he could enjoy his small victory against his parents' tyranny. He still never saw a graduation present, but he felt like he had when the money painfully departed from their savings account.

This company he was breaking into now was just to kill some time, nothing fancy. He had searched the Internet blindly as usual to find a target. Using his favorite search engine, he entered a random word from the dictionary, then when the engine returned a list of responses, he pressed the "Next" button an uncounted number of times and followed down the resulting page to the first company listed. No matter how large or small they were, he would break in with little effort.

He smiled smugly to himself as he pulled up a page for Moonshine Brewing Company in Rhode Island. This would be a piece of cake. They were just a small microbrewery and probably had no money for a decent firewall. He employed a password breaker and popped the lock easily. He was in!

Johnny pulled up the personnel files and lowered a few of the larger salaries. The bigwigs—they've got enough money; they won't miss a few dollars. But Sam Willis doesn't seem to earn too much; give him a couple extra zeroes on his paycheck and he'll be glad for about five minutes until they track his sorry ass down and blame him for the changes. Willis probably doesn't know his way around the Internet, much less how to hack into a site, but they'll hassle him. Johnny popped on over to the shipping and receiving screen where he erased a few deliveries that were already en route to the microbrewery and deleted several large orders that were bound for stores around Rhode Island. That should cost them a few bucks, he mumbled aloud. What a rush!

He was finished with his fun for the day; his parents would be home soon and Johnny didn't like to play these games when they were around because they always snuck in and peeked over his shoulder, worried that he would be looking at porn or something. Johnny hated porn. It was gross to watch people get it on. He wasn't really even old enough to appreciate looking at the women. He just liked to hack.

Johnny covered his tracks as he backed out of Moonshine Brewing. Just like dragging a pine bough through the dirt behind you, he thought. He shut down the computer and picked up his schoolbooks. Even if his parents didn't pay for it, he was going to college some day. He had to keep up his grades.

What Johnny didn't know about Moonshine Brewing was that Sam Willis owned the company. He was not in a position to appreciate the extra dollars added to his paycheck because Sam didn't want his ownership of the company known. He was a simple man with a very greedy ex-wife who would eagerly take every last penny from him if she knew how many pennies he had. To keep her hands out of his pockets, Sam hid the truth and took a meager salary every week to put into an account boldly bearing his name. Then, once a month, Sam wrote a check to the bitch with the good lawyer for seventy percent of that salary. He did not live an extravagant life and the leech never guessed that there was more treasure to be had. The rest of his paycheck was filtered out of the company to an offshore account; but now with his expensive new lawyer who had "donated" his services to Sam, an "old friend"—the lawyer was actually being paid quite handsomely under the table—Sam would soon be free of this cloak of secrecy. The bitch would not receive another red cent after their next appearance in court. And if the judge didn't see to cutting her off, Sam would earn enough over the next few years to just disappear to a warmer, friendlier climate where she would never find him.

When Sam received his paycheck in the amount of $50,000 for twenty hours of work, he was not as happy as he might have been were he any other employee of Moonshine Brewing. He went straight to the payroll office to check on the error, explaining to the clerk that, although it was a nice gesture and he would like to take the company up on their generosity, he knew it would come back to haunt him eventually. He preferred to get it taken care of now. The girl behind the desk laughed at his light sense of humor. She didn't know his true position in the company.

As soon as the payroll error was fixed, Sam had the president of Moonshine Brewing call a friend who worked freelance, tracking down hackers like the little shit who had broken into his company. This man was good at his job, too. There had never been anyone he could not trace—he knew his business. He was good with security, and obviously, Moonshine Brewing could use a bit more of that on its computer network. This asshole hacker had actually done him a favor, Sam thought. Now he knew he was vulnerable. Imagine if his ex or worse, if the government spooks, had hacked in. They would run him in for tax evasion when all he was really guilty of was wife evasion, though he did evade taxes on the money he'd hidden from her. If the government had found out his little secret, all he had, including his freedom, would be lost. And it's not as if he were filthy stinking rich, either. He had enough to enjoy: a really nice boat, a forty-seven foot Catalina with two decent-sized cabins. He loved to sail and it was sailing down the east coast one year in an old twenty-two foot Hunter that had put him in the position he was in now.

Sam had always liked to sail into Newport Harbor, pick up a mooring, and go ashore to hang out on the strip. Newport was his favorite harbor—the strip was usually a hopping place and he especially liked some of the pubs that overlooked the water where he could look out at his dream boats while sipping on a margarita.

He never made it to his favorite pub on that trip, though. He pulled into the harbor just behind an oversized luxury motor yacht, pulled down his sails, and powered up his little diesel engine. He was motoring in about thirty yards behind the yacht when it hit an unusually large swell spawned by a reckless cigarette boat speeding across her bow. The luxury yacht's bow rose up and then dropped down so suddenly that a middle-aged man standing at the bow lost his footing and fell overboard into speedboat's wake. The pilot of the yacht was so busy cursing at the boat's driver that he didn't even notice the man's disappearance over the rail. The ship continued on at its steady pace, headed for the harbor.

Sam had seen the accident, though, and acted quickly, maneuvering his little sailboat to the spot where he had seen the man fall. The man's head rose above the crest of a wave, about a hundred yards offshore as he stared helplessly at the yacht now a hundred feet away. Even if he could swim the distance to shore in the choppy waters, the unusually warm weather had attracted all sorts of speedboats that crisscrossed rapidly outside the harbor, and without a lifejacket, the man was almost invisible to them. Still, seeing no other choice, the man struck out in a haphazard crawl toward the nearest shore as Sam guided the Hunter in his direction. He was within ten feet before the swimmer turned and saw him. The man's relief was easily visible as the creases diminished on his brow and he waved.

Sam grabbed the life ring and tossed it over to him, landing it beside the bobbing head with a loud smack. He had saved the life of a wealthy American businessman and his own life soon changed forever. Moonshine Brewing Company was a gift of gratitude. The businessman, John Harp, had purchased the Company as part of the hostile take-over of a large conglomerate. The extravagantly wealthy Mr. Harp sold off each piece at an obscene little profit. Many people would lose their jobs and livelihood, but that was never his concern. Money was all that mattered. But when Sam saved his life that day, he also saved the lives of the workers at Moonshine Brewing. John Harp gave him this small company, one of the most viable and prosperous of all the small companies formerly part of the large conglomerate and the only company located in Sam's home state of Rhode Island.

Previously a poor man who survived paycheck to paycheck after his ex-wife took all she could, Sam Willis never wanted for anything again.

# Chapter 7

It was Friday and Laurie was in a slump. It was now officially two weeks gone by since she had caught Jeff with his trampy neighbor. She was at the end of her workweek—no closer to finding the Neighbor's Bank robbers, and certainly nowhere near a reasonable clue in the Wilson murder. She had exhausted all current leads in both cases—leads that could have kept her mind occupied—and now she kept turning thoughts of Jeff over in her mind. He had simply used her, she knew. There are men out there who do this, who lay out elaborate lies to suck women in and then just play the game to get whatever they want until, one day, they either grow bored, or the truth comes out and the woman gets hurt. It happens, she consoled herself. Life went on and she would get over it. But it would take some time. Even though Laurie went to every extent to lead everyone to believe she was tough and unbreakable, that was really only true about the way she handled police work. When it came to love, Laurie was weak and she knew it. She was most comfortable when she was around people she knew she could drop her guard with. Jeff had almost felt like one of those people. Now she had only Jessie and though she loved her friend, Laurie really yearned for that same feeling of comfort with a man whom she could love and share everything with. Someone who would love her as much in return.

She had almost taken her last toe off of solid ground and let herself fall for Jeff and if she had, Jeff's actions would have crushed her. But maybe somehow she had known and now she was just angry and disappointed.

Laurie was staring blankly at her desk, absorbed in self-pity when she realized dazedly that her phone was ringing—it was already on the third ring. She cleared her throat and hesitantly lifted the receiver.

"Laurie Sharpe," her voice rasped.

"Is this the detective bureau?" asked a voice in a deep bass tone.

"Yes, this is Detective Sharpe. What can I do for you?"

"My name's Brandon Doyle. I'm a free-lance computer security consultant. I'm working on a hacker case right now and I think I may have found my culprit here in Worcester. I'll need the law to help me apprehend the person, probably a kid."

"I thought you said you knew who it was?"

"I can only be certain of the location of the computer used to break in at this point. But it happens to be in a private home, so it's certainly someone there, but I can't be sure until we question the family. Usually for something like this, unless the parents personally know and want to intentionally harm or embarrass the victim, it's generally a kid playing around."

The man at the other end of the phone was very professional and Laurie liked the sound of his voice. Besides being a deep voice, it had a certain breathless quality to it that sounded as though he might be smiling while he spoke.

"I'd like to set up a time to come in and speak to someone about the specifics of my case so I can move on this as soon as possible. The company I'm doing this for wants to nail this hacker—they made quite a mess of things for the company they hacked. Do you have any time for me today or tomorrow?"

Laurie pulled out her organizer, the old-fashioned paper kind. She had never gotten used to the idea of trusting her life to something that required batteries and could eat her whole schedule in a moment's notice if it slipped out of her hand and fell to the floor. She liked paper, thank you very much.

"I have some time this afternoon. How's one-thirty sound? Are you in the area?"

"Yes, I can be there." The smiling man at the other end of the line made certain he had the correct spelling of her last name and got her first name as well. He used the latter as he closed their conversation and promised to see her later.

Sounds like a date, Laurie thought. He's probably short, fat and sweaty. He's out of breath, not smiling breathlessly. I need to quit thinking about men. Damn Jeff!

A moment later, the phone rang again and the dispatcher downstairs described a robbery to her. A gas station on the far side of the city had been held up and the kids, barely out of high school, if that, had made off with several hundred dollars in cash. Why on earth did the clerk even have that much cash on hand in the register? Dozens of convenience store robberies had taught her that the cashier always dumped everything over a hundred dollars into a secure safe in the floor. The cashier never had the key or combination, so the thief never got much for the risk he took. This clerk probably doesn't bother with the rules and the thieves not only got away with the money, but probably cost the clerk his job, too.

She looked at the clock. Gunnar wasn't due in for another hour. She grabbed her keys and headed out to the call alone.

Laurie saw that the sign in the window read "Closed" as she brought her cruiser to a stop and threw the transmission into park. A resounding clank met her ears. One more thing for the mechanics to check out, she thought. Many of Worcester's police cruisers were in poor condition; some of them were so bad that a rough ride on a dirt road could result in lost parts from the car. Although the officers usually arrived in one piece at the station when their shift was done, the cruisers were not always so lucky.

The clerk was hysterical when he met Laurie. He kept running his hands through his hair, grabbing hold and tugging at it, then folding his arms across his chest and starting the nervous jitter all over again. He started rambling off one long incoherent sentence, hanging over Laurie as she climbed out of her car. He waved his arms around erratically as he tried to describe the thieves. "There was two guys, high school maybe."

"Were they white, Hispanic, what?" she prodded as she began writing in a notebook.

"White dudes, one had blonde hair, one brown," he replied, wringing his hands. He kept his eyes averted from Laurie while he spoke.

"What were they wearing, do you remember?"

"The blonde dude had on a leather jacket. I guess they both had jeans on. The other guy pulled a gun on me. I gave him everything in the register and some butts. Then the asshole hits me over the head. This guy out here woke me up." He pointed to a man in his early thirties who was waiting patiently, leaning against his pickup truck.

"You want to go get that checked at the ER?" Laurie asked. "They could have done some damage hitting you on the head like that."

"Naw, I feel fine. I think I was out for a while, but I'm good now." The clerk turned his head away from Laurie as he waved off her concern. Laurie took a moment to assess his clothing and saw that the cashier was a walking jewelry store, wearing not less than five thick gold chains around his neck, a couple gold bracelets, three other gold rings on his left and a large gold ring in the shape of a lion's head on his right.

"Are you the only cashier on duty here?" she asked.

"Yeah. They probably wouldn't have done this if I wasn't alone." His tone had calmed somewhat.

"Did you see which way they ran?"

"They knocked me out cold." He paused as he rubbed the back of his neck and grimaced. "They was history when that dude woke me up. I didn't recognize them, I don't think they come in here usually."

"And they're probably long gone by now," Laurie pointed out. "Maybe since you have your 'closed' sign up, you might come down to the station and go over this there. Can you get in touch with your boss?"

"I shouldn't really leave the place," he replied. "Can't we just talk here? I don't wanna lose my job."

"I really should have you come down to the station. I'd also like to get a look at the video in that camera over there." Laurie wondered whether the cashier had accomplices to make the robbery appear realistic on video or if he'd foolishly forgotten the camera and simply taken the cash on his own. If she got him down to the station, she could weaken his story until he cracked and maybe there was something on the camera that could help with that. "I can talk to your boss and explain it to him, but I really think it would be best if we discussed this at the station. The video could help jog your memory a little."

The cashier seemed unconcerned about the video, so there must be accomplices, Laurie figured as the clerk led her to the phone and dialed up the bosses' number. He explained the situation to whoever answered at the other end, wincing as Laurie could hear shouting from the other end of the line, then handed over the phone.

The cashier sat alone in the interrogation room as Gunnar entered the viewing room and joined Laurie in watching him through the one-way glass while he fidgeted in his seat.

"There's no way he was robbed at gunpoint and knocked out and the kids that did it left all that gold on him. The rings I could understand, since it's pretty tough to get a ring off someone else's finger, but the gold chains should have been gone." Laurie relayed the reason for not believing the cashier's accounting of the robbery. They had both seen several cases where an underpaid cashier decided to make off with a little bonus. Laurie was certain this was one of those instances.

"Well, should I be the bad cop as always?" Gunnar offered.

"You know I'm just not convincing as a bitch," Laurie replied.

"That's debatable!" Gunnar laughed. "Here I go, then." He opened the door and walked into the little room while Laurie remained unseen behind the glass.

"Hi. My name's Detective Hincks. Do you know why you're here?" Gunnar shot at him.

"Yeah." The cashier shifted nervously in the shaky little chair as Gunnar's threatening tone caught him off guard. "I was robbed and the assholes knocked me out. I think I got a concussion. Maybe I'll file for workman's comp." He rubbed his head and winced painfully for effect.

"Well, that is the story I hear you're telling." Gunnar walked slowly around the table and then around behind the cashier who adjusted himself nervously, trying to keep his threatening visitor in view.

Suddenly, Gunnar grabbed a handful of gold and pulled upwards, choking him. "Then why are you still wearing these? Aren't these worth stealing?" Gunnar pulled a little harder on the chains, then released them and walked back around to face the cashier while he continued his barrage. "If I was going to rob someone and knock him out, I sure wouldn't pass up gold like you're wearing. Those chains are another couple hundred easy. And what about the six hundred dollars you had in the drawer. I thought you guys were supposed to keep the drawer empty—no more than fifty dollars is what it says on the door. Why did you have so much in your drawer? Were you waiting to get robbed? Maybe by some friends? What will we see when we look at the surveillance tape? Are you chatting it up with your buddies before they clock you on the head?" He strode menacingly back toward the cashier who cringed with fear. Then Laurie walked in.

"Oh, I see you've had a chance to meet my partner." Laurie smiled at the clerk as she closed the door behind her. "So, did Detective Hincks explain why your version of this robbery sounds like bullshit?"

The clerk's expression displayed his shock that Laurie, who'd thus far seemed to believe his tale, was no longer on his side. "I was robbed and knocked out. My head hurts and I wanna see a doctor!" He glared at Laurie, then Gunnar.

"But you told me that you were fine." Laurie replied calmly. "We'll talk some more and maybe you can see a doctor later." The clerk folded his arms across his chest and said nothing.

"Your boss is bringing in the tape. What're we going to see on it? Is there really a robbery? Did you even bother to fake it with friends or did you just stuff the money in your pockets or in your car? Should we search your car?"

The cashier shifted in his seat. The fear was plain on his face. "I was robbed and knocked out. What do you want from me? I don't know what that tape's gonna show because I was out cold. I wanna see a doctor," he complained again.

"How about the truth," Laurie replied softly. "You did a poor job of making this look like a robbery, Carl, so just come clean. Maybe they'll go easier on you if you don't waste too much of our time."

"Or I could just throw you in the lock-up downstairs," Gunnar interjected. "You're kinda cute, ya know. And no one really keeps an eye on the cells down there. You'd be on your own. Hope you like getting cozy with a bunch of big, tough, sweaty guys. Hell, it's probably nothing new to you, anyway." Gunnar shoved his face close enough to the cashier's to see the veins popping up red in his eyes. He was frightened. They had him.

"All right," he whimpered. The confession came out in a long jumbled mess. The two kids were his cousins; they needed the cash to go get an eightball of coke for the weekend. They were having a few girls over and wanted to show them a good time.

Laurie felt a rush through to her toes. She loved it when they confessed. But she actually felt a bit sorry for this kid. He wasn't bright enough to know that there were better things in life than doing drugs. And he would probably never learn.

# Chapter 8

At precisely one-thirty, the desk clerk buzzed Laurie's line. "A Brandon Doyle is here to see you," the clerk droned out in his nasally voice.

Hmmmm. Mr. Breathless or is it Mr. Out-of-Breath? I guess I'll soon discover the truth. "Thanks, Jim. I'll be right down." Laurie made a vain attempt to quickly straighten up the piles of paper on her desk, before hurrying off to the elevator.

"What's with you, Sharpe? Got a hot date?" Gunnar asked as Laurie nearly plowed into him on her way to the elevator.

"Watch out, Gunnar. You keep worrying so much about my sex life, I might just have to claim sexual harassment," Laurie shot back with a smile before she realized her face was hot. She was blushing! What was the matter with her? This computer geek in the lobby was going to turn out to be fat, bald, and sweaty, so why was she falling all over herself?

But he wasn't fat, bald, and sweaty. When Laurie emerged from the elevator, he was waiting casually by the glass doors, looking out at the parking lot. Brandon Doyle was tall, lean, and absolutely everything that Laurie considered sexy. He was as attractive as his voice had been earlier, and even more so. Laurie glanced over at Jim behind the desk and was silently thankful that he wasn't looking over at her as she could feel the crimson in her face deepen. God, she needed to stop blushing! She took a deep breath, then another, and finally walked over to where Mr. Breathless stood at the door.

"Mr. Doyle?" He spun around to face her and the smile that spread across his face nearly made Laurie's knees slide out of joint. His blue eyes latched onto hers and it was every effort she could make to fight a smile of her own, put on a stone face, slightly red, and thrust her right hand out in greeting. Mr. Doyle grasped it firmly, but did not shake. Instead, he held her hand a moment then eased up on his grip and let his hand slide slowly out of hers.

Butterflies fluttered around in Laurie's stomach, but she did her best to ignore them. "Follow me?" Mr. Doyle nodded and climbed onto the elevator behind her. Laurie tentatively tried her voice as the doors closed, "So where does this hacker live?"

"Tatnuck area, down off Salisbury Street."

"The neighbors won't like seeing the police down in their neighborhood, at one of their houses. So what do you think, race in with lights and sirens or keep a low profile and let these people save some face in case, as you say, it turns out to be their kid playing around after school?"

Mr. Doyle wrapped the tip of his silk tie around his finger as he feigned serious pondering on his reply. "Low profile, I think. The neighbors will start enough rumors without any extra help from us, though lights and sirens would definitely be a bit more exciting." He smiled.

Laurie allowed the corners of her mouth to ease upward. "Nice tie. Are you a Marvin fan?" Mr. Doyle held out his tie, which displayed Marvin the Martian peeking out from the black silk.

"Since I was a kid. Always wanted his Illudium Q-36 Explosive Space Modulator." He smiled again, a warm, confident smile.

The elevator opened onto an empty granite hallway and Laurie stepped out first, turning her head away from Mr. Doyle in an effort to hide the color that was once again rising in her cheeks. This man was everything she had pictured from his voice and she liked him at once! But she was only a few weeks out of her relationship with Jeff, so this would just be a rebound, right? But what was she thinking? He's probably attached. Not married, of course. Laurie had noticed the ringless finger immediately, but certainly this man had a woman in his life. No, this is just work, she thought, and he's just being nice. He's not flirting with that unbelievably sexy smile, that's just the way he smiles for everyone.

"Would you like a seat?" Laurie motioned to a plain, steel armchair with a worn plastic cushion that was positioned in front of her desk, while she quickly made her way to her own seat and gingerly sat, aware that he was watching her.

"So, Mr. Doyle, what's your evidence pointing to this particular address for your hacker? And I need something that a judge can understand."

"Please, call me Brandon. If we're to work together on this, we should at least drop some of the formalities, don't you think?"

"Call me Laurie then," she returned in a stark tone.

Brandon opened his briefcase and pulled out a short stack of paper held with a binder clip and handed it to Laurie. "A judge probably won't understand most of that, but I've included a summary letter on top that outlines how the information printed out in the attached report points directly to that address in Tatnuck." Brandon closed the briefcase, placed it on the floor beside his chair and casually leaned back, crossing one leg over the other as he watched Laurie study the papers.

"I can also speak to the judge if he or she has any questions about what's in that package."

After a moment, Laurie responded, "This summary seems pretty clear. As long as the bulk of the information is in order, I don't see any problem. Amazing how you can trace this back to someone. A lot like my job." She smiled and her stomach rolled as he met her eyes with another of his smiles.

"I will get a judge to issue a warrant for the house. It should take a couple hours since this isn't really a life or death situation. Then we can head over to the house. I think just a couple of cars to the house should suffice."

"Right. I don't think there'll be any physical threat from this person, whoever they are," Brandon agreed. "Of course, don't neglect to cover the computer itself in the warrant, since that's where we'll find the evidence we need."

Laurie nodded. "Then we determine who did the hacking and arrest them if they're home."

"All right. Should we meet back here around five then? I will certainly have the warrant by then. I shouldn't need any further explanation for the judge. Then we can hit the house around six o'clock?" Brandon's eyes held hers as she prepared to close their meeting. His manner was very professional, but the way he held her gaze in that moment hinted at other thoughts going through his mind. He liked her, too.

Brandon returned to the Worcester Police Station at exactly five o'clock with a broad smile spreading across his face when Laurie greeted him. Gunnar joined them at Laurie's desk and she introduced them.

Gunnar greeted Brandon gruffly and held out his hand. "How are you?" he asked, putting little effort into the handshake before turning back to Laurie.

"I've already filled Detective Hincks in on the details of the break-in. We can get started at any time. Officers Lobel and Brooks will join us as back-up in case things get ugly. You can imagine people can get a little testy when you force your way into their home waving a piece of paper." She held up the warrant, then folded it and placed it into a folder.

She looked from Gunnar to Brandon, ready to urge them toward the door, but suddenly it occurred to her how much these two men looked alike. She shifted her eyes from one to the other again and again, noticing each individual similarity—the clear blue eyes, the nose, the same strong, square jaw, the same height—both were six feet, two inches tall. Gunnar and Brandon, standing together side-by-side looked so much alike they could have been brothers. They weren't twins; if they were that much alike, Laurie would have noticed the similarities when she'd first spoken to Brandon earlier, but except for Gunnar's military style haircut, his lighter hair color, and his military stance, one could easily be mistaken for the other. So why had she never been attracted to Gunnar the way she was to Brandon? Most likely it was Brandon's confident and casual manner that drew her to him. She did find his manner very appealing. Gunnar, however, was cocky rather than confident and he was far too uptight to ever properly relax. Laurie couldn't ever remember Gunnar just letting his guard down, but she was certain that Brandon relaxed easily. That was probably why Gunnar had never committed to any one woman, because to commit would mean he would have to trust a woman and let her trust him. That meant he would have to drop his guard and at least to some degree, around Laurie anyway, Gunnar could never do that.

Laurie suddenly realized that both men were staring at her. She had been silently comparing them for more than a minute and they probably wondered at the surprised look on her face. "Do you two realize just how much you look alike?"

"What are you talking about?" Gunnar asked, a little confusion in his voice.

Brandon reacted more quickly to Laurie's observation and took a moment to study Gunnar's profile before Gunnar glared at him, sizing him up while he threatened him with his eyes.

Brandon grinned and slowly nodded his head. "You're not imagining it. You're right." He gave a short laugh and turned his eyes back to Laurie.

Gunnar huffed as he also noticed features on Brandon that he knew were similar to his own. "I'll have to talk to my mother," he smirked. "She never told me I had a second brother. I thought it was just the two of us."

As Gunnar spoke, he noticed the look of interest that Brandon was giving Laurie and saw how she was responding to it. Was it too late to decide how much he, himself, really cared for her? If he told her, would she ever look at him the way she was looking at Brandon now? Certainly Brandon was just toying with her, just flirting. But Gunnar had seen that look before. That look had resulted in his brother's marriage. Love at first sight! Gunnar suddenly realized Laurie was again out of his reach and he'd not even had a chance to consider the possibilities.

Laurie led Brandon and Gunnar as they climbed the front steps of the large Tudor style house on Salisbury Street, one of Worcester's most prestigious neighborhoods. There were two cars in the driveway and lights on in the first floor of the house. Both parents were home, visible through the large bay window. She used the brass lion's head to knock firmly on the front door. There was no bell. Shuffling and footsteps could be heard from the other side of the door before it opened to a middle-aged man with thinning brown and gray hair. His tired eyes suddenly came to life as he saw who was standing on his front porch. He was a short man, but as he straightened up, he seemed to grow a couple inches and lose a few years.

"Can I help you, officers?" He eyed the badge around Laurie's neck and took the search warrant as she presented it to him.

"We would like to speak to you and take a look around your house," Laurie said softly. She saw no sense upsetting this man when it was most likely his son who had done the hacking. This man might not even know how to use a computer, being from a generation that had none.

"Do you own a computer, sir?" The man nodded. "Do you know that your computer was used to hack into the Moonshine Brewing Company and wreak havoc on their personnel files as well as costing the company thousands in lost shipping orders?" Laurie paused as she saw the confusion on the man's face. "Do you use your computer much, sir?"

The man slowly shook his head. "I use it for building design is all. I'm a contractor. My son uses it for his schoolwork. My wife hates the thing and won't touch it. How did someone break into a company from my computer?"

"That's what we'd like to find out," Gunnar spoke. "Can we come in, sir?" He pushed the door gently and the man stepped back, allowing them to walk past him into the house.

"Wait, do I need an attorney?" the man began to object.

"Yes, you can call your attorney. We may need to talk to you or your son, Mr. Bryant, and you may wish to have your attorney present. But we are here to exercise this warrant at this time to collect evidence. Could you show me where the computer is?" Laurie was certain this man had nothing to do with this. He had no record and seemed genuinely confused by their presence.

"I can't wait for my attorney before you come in?"

"No, Sir. The warrant is exercised immediately to limit destruction or damage to evidence present."

"No one is going to destroy evidence," Mr. Bryant grumbled. "I'm going to call my attorney."

He picked up a cellular phone from a table near the door and punched in a number he'd apparently memorized. Suddenly, the entry echoed as the man bellowed out his son's name and Laurie's heart nearly leapt from her chest in surprise. The strength of Mr. Bryant's booming voice far surpassed his timid appearance.

A mousy-haired boy with a face full of red zits appeared quietly in the doorway of the living room. He cringed noticeably when he saw the badges.

Mr. Bryant held the phone to his ear a moment, then punched in several digits on the number pad, apparently paging his attorney to call him back, then disconnected the call. Maybe Laurie and Gunnar would get a few minutes of free time with him before the attorney stepped in.

"These officers need to have a word with you." Mr. Bryant's face was turning bright crimson as the knuckles of his hand that still gripped the phone went white. He leaned threateningly into the boy. "What have you been doing out on the Internet, John? Vandalism?" He took the boy by the shoulder with his free hand and pulled him toward the officers as if to hand him over.

Great guy, Laurie thought. Doesn't even have the slightest bit of curiosity as to whether his son is innocent or guilty. I guess it's guilty until proven innocent in this house. Poor kid.

Reluctantly, she took the boy down the front stairs to the cruiser parked in the driveway. His father followed, his demeanor still very threatening. Laurie carefully guided Johnny into the back seat of the cruiser and closed the door behind him.

"I should get in with him," the man dictated.

"He'll be fine there for now. We need to go get that computer. We'll need to go through it for evidence. Then you can come down to the station while we talk to him. You may want to follow us in your own car, though."

Mr. Bryant hesitated, glaring at his son through the glass, then turned with a huff and led Laurie back into the house.

They left the hacker to sweat alone in the interrogation room while his father was out in the lobby, again calling the lawyer who had not yet responded to his page. Gunnar stood outside, watching Johnny through the glass as if he were a caged animal. Laurie had run out with Brandon to the nearest shop that had decent coffee. *Let the boy worry!*

Laurie was growing at ease in Brandon's company. Since he'd first entered the station earlier that day, it seemed she met his eyes whenever she looked his way and now she found herself glancing sideways at him from time to time, excited to find his eyes upon her, watching her while she drove.

"Do you always check out the guys you work with?" he asked, his voice suddenly smoky and hesitant.

"One of the perks of my job," she countered with a smile. "A woman with a badge can do anything she wants. Besides, I thought it was you who was checking me out." Laurie felt her cheeks turn cherry red as the words escaped her before she could stop them. What was she saying? She was never this forward with a man she barely knew. But Brandon was certainly not like any man she'd ever met. Or was he?

"You know, I don't usually try to pick up women with badges since I occasionally like to live a little outside the law." He gave a sly smile, paused, and asked, "I wonder if you would have dinner with me tomorrow night. Are you free?"

Laurie was silent for a moment. Had this perfect man just asked her out for a date? And was he really perfect, or was she just rebounding from Jeff? It had only been a few weeks after all. But again, before she could stop herself, the words burst from her in a rush. "I'd love to! But I confess, I don't usually bring my handcuffs out on dates." She cringed inwardly, but fought to keep her face from wrinkling up in her embarrassment.

"Too bad. I'll have to find some ropes then, just in case." But Brandon had seen her dismay at the words she had blurted and offered solace. "Honestly, just dinner. I'll try hard not to take advantage of you if you'll tell me where to pick you up. And your phone number, as well, of course." He smiled and pulled out a PDA, removed the stylus from its sleeve and held it poised, waiting. "Shall I pick you up around seven?"

Laurie hesitated, her eyes glued to the road ahead.

"Sounds good," she said finally and dictated the information as she guided the cruiser into the drive-through, then ordered four coffees and a soda. She always tried to butter up her prisoners before an interrogation. It helped loosen their tongues enough to tell her the truth about why she had to bring them in.

Laurie was now shaking with anticipation for Brandon when the cashier handed her the tray of coffees. Her hands shook so badly; she nearly toppled the coffee into his lap as she handed the tray over to him.

"Careful there." He chuckled. "I don't have a change of clothes with me and having a large coffee stain in one's lap is hardly an effective interrogation tactic. Not to mention the nasty burn all that coffee would make."

Laurie blushed again. Get a hold of yourself, Laurie! Spilling coffee on a man is hardly the way to his heart. Still, she smiled uncontrollably in spite of herself and met Brandon's eye as he grinned back at her, clearly entertained by the nervous wreck she'd become. She didn't look his way for the remainder of the ride and they drove back to the station in silence, staring straight ahead like two children playing a game of who could be quiet the longest.

The Bryant's lawyer had arrived and sat impressively, confidently beside his client. He glared and raised his nose as Laurie and Gunnar walked into the interrogation room and Laurie introduced them both. Brandon remained behind the glass, watching with interest.

Johnny was now shaking from head to toe. He had never been caught before and was still coping with the idea that he was actually sitting in the police station with a lawyer beside him. His father had left him and though he felt angry at the desertion, he was thankful that at least he wouldn't have to listen to him yell. But where had he screwed up? He'd always been so careful. Was it the IRS that had caught him? Had they finally uncovered tracks from his trip into their system when he'd reinvented his parents' tax returns? But that was months ago. Surely they would have caught up to him before this if they suspected anything? If it was the IRS, his father would disown him if he hadn't already. This high-priced lawyer sitting next to him would disappear and he'd be left with some public defender ass. He'd go to jail for sure. It couldn't be the IRS!

Laurie handed Johnny the soda, but he wouldn't take it, so she set it on the table in front of him. Meanwhile, she sipped at her coffee, enjoying the warmth as it caressed her throat, readying her for the attack.

Gunnar cast the first question while Laurie sipped casually, eyeing the teen. "How did you happen to choose the Moonshine Brewing Company to vandalize over the Internet?"

The shock of relief left Johnny speechless for a moment. It wasn't the IRS? If the IRS didn't catch him, then his dad wouldn't yank the fancy lawyer. No dumbass public defender. He would be okay! "What's the Moonshine Brewing Company?" The words came out easy now and he was calm.

Gunnar smiled smugly. He had not expected any other answer, but he didn't explain. Instead, he suggested that Johnny should be more careful about who he tries to pin his little acts of vandalism on. Gunnar was unaware that Sam Willis was the owner of Moonshine Brewing, but he told Johnny of Sam's immediate reaction to his extraordinarily large paycheck and how he brought it straight to the payroll department to have the mistake corrected.

"The guy probably found out they were on to him. So, what's this got to do with me?" The boy fidgeted in his seat. What could they do to him, really? He was too young to do jail time for something as trivial as this. Right?

Laurie saw what Johnny was thinking. It was a pretty standard thought. Kids never seemed to think that the laws applied to them. They always figured that they would get a free ride until they were eighteen. And sometimes that was true. But Laurie liked to at least try to teach them a lesson; make them better adults. And in Johnny's case, she thought there was hope—he didn't seem like a bad kid, just troubled. Who wouldn't be with a father like his? She figured the attorney was only there to save his father's reputation, not Johnny's.

"You do know they traced the break-in back to your computer, so there's really no sense denying it." Laurie leaned over Johnny while he squirmed in his seat. "The evidence is all right there in your computer to backup what they got off the Internet. Just come clean with it and maybe we can put in a good word; ask them to go easy on you. Lots of kids like to toy around with the Internet. I'm sure they can cut you a deal since this is your first offense."

"I-I h-have no idea what you're talking about," Johnny stammered. He could tell Laurie was no computer genius but knew there must be something on him if they knew about Moonshine Brewing and Sam Willis. Johnny was sure she didn't spend that much time on the Internet and certainly not enough time to learn how to break into corporate networks. But if these two stupid cops hadn't tracked him, who had? He was always careful. How much information did they really have?

Johnny said nothing; he merely glared, shifting his eyes back and forth from Gunnar to Laurie. Until they could show him proof of how they tracked him, he would deny everything.

Again, Laurie read his thoughts. She smiled at him, left the room and ushered in Brandon, who strolled confidently into the small interrogation room. Laurie watched from behind the glass; the room was too small to have all of them remain in there comfortably. Besides, not only did Laurie get to watch the kid squirm and sweat, she also got to watch Brandon; got to appreciate that calm demeanor without interruption and certainly without blushing.

Brandon smiled at Johnny. He didn't often get to sit face-to-face with his prey, but when he did, he loved to make the punks squirm. Nothing wrecked their day more than knocking them off their high horse of computer knowledge. Hackers are an interesting group. Most of them think they know more about computers than anyone else on the face of the earth. But when someone comes along with some real knowledge and real skills and they realize how truly little they know, they are horribly shocked and confused. Brandon had yet to meet a hacker who even came close to understanding computers and the Internet as well as he. And those hackers he did meet simply couldn't comprehend the magnitude of technology when Brandon shared his knowledge. All that many of them had ever seen was their own desktop computer and what can be done with that alone is very limited. Brandon, on the other hand, had worked with several agencies over the years and had enjoyed access to all sorts of hardware, software, and the latest technology in gadgets. He knew it all. He had even worked with the NSA and, although they did not show him everything, he was sure they had shown him many tools and toys that the rest of the world never sees.

Johnny, like the other hackers, was taken aback with the details of how easily he was traced. He wondered why he'd never been caught before this, but Brandon was not surprised. He knew that the steps that Johnny had taken to cover his tracks could easily throw anyone off the trail. Johnny's only mistake here had been in choosing Sam

Willis to lay blame on. Sam had known Brandon since college, when they shared a few classes and had become good friends. And Brandon was always eager to help his friends.

Johnny wilted as his mistakes were explained to him. He suddenly felt much younger than his thirteen years. He hated computers! And he hated this man! Yet he felt the immediate need to tell him everything and beg forgiveness as though Brandon were the god of the computer world. His attorney tried his best to keep him from spilling all, but soon realized it was hopeless. Johnny was a waterfall of information.

Laurie did her best to stifle a laugh as she watched through the glass. She could tell Gunnar was doing his best not to laugh—the corners of his mouth were pinched tight with the struggle to keep them from turning upward. Boys had the most unexpected reactions to being interrogated. Some of them cried; some just got a silent angry look, but Laurie thought Johnny Bryant would start kissing Brandon's feet at any moment. Brandon, the almighty computer guru!

When Johnny was through spilling his guts, his lawyer asked for a moment alone with his client and Gunnar and Brandon joined Laurie behind the glass. It was all over now. Regardless of any advice his lawyer gave, the truth had been spilled. But Laurie hoped silently that the courts would go easy on him. Brandon's bursting his bubble had been punishment enough. She didn't think he would be out hacking into new companies anytime soon, if ever.

"I guess my work is done here. You shouldn't be needing me around here anymore today and I have preparations to make for tomorrow evening." He winked at Laurie, and then held out his hand to her and to Gunnar before he left.

"I know you two are up to something," Gunnar accused when Brandon was gone. "You have a date, don't you?"

"Why Detective, I have no idea what you're talking about," she smiled without looking away from the glass and the room beyond. But Gunnar knew. Whatever chance he might ever have had with Laurie was now gone for good. Laurie was in love.

# Chapter 9

Y ou're canceling our first-rate plans this evening to go out on a date with some gorgeous guy you just met and know nothing about? Of course I understand," Jessie chided Laurie from the other end of the phone.

"Thanks. I knew you would."

"So, where is this Mr. Gorgeous taking you?"

"I've no idea. Dinner, of course, but I don't know where. I'll wait to see. You can tell a lot about a guy from what he chooses for a first date, and I don't want to influence that first impression."

"Right. Coffee is casual, noncommittal, no passion? Straight to drinks is hoping that you'll have one too many to loosen you right up, then a quick one-night stand and never hear from him again."

"Come on, Jessie. That's bringing it to the simplest level. I'm talking about the restaurant he chooses."

"Isn't that usually based on the kind of food he likes?"

"Sure. But more than that, it says something about his personality. For instance, a guy that takes you out for Italian likes to eat family style, break bread together, and share lots of conversation."

"Or, he's just playing it safe by picking food that most people like," Jessie countered.

"That could be. But I think that Chinese is more the safe food and actually, I think I'd prefer Chinese to Italian for a first date. Chinese is fun, casual food. You get to share dishes, serve each other, share a scorpion bowl. I think going for Chinese shows a guy is casual and easy-going."

"Or he just lacks imagination. Everybody goes for Chinese. What about something more exotic like Japanese or Indian?"

"I like those, but they can be dangerous choices for any guy to make without consent, and for a first date, I don't think I'd like it if a guy chose something exotic without knowing ahead of time whether I could handle exotic or not."

"But Chinese is cheap. Wouldn't you rather go to someplace like The Sole for seafood?"

"No way. Too preppy, and too noisy. I'd much rather a place where I can hear what he says without straining."

"I don't know, Laurie. Personally, I'd rather go to a really nice restaurant on the first date. Then I know he's not just trying to score."

"On the contrary, guys who have taken me to expensive restaurants for a first date made the most advances afterwards, were the most disappointed at their lack of success, and were the least likely to ever call me again."

"Well, then for your benefit, I hope he likes Chinese food. Have fun and if it starts going bad and you need an out, call me and let me know to ring you back with a fake emergency so you can slip away."

"Thanks, Jess. You always look out for me."

"That's what friends are for. That and gossip—I want a recount with all details later."

"I'll call you tomorrow," Laurie agreed.

Laurie hadn't been so nervous about a date since her very first in high school. Maybe Jeff's indiscretions with that plump little housewife had been a good thing. If Laurie hadn't discovered that she was sharing Jeff, he'd still be in her life, she wouldn't have been flirting with Brandon, and certainly wouldn't have accepted his invitation. Timing *is* everything. Had her luck with men finally changed for the better? Or was there really such a thing as fate? Because Brandon seemed to be everything she had ever dreamed of in a man.

Laurie only hoped that she wasn't deluding herself; that she wasn't going out with Brandon tonight and wasn't thinking so much of him simply because she was hurting and needed some release for her pain. No. This wasn't just a rebound reaction, she was certain of it! She felt all this anticipation because Brandon really was just so damn attractive and so right for her! She wasn't going to blame this feeling on needing to rebound from Jeff. *I think that even if I hadn't found out about Jeff running around, I'd still have said 'yes' to Brandon's invitation!* Even just to spend time with him once to get to know him. It's not every day someone so perfect passed through Laurie's life. At the very least, she and Brandon could have become good friends. But now she wouldn't have to stop at being just friends if this date went as well as she hoped. *I won't have to hold back because now I'm totally free!*

She adjusted the clip in her hair and pulled a few strands of blonde out from its grasp to let them fall across her forehead. Not bad. But was it the right look she wanted? More importantly, if he wanted to touch her hair, a banana clip was hardly an invitation to that and it did look a bit rigid. She pulled the clip out of her hair and the strands trickled down the delicate curve of her neck to her shoulders. She contemplated the look in the mirror, poking at a few of the curls with her fingers before taking a brush to them. Then she tamed the style by tucking a lock behind each ear.

"Better," she said to her reflection. She eyed the bottle of hairspray and decided against using it and turned her attention to her attire. Straightening her short black skirt, she brushed a few flecks of white off, and then checked the cloth under her sleeveless arms for deodorant residue—there was none.

"All I need now is shoes," she murmured, sizing up her overall appearance again before rummaging around the floor of the closet until she'd located of a pair of leather pumps that were both comfortable and stylish.

The doorbell rang as she was slipping her feet into the shoes and she suddenly felt goose bumps pop up on her arms.

"These nerves had just better calm down," she mumbled to herself. "No surer way to scare a guy off than to be too nervous, so I have to relax." She drew a deep breath, and met the eyes of her reflection. "I hope this guy's for real." She paused, and then tore her eyes from her own and headed for the door.

85

Her hesitation over, she grabbed the doorknob boldly and quickly pulled the door open.

Brandon stood on the doorstep, a shy smile turning up the corners of his mouth, his eyes meeting hers from beneath dark brows that accented the shape of those blue eyes with a bold, symmetrical curve.

"How are you, Detective?" He offered a single red rose that she failed to notice until the delicate leaves brushed against her trembling hand.

With enormous effort, Laurie shifted her gaze to the flower, then slowly took it from his hand. She raised the bud to her nose to inhale its perfume when she realized she wasn't breathing, hadn't actually taken a breath since she'd opened the door. Now, aware of her need for oxygen, the air rushed into her lungs, pulling the petals greedily to her nose. She pulled it back quickly as the petals blocked her breath.

Her eyes darted quickly to his, hoping he hadn't noticed the mishap, but his eyes were on her, watching her, wrinkled at the corners in his amusement.

"I can get you more if you inhale that one, but I don't believe roses are meant to be breathed in."

Laurie blushed crimson. "A little nervous," she confessed.

Brandon was positively irresistible in a pair of faded Levi's and a tweed sport coat, but she barely noticed anything but his eyes. They were glued to hers as she backed into the house, stepping aside for him to enter before she closed the door.

He spoke first as they stood in the entry, eyes still locked together. "Do you like Chinese food?"

Laurie nodded slowly.

Brandon grinned and Laurie's trance was broken by his continued amusement.

She laughed and let her eyes shift to her toes a moment to regain her composure.

"I'm sorry, I'm acting really strangely. I'm just unaccustomed to meeting any man's eye for so long unless I'm interrogating him." She looked into his eyes again, this time to share in his amusement.

"Are you planning to interrogate me then?"

"Just a few questions over a scorpion bowl."

"Ahhh. Favorite interrogation technique, huh? Get the man drunk and make him tell all?"

"How else could I get past those first date lines, stories, and untruths?" Laurie raised a brow then turned on her heel and headed to the kitchen.

"I'll put this in water, then where should we go?" She pulled a narrow blue vase from the white-painted overhead cabinet beside the sink as she spoke and filled it with water, then added the rose and placed it on the table in the center of the kitchen.

"I know this great place in Westborough," Brandon replied. "We could eat and maybe catch a movie."

"The Chinese and scorpion bowl sounds great! Let's skip the movie, though?" She daintily cleared her throat when her words crackled, catching in her throat. Still a little nervous. "Let me just grab a jacket." She disappeared and returned with a short, black leather jacket.

Brandon took the jacket from her and helped her into it. He stood close to her, appreciating the scent of her hair and its subtle shades of gold. He wanted to run his fingers through it; feel if it was as soft and silky as it looked. Instead, he cupped his hand tenderly onto her shoulder and encouraged her toward the door and out into the night.

They took the last empty table near the front of the restaurant. Brandon took Laurie's jacket as she slid onto the bench seat.

"Brandon?" A familiar voice greeted him from behind and Brandon turned around.

"Spence? You didn't tell me you were in town. How are you?"

"Good. I got a last minute assignment to test out some networks. I didn't get a chance to call you before I came out and the company's got me running around like a nut these past couple of weeks."

"You've been in town two weeks and you're not staying at my place?"

"Nah. Company's dime, so I figure they can cover the Crowne Plaza. I should have known I'd bump into you here for Chinese food. Didn't think you'd actually bring a date to this place, though." Spencer looked toward Laurie and smiled warmly.

"I'm sorry, Spence." Brandon stepped aside to introduce Spence.

"Spencer Kinney, this is Detective Laurie Sharpe."

"Detective? Very nice to meet you." Spencer let his eyes linger a moment then turned back to Brandon.

"Well, I should go. You two are here for a quiet dinner, I'm sure, and I've already eaten and have to run. You two have fun." He smiled at them both, patted Brandon on the shoulder, and headed for the door.

"I get the impression you've known each other many years," Laurie observed.

Brandon chuckled. "That's the truth. Spencer and I have been pretty tight since high school. We even dated some of the same girls. Teachers always thought we were brothers and could never get our names straight. Not that we look that much alike, except for this chin." He rubbed a hand across his square jaw, noting that the skin was still smooth from his five o'clock shave.

"It's nice you still have friends from high school. I keep in touch with a few, but it's difficult to find the time," Laurie said.

"I really only keep in touch with Spence. He and I are both in the same business, so we can always connect on something. He handles network security for Ernst & Young and we're always on the phone talking about computers. He usually stays with me when he's in town unless, as he says, he's got a really big job. Then he's in and out at weird hours and doesn't want to bother me. Personally, I wouldn't mind, but he's more comfortable this way."

A petite Chinese waitress appeared and Brandon quickly ordered a scorpion bowl and sent her on her way while they looked over the menu. When she returned with the drink, Brandon pointed out what they wanted on the menu to be sure she understood their order, since she spoke very little English. Then she scampered off again like a little girl headed for the playground.

"So how long have you been tracking down hackers?" Laurie asked as they sipped together at the large bowl of alcohol and fruit juice. The sweet pineapple helped her keep her cool as she met his eyes over the blue flame rising off the rum in the center of the bowl.

"About five years," Brandon replied between sips.

"That's all? You seem to know so much. I was certain you'd been doing this much longer."

"Well, I was the hacker for many years before that."

Laurie raised an eyebrow and Brandon grinned at her surprise.

"I hacked for fun from the moment I could afford a computer that could access the Internet. That was before they were really affordable to the average person. But I had some extra money at the time and I just went for it. I was about twenty."

"Wow, you started early. I didn't even get onto the Internet until I joined the police force at twenty-four. I used a computer for word-processing in college, but that was all. Of course the Internet then was much less useful and exciting than it is now.

"So, what did you hack into?" she asked.

"Whatever I could. Until I got caught, that is."

Laurie covered her mouth in surprise. "Like our little friend, Johnny?"

"I was a bit luckier than Johnny, although he might yet come out of this smelling like a rose. But I had a distinct advantage over our little friend. When I got caught, the Internet was still new. They determined that I had a special and valuable talent that few people had then. Today, hackers are commonplace. But back then, instead of going to jail, I got recruited."

"By who?" she asked.

"I got caught hacking into the government. I didn't do anything to their site; I just wanted to see if I could get in. So, they hired me. I did a lot of work, both hacking and security for the next five years before I branched out on my own. I get to travel a bit more freely now and the money's certainly better. But, enough about me. How about you? Why did you decide to become a police detective?"

Laurie smiled shyly as the spotlight shifted to her and she took a long drink. She much preferred asking the questions to answering them.

"My story is far more predictable, I'm afraid. I'm from a small town, Clarendon Springs, in Vermont. My father is a district attorney in Rutland, nearby. My uncle, his brother, is a detective in New York City. My uncle on my mother's side is a cop in Fair Haven, Vermont. The thought of being anything but a cop never crossed my mind after listening to the exciting stories they shared over holiday dinners. My brothers took the same path. One's an MP and the other is a cop in Hartford. Myself—I weighed the small town stories with the big city ones and decided on Worcester for something in between. There's just enough action around here to keep the job exciting, but I'm not overwhelmed like my uncle in New York."

The waitress appeared with their food—Peking raviolis, fried rice, and spicy chicken with cashews. They waited patiently while she arranged the plates on the table, lifting each lid to show them what was underneath. Then they requested another scorpion bowl before she departed.

Brandon took a long sip from the bowl that remained on the table as Laurie asked, "You haven't said much about your family. Are they close? Do you get to visit much?" She started to reach for the plate of raviolis when she noticed the change in Brandon's expression.

Brandon's eyes dropped to the table as he gathered strength to respond. "My parents were killed in a car wreck when I was nineteen. My father lost control of the car on the way home from a party. He hadn't even been drinking."

Laurie covered his hand tenderly with her own. "I'm sorry," she offered.

Brandon continued, his eyes misty. "I was at college, WPI here in Worcester, when it happened. That's when I decided to stay. I bought a condo here and another in California with the inheritance and insurance from my parents. I like to spend time in both places, visit with friends and such. I also do a lot of work out in California, so it's nice to have a place to come home to."

"Where's your home in California?"

"San Francisco. I've always liked it there—it's very quaint and there's always lots to do in and around the city. But again, enough about me," he said as he encouraged Laurie to continue with serving up raviolis. "I still haven't heard much about you. When did you move here to Worcester?"

"Just like you, I moved here for college also. I did four years of Criminal Justice at Anna Maria College. I took the civil service exam during that time and as soon as I graduated, I had a job here in Worcester. It wasn't easy at first, though. The guys here can be pretty tough on women, especially back then. But after a couple of years, they finally started to treat me as an equal instead of a pair of pants to try and get into."

"I can imagine being on the police force is difficult for any woman, but for you it must have been horrible. I hope you'll forgive me for saying so, but you are an extraordinarily attractive woman."

Laurie blushed a deep crimson.

"Do you still enjoy your work? I mean, it must be difficult to handle cases like that poor girl they found murdered. Did you have to work on that?" Brandon covered a pile of rice with a spoonful of the spicy chicken.

"I was the first detective on the scene for that actually," Laurie replied softly, disheartened by the image of the dead girl that entered her mind.

"I'm sorry," Brandon said when he saw her mood change. "Are you OK talking about it?"

Laurie nodded and the sadness faded a little. "It's alright. This is my life. I can't be afraid to talk about it."

Brandon studied her eyes then continued softly, "How do you handle seeing something like that?" His eyes were glued to her intensely, trying to see as well as hear how this beautiful woman handled gore.

"It's not easy. That murder scene is the worst I have come across in my career. It was everything I could do to keep from running out of there, if you really want the truth. Of course, don't ever tell anyone that." She smiled a sickly smile. "I have to maintain the respect of the guys. Even though I know some of them were equally ready to puke, they would lean into me if they knew I had barely held it together."

"Your secret is safe with me. I'm sorry that you had to deal with such a nasty scene, but I'm pretty impressed that you're able to work through the horror of it to get the clues you need to solve the case."

"If there were any clues," Laurie mumbled as she took a sip of the new bowl the waitress brought.

"How do you mean?"

"This guy, whoever he is, left nothing behind that we could use. No hair, no DNA, nothing. Just some fibers, but they were pretty common. And it doesn't seem like anyone really saw anything at the bar she was picked up from, either." Laurie shook her head in frustration.

"I'm sorry." Brandon studied her a moment, fork poised, as he noted the sadness in her eyes. "Enough of that then. I can see this case bothers you and I didn't bring you out to cause you stress. I apologize for bringing up your work. Have another drink with me and relax." He motioned toward the scorpion bowl and took a sip through his straw as Laurie joined him in doing the same. Their eyes met over the small rum flame and Abra Wilson's mutilated body was forgotten.

"Do you ever miss your parents?"

"To be honest, I don't think I ever really knew them that well. I know that might sound cold," he cleared his throat, "but my father was a salesman, always on the road. I never saw him that much, and my mother was very quiet. I remember she hummed a lot, but she didn't say much."

"But you turned out perfect anyway."

Brandon smiled and held her gaze in response to her compliment before he turned the questions back on her.

"Were you this beautiful in high school? I'll bet you were a cheerleader, or did you play sports?"

Laurie shook her head. "I was pretty quiet and shy in high school, really. I had gotten this mouth full of braces in my freshman year and didn't get rid of them until just before the senior prom. Talk about ruining your high school years. I mean, is there anything more unattractive than a mouth full of metal? Especially in high school."

Brandon shook his head and laughed. "Actually, I think braces are somewhat of a turn-on. Course, I never had to deal with them myself, so I don't have any opinion from that side of the fence."

"Oh, I guess you were the perfect boy with the perfect smile. Were you the boy that every girl wanted to go out with?"

"Hardly," he looked away again, toying with his food. "I had a few girlfriends and even took one to the prom, but nothing that ever lasted very long. I just wanted to have fun then. Now, I guess maybe I'm a bit older and wiser. I want a little more than that."

Laurie smiled at this. Did he mean he wanted more with her? But it was a little too soon to think about that, wasn't it?

But she couldn't help thinking more and more that this first date would turn into something more. The awkward silences that Laurie always feared on a first date when she found herself searching for a new topic just didn't happen with Brandon. He told more stories of his work and Laurie shared some of her own, less gruesome, and sometimes comical cases. Brandon shared stories of places he'd traveled to. He liked to travel; he tried to get to as many new places as he possibly could. Laurie was fascinated — she had traveled so little herself. Brandon could see that she was eager to join him in his adventures and he promised her that he would try to show her something new each time they got together, which he hoped would be often.

The waitress brought the check along with a couple fortune cookies at the end of the meal. As Brandon placed several bills into the black folder that held the check, he met Laurie's gaze over the table.

Laurie's heart began to flutter and she felt as if her eyes could just melt into his. She knew by the beat of her heart and by the feel of the little hairs rising off the back of her neck that she had already lost all sense of control. There would be no toe left on solid ground like there had been with Jeff. She had already taken the plunge and Brandon hadn't even touched her yet.

Suddenly, Brandon leaned forward across the table and gently kissed her mouth.

"Would you like to leave?" He asked softly as he held his face inches from hers.

She nodded silently, her eyes never leaving his.

They stood up from the booth together. Brandon took her jacket and draped it onto her shoulders, then placed a tender hand on the small of her back and guided her toward the door.

Laurie's body quivered with excitement. The small of her back bristled with goose bumps where Brandon's hand rested; the space between her legs ached with a passion that traveled like quicksilver through every artery, every vein. Her body tensed like taut elastic and when the cool air caressed her as they stepped outside, she could stand it no more. She and Brandon turned toward one another in a single motion and embraced. Laurie had never imagined passion like this. Every inch of her craved Brandon's touch and she felt powerless to deny him. She shivered uncontrollably as his strong hands made a quick exploration of all her curves before she pulled herself away from him.

"Are you alright?" he asked.

The dry smile Jeff had given her as he bid goodbye to his neighbor flashed into Laurie's mind and just as instantly, it disappeared as she looked into Brandon's eyes. Passion flared through her again and she pulled him close for another kiss.

"Not here," she whispered to him as their lips parted.

He nodded and ran his hands quickly up her front, brushing them over her breasts, before sliding an arm around her waist and hustling her toward the car.

Brandon held the door for her as she slid into her seat, letting his gaze linger upon the area between her now partially unbuttoned blouse. Laurie looked up at him longingly and he met her eyes before he closed the door and jogged around to the other side. They indulged once more in a long, passionate kiss within the confines of the car, Brandon tenderly cupping her breast and running an errant thumb across the nipple, encouraging it to stiffen and throb.

Laurie forced herself away from him. "You've seen my place; I haven't seen yours."

"It's not far. I can take you there."

Laurie smiled. "I don't think it's too healthy to end the evening at this point."

"No," Brandon agreed. "I'd much rather end the evening tomorrow."

Laurie smiled again and placed a hand on his thigh. Brandon removed it.

"Scorpion bowls and driving don't mix, but scorpion bowls, driving, and groping.... Well, I do have to draw the line."

Laurie pulled away; looking for a moment like a scolded child, then smiled. "Well, then. I think you'd better start driving. Unless you think I should administer a field sobriety test."

Brandon grinned. "I've been a good boy this evening. But I see that you've got a bit of a flush in your cheeks. Are you sure you wouldn't rather I take you home?"

The question blasted her with uncertainty and she could feel herself desperately trying to grasp at the cliff she'd fallen off and pull herself back to the top. But at the same time, Laurie couldn't fathom the idea of leaving Brandon's side for the night. She'd never felt this way toward any man she'd just met. Both her body and mind were ripe and eager for him—eager to feel his touch. Suddenly, she didn't care if she might have him for only one night.

She smiled shyly at his intense gaze. "To your home, yes."

Brandon studied her a moment, then returned her smile and put the car into gear.

Laurie felt isolated, forced to sit far away from him as he drove at a steady speed along busy Route 9 toward Worcester. She studied his profile as she longed to reach over to him.

But once again, she thought of Jeff and of how many times he had claimed to love her, while at the same time cheating on her with his neighbor. I trust too easily, she thought. Jessie would have the right words for tonight: Chinese food, scorpion bowls, and sex—classic ingredients for a one-night-stand. And Jessie was probably right, she thought, but she didn't care. Even if it was a one-night-stand, she knew it was still going to be the best sex she had ever had. She didn't care what the final score would be; she just had to touch him, just once.

Brandon turned left off Route 9 just before they crossed out of Shrewsbury and followed a winding road a short distance until he turned the car into a complex of large townhouses.

Brandon's place was a comfortable, tri-level condo that hung on the edge of Lake Quinsigamond. He took her jacket as she walked in the front door, and then closed the door behind him. "I bought this at auction back when the real estate market fell apart." He turned on a few dim lamps, but avoided the overhead lighting.

Laurie pushed her impulses aside as she looked around the townhouse. "Great place! I wish I'd had a bit of cash back then to take advantage of some of the deals that were around." She looked toward the kitchen, but she wasn't interested in seeing the condo just then.

She turned toward him and her body was immediately light, floating as she leaned close.

But he didn't reach for her. "Would you like the grand tour?"

Laurie contemplated the delay to their passion, then grabbed a handful of his shirt and pulled him firmly toward her. "Not now," she said.

She turned her face up toward his and felt her heart skip as his lips met hers. Here, behind closed doors, there was nothing left to keep them apart. Brandon fell upon her, pushing her up against the wall. Her passion rendered her powerless to resist as his skilled hands quickly peeled away at her clothing until her bare skin glowed in the dim lighting. He stepped back, admiring the beauty of her slim figure and pale, perfect skin, then slowly he began to remove what remained of his own clothing. She ached to help him, but with a mixture of fear and excitement, she merely watched him undress, wanting the moment to proceed slowly, yet impatient to satisfy her desires.

Brandon moved upon her tenderly, slowly lifting her up as she wrapped her legs around him. He pushed her firmly up against the wall and pressed himself inside her. Laurie felt a wave of pleasure and relief wash over her. She knew this was the man she wanted to be with forever! She held him tightly and made love to him more passionately than she ever had with any man. Her every sense was alert to his presence and her body moved in smooth rhythm with his until finally they collapsed together in a heap on the floor. They lay silently for a moment, breathing heavily. She studied his profile while he stared up at the ceiling.

"Don't be scared," she said, "but I think I love you."

He rolled his head sideways to face her. A bead of sweat rolled down his brow. "Yeah." He smiled. "I know what you mean and I'm not scared," he said softly. He pulled her close to him and wrapped his arms around her. "I loved you the second we met."

# Chapter 10

Laurie found herself naked beneath a thin summer quilt atop an overstuffed feather mattress. Brandon was nowhere in sight. She rolled over tiredly and crumpled a note that had been handwritten on a plain piece of printer paper folded over once. The scent of Brandon's cologne tickled her nose. She picked up the note and focused her sleepy eyes upon the swirling penmanship.

"Last night was incredible—the first of many wonderful memories," he wrote. The corner of Laurie's mouth turned up a bit as she read on. Brandon had run out to meet with a friend and client who was having trouble with his network. He figured she had to work today, so if he had missed her when he got back, he would call her house later. That would be just fine, she thought.

Laurie wasn't scheduled to work that day, but she didn't want to stay in bed alone. She rolled out from under the quilt and settled her feet into the thick gray pile of the carpet. Typical bachelor décor—soft grays, taupe, and white—devoid of anything resembling color. She smiled again. Maybe she would bring a little color into his life.

She found her way to the master bath and discovered a small whirlpool tub. It was just what she needed. She turned the water on as hot as she could stand to touch and let the tub fill to six inches from the rim. Then she stepped in gingerly, feeling the burn on her skin.

She settled pleasurably into the scalding pool and laid her head back on the rim. She could get used to this. She pulled a book from a shelf beside the tub and began to read from somewhere in the middle. Some psychopath was taking the life of a prostitute down in Brazil. His first murder. She guessed from the description of his state of mind that it would not be his last. She finished the chapter and put the book back in its place upon the shelf, then settled herself back into the soothing jets and let them work the stiffness from her muscles.

Laurie woke with a start, gasping for air. Her chest felt heavy and she feared the weight would keep her from her next breath. A shadowy figure had filled her dream and threatened to take her life. He held a long, shiny hunting knife covered in blood. Instinctively, her hand went to her throat. There were no cuts. Her throat was wet only with water and bubbles from the bath. Shaken, she reached over and turned off the jets.

She wrapped her arms around herself for a moment and held tight. The dream had been all too real. Silly, she thought. She wasn't one to get freaked out like this. Maybe the Wilson case had spooked her. Worcester was not prone to such vicious murders as that one and it thus far seemed a random killing, too. Laurie wondered if a serial killer of sorts had visited his insanity upon her town. Or maybe the Wilson girl just had a very nasty boyfriend or stalker that no one knew of.

Laurie opened the drain and stood up from the warm water. She grabbed a towel from the hook and stepped out onto a black bathmat on the white tile floor. She felt her tension subside as she dried herself off. Back in the bedroom, she found her clothing carefully folded and lain out on a fluffy white chair in the corner of the room. She pulled on the skirt and slid her arms through the sleeveless holes of the red top. She felt a bit awkward heading out in the bright morning sun in such obvious eveningwear, but she smoothed out the wrinkles and called herself a taxi.

She took the note that Brandon had written and turned it over so that she could leave one of her own. 'I can't wait!' was all she wrote. Then she drew a thick set of cartoon lips puckered up in a kiss and scribbled her name at the bottom. She made the bed and left the note propped up on the stack of pillows.

SERIAL

Laurie hopped into the yellow cab as it pulled up to the condo and called Jessie from her cell phone as the cabbie pulled out onto Route 9. "Hey, I'm not working today. Have you got time for a cup of coffee?"

"Plenty," was the response. They planned to meet at a small breakfast place in Greendale where the coffee was great, and the omelets were better. Laurie could already taste the coffee.

"I can't believe you slept with him on the first date! Even I wouldn't do that and you know what a slut I can be!" Jessie scolded her friend in a hoarse whisper. The waitress had put them in a secluded corner at the far end of the restaurant, so there was little chance of being overheard. "And you told him that you love him? I mean, you don't really expect to see this guy again, do you? You made every single major dating error all on the first date!" Jessie paused and cut off a large section of a sausage and cream cheese omelet that she had stubbornly insisted would taste good if they would only make it for her. She stuffed her mouth and closed her eyes briefly in pleasure. "I can't believe they actually made it right! Mmmm!" She glared expectantly at her friend.

"If you only could meet him. Haven't you ever gone out with a guy and just known that he was the right one? Everything just clicked between us. It was wonderful. Best sex I ever had, too." Laurie ignored the broccoli and cheese omelet in front of her and concentrated on the coffee.

"Well, as long as the sex was good! I'd be awfully disappointed in you if you couldn't at least tell me that much!" Jessie giggled and Laurie joined her.

"Just do me a favor." Jessie paused in stuffing her face. "Please don't take this guy at his word like you did with Jeff. I mean, it sounds like you've already fallen for him. That's not healthy. Guys are generally scum, you know that."

"We're all scum to someone along the way, though, right? But eventually we happen to run into someone who's just perfect for us. This feels like the guy. I know that sounds strange." Laurie took another sip of coffee that was growing cold. "Besides, I didn't take Jeff on his word. I kept my senses. Maybe subconsciously I knew he was a lowlife. Brandon feels different to me."

"If you say so, girl. I just want you to be careful because I love you." She paused for a moment and smiled coyly. "Not the same way, of course." The waitress came over and refilled their cups with more steaming brew.

"Honestly, I think I'm a bit jealous," Jessie continued. "I mean, I don't think I've ever felt that way about a guy. You know me—I'm generally a skeptic. I wish just once that I could fall head over heels for a guy, even if it turned out to be bogus later. It would be nice to feel that way even for one night."

"At least you haven't been hurt like I have," Laurie countered. "You would think I'd learn. But I really do think that Brandon is different. Honest. It's just a weird feeling I have."

Jessie met her friend's eyes and smiled. "I hope so. Maybe I'll get to be a bridesmaid."

Laurie laughed. "Now look who's rushing!" She tipped her cup to her mouth and emptied it.

"Come on, let's get out of here." She pulled some cash out of her pocketbook and checked the bill. She put in her share and passed the check on to Jessie who did the same.

Outside the restaurant, Jessie commented on her outfit. "I hope you don't plan on hanging out in that today. It screams one-night stand, you know."

Laurie looked down at herself and smiled. "It's sleeveless, at least, and it's supposed to be hot today. Hey, any chance I could get a ride out to Auburn?"

Jessie was taken aback for a moment. "He couldn't even give you a lift home or cab fare?"

Laurie flushed a little. "I didn't really think about it. Maybe he didn't either. I was asleep when he left."

"Well, he is a guy."

"A really great guy."

# Chapter 11

Since she was off work on a sunny day, Laurie chose to spend some time in her garden. The flowers had come and gone and it was time to add new annuals to bloom for the current season. After Jessie dropped her off, she changed into a pair of comfortable shorts and a t-shirt that she reserved for gardening, then drove out to the nearest garden center. She pulled into a spot near the exit, leaving her little distance to travel once her arms were filled with flats of flowers and headed back to the car.

"Hi Laurie, how are you today?" A middle-aged woman greeted her as she entered the garden area. Her brown skin had loosened over her plump face, allowing a few soft wrinkles to form. She gave Laurie the impression of a young grandmother who spent hours working the earth and planting flowers in her own garden. And in fact, this was the case Laurie had learned in talking with her each time she visited the garden center.

"Hi Sarah. I'm very well. I stopped by to get a few annuals to brighten up the front of my house." Laurie knew little about flowers herself, so she was thrilled that Sarah was there to share her immense knowledge and experience in this.

"I have just the ones for you." She led Laurie toward the racks of annuals and began pulling down flats of bright yellow, brilliant red, and delicate purple. "These just came in today," Sarah gushed with pride. "They'll look wonderful along your front walk and they'll do really well in full sun."

Laurie nodded agreement and loaded the flats into her cart. "Thanks for your help. You're always so good to me."

"Always glad to help, dear. You seem very happy today—is it this wonderful weather or something else?"

"A little of both, I guess," Laurie confided as she opened her purse. "I've met the most wonderful man." She smiled shyly as she shared a few simple details about Brandon.

"Splendid! But whatever happened to that boy, Jeff, you were seeing?" Sarah asked as she took a few bills from Laurie's hand and returned change.

Laurie explained as little about Jeff's indiscretions as she could without disappointing Sarah's ear for gossip.

"I'm sorry, dear," she replied when Laurie finished. "But if you want the truth, your face was never lit up over Jeff the way it is lit up over this Brandon lad."

Laurie smiled and blushed. "Thanks, Sarah. And thanks for the flowers. I'll see you later."

"Anytime, dear. You take care."

Laurie felt eyes upon her as she loaded the flowers into the trunk of the Camero. Her spine tingled with the sensation and knots crept into her stomach. With her hands on the rim of the trunk, she slowly turned her head side-to-side, scanning the parking lot over each shoulder. Nothing. She closed the lid of the trunk and wheeled the cart back toward the store and returned, looking around the lot as she walked, but she noticed no one watching her. Still, the feeling of being watched was there and it was unmistakable. She started the car and noticed the cars around her and in her mirror as she drove away from the garden center. No one followed her and as the distance between her and the lot increased, the feeling of being watched faded. Maybe it was just her imagination, the same as the dream she'd had that morning while she slept in Brandon's tub. She admitted to herself that images of Abra Wilson's body still floated beneath the surface of her mind. Would she ever be able to forget that morning; forget stepping around the pools of blood; forget the way Abra's open windpipe gaped at the sky?

The Hunter watched her as she loaded the trunk of her car. Even in worn work clothes she was attractive. Her delicately chiseled knees, slender thighs, perfectly carved buttocks. He admired her movements as she bent and stretched, reaching far into the trunk to load the flowers. He saw her pause, head still under the lid of the trunk as she looked out at the lot. What was she looking for? Did she know he was there watching her? He slumped down below the level of the dashboard as her eyes turned in his direction, hoping she had not seen him, but she looked away, continuing her search of the lot. Then finally, he breathed easier as she climbed into her car and drove away.

The phone rang as Laurie finished washing the dirt from her hands. The flowers now brightened the walkway to her front door.

"Hello?"

"Hello, Detective."

"Brandon! I didn't expect to hear from you. I thought you had work to do."

"I did, and it's done. Listen, I have a proposition for you tomorrow, but it might be best if you stay here tonight so we can get an early start in the morning."

"Well, I don't know. Would you be planning to take advantage of me as you did last night?"

"I hardly thought I took advantage of you. Rather, I thought it was you who took advantage of me."

"I see," Laurie smiled at his twist in responsibility for the events of last night. "A truce then. No fault to either of us."

"Done. Come by at six for dinner?" Brandon's voice was breathless as it had been the first time she'd heard it. Had he been smiling as much then as she knew he was now? She made a mental note to ask him later if the chance arose.

"Great! I'll see you at six. And this time, if you don't mind, I'll bring a change of clothes."

"Right. Bring along a light jacket and a hat if you've got one. You may need them tomorrow."

"Hmmm...sounds mysterious. I don't suppose you'd let me know what I'm agreeing to."

"Not a chance."

# Chapter 12

Brandon guided the Mercedes into the Ted Williams tunnel. There was very little traffic this time of the morning and they cruised through easily to East Boston.

"Are we taking a plane?" Laurie asked. She had never been into the tunnel unless headed for Logan Airport. "I haven't packed a thing, if we are," she added. But Brandon simply looked at her and smiled his mysterious smile. She loved surprises like this and as she glanced over at his profile, she couldn't ever imagine growing tired of him.

"Just wait and see," he said. "If you haven't heard, the Tall Ships are in town. I hope you like them because I have connections for a great way to see them up close." He turned away and focused his attention on the road, looking for landmarks he had been given in the directions to their destination. He maneuvered the car through dingy side streets with aging brick buildings until the road ended at a pier that housed several brightly painted tugboats.

"What's this?" Laurie asked. "I don't see any ships."

"We won't see much of anything from this pier," he smiled. "But we have a firsthand view of the boats from aboard those tugs." He cast Laurie a sidelong glance to observe her reaction. She appeared both elated and puzzled.

"What's wrong," Brandon queried. "Don't tell me you get seasick."

"No, not at all," she replied. "I'm just a little confused as to what we'll be doing today with the tugboats. Do we just hang out around the harbor?"

"Not that simple, my dear. You really do need to get out more," Brandon laughed. "The tugs pull the ships out of the dock and turn them around so that they can get under power and head out into the harbor.

"Can't the ships do that on their own?"

"Not really. Many of the ships don't have the proper maneuvering capacity to pull away from the dock on their own without bumping the dock or another ship in the process, either of which could be disastrous. So the tugs pull them out and send them on their way. It's a lot of fun, you'll see." He pulled a large cooler and a duffel bag from the trunk of the Mercedes and led the way toward the docks.

"Hey Brian!" he shouted to a man at the bow of the nearest tug. "Where should we drop anchor?"

The man responded with a wave, then motioned them over. "Why don't you drop your stuff here. I was starting to wonder about you two. Did you bring any coffee?"

"Nah, we were running a bit late and I'm not too sure what's open at this time. Do we have time to run out? Is there a place around here?"

Brian looked at his watch, a beaten and battered old Timex. "Ehh, could be tight. Spencer called. He's still a few minutes out. Maybe he can grab us coffee. We got a job to run out on soon, but he may have time to grab us some brew. I'll give him a call. Why don't you two just hop aboard and get yourselves settled for now. Toss me your stuff." He held out his hand and Brandon tossed him the duffel, then more carefully, he handed over the cooler. "Hey, no drinkin' on my boat," Brian winked. "Wouldn't want you to be feedin' the fish, now would we." He lifted the corner of a white canvas, which hung over the side of the boat, exposing two large old truck tires that had been tied to the side of the tug to serve as bumpers. He offered his hand out to Laurie who took it gingerly. "Just step here on the tire, then you can get a foot on the rail here and hop in." Laurie eyed the tire, which rested a foot below the rail.

"Actually, if you don't mind." She took a little leap, landing her foot onto the rail and following with the other foot. She paused atop the railing. "Stepping on that tire seems a bit shaky to me." She smiled, and then hopped down into the boat.

"Ah, a natural," Brian laughed then turned his attention to helping Brandon who simply followed Laurie's footwork and hopped lightly into the boat.

"So, Spencer's joining us?" Laurie asked.

"His connection," Brandon smiled. "He does a bit of computer work for these guys. You don't mind it's not just us, do you?"

"Of course not. Maybe Spencer can tell me some embarrassing childhood moments of yours," she teased.

"Yeah, there's a way to start off a relationship," he chuckled. "Of course don't think I didn't pay him off already to say nothing but good things about me."

"I'll bet you did."

"Someone here order coffee?" The boat rocked a little as Spencer jumped aboard, followed closely by Brian.

"Caught him sitting at the light across from Dunkin' Donuts. Perfect timing. Got a dozen, too."

"Excellent!" Brandon reached for the donuts, while Laurie went for the coffee.

"Good to see you again, Laurie," Spencer smiled at her. "How's things with you and the geek, here?"

"It's going well, thanks." She leaned a little closer to Brandon.

"Good. Good. Glad to hear it. But you know if you ever get tired of him and want a real geek...."

"Watch it, Spence. No hitting on my girl. She'll kick your ass. Remember, she's a cop." Brandon grinned.

"Hmmm. Your girl, huh?" Laurie teased. "But I have to take care of myself?"

Brandon smiled warmly at her. "I'd like you to be my girl. And you don't have to take care of yourself. I'll take him out if he starts putting any moves on you." He kissed her gently on the cheek.

Laurie smiled back at him and leaned into his open arms.

"Here comes the pilot," Spencer said, pointing to a toughened old seaman in a bright yellow slicker making his way down the pier. "Looks like we're off."

The tugboat eased out from the dock and headed toward the harbor. Another tug stood solidly in its way, but the captain ignored it, bumping its stern solidly like she was a bumper car, and pushing past her into the open water. Laurie and Brandon found a vantage point on the upper deck from which they would have an unobstructed view. Spencer stayed below with Brian.

It wasn't often that the Tall Ships, including sloops, frigates, ketches and other sailing ships of all shapes and sizes, as well as battleships and other boats visited Boston. But when they did, thousands flocked to the little hub to see the grand parade of sails and tour the ships while they sat docked in the harbor.

The news had described enormous crowds and congestion and Laurie, hating crowds, would probably never have attempted the drive into Boston for the event, yet here she was in the best seat imaginable. The weather, though a bit foggy, was perfect and she settled down beside Brandon and kissed his cheek as he put his arm around her.

"You really have some great connections," she said into the wind.

The Tugboat slowed a few knots as they approached a large destroyer docked in the harbor. The crew of the Vicksburg was all aboard deck in their Navy blues, intermingled by officers in striking whites. They had started the ship's engines and were letting them idle while they awaited assistance from the tugs. A long barge was alongside the destroyer, accompanied by a tugboat. Hoses ran between the barge and destroyer like giant umbilical cords.

Brandon shouted down to Brian. "What's that boat?"

"That's the honey barge," Brian shouted back. "Shit collection for a thousand sailors. The tugs will pull her out, too. Wouldn't want any accidents with her. Pollute Boston Harbor in the nastiest sort of way." He laughed.

He turned to Spencer who stood at the bow of the tug. "We're gonna go tie up to the bow of the destroyer. Then, once the other tug there pulls out the honey barge, they'll tie up aft and we'll pull the Vicksburg straight out from the pier."

The captain guided the tugboat up close to the stern of the Vicksburg. The pilot joined Brian and Spencer at the bow and waited until the bow of the tug was pushed up against the stern of the destroyer. Carefully, he climbed onto the rail and stepped out onto the tires strapped on the front. He grabbed hold of the rail of the destroyer and, with assistance from her crew, pulled himself up onto the ship. The tug pulled away, leaving him to join the captain of the destroyer in guiding her out from the dock.

On the top deck of the tug, Brandon wrapped his arms around Laurie as they watched the crew tie the tug to the ship at the bow. The second tugboat tied up to the stern after maneuvering the honey barge away from the destroyer.

Laurie was startled as two short sharp whistles pierced the air beside her, prompting a two-blast response from the tug at the stern of the ship. In unison, the tugboats revved up their diesel engines and began to pull backwards. The ropes tightened and popped under the stress and the water around the tugs turned a light shade of green from the air that the engines churned into it. Slowly, the destroyer eased out from her docking place twenty or thirty feet. The tug at the stern released her ties and moved to the bow of the destroyer. Together, the two boats pushed at the ship from both sides of the bow, forcing her backwards out into the main harbor. When she was clear of the docks, the tugs slowed their engines and let the ship go. She backed and turned then under her own power and faced out into Boston Harbor.

"Beautiful!" Laurie shouted down at Brian. "Tough, boats! Very cool," she smiled broadly.

"Well, that's it for now, I think," Brian shouted. "We're gonna grab the pilot and head back to port for a bit." The tug moved to the stern of the destroyer to collect the pilot who climbed aboard as carefully as he had left. The Vicksburg's crew waved thanks as the two tugs turned and headed back toward home.

The rest of the day was glorious. They had a front row seat to various shows put on by the ships' crews. A Japanese crew climbed a hundred feet in the air to stand atop the yardarms and present a formal ceremony before the ship was pulled away from the dock. Of course since the ceremony was in Japanese, Laurie didn't understand a word, but the spectacle of twenty barefoot men and women lined up along the yardarms was incredible.

On another ship, the Indonesian crew wore brightly colored silks while one man in a walrus costume danced on the bow as the ship was maneuvered out from the dock. Each ceremony by each crew was unique and Laurie, Brandon, and Spencer clapped and cheered for them all.

The afternoon was nearly over when Brian dropped them off near the mouth of the Charles River to watch the return of The Constitution. A Boston fireboat escorted the ancient battleship, spraying a plume of water thirty feet into the air, which blew backward like a giant banner. Cloaked in the mist, "Old Iron Sides" approached the docks. She fired her guns one by one, sending out puffs of gray smoke as the crowd cheered. War veterans and police saluted the old ship as she was brought home. A shiver ran down Laurie's spine to her toes as she joined in the salute.

"Well, I guess that's it," Brandon put an arm around her and pulled her close. "I hope you liked the sights. Did you have fun?" He kissed her lightly on the cheek.

"Now, that's a foolish question. This was fantastic! I've never had such a great view of ships like these."

"Oh, look at this. It looks like our ride is here. Shall we go?" He followed Spencer as he walked toward an approaching tug and waved her in. Brian recognized them from the tug and motioned the captain to pull in. The three of them stepped out onto the dock followed by a few straggling tourists. One held up a pass for the subway, flashing it to Brian as the boat pulled alongside the dock. "Can I use my T-pass to catch a ride with you?"

Brian did his best to stifle a laugh. "Not on this boat, pal," he said. The man cast a disgruntled look at Brandon, Laurie, and Spencer as they hopped onto the boat. He stuffed the pass back into his wallet and stormed away.

"Spence, you up for some drinks?" Brandon asked.

"I got client work, remember?" Spencer replied.

"Right, I forgot." He turned to Brian. "Hey, Brian. Are you through for the day? Maybe you and the guys might want to join Laurie and me for a drink? I figure we can head down to Marina Bay in Quincy," he glanced at Laurie to be sure she did not disagree, "if you're up for a drink or two."

"Nah, you guys go. We got enough work here to last us several more hours and I could use the extra money. Maybe if things change and I get out early, I'll give you a ring to see if you're still around, but most likely I'm here til late."

"Alright then, maybe some other time." Brandon held out his hand for Brian to shake. "Thanks for a great day. We really enjoyed it."

"Yes, very much so," Laurie chimed in. She smiled and shook Brian's hand when he offered it.

They gathered their things and waved a quick goodbye to the captain of the boat.

"Thanks, Spence, for hooking us up here," Brandon clapped his friend on the shoulder.

"Anytime. Glad you guys could make it out here. And don't forget, Laurie…when you get sick of him, I'm here for you."

"Don't hold your breath," she smiled.

The club at Marina Bay was not yet too crowded and Brandon easily located a parking spot near the front. He got out and opened Laurie's door.

"I guess we're a bit roughed up from the long ride," Laurie observed. Brandon's hair was windblown in many directions; both had smudges of black on their clothing from the grease and dirt around the tugboat.

"I have mixed feelings about not having worn decent clothes on the boat. At least I wouldn't be quite so underdressed going in here," Laurie said as she examined the spots on her clothes. "But on the other hand, I would have ruined some better clothes."

Brandon laughed as he threw an arm around her waist. "You look wonderful, my dear. Grease is absolutely your color."

# Chapter 13

It was Thursday and the sweltering sun and the lack of even the slightest breeze throughout the day had made the night air sticky and stagnant around Boston. What better relief than to slip out to the waterfront in Quincy for drinks and a little fun? The hunter leaned casually against the wall in a back corner of a lively club facing the direction of the bar, his eyes roving over the crowds that had gathered for the evening. It had been a long time since he'd played his game around Boston—at least a year. He'd stayed away when someone else began playing games in the city. That player hadn't been as efficient as the hunter was in covering his tracks, though. He left witnesses, having been foolish not to kill them when he was through with his fun, and one of them had identified him. But even after they'd caught that one, the city remained on edge, so Hunter stayed away; played it safe. Now, he was glad to be back, close to home, but not too close for comfort. His victim's death tonight would be swallowed by other news events and her fate would soon be forgotten.

A group of three gossiping woman walked past him, so close he could have easily sliced the skimpy black dress off the tall, slutty one with the short spiky black hair. He wondered if what she wore under that dress was as risqué as the rest of her looked. She winked a heavy lash at him from under a gold-ringed brow. Hunter smirked and her eyes turned acid in response. Even on a truly bad day, he could not fantasize playing with that one. Her friends were less conspicuous: one in a knee-length skirt, the other in a black cat suit, but neither was worth a second glance. Besides, he wasn't interested in playing with women that had friends who could describe him later. Even if he was disguised, a woman who sat alone was the safest choice. No one would notice whom a lone woman left the bar with. His falsely-colored eyes, green tonight, roved the bar, looking for a likely woman to satisfy his desires for the evening. He ignored the bartenders scurrying back and forth, fixing drinks for the eager patrons who pushed their way through the crowd to be served. His eyes moved slowly over each woman at the bar, determining if they were alone, with friends, or with men. He cursed that he had not arrived as early as he would have liked. Traffic on the Turnpike had been stalled for over an hour as fire trucks doused two blazing cars with water before tow trucks and a flatbed truck cleared them off the road. Hunter had been close enough to see the excitement as it unfolded, but not close enough to determine if the victims carried away in the two ambulances had been dead or alive. He hoped they were dead, having crimped his plans for the evening. Hunter liked to arrive before the heaviest crowds filled the bar, but tonight the crowds around the bar were already thick. Experience had taught him that many women who went out alone liked to arrive early to get a seat at the bar where they could stay comfortably late into the evening. Hunter also tried to arrive early so he could get a seat beside them and strike up casual conversation to put them at ease, leaving them open to his fatal move when the bar was filled with noisy patrons. But with an arrival as late as his was tonight, it would be difficult to get close to the women at the bar. And although a lonely woman might, by this time, be more eager to strike up conversation with an unknown man, having had a few drinks to dull her nerves, without a seat beside her, it would be difficult to slip rohypnol into her drink without being noticed.

His eyes stalled on a shapely blonde seated, speaking to the bartender. He was hopeful a moment. She was certainly attractive. Two women seated beside her were engrossed in a conversation to one side of her while a couple were laughing and chatting on the other. The bartender left her and she turned to cast her eyes around the bar. She certainly was attractive. The hunter moved toward her.

A group of young businessmen jostled their way across his path, blocking his view of the woman. A shame, he thought. The closer he got, the more attractive she became. He envisioned her full, pouting lips stretched wide in a scream as he shoved the point of his blade into the small hollow at the base of her throat. He waited patiently as the group of men pushed their way past, joking and laughing. When his view was again clear, he started toward the woman again, admiring the bounce of her hair as she turned, turned and nudged the woman beside her, drawing her attention away from the man she'd been conversing with. She waved the man off and took up conversation with the blonde. They were together.

Hunter fumed and tossed back the remainder of his drink, catching a waitress by the arm as she weaved her way around him. He ordered another drink and let his eyes slide easily down her backside as she turned away and continued to wiggle her way through the crowd.

Though his late arrival tonight might deny him a target, it wouldn't be the first time he'd left empty-handed; he liked the game and always played it safely. Better to go home unsatisfied one night than to throw caution aside. Caution kept him alive, kept him playing, and since he never played in the same town twice, at least not too frequently, his caution left very little to connect the women he killed. Many of his victims only appeared in the local papers and since his game brought him to different cities and across state lines, it was unlikely that anyone would ever make any connection between them. Being cautious meant he was free to play as long and as often as he liked.

He leaned back against a support column while he waited for the waitress to return with his drink. The blonde was now engrossed in chatter with her friend. He continued to watch her as he reminisced on his most recent successful hunting trip to a small town in Vermont. He scratched at the glued mustache on his lip, checking before he lowered his hand to be certain the strip of false hair was firmly attached. His mind wandered.

The girl had been so young and tender, just barely eighteen. She had borrowed her cousin's identification to go out that night. She had been so proud of that, he recalled with a smile. Young girls were so gullible. She liked it when he commented that she appeared more mature than her eighteen years, and blushed a rosy red when he guessed correctly that the doorman hadn't even asked for her identification. She had simply flirted her way through the door. The fake ID was only a backup. Charming her way in was more fun. Hunter glanced around at the doorman once or twice when she told him this, but the doorman apparently had lost interest.

Hunter remembered dancing with that one. He rarely danced with his conquests, but she had such a beautiful body and such lovely long legs that he just had to see her move to the music. She was a slow and sensual dancer and he remembered how easily she had excited him. *She* wanted to take him outside before her friend arrived who would, in truth, not be coming until almost midnight and it was only nine o'clock.

What a treat, he thought. A quick bit of mutual passion was always welcome, although he did like that feeling of ultimate power. But he also liked to just sample a variety of women, willing or not.

His eyes lingered on the perfect features of her face and body as he imagined touching every point and curve. She guided him out of the little club around to the side of the building where there were a few trees, but no real cover.

He moved on her gently there, coaxing. She kissed him pleasurably and he slowly moved his hands over her, testing her. He placed them on her firm rump, kneading gently, and she responded by pressing her body harder against his. He moved his hand to her breast and she moaned with pleasure. But when he gently slid her dress up to remove it, she wriggled in his arms in protest. He mumbled a brief apology, but did not fix the dress, instead leaving it pulled up exposing the naked lower half of her slim figure. He continued to kiss her and she relaxed a little, then his mouth left hers and moved down to her breast, nipping gently at the material and nipple beneath.

She pulled away completely then, blushing with desire, but controlling herself with fear. "Don't," she said. "I've never done any of this before. I think you're really attractive, but can we just not do so much right now?" The man apologized, blushing for effect, and offered to accompany her back to the bar then. He was disappointed, but he knew he would have her yet. And she would wish she had not refused him.

They left the bar again later to get some fresh air and walked to a tiny airport just down the road. He had not given her too much of the drug. He so hoped to feel her passion. She was strikingly beautiful with her waist-length red hair blowing gently in a passing breeze.

They walked along the packed road between rows of planes tied down for the night when he abruptly stopped and pulled her to him. She did not refuse and he was suddenly aroused. She kissed him passionately and forcefully and he touched her in ways that had frightened her before, but now she did not object. He raised the hem of her dress and slid his hand between her thighs and she kissed him harder.

He was driven by confidence and desire. If only all women would just give in to desire without playing games, he wouldn't have to drug them. He grabbed hold of her dress and pulled it up over her head, leaving her naked, since she had worn no undergarments. Her ivory skin glowed white in the light from a nearby street lamp.

The girl looked down at herself as though she had never before seen her own body. A shame, he thought—it was exquisite. He ran his hands slowly up and down her front, caressing her breasts and tugging lightly at the small patch of hair between her legs. She blushed but did not object, though he could see uncertainty in her eyes. Then, as he began to pull at his belt and unfasten his jeans, she backed away from him and began to look around for her dress.

Hunter's patience ended then, he recalled. If only he had had a bit more patience, she might have softened, but he had grown tired of her games. She did not have enough drug in her system to keep her from screaming, so he pulled the hunting knife from his travel bag while she fumbled along the ground for the dress. Viciously, he grabbed her by the hair, lifting her from the ground. He ripped the dress angrily from her hand and threw it aside, and then he pushed her back until she sat down on the wing of a plane behind her. The foolish little tease had started to yell at him when the flash of the blade caught her eye. He remembered how easily she had submitted then and he made her do all the things he knew she wanted to. And then he killed her. A shame, he thought. She was so beautiful, but it had to be done or his game would have quickly ended. He left her lying on her back over the wing of the plane. Her body glowed in the light of the street lamps and he immortalized her with two clicks of the shutter.

The waitress stopped in front of him, a tray of drinks held high over her head, and brought his thoughts back to the present. He fumbled in his travel bag, removed a few bills, and handed them to her. She pocketed the cash then lowered the tray. She carefully selected his drink, maintaining the balance of the tray, handed the drink to him, and with a quick smile, spun around and pushed her way back into the crowd, the tray once again balanced high over her head. The man who called himself Hunter watched her disappear, then refocused his attention on the game at hand. The sight of an attractive woman in a plum-colored business suit rewarded his attention as she sauntered confidently toward the bar. The young men crowded in her way parted like water before the bow of a boat and made a path for her to the bar. Her confidence was extraordinary as was she. He watched as the bartender sloughed off the attention of other patrons to get near enough to take her order, leaning over the bar and encouraging her to speak into his ear. This striking woman would be his next conquest, Hunter decided as he strode slowly toward the bar to join her.

The woman was here to meet someone new, he could see, and when Hunter offered to buy the drink she had just ordered, she did not decline. The hunter could tell that this woman had had her share of short romances and one-night stands. He knew he could charm her into bed with a few drinks and some witty conversation, but that wouldn't be any fun with this one. There was no challenge in taking something that was given so easily, so smugly. He wanted to break that confidence that kept her head high and made her walk above everyone in the club. He wanted to see the fear in her eyes as she realized that he intended to take her life and that she was powerless to stop him. He wanted to hurt her; he wanted to make her scream out in pain, and then stifle that scream. He would gag and tie her just enough to keep her from screaming or pulling away. Hunter liked a good fight. In fact, he thought, he wouldn't even drug her. No, he would entice her into a walk down on the docks. He knew how to appeal to the weaknesses of this type of woman. He knew she would go with him.

"Thanks for the drink." She smiled and held out her hand, her palm turned toward the floor. "Cassandra," she offered, awaiting his name in return.

"Hunter," he obliged and gently shook the hand she offered.

"Not my usual place to hang out, how about you?" She edged closer to him as the crowds jostled her from behind.

"Sometimes. Certainly a relief from the heat to be near the water anyway, though we don't get to appreciate it stifled in here with this crowd." He smiled. "Where do you usually hang out?"

"I like the pubs around Boston, usually. Better there with friends, though. This is one place I don't mind coming to alone."

"I know what you mean. Good atmosphere. Good crowd if you like to watch people."

"A man after my own heart. I make my living off watching people."

"Really? What kind of living would that be?"

"Lawyer."

"Ahhh. Watching people does come in handy for you, doesn't it? Like playing poker. Where do you work?" he asked as a couple working their way across the bar jostled him toward her.

"One of the local firms in Boston, to remain nameless," she replied with a mischievous grin. She didn't step back as he encroached. "What do you do," she asked while her long, slender finger poked playfully at the ice in her glass.

"I'm an exec for a small high-tech company in Dedham," he lied. He certainly wouldn't give her any real information. And she didn't seem the type of woman who would be turned on by anything less than a company executive. She was probably the type to seduce her boss in order to climb the corporate ladder.

"Are you one of those geeky high-tech guys? Or do you live a little once in a while?" She eyed him seductively with mischievous brown eyes. She was taking the bait. Too easy, he thought.

He laughed at her statement. Most guys he knew in the high tech industry were a little uptight. "I like to live a little," he confessed. "A lot, in fact. What do you like to do for fun?" He searched her eyes for a moment to determine her level of humor before he continued,

"Besides trying to pick up single, good-looking guys like myself and seduce us."

The woman was momentarily shocked. He had misread her, he feared. But she quickly regained her composure to continue the conversation as she was bumped from behind. The man making his way to the bar took the opportunity to put a hand on her shoulder and apologize, holding his lips close to her ear while he glanced jealously at Hunter.

"I do no such thing," she smiled slyly when the opportunist was gone. She liked this bold, attractive man. Usually they were too busy telling her a bunch of sordid lies to get to the point of what they really wanted. "Unless, of course, you have a boat tied to one of those docks out there." She didn't expect that he did, but she gave him a slow wink and put her drink to her lips while she awaited his response.

"I do," he smiled as he lied again. "A very nice one, too. Would you like to see it? It would give us a chance to get out of this crowd, away from the bumping and shoving."

"Agreed," she smiled. The woman tilted her drink and sucked out the last of the liquor. "I'd be delighted to see your boat." Her smile spread to show her teeth as she handed him her empty glass.

Hunter moved between the people at the bar and placed the glasses on the counter, then turned and held out his hand to his latest conquest and led her toward her death.

An elderly man found her the following morning when he climbed into his boat to prepare it for a day of fishing with his grandchildren. The woman's bulging eyes stared glassily up at the orange sky, as she lay nude upon the bow of his boat, the plum-colored suit in tatters on the floor of the cockpit. Her mouth bore a strip of silver duct tape and a length of rope had been tied snugly about her throat. She had died slowly, the man guessed, though he was not sure which had actually killed her—the rope about her neck or the numerous wounds inflicted upon her flesh. The bow of his boat was red with blood, a rivulet of which had made its way along the deck and pooled in the cockpit. This had been his first indication that something was amiss. He thought perhaps a prank by kids from the nearby clubs, but then he had seen her body on the bow and had immediately lost his breakfast into the water beside the boat.

He cast a glance around the docks and, seeing no one, made his way as quickly as he could back to the boardwalk where there was a pay phone. He cursed himself for not owning a cellular phone and vowed to get one after this. When he returned to the boat, seagulls had gathered on the corpse; one was pulling at her left eyeball, its head bobbing up and down in frenzy as it worked to break its prize free of the tissues that tied it to the socket. The man turned again and lost what little remained of his breakfast.

The hunter chuckled as he watched from shadows along the boardwalk. Although he knew he needed to leave, he took a moment to appreciate the way he had laid her out on the bow of the boat, her limbs spread out from her body. The sounds of the water around him brought another image to mind. Fifteen years ago he had left Karen lying beside the water, drenched in blood and staring at the sky. He was disappointed he wouldn't get to wait for the police to come. In the enclosed marina, he would certainly be questioned if he were caught standing around. The killer always returned to the scene. At least that was the theory, and although he liked to witness the discovery, Hunter didn't take any chances.

He leaned against the wall in the shadow and thought back to the day he last saw Karen. The sounds of snapping twigs popped like gunshots in his mind as he remembered tearing through the woods at a dead run; fallen branches grabbing at his ankles and adrenaline the only thing steadying his feet and plunging him through tangled growth. He remembered the fear tearing at his chest, and the pain in his lungs as he struggled to put distance between himself and his deed. He felt no fear now.

He was only fifteen then, and not the sort who would lose his cool. But his fear had sent him running haphazardly out of the woods into an open field in full view of several houses. Anyone looking would have remembered him running out of the woods alone. It was the middle of nowhere. Fortunately, though, good sense stopped him dead in his tracks. He made certain no one had seen him, then walked casually away from the trees.

Before him, the hunter watched vacantly as the man paced the dock, but his thoughts focused inward to Karen's pleas for her life. He hadn't listened to her. His anger and pain had prevented that. He thought only of how she'd dropped him and stomped on his heart though she knew how he loved her.

She'd called him selfish. Him, selfish? All he ever did was give her things—roses, candy. He took her to movies and out to dinner. Every day after school he worked his *ass* off just so he could have money to spend on *her*, and she had the audacity to call him selfish! And, boring! He had taken her every place she ever asked to go and done everything *she* wanted to do. How could he be boring? Well, she's certainly bored now—in more ways than one. She's dead and it serves her right.

The hunter remembered that evening, listening intently to the old police scanner as he struggled to appear engrossed in his homework while Mother quietly dusted the woodwork. He had tried hard not to look at her, hiding his face in a book. Mother was so perceptive when it came to reading his moods and if she sensed his turmoil at that moment, life would be over. She would needle and pick at him like someone working out a sliver. Sooner or later he knew she would tweeze it out of him if she sensed something occupying his mind.

The scanner sputtered out static and a few broken words as an officer announced his position on 44. He had a car pulled over for speeding—nothing worth listening to.

Man, what a dull town—nothing ever happens here! But soon that would change. Something *had* happened and soon they would find her. The pond was a favorite skinny-dipping spot, though maybe it was a little early in the week for that. Still…the cops always stopped there at least once or twice each night. Man, they'd shit themselves.

The hunter remembered exactly how he had heard it. One of the cops was out at the pond to check on a parked car—Karen's car. The boredom in his voice as the scanner sputtered out, "Ah shit! Someone's up on the rock again. Damn, I'm not in the mood," he drawled. "Who's up there?" he called. "Shit. Gotta do some climbing. Stand by."

The young hunter had envisioned the scene through the officer's eyes, trembling with excitement. Getting no response and unable to see the top, the officer had climbed up on the craggy rocks that formed an uneven staircase. Karen was lying there on the boulder, blood pooling around her naked form, eyes staring blankly at the quarter moon.

"Jesus Christ!" The officer had gasped into his radio. "I need some backup down here. Now! You better scramble this."

The words from the speaker were suddenly garbled when the dispatcher hit the scrambler, but Hunter flipped a switch on his scanner and they were clear again. His best friend at school was a whiz with electronics and had installed an illegal descrambler. It gave them a strange sense of power to hear what they weren't supposed to hear and that night, Hunter had thrilled to be there at the scene with the officer as he found Karen and poked at her body, hoping she was still alive.

The following day, they showed up at his door, just as he'd known they would. Karen had been his girlfriend, not for very long, but time didn't matter—they were dating. He was a suspect and he knew it. But he had left nothing at the scene, he was pretty sure of it. He'd checked Karen's body over for hair and stuff like he had read about in crime novels. The clothes he'd worn had been discarded in a trash compactor at the shopping plaza. He should be safe. And even if he did leave something, she was his girlfriend—it could be explained. He greeted the detectives calmly, with a genuine expression of curiosity about their appearance on his porch.

"Can I help you?" He ran a hand through his thick brown hair before folding his arms across his chest.

The detectives flashed identification inches from his face and barked their names at him. "You have a minute?" the tall one asked. They watched carefully for a reaction but he betrayed nothing.

"My mother's not home," he replied with feigned hesitation.

"That's okay. It's you we really need to speak with. You knew Karen Callahan?"

"I know her, yeah. She's my girlfriend."

"We'd like to come in, if you don't mind," the shorter detective on the right said. He put a hand on the storm door and took a step forward.

"Sure, I guess. Come on in." Hunter stepped aside, motioned toward the living room and offered them a seat while he remained standing.

"Were you with Karen yesterday?" The detectives' eyes bored through him.

The hunter let himself show a little discomfort. That's only natural, right? It might look suspicious if he was stone-faced.

"I walked her to school in the morning, yeah. That's about it. We were supposed to get together after school, but I never saw her. I figure she headed off with her friends. She does that a lot. What's wrong?" He deftly showed concern.

"You didn't call her last night?" the taller detective asked, leaning back and propping an ankle up on his knee.

"Naw, I had a lotta homework and I don't like calling her after she's stood me up. Not into the chase, ya know. She'll call me later to take her out. We always do something Saturdays."

The detective locked eyes with him. "She was killed yesterday." He waited for a reaction.

The hunter hesitated. "Wha...?" Disbelief showed in his eyes, then he buried his face in his hands. He could not force himself to cry, but water welled in his eyes as he quickly brushed a fingertip across the iris of his left eye and he held his breath until his face turned crimson. His shoulders shook voluntarily with mock sorrow. He knew how to fake it and he laid it on thick while he hid a smile with the palms of his hands.

The shorter detective put a comforting hand on his shoulder, offering a few soothing words. Hunter was silent for a moment, then carefully, he drew in a breath and turned wet eyes upon the detectives. He asked tentatively how she died. He chose his words carefully. He couldn't give himself away. Not now.

The detectives described briefly some of the details of the scene and the hunter could see that they were having difficulty with the thought that this had happened here in Susanville, where nothing ever happened. The cunning young killer gloated inwardly, but his face never lost its look of shock and sorrow. Damn, but he was a good actor!

A major investigation was launched into the murder of Karen Callahan. The small town police department poured every ounce of effort into locating the killer of the fourteen-year-old popular cheerleader. They called upon the hunter a few more times, unsure of his guilt or innocence, but he offered them nothing but skillfully manufactured grief.

After several months, the case grew cold with no leads. There were no witnesses and no important evidence had been found on the body or in her car. There was nothing to go on.

Eventually, the shocked and shaken town forgot her and the file found its way into a drawer of pending cases and was never opened again.

The hunter was jarred back to the present as a door slammed nearby. He turned to see a shopkeeper coming out, looking with wonder at the man pacing the dock below. Then slowly his expression turned to one of horror as he noticed the naked, bloodied woman lying on the boat beside where the man was pacing.

"What's going on down there?" he hollered to the man on the dock?

The hunter casually left the shadows and disappeared between the buildings. As he walked back toward his car, he could hear the sirens approaching in the distance.

# Chapter 14

The robbers in black pulled up in front of their next target. They positioned their car where it could not be seen through any of the windows, then stretched black nylon down over their faces.

"Alright, no shooting this time. We don't want to leave any more evidence behind that could help to identify us and, as we all know, a bullet can easily do that if they trace the gun back to us. I had to ditch the last gun, but at least it was unregistered. We have to be a little more careful with these since they are registered to us. It's risky trying to get our hands on unregistered pieces, so no shots." But he checked his revolver to see that it was fully loaded and there was a round chambered. Just in case.

"You wait here, honey. Keep that motor running. Both of 'em." The tall man gave the driver's thigh an affectionate squeeze as he kissed her gently on her chocolate-colored cheek. Changing her white skin to black had been the easiest solution to disguise her face inconspicuously for this job. A pedestrian walking by would take notice of a driver wearing a nylon over her face, but not of a well-dressed black girl sitting in a car, even if the engine were running. And although they planned to be in the bank less than a minute, they preferred she didn't advertise the robbery.

She looked around at the interior of the car she was sitting in, a blue Mercury Sable. Not a bad choice for a stolen car. It had enough power to fly if they needed it, but wasn't so flashy that everyone would notice it. They could get away on the side streets easily in this and switch cars up on Vernon Hill. Someone might see them do it, but it would take much longer to find a witness who would think to report such a trivial matter as suspicious. Then they would park the second car in a mall somewhere and walk away free.

She wondered how much money they would walk away with this time. This bank was a little more difficult than the last because it had bulletproof glass at the teller windows. But that didn't stop them from handing over the cash. Bulletproof wasn't one hundred percent and they wouldn't take any chances.

Suddenly, the door of the bank flew open and the two men hurried out. The tall man ran to the door behind the driver while the shorter one slid into the front seat on the passenger's side.

"Whew, we did it!" shouted the tall man. He reached over the seat and grabbed a handful of the driver's breast.

"Drive, babe!"

The girl already had the car in gear and was pulling carefully out of the parking lot and out into the street. She guided the car quickly along the empty side streets and up into the more populated streets on Vernon Hill. There were not too many cars on the road at eleven o'clock in the morning. It was the dead hour before lunchtime and it was only a matter of minutes before they pulled up behind a white Subaru parked neatly in front of a long row of three-deckers. The tall buildings with their dilapidated and out-of-date facades loomed over the group like a protective wall. The neighborhood was quiet; they were safe.

Casually, they abandoned the Sable and climbed into the new car. They had removed their nylons and gloves already and had donned colored shirts, one blue, one green, over their black jersey shirts. Two men all in black might stick in someone's mind, but now they looked a little more casual, unremarkable. There were no other cars visible anywhere along the street as the new driver, the shorter of the two men, tied two wires together that had been left beside the steering column. The car started instantly. He pulled the transmission into drive, pulled away from the curb, and drove slowly up the hill toward the main road and freedom with over four thousand in newfound wealth. And no one had seen them at all.

The first officers arrived at the bank only three minutes after the alarm had sounded, but the robbery team was well out of sight by then. Laurie and Gunnar pulled in shortly after.

"What is this, two in two months?" Gunnar mused as they walked to the door of the bank. He pulled it open for Laurie and walked in behind her.

"Actually, I would have expected a second robbery sooner if they're making a habit out of this," Laurie replied. "Maybe this is just mad money for these guys. They took eight thousand in the last one. Maybe that was enough to last a while." She paused inside the door and her gaze panned slowly around the bank.

A group of five tellers were gathered in the back corner of the bank's lobby. One was seated in a chair set aside for customers waiting to open a new account or apply for a loan. She was weeping uncontrollably while two coworkers, a man and women, comforted her. The other two women stood back a few feet from her, chatting quietly while they watched the weeping women, gaining their own strength from her distress.

"You get that group over there." Laurie pointed at the women and man. "I'll start with the customers over here." She turned toward a man and two women huddled in another corner away from the bank personnel.

The man started talking as she approached and the women looked up to him as if to a leader. They had probably elected him to speak.

"Not much for us to see," the elected speaker declared as he locked his thumbs through the loops of his jeans and hung his hands beside his hips.

"What can you tell me about them? How tall were they, how big or how heavy? What color skin?" Laurie rattled off a few suggested features for them to describe, then waited while he rolled his eyes to the ceiling a moment before he responded. The two women just watched him.

"Well, there was a tall one and a shorter one." He rubbed his bristled chin a moment, eyes still on the ceiling, before he continued. "The tall one was at least six and a half feet, I'd say." Laurie noticed the two women nodding in silent agreement with the man as he continued.

"The shorter one was a few inches short of six feet. They were both pretty well built. Didn't look to be any fat on 'em. Not big guys, though. Just sort of average build, I guess. Not like this here." He grabbed both sides of his belly and shook the small pot of flesh that hung over his belt.

The two women still watched him, and one stepped forward with more input. "They were all in black too, don't forget." The space between her eyes knotted with the effort it seemed to require for her to voice her thoughts.

"That's right," the man continued, smiling encouragement for her to let him do all the talking for them as he continued speaking. "All in black, head to toe. Nylons over their heads. Black jerseys, black jeans, and black shoes. Well, actually, one had black jeans, the other had casual pants, like them Dockers my wife makes me wear when we go out to dinner." He grinned.

Laurie nodded as she jotted down notes. "What about their voices, the way they talked, anything."

The man glanced toward the women. One boosted her shoulders in response; the other just gave him a blank look. "Nothing special, I guess. Local accent, I think. Only the big guy said anything. He kept yelling at us. The only thing I could say is he was loud. They kept swinging their guns around at us, got us down on the ground. I quit looking after that."

"Ladies?"

They shook their heads in unison. "I put my head in my arms and prayed. I didn't see anything after we laid down on the floor." The knot between her eyes had thickened. The other woman remained silent.

"Alright. Thanks," Laurie tried to hide her disappointment. Nothing new.

Gunnar had as much success with the tellers. "Well, if you're right about the mad money idea, they should be back next month," Gunnar mused as he returned from interviewing the group of tellers. "The tellers couldn't tell me much. The tall guy did all the talking again. The other one never said a word."

"I wonder why that is," Laurie mumbled. "You would think he'd say *something*. Maybe he's got a distinctive voice he doesn't want recognized."

"Or maybe he's stupid enough that the leader is afraid he'll say the wrong thing, so he just tells him to keep his mouth shut. One of the tellers said when she hesitated in giving him money, he just shook the bag and pointed his gun at her. If he was going to say anything, that would have been the time to do it, but he didn't."

"Yeah, maybe. But I'd say it's probably his voice. But why would he even worry unless he thinks someone here knows him?" Laurie closed her notebook and turned toward the door.

"Or maybe he thinks one of us will know him. Remember the shoes?" Her eyes lit up as the thought escaped her lips. "I'll bet they're in civil service somewhere. I hate to even suggest that maybe they're cops, but they could be."

"Yeah, they could be, but we would need some pretty good evidence before we even suggest that," Gunnar cautioned. "Even hinting at that could bring down department morale. We need more than shoes and a guy who never says anything."

"Yeah, but I've just got this feeling," Laurie mumbled.

"You and your feelings. You know I don't believe in instinct. You're not a dog, you know. Definitely not a dog," he grinned and winked.

"Thanks for noticing." She smiled as she climbed into the car. "Just wait. Someday, you'll have a gut feeling that you won't be able to shake."

Gunnar held up the surveillance tapes as she started the engine. "Don't suppose we'll get lucky with these?"

"Maybe. Cross your fingers."

They viewed the tapes at the station but still learned nothing about the robbery team that they didn't already know from the previous job. The gunmen had again dressed in black, covering every inch of skin and leaving no clues to help identify them. There had been no shots fired this time. The tellers had cooperated quickly as they had been trained to do and sent the team away with just over four thousand in cash—only half the amount they had taken in the first robbery.

# Chapter 15

So, what will you be doing while I'm up visiting my parents?" Laurie asked as she snuggled her face into Brandon's chest.

He wrapped his arms around her and pulled her into him, gently kissing the top of her head. "Spencer is in town again, so we were going to head out on the boat and do some fishing. Gunnar's coming down too."

"Fabulous!" Laurie chuckled. "Three guys out on the water, drinking beer of course while driving a rather large boat, and catching fish that might well kill you if you ate them. Sounds like a very productive day."

"Oh, I think the fish appreciate a little fresh air before we throw them back." He kissed her head again and she turned her face to his.

"I won't see you for a couple of days," she murmured and reached to kiss his lips.

"I guess I'll just have to keep you thinking of me while you're away." He pulled her closer and kissed her deeply, rolling onto her and pinning her beneath him. "I want you to miss me so much you'll come running back."

"Oh, I'll be back alright. You're not getting rid of me that easily." She smiled warmly and kissed him again.

He made love to her tenderly, his eyes finding hers between kisses.

When they'd finished, she kissed him and slipped out from between his arms. "I really have to go or I won't get there at all. What time are the guys coming?"

Brandon glanced at the clock. "Soon, actually. Mind if I share your shower?"

"Not at all," she smiled, reached for his hand, and pulled him out of bed and to her. He lifted her up and she wrapped her legs around him as he carried her to the shower, turned on the water and stepped inside with her.

"You know, I could keep you in here and make love to you all morning, but I do think our time is short before they arrive."

"Yes, I know you're right," she sighed as she unwrapped her legs from him and he gently set her down. They stayed apart while they showered, though they never took their eyes from each other. When the water was off, Brandon embraced her and kissed her forehead before he wrapped her in a towel and took a towel for himself.

Once dried and dressed, they embraced again, then parted reluctantly as the doorbell rang. "Good timing," she grinned as she opened the door.

"Hey, Laurie," Gunnar greeted cheerfully as he sauntered in through the open door. "I thought you'd be long gone by now."

"I would've been, but I got held up." She smiled as she motioned her head toward Brandon.

"Sure. Blame it on the man," Brandon chided.

Laurie simply smiled coyly in response and kissed Brandon on the cheek. "Have fun. See you back at work, Gunnar." She grabbed her weekend bag that she had placed by the door and headed out.

"Sure thing," he grinned.

She encountered Spencer pulling in to park as she reached her car. She smiled warmly to him as she waited to greet him. He parked his car and climbed out. "How are you Miss Laurie?" He walked to her and gave her a warm hug and peck on the cheek. "So you're gone for a couple of days?"

"Yep. And I'm leaving it up to you and Gunnar to keep that man out of trouble, at least most of it."

"Good. So we're allowed a little bit of trouble," he grinned.

"Just a little. Take care and have fun." She threw her bag in the trunk and climbed into her car as he turned toward Brandon's condo.

"So, what sort of shape is the boat in these days?" Spencer asked as they left the condo.

"Good, I hope. I haven't been on her much since Laurie and I met."

"Busy with other things, I bet. Hope the old girl's not jealous. I'm not much for hanging out waiting for a tow if she decides to crap out on you in the middle of Quinsig," Spencer warned.

"Just means we have to bring a good supply of beer," Brandon replied.

"I brought a couple of sixes along," Gunnar chimed in. "Let me just grab them out of the car." He opened the trunk of the Monte Carlo and pulled out a brown bag. "Little bit of Wachusett's finest," He smiled as he closed the trunk lid.

"Great! So, we're good to go. I've got plenty of beer in the refrigerator on the boat already. We can add that to it. All the gear and bait is packed, so let's hit it."

"Now we're talking," Spencer said.

They walked down to the dock where a 26-foot Sea Ray floated peacefully, swaying with gentle undulations of the water. The scent of morning mist filled the air and the lake was free of traffic save for a few boats that drifted quietly in the middle, their captains wistfully watching the lines of fishing poles that tied them to the water.

"Find what room you can in the fridge for that beer. Actually, I'll take one while you're at it," Brandon directed.

"Same goes for me," Spencer agreed.

Gunnar lifted the lid of the cooler that was mounted into the boat's galley counter and dropped the beer inside. He pulled three bottles from the bag before he closed the lid. He popped the lids off with an ancient bottle opener, then headed for the open air.

"Man, you've definitely got it made down here," Gunnar commented. How can you not be on this boat every day. I mean, Laurie's great and all, but you've got to take time for this."

"I'll take any second I can get with that woman. I haven't even thought about this boat since I met her, to tell the truth." Brandon put the key in the ignition. The engine hesitated, but then turned over smoothly and came to life. Brandon applied the throttle and revved it up.

"I have," Spencer added. "We have to get you back on your boating schedule." He untied the lines from the cleats and held the boat in place until Brandon slowed the engines and put the transmission in gear.

"Hell, you guys don't need me to get out on the boat. Just come on out whenever you want. I'm not giving up any of my time with Laurie, though. You know, I think I love her." He pulled the boat away from the dock as Spencer climbed aboard.

"That's pretty intense. You should think about that before you say anything to her. You know she's had a lot of bad luck in the past. Guys tell her all sorts of things, then dump her because she's a cop and that's eventually a turnoff."

"Hell, I don't think that's a turnoff," Spencer interjected. "I think it's hot!"

"So do I," Brandon agreed with a grin. "But I understand your point. I worry about her everyday while she's out there dealing with things like that girl that was murdered recently."

"Hey, I heard about that. That was some nasty stuff," Spencer chimed in.

"Yeah, we don't get much like that around here, but I can say that definitely affected her. She wasn't herself for days. Even now, I can see how it haunts her when she's working that case. That sort of pressure can weigh on a guy when his woman is stressed out like that."

"That doesn't discourage me. I'm always here for her," Brandon countered.

"All I'm saying is realize what you're into before you start telling her you love her," Gunnar reasoned. "You better not hurt her. If you tell her you love her, then walk away, I'm just going to have to hunt you down."

Brandon chuckled. "Oh, I don't think I'll be walking away any time soon." He slowed the boat as they neared the Route 9 overpass. "Spencer, you want to go up and drop the anchor?"

"Sure thing, captain." Spencer left his beer and proceeded to walk along deck to the bow of the boat. He opened up the locker located within the deck, pulled the pin back that held the anchor into its seat in the anchor roller, then dropped the anchor into the water. The chain attached to the anchor disappeared quickly and coils of rope leapt into the water after it. When the rope rested and went slack, Spencer tied it off to a cleat on the bow, closed the locker, then turned back along the deck and rejoined the other two men in the cockpit.

Brandon and Gunnar were discussing the Wilson case when Spencer settled back into his seat and took a long pull on his beer.

"I haven't asked Laurie about it lately. Have you found anything further on that girl's murder?" Brandon asked Gunnar.

"No. The guy didn't really leave anything behind. He raped her, but wore a condom. He didn't even leave any hairs behind on her, which is odd. There's always hair. These days, we can even pull fingerprints off of skin, but he didn't leave any of those either. He did leave some clothing fibers, but they're pretty standard materials and would be hard to trace. It just doesn't make any sense. Usually, perps leave carpet fibers from their house or car, hair from themselves, but there just wasn't any of that. The only thing he did leave was a smear of blood from the knife he wiped off on her shirt. But even that wasn't very definitive." Gunnar took a long pull off of his beer.

Brandon shook his head. I really worry about her with this case. It's really got her down.

"That sucks!" Spencer said solemnly. "But we're here to fish. No more talk about work." He grabbed a pole and opened the bucket of bait they'd brought: scraps of chicken, raw beef, several large nightcrawlers, a block of mild cheese, a few raw scallops and other bits that he didn't recognize. Spencer grabbed a nightcrawler and began to thread it onto his hook.

Brandon watched him a moment, then grabbed a pole and a piece of raw beef. "You're right," he said. "We didn't come out here to talk about our work: mine, yours, or Gunnar's."

Gunnar stayed seated, watching the two of them prepare their hooks. "I'm just going to sit here and watch the two of you while I drink my beer," he grinned.

"You're not going to fish?" Brandon asked.

"Not just yet. It's a beautiful morning and I'm just going to enjoy it and see if the two of you start pulling anything out of the water."

"Suit yourself," Spencer said as he cast his line into the water. He stood holding the pole a few moments, then put the butt of the pole into a steel tube designed to hold it and sat down.

Brandon did the same with his pole.

"Do you guys ever catch anything?" Gunnar asked.

"Not really," Brandon answered. "Fishing is just an excuse to come out here and drink beer in the early hours of the morning."

"Hey, works for me. But I don't need to dip my hands into slime to feel justified drinking a beer this time of the morning," Gunnar grinned. "But you guys do whatever you have to do." He tipped his beer back and finished the bottle. "Anyone ready for another?"

"You bet!" Spencer said as he finished his also.

"One for me, too." Brandon and Spencer both handed an empty bottle to Gunnar who disappeared into the cabin.

The tip of Spencer's pole pointed down at the water and quivered. "That's a surprise," Brandon mused as he pointed at the pole. Spencer grabbed the pole and began reeling in the line.

"Feels pretty good size," he grinned. "Putting up a pretty good fight."

"Thought you guys never caught anything," Gunnar said as he reappeared with three open beers in hand.

"Don't usually," Brandon said. "But every once in a while we get lucky. Keeps us coming back out here with the poles."

Spencer worked the pole until a fish appeared on the surface of the water, wriggling and fighting to free itself from the hook. Brandon grabbed the net and lowered it to the water to scoop up the fish.

"Nice. About twelve inches," Brandon commented. "If we were crazy enough to eat out of this lake, that would be a keeper."

"Nope. Back it goes," Spencer said as he quickly worked the hook out of the fish's mouth and tossed it back into the water. "Let's see if he gets stupid again." He baited another worm onto the hook, tossed it back into the water and set the pole back into the holder.

"So, you've busted me about Laurie, how's your sex life these days, Gunnar?" Brandon asked.

"Hell, my sex life is great. Still plenty of women calling out my name."

"No one in particular?"

"Nah. I don't like to get too close. I don't need anyone nagging me about what time to come home. That's just not for me. I make them scream out my name a few times, then leave them for someone else."

"I hear that," Spencer said. He held up his beer as a toast and Gunnar touched his bottle to it. "I'm on the road too much. I don't need someone asking where I've been. One-nighters: they work for me."

Brandon chuckled and shook his head. "Laurie turned me around from that. Spencer, you know my story. Mostly one-nighters, never long with any woman. But Laurie is special. She's fun, she's smart, sexy, and yes, she's incredibly good in bed. But I'm not going to tell you about that. I do believe she's just the perfect woman. I don't know what she sees in me, but I hope she continues to see it. I just hope she doesn't learn any secrets about me that'll drive her away."

"What secrets? You?" Spencer asked.

"If I told you, they wouldn't be secrets, would they?" Brandon grinned.

"Come on, we've all got secrets," Spencer challenged. "I know I've got mine."

"Hell, I live my secrets. Never can reveal too much while you're on the job," Gunnar pulled a long drink from his beer. "As long as your secrets aren't anything that hurt Laurie, you can keep them as far as I'm concerned. But remember, you do anything to hurt her, and I'm going to hunt you down."

"I remember, but looks like we've got company, guys." Brandon pointed to a patrol boat that was approaching slowly. He waved to them.

"Hi. How's it going today?" he said as the boat pulled up alongside.

"You boys drinking out here?" the captain asked.

Gunnar stood up and reached out to shake the captain's hand. "Hi guys. Gunnar Hincks, Worcester Police. We're just hanging out here doing some fishing. How are you today?"

The captain shook the hand offered. "One of Worcester's finest, huh? I've heard of you, detective. You've done some fine work in this city. Good to see you taking some time to relax. Just keep the beer out of sight, alright?"

"Will do, sir. Take care and don't work too hard, yourself," he smiled.

The other patrolman in the boat pushed them away from the Sea Ray as the captain applied the throttle. They exchanged waves as the patrol boat pulled away.

"Thanks for covering us, Gunnar. They don't usually harass us like that. They must have orders to crack down on drinkers," Brandon said.

"Glad to help. So how about another beer? Maybe we pour them into glasses to help hide them?"

"Good idea," Brandon said as he took the empty bottles and headed into the cabin.

# Chapter 16

Laurie took a moment to admire the last pink of sunrise. It was going to be a beautiful day for her ride up north, though she was disappointed that Brandon wouldn't be riding with her. She was really looking forward to his meeting her family, but she wasn't ready to share him yet; it was too soon for that and she knew it. As she started the engine, the corner of her mouth turned up slightly as she thought how much her family would like Brandon. She put the convertible top down so she could enjoy the feel of the rising sun's warmth, then reached around, grabbed a baseball cap from the floor behind her seat, and pulled it down onto her head.

It had been three months since she'd been to Vermont, since before she'd met Brandon, and Laurie didn't expect anything less than sheer excitement from her mother when she told her about him. Though she had talked to her mother a few times since then, she had been afraid to share this secret and jinx the relationship. Besides, she really wanted to tell her mother face-to-face, over a glass of wine or two, rather than over the phone.

Laurie had waited several months before she had introduced Jeff to her family and it seemed that not long after, things had ended between them. The same had been the case for the previous love she'd brought home to Vermont. He had decided it was time to "see other people" the following week.

Jessie insisted that those men weren't ready for the kind of commitment that meeting parents suggests, but Laurie wondered if they hadn't really held out the hope that she would leave police work, only to have those hopes dashed when they met her family. She didn't think leaving police work was something she could ever do and, although she never concealed the passion she felt for her job, she didn't think they believed in her commitment until they saw her family in uniforms, guns, and badges, displayed in photo after photo around her parent's home, or heard the excitement around the table as they all shared their stories.

She weaved in and out of the light traffic, enjoying the wind in her face as she made her way along the Massachusetts Turnpike toward Springfield. The sun was now high enough to begin sharing its heat and she straightened in her seat a little to better appreciate its warmth.

The traffic thickened as she approached Springfield's city limits, but by the time she'd reached the far side of the city and turned north on Route 91, the traffic had died. Farmlands began to appear on both sides of the highway the farther north she drove. Cows dotted lush, green pastures where quaint, red barns stood like matrons watching over their children. It was a different world from the congestion and population of central and eastern Massachusetts cities. In Vermont, life passed at a different pace and Laurie loved to escape to that; she loved to let her tension unwind over a cup of coffee in the morning as she watched the mist evaporate off the valley.

Laurie had failed to appreciate the lackadaisical life of the country when she was a child in Clarendon Springs. She had longed for the city then, had longed for more contact with human life than with animals and nature. Now, though, she felt differently and warmed to the times when she could escape the city and its people. The wind whipped strands of hair into her face as the countryside raced by and her thoughts returned to Brandon.

Brandon had given all of his time to her since they'd met. She had a key to his condo and spent as much, if not more, time there than at her own little Cape in Auburn. They'd discussed her moving in with him, but decided it would be prudent to wait at least another two or three months. Laurie wasn't yet ready to sell her house, though. She would have to rent it, she'd decided, and so she began to put as much time as she could spare into fixing those little things she'd learned to live with—a broken tile here and there in the kitchen and bathroom; the blue and yellow-flowered wallpaper in her bedroom that she'd vowed to remove right away when she'd first bought the house finally came down to be replaced by a fresh coat of soft green paint. Window and door trim that had been painted brown in the past was now white and the leaky faucet in the kitchen had been replaced.

Brandon had offered his help with each home-improvement project, but Laurie refused, saving the projects for when he was away from her so they could share more romantic times when he was near. His work took him out of town frequently, and though he usually returned within a day, Laurie felt lost when she couldn't be near him. Finishing projects around the house kept her mind entertained and Jessie often stopped over to share drinks and critique her work. It seemed to be the only time that Laurie had to spend with her best friend since she'd met Brandon, and Jessie spared no chance to chide her for her neglect.

Laurie exited Route 91 onto VT-103, stopped for gas and a coffee and continued north. The sun was now high overhead and beat down mercilessly upon her but she never considered raising the roof of the car to hide from it since that would stifle the feeling of freedom she felt when it was down.

When she finally turned into the long, narrow driveway, it was approaching noontime and her stomach complained loudly at her. A fluffy, Newfoundland, blacker than the night, bounded out from behind the house and raced over to greet her, tail wagging furiously.

"Hey, Whiskey. How are ya, furball?" Laurie looped her free arm around the enormous black head and gave an affectionate squeeze, then threw her travel bag over her shoulder and gave the dog a gentle nudge. He backed away obediently but clung close to her heels as she walked toward the house.

The door was flung open before she reached it and Laurie's face lit up as her mother rushed out to greet her.

Evelyn Sharpe was a striking woman at fifty-one with golden blonde curls that fell to her shoulders and soft jade eyes that glowed with pride at the site of her only daughter. An active woman, Evelyn had maintained the same figure she possessed in her twenties—

slender, graceful, and perfectly proportioned. She greeted Laurie with a warm hug that made her think she would break a few ribs if she squeezed any tighter.

"How have you been, Sweetie? I haven't seen you in so long. You usually visit more often." She held her daughter at arms length and looked her over from head to toe before pulling her into another hug. Then she threw an arm around her waist and hurried her toward the open door.

"What can I get you to drink, Sweetie?" In the kitchen, Evelyn wasted no time. She loved to wait on her family. Before Laurie could respond, her mother retrieved a bottle of tomato juice from the refrigerator, filling two large glasses to the rim.

"What have you been up to that I haven't seen you? Have you been spending all your time with a man?" She smiled, her eyes twinkling expectantly as she handed a glass to Laurie and raised her own up to touch its rim in a quick toast.

"As a matter of fact, I have," she smiled broadly. The last news Laurie had shared about her love life had been about her break-up with Jeff. She hadn't even mentioned Brandon, and she was eager to share every detail now. But she delayed the news a moment, motioning her mother to the kitchen table.

"Let's sit and relax. Should I open us a bottle of wine?" Laurie asked, fighting a smile as she intentionally withheld her news.

"Not yet, dear. Now quit stalling and tell me about this new man in your life," Evelyn demanded as she took Laurie's hand and gently motioned her to her seat.

Laurie grinned, sat, and took a sip of tomato juice before elaborating. Her mother was visibly bursting with expectation as she waited on her daughter's next words.

"I think I've met the man I'm going to marry!"

Evelyn screamed with delight. She pushed her chair back from the table, stood, and pulled Laurie up from her seat to give her a bone-crushing hug. "I'm so happy for you!" she cried. She let her go and held her out at arms length again, demanding to hear every detail.

"Oh, Mom. He is just absolutely wonderful! You know how you always said it was with you and Dad? That it was love at first sight for the two of you? It was even more than that. I think I was in love with him when I first talked to him on the phone."

"On the phone? What did he say?" Evelyn motioned her back to her seat and Laurie obliged as Evelyn sat back down across from her.

"He said that he needed me to help make a bust."

"So he's a cop?" Evelyn clasped her hands together, excited that Laurie was in love with a man who could appreciate her family's love for the job.

"No, Mom. He's not a cop. He's a computer geek. But, Mom it wasn't what he said, it was something in the sound of his voice. After talking to him on the phone, I just couldn't wait to meet him. And he was just everything I'd expected."

"What's his name?" Evelyn pressed.

"Brandon. Brandon Doyle."

"He's handsome?"

"Oh, yes." Laurie smiled.

Evelyn eagerly propped her elbows on the table and rested her chin on her knuckles as she listened.

"He is just so gorgeous! And to answer you're next question, he's well off, too. He's got a place here and one in California. He works for himself as a computer consultant and travels all over for that. We've been together every free minute that he *is* in town. That's why I haven't been up here. I'm sorry, Mom. I didn't want to jinx this by telling you, but everything's going so well. I don't think it could be any better."

"Oh, I just worried about you when I hadn't seen you and I could tell you were holding something back when we talked on the phone. I'm so happy for you!"

"Thanks. Me, too. I can't wait until you can meet him. But I don't know if he's ready for that yet. I want to give him a bit more time, at least until I've had a chance to gauge whether he's ready. Brandon said he wanted to come with me today, but I could see he was hesitant, so I sent him off fishing with the guys instead. You know how men are. Even if they say they're ready, they're not really ready."

"Yes, dear. I know how men are. Your father is the worst of them," she said affectionately and sipped her juice. "How long have the two of you been together?"

"Only about two months. I know it's really soon to feel this way about him, but I love him. It feels like I've known him forever and I really love him."

"I'm so excited for you. I can see in your eyes that he really is the one. I never saw that when you talked about the others," Evelyn observed.

"This really is different." She paused reflectively, then rubbed her belly. "You know, I'm really starving. Is Dad working? You and I could go grab some lunch."

"That's a fantastic idea. I haven't eaten yet. I was waiting for you to arrive. Just give me a minute to change out of these house pants." Evelyn indicated the ragged pair of sweatpants she wore that bore several splotches of old paint and a tear at the left knee. She hurried away upstairs.

Laurie picked up her glass of tomato juice and turned her attention to the morning paper, *The Rutland Herald* that was still spread out on the table. Since she hadn't seen her family, she hadn't been informed of the latest events, but in Rutland and its surrounding suburbs, even the smallest events were news. She flipped back to the front page to see what, if anything, was happening in her hometown. Nothing exciting on the first few pages. But it was a headline at the top of the fourth page that caught her attention: *No Leads in Clarendon Murder.*

Very little ever happened in Clarendon, so when Laurie read about the lack of progress in the case of a young girl who had been murdered a couple months earlier, she was very surprised that blood had been shed in the tiny, peaceful town.

She read carefully through each line of the article as it briefly described the facts of the case and slowly her blood chilled in her veins as she held the pages up closer to her eyes. The chill passed quickly to her spine, raising the fine hairs on the back of her neck as she read the details again and again, noting the similarities between how this girl had been found and how she remembered Abra Wilson's body just weeks before this girl had died.

They still had made no progress with the Wilson case. But now, here was something. Laurie scarcely dared to hope that the man who had butchered Abra Wilson had also taken the life of the girl in Clarendon. But why here? Clarendon and Worcester were at least a three-hour drive apart. What connected the two?

"Well, I'm ready, Sweetie. Let's go." Her mother bounced into the kitchen like a teenager but stopped short when she saw the mixed cloud of trouble and elation on her daughter's face. "What's wrong, Honey? Everything OK?"

"Mom, what do you know about the girl that was killed over in Clarendon?" Laurie asked.

Evelyn Sharpe's face was immediately dark. "That poor girl," she replied. "They found her dead at the airport. She was just cut apart."

"Any idea who's handling the case?"

"Gary Morris is handling it. Why?" Her brow furrowed with puzzlement.

"I know there's probably some other explanation, but I've got a case just like this in Worcester and it almost sounds like the same MO. I need to talk to Gary." Laurie reached for the phone on the wall beside the table.

Evelyn smiled with pride as she took the handset from her and replaced it in its cradle. "You're not getting out of telling me all about Brandon over lunch." She put her hand up to shush Laurie as she started to protest.

"Work can wait. Gary should be on the clock today. We'll have lunch, you'll tell me everything a nosy mother needs to hear, then we'll swing by the station and talk to Gary afterward."

Laurie tensed with the overwhelming need to attack this first lead in the case that had confounded her, but the calm demeanor of the woman who had held her family together through countless cases, all needing immediate attention snapped her back to the moment. Her tension melted and she smiled at her mother. "You're right. Lunch and girl-talk first."

# Chapter 17

The Piccadilly Pub was as crowded as it usually was at this time after work. Laurie pushed and squirmed her way through the tightly packed throng of after-work drinkers to a group of off-duty officers gathered around the large wooden table in the center of the lounge. It was a tough table to get unless you had connections and theirs had arrived very early in the evening and were now loud and boisterous with the influence of the alcohol they had consumed, unchecked, since then. Laurie selected an empty square of space next to Gunnar in which to stand, but he immediately got up, offering her his seat.

"And they say chivalry is dead," she said with a touch of sarcasm, giving him a slight jab in the arm. "Really, though, thanks." She smiled up at him from her seat. "It's been a long day and I really need to sit."

"Not a problem," he said. "What are you drinking? Manhattan?"

"Yeah. Sounds great," Laurie sighed and rubbed her neck.

"So how were your days off?" The waitress stopped by and Gunnar ordered Laurie's Manhattan as well as another beer for himself. "Gotta stay on the light stuff tonight. I had enough the other night."

"Oh? Where'd you go?"

"Had a date out in Boston. I took her to see the Blue Man Group. You ever see them?"

"No."

"Fantastic!" Laurie saw his face light up. "Course I won't tell you all about it. You really should get to see it yourself sometime." The drinks arrived and he thirstily drank the first third of the beer.

"Maybe I'll ask Brandon to take me."

"Ah, Mr. Wonderful. How's it going with him? You guys spend so much time together. Are you getting married yet?" Gunnar jostled her with his shoulder and she blushed a faint red.

Laurie's drink arrived and she nervously picked it up and took a sip, making a face at the strong taste of it. She picked a few ice cubes from the glass that had been served with it and dropped them in, then sipped again. Satisfied, she replaced it on the table before she replied. "I only just met the guy a couple months ago! The way things are going though, I don't think I'd mind if he asked." She lifted her drink again. This sort of talk made her nervous, even with Gunnar, who was closer to her than even her brothers at times.

"What about your date?" she changed the subject. "You said you had a great time. You going to call her or did you already get what you wanted?"

Gunnar stifled a grin. "You know I like to leave things on a high note. Besides, I don't think this girl wanted anything serious."

"Typical guy." Laurie sipped her drink. "I found something interesting and I want to know what you think."

He set his drink on the table and leaned over it on his elbows when he saw the seriousness on her face. "What is it?"

"While I was up to see my parents these past couple days, I took a look through *The Rutland Herald*. There was an article about a girl killed at a little local airport a couple of months ago. Apparently, this girl had been at a bar near the airport and it seemed whoever killed her had given her Rohypnol." She paused to take another sip of her drink.

"Ruffies are pretty common for date rape," Gunnar commented. "So, what's the issue?"

"She was cut up pretty badly, throat cut, and they found her body laid out on the wing of a plane," she responded.

"Sounds a little like the Wilson case," Gunnar mused.

Laurie nodded excitedly, "Exactly what I thought! I talked to the detective on the case." She paused a moment, then continued. "They didn't really find any physical evidence on her that they could use— no hairs, no DNA, no semen, just some fibers, but nothing easy to trace. And no one in the bar could remember much about the guy she was with. Just that he had dark hair, a beard. That's it."

"You think it's the same guy?"

"Yeah, I do. The detective in Clarendon was a little skeptical, but there are too many similarities. He said the killer had cleaned his knife on her dress, so I asked him to send me the dress to compare it with the stain on the Wilson girl's blouse. Maybe we'll find it's the same knife or at least the same type of knife." She paused to take a deep breath. "So, what do you think? If this is the same perp, there's no telling how many other girls he's killed. And how big a circle."

Gunnar nodded agreement slowly and sipped his beer. "It really is a long shot that this guy kills a girl here in Worcester, then winds up in a tiny town in the backwoods of Vermont and does another girl there. That's a long way to travel to commit a random crime, don't you think?"

"But not so far away that it doesn't warrant looking into," Laurie concluded. "Tomorrow I'm going to send out a teletype message around New England for information on similar cases. But to be sure we're heard, I'm going to start making phone calls, too. You know they miss those little messages all the time, but they always remember a phone call."

"Don't be too surprised if nothing turns up. It really could just be a coincidence. Or, maybe it is our guy and he just happened to be out in our neck of the woods when he happened upon the Wilson girl. Maybe she was even his first and then he figured he'd try it on his own turf." Gunnar took another drink of his beer. "Anyway, check it out, but if there were a bunch of girls dying out there, I'd think some reporter would've made the connection. They read through all the papers all the time. They would've caught on and written up some huge story by now. It's probably just a couple isolated incidents. That, or maybe the guy is trying to get your attention."

Laurie's stomach knotted up and she didn't understand why. "What do you mean?"

"Come on, Sharpe. Both murders are in your hometown." Gunnar grinned and held up his beer. "See? I got it all figured out."

"Not funny, Gunnar. Now are you going to help me make phone calls?"

"Yeah, I'll help. You are my partner. But I think you're barking up the wrong tree."

"Well, then. Here's hoping we don't find a whole lot of bodies out there." She solemnly held her glass up to him.

Gunnar raised his glass and tapped it against hers. "I'll drink to that."

"Hey, what are you guys toastin' over there?" One of the off-duty, slightly drunk patrol officers shouted from the far side of the table. "You havin' your own private little party over there? If we didn't know any better," he looked around the table, "and who's to say we don't, I'd say it looks like you two have been getting' it on the way you're huddled together."

"Alright, Donny," Gunnar retorted. "Just cause you ain't gettin' any lately doesn't mean everyone else is." A few of the other officers snickered a little. Gunnar's dating habits were well known around the department. He almost never took anyone out for a second date.

"Hey, speak for yourself," someone countered in a slurred voice. "I got laid last night."

"Hey, thanks for the info, Tommy. Rotten sex life, Gunnar?" Another chimed in. "Maybe you oughta try your luck on Keno, 'stead o' women. You need a card?" He offered him a ticket.

Gunnar refused. "I don't need to throw my money away on that shit. How much you guys bet so far?"

"About twenty bucks."

"Win anything yet?"

"Yeah we won a couple bucks. I dunno, does anyone really come out ahead with this stuff?"

"Exactly my point. You play; we'll drink."

"Problems?" Gunnar asked when he found Laurie slumped over her desk, holding her head up by clumps of blonde entwined around her fingers.

If he had walked in a moment sooner, he would have heard her cursing openly, something she rarely did—Laurie was always calm, rational and levelheaded, no matter how bad things got. But she had been alone in the room before his arrival, and had given in to frustration.

Laurie untangled her fingers when he approached and looked up at him. She struggled with a smile, but failed miserably.

"Oh, just frustration from a complete lack of success after several hours of hard work."

"Well, cheer up. I have the world-renowned solution to everything right here." He held up a steaming cup from the local coffee stop.

"Oh, you are a life saver," she sighed and felt a tingle of life rush through her as she reached for the cup. The warmth of it in her hand began a chain reaction of relaxation that spread quickly up her arm toward the knotted muscles in her spine. Coffee was just what she needed!

"I haven't had any coffee yet today. Now I'm in cop heaven."

She wasted no time tearing the lid off and boldly put the cup to her lips. She didn't care that it was hot enough to burn; she drank heartily, ignoring the scorching sensation as it seared its way down her throat. "Oh, that's good! You are a lifesaver," she said again. She managed a tired smile before attacking the coffee again.

"So what's all this frustration?" He pulled up a chair and turned it around, sitting on it backwards with his arms folded upon the backrest, and stared at her intently.

Laurie curbed her delight in the coffee, setting it down on the desk.

"It's the Wilson case, of course," she sighed. "Two days of calling since I found the info on the girl in Vermont. I got her dress and the crime lab says that, based on the bloodstain, the knife is a ninety percent possible match. So we've got a good possibility that this is the same killer, at least it feels right, and then, that's it—dead end! I've made a bunch of calls to cities and towns all around Massachusetts and into Vermont and New Hampshire—nothing! I can't find a thing! But I just *know* that there's something else out there. I *know* it! I just can't find it," she groaned and threw her hands up in the air.

Gunnar grinned disarmingly and put a hand on her shoulder. "You know I'm a skeptic about gut feelings since I don't get them myself. "You've gotten really wound up on this case. Are you sure you're not just pushing too hard for this connection to be real with the Vermont case? It's a long way from here and the Wilson crime scene wasn't really all that unusual for a murder/rape. You should give it a rest. You look wiped." He patted her shoulder gently.

"Maybe you're right. But I don't know. I just really feel like I'm right, here. I guess I just need to make more calls."

Gunnar shook his head skeptically. "How many towns have you called? Do you have a list?" He leaned over a map on her desk upon which she had circled the names of several towns with a blue ink pen.

"No," Laurie replied. She pointed to many circled towns, of which Clarendon, Vermont and Worcester were circled in red. "These are all the ones I've called. Clarendon and Worcester of course are the only hits so far."

"Alright. You keep working around Mass, for now. I'll start calling up some towns in New Hampshire. Okay?"

She smiled. "You're a prince," she said. "Even if you are a cop."

"Excuse me? And what are you?"

"Yeah, but you know that bit about boys in uniform," she taunted.

"Well, we've got a few sayings for women in uniform, too," he fired back.

"Yeah, they're probably all sexually explicit."

"Well, we do have our priorities," he smiled coyly. "Now get to work; we've got a lot to do." He picked up the phone and began to dial.

A half hour went by, then an hour. They dialed one town after another, but the responses at the other end of the line gave them nothing. Other officers came and went, stopping by only to gather items needed to conduct their work on the streets of the city.

Laurie was just about to give up for the day when Gunnar, who was still in conversation on the other phone, held up his hand in a manner that told her he had found something. Laurie tried to listen in on his conversation, but could determine nothing from the one side that she could hear.

Finally, he hung up. She felt her heart beating against the walls of her chest with excitement. *What is it?* her eyes pleaded.

"That was the Concord Police Department in New Hampshire. They had a girl go missing from a bar up in Chichester. It took them a few days, but they finally found her body in Giddis Brook near there. She appears to have been raped, but they're conducting the autopsy now and they'll call us back later with the results." He smiled triumphantly. "Maybe you're right. Maybe there are more."

But Laurie did not share his enthusiasm. She was puzzled. "They found her body *in* the water? Did she have any clothes on?"

Gunnar dropped a pen he'd been twirling through his fingers. "She had what was left of her dress on and the detective said she was floating near the bank, so I assume that means she was in the water. What's wrong with it? She's a rape victim from a local bar. It could be the same guy."

"No, this guy likes to display his women. The Wilson girl was left on display either for us or maybe even for him, so he could remember her. Throwing a body into the river is impersonal, don't you think?"

"I don't know. Let's wait for the report. Maybe they can get a decent rape test from her, even if she was in the water for a while. That will tell us for sure. Well, we really should get some outdoor exposure for a bit, don't you think?

"Yeah, I suppose. We should go check out that accident over in Kelly Square yesterday. A call came in from one of the shop owners this morning, said his son saw the car that took off."

Kelly Square was Worcester's worst traffic nightmare. Four roads and an off-ramp from the expressway fed vehicles into a hexagon with no signal light to help sort out the traffic. It was a free-for-all, barely slowed by stop signs, with drivers fighting their way toward any one of the five outlets. The drivers were rarely courteous and the traffic flow was certainly not organized as cars darted through tiny holes in the flow to reach their outlet.

Two cars had collided as one turned left across the path of the other. One of them had fled without stopping, leaving an elderly woman dead in the other car. No one at the scene had been able to give them more than a vague description of the car—a faded blue Toyota Celica.

Now, almost 24 hours later, someone suddenly decided to remember something. Guilt was always a detective's friend. Laurie wondered what he was hiding that he had not spoken up sooner.

"I'm sure the girl in Concord's not related to our guy but I am sure he's left other dead girls out there," Laurie pondered aloud as she guided the car around the rotary at Posner Square.

"You don't know that," Gunnar argued. "The case in Vermont may not even be related to the Wilson case. It's probably all just a coincidence. And you know what's an even bigger coincidence?"

"What?" Laurie grumbled.

"That both girls were killed a four hour drive apart and you just happen to have connection to both places."

"You said that, already," Laurie fumed. She was silent a moment, but Gunnar could see her thoughts in the movements of her face. The coincidence made her nervous. He wanted to laugh, but held back.

"I...." Her forehead wrinkled in confusion as she searched for an explanation. "Do you think he's taunting me? He couldn't know I'd hear about the girl in Vermont, right?" She cast a worried glance at Gunnar.

He let go the laugh like a loud bark. "You can't be serious!"

"No. You're right." She brought the car to a stop in front of the witness' shop.

"Listen, Laurie. If he had his eye on this investigation and wanted to taunt either of us, he'd kill another girl in Worcester. It's just a really weird coincidence that Clarendon happens to be your home, also. Don't even get into the bad movie plots with killers picking a cop to play cat and mouse with. This is just a coincidence." Gunnar watched her dubiously.

"Come on, let's go interview this witness," he urged.

Laurie nodded silently, but she couldn't shake the feeling that Gunnar was right, even if he was only joking.

Abra Wilson's killer was watching her.

# Chapter 18

A few weeks had passed with no word back from any of the cities or towns they had spoken with. Nothing had come across the teletype either. Their case was dead again, as dead as the case in Clarendon, and as dead as both young women, cut to ribbons in their youth.

"There's a Sergeant Johnson on the phone for you." Gunnar held up the phone for Laurie to take.

Laurie's eyes lit up with sudden recognition and she hastily grabbed the phone from him and spun away, wrapping herself up in the cord before she could pull it over her head and out of the way.

"Wow!" Gunnar exclaimed not without a little friendly sarcasm. "I don't think I've ever seen you grab for the phone so fast. Sheesh!" Gunnar took a seat at his desk, watching Laurie for a moment before shuffling through some papers on the desk in a half-hearted attempt to make sense of them.

He glanced up occasionally as he half listened to her conversation. Excitement and horror alternated like waves as she spoke and he guessed she was probably getting some key tidbits on one of her cases. She grabbed a pen and began to scribble feverishly on a yellow pad. He leaned toward her, trying to read the words from a distance of five feet, but they were illegible, probably to anyone but Laurie herself.

"Thank you. Let me know if you hear of anything else like this." Finally, she placed the phone tenderly in the cradle and silently met Gunnar's eye with a twinkle in her own.

He stared at her with his usual intent expression as he awaited information. "Hot date? Really great seats at a sold-out concert? What?" He asked with joking sarcasm. He knew what she'd just heard was important and he used the sarcasm to hide his eagerness.

"The Wilson case."

Gunnar was instantly forward in his chair, eager for any information that promised some sort of closure in this case.

"He said they have a case on the books from a few weeks ago. They found a woman dead near a club in Quincy," she said. "And you want to know what's weird about it?" She paused as though she was actually waiting for an answer, but Gunnar just shrugged.

"What's really scary is that I was at this same club, not long before this murder happened. Remember, I told you about that neat little place Brandon and I went to in Quincy called Marina Bay?"

Gunnar shook his head uncertainly.

"After Brandon and I took our little trip out on the tugboats when the Tall Ships were in town."

"Oh yeah." Light dawned across his face. "I remember. The little club on the water."

"Right. This woman was in that club before she was killed. In fact, the bartender said she was a regular there. Always came in alone and often left with a guy she'd just met. The bartender says he stopped noticing her, though, so he couldn't really give any great description of the guy she was with that night."

"Wait a minute," Gunnar held up his hand in a gesture for her to stop. "What's the MO? Why is this related to the Wilson case? Was she drugged? Did he cut her throat?"

"No. Actually, she wasn't drugged and he didn't cut her throat, he strangled her. It's just the way he left her—completely naked, laid out on her back with very deep cuts on her body from a very large knife. I don't know, maybe it is completely unrelated, but the way she was left is just too similar and I just have this gut feeling that this is our guy."

"It sounds like a different MO if he didn't drug her and didn't cut her throat. You sure you're not seeing a connection because you're worried this guy is following you and you were at this club?"

"You're probably right," she responded half-heartedly. But in her mind, her thoughts still churned.

"Maybe some caffeine will help get you thinking straight again. Because at this point, I just don't see a relationship between these cases myself."

Gunnar stood up from his desk and picked up the car keys. "Are you coming?"

Gunnar brushed the coincidence aside, but Laurie felt that her connection to the sites where the murders occurred was significant—she didn't get outside Worcester all that often. She felt the hairs rising on the back of her neck and along the crown of her scalp. The killer was following her.

Midday traffic was heavy as workers escaped their offices and piled into the streets, searching for food and probably a few lunchtime drinks.

Gunnar guided the unmarked car cautiously up Park Avenue, stopping for a few pedestrians that stepped out casually in front of him. A car on his right cut sharply across his nose to catch the street on his left. His foot landed heavily on the brake as he narrowly missed the rear bumper. "Shit! I just love Worcester drivers!"

Laurie laughed.

"He's just lucky I'm on my way to get coffee, otherwise I'd play traffic cop and nail him for that move. But he's probably just lost, so I'll cut him some slack."

"Yeah, right. You just want your coffee."

Gunnar grinned. He maneuvered into the right lane and pulled into the coffee shop's tiny parking lot. Fortunately, lunchtime didn't bring crowds in search of coffee and there was ample space to park.

The shop was empty. Niko, the teen whom Laurie had pulled out of Great Brook Valley to a more hopeful life on the west side of the city, was not working today. She collected her coffee from the unrecognized clerk behind the counter and proceeded toward the row of stools facing the windows and Park Avenue.

"So, what're you doing with the extra day you're taking off tomorrow? Are you and Brandon off to someplace new this weekend or are you just staying in for a sex marathon?" Gunnar put his coffee down on the counter and slid onto the stool beside Laurie.

Traffic sped through the intersection outside as the two detectives watched through the window. There were a couple fender benders here every week and Laurie and Gunnar had personally witnessed a few of them. They relished the change of expression on the guilty party's face as they realized that their trip through a red light had not gone unnoticed as the cause of the accident.

"Talk like that could get you in trouble and I might just be inclined to file a sexual harassment suit against you," Laurie grinned.

"Right. Like anyone would believe that an honorable officer of the law would ever consider harassing his gorgeous female partner," Gunnar shot back with a healthy dose of feigned sarcasm.

"Who said anything about honorable? Anyway, since you asked, Brandon is taking me up north. We're going to canoe the Saco River."

"No shit? I'm going fishing up there. Where are you dropping in?" He popped the lid off his cup of coffee and sipped at the scalding liquid.

"I think we're starting around North Conway. We're floating down about five miles. I'm a little nervous, though. I haven't been in a canoe for at least ten years. I'll probably dump us into the river." Laurie peeled the paper off a chocolate chip muffin and set it back down on the wrapper.

"Well, I wouldn't worry too much if you do. That part of the Saco isn't going to do you any damage. It's as calm as a lake around there. You'll have fun, I'm sure."

"That's good to hear. Brandon said it was safe, but I'm not sure how his canoeing skills are and what he considers 'safe'.

"Where are you going fishing?" She wished Gunnar hadn't told her his plans. She would have preferred thinking that she and Brandon would be miles away from everyone they knew.

"Just below Swans Falls. My dad used to take me up there when I was a kid. I have to go back every so often, now that he's gone—memories and that sort of thing."

"That's nice you can still bond with him even though he's gone."

"Yeah. He was really into fishing and got me excited about it, too, from when I was just a kid. I really miss having him around. I talk to him when I'm out on the Saco. Makes me think he's still around."

"Maybe he is," Laurie smiled.

"I think Brandon and I will be pulling out before Swans Falls. I remember him mentioning the falls and I'm pretty certain we're pulling out before we get to them. The canoeing company picks us up at a specified spot and brings us back up to the car. Brandon's got it all set up. If we do see you there, though, we'll be sure to herd the fish your way." Laurie returned her gaze to the busy intersection outside just in time to see a red Volvo wagon smack into the back end of a blue Ford Focus.

The driver of the Volvo, a middle-aged woman in designer clothes with several bands of gold on her right wrist, clambered angrily out of her car and stomped up to scold the other driver.

A teenaged girl, her hair pulled back into a tight pony tail and a frightened look on her face, stumbled from the Ford to meet the full fury of the angry woman, who shook a clenched fist inches from her nose. The woman's face deepened to an unhealthy red as she proceeded to read the terrified girl the riot act.

The girl cowered back from her and held up her hands as a shield from the woman's onslaught. This sign of submission from the girl encouraged the assault and soon it began to look like the woman would start beating her.

"Looks like we better intercede before that rich bitch punches the poor girl's lights out." Laurie replaced the lid on her coffee and she and Gunnar approached the now frenzied woman, stopping to leave their coffee safely on the roof of their car.

The woman saw the two officers approach and her demeanor changed in an instant as she eyed the shields hanging from their necks. Every word she spoke to them was heavily coated in several layers of oozing sweet syrup as she condescended to the teenage girl who was now cowering against the door of the Ford.

Laurie passed the woman by without a second glance and approached the girl.

"Are you all right?"

The girl nodded; her eyes were cast downward. "I didn't think I did anything wrong," she whispered hoarsely. She was close to tears.

She's probably only had her license a week, Laurie thought. She asked to see it and the girl's knees nearly collapsed from shaking as she reached into the car to retrieve it.

"You didn't do anything wrong," Laurie responded once she had assured herself that the girl did in fact have a license. "You were in the left lane with your left blinker on to make a left turn. My partner and I just happened to be watching the intersection, so we can confirm that for you. You did all you were supposed to do. I'll need your registration, too." Laurie scribbled some notes on a pad while the girl retrieved the other document from the car.

Gunnar was having a far more difficult time with the driver of the Volvo who, upon learning that they had witnessed the accident and were convinced that she was to blame, had grown less than sweet and was now shaking her fists at him. "You can't put this on me," she bellowed. "I'm a good driver. I drive a Volvo, for God's sake. This is her fault!" She thrust a finger in the direction of the other driver, bracelets jingling loudly.

Gunnar had his hands up, palms down and was gesturing for her to calm down, but Laurie could see the woman's anger mounting to dangerous levels. And then she snapped. Her punch caught Gunnar between his cheek and nose and snapped his head back. Blood oozed from his left nostril.

Laurie was immediately behind the woman. She grabbed her arms from behind and pushed her roughly up against the Volvo. The woman fought, but Laurie held her tight while Gunnar recovered and assisted with getting her hands locked behind her back. When her wrists were locked in steel, she spat at the teenager who now stood wide-eyed and paralyzed, watching the scene, shaking from head-to-toe.

"Lady, I don't care what you drive and what kind of clothes you wear, you just earned yourself a ticket to jail." Gunnar held her strongly and muscled her across the street while Laurie held the traffic back. He guided her into the back seat of the car and returned to the two cars blocking the intersection. He pulled a two-way radio from its clip on his belt and called for a route car and tow truck as he watched the teenage girl break into tears.

"Can you believe that?" Gunnar asked as he approached Laurie. He pulled a napkin from his pocket and held it to his bleeding nose.

Laurie fought to keep from laughing. The girl, seeing Laurie's amusement stopped crying and the corner of her mouth turned up slightly. She accepted her license and registration back from Laurie and shyly thanked them both for coming to her aid.

"Not a problem," Gunnar responded gruffly. "Your car doesn't seem in too bad shape." He quickly examined the rear bumper of the car, which had been creased in the middle and was pushed in against the body of the car. "I'm sure the other driver has plenty of insurance to cover the repairs, so make sure it gets done, alright?" He smiled and clapped a hand gently on her shoulder.

She nodded, keeping her eyes directed at the ground, then climbed back into her car, completed her left turn, and drove away.

Gunnar looked toward the woman in the back of his car. "Man that woman is a drippy gash!"

"A what?"

"On the rag. Probably all the time too, from the looks of her." He shook his head and scowled at Laurie.

Laurie chuckled. "Do you have this much luck with all women?"

"Very funny. I can't wait to see that lady before a judge." He cast an angry look at the woman who was throwing a tantrum in the back of the cruiser.

"Of course you threatened her. That's what she'll say. And I might have to agree with her." She winked as she taunted him.

"Great! That's the kind of support I need from my partner. Why don't you just stay here and play in traffic while I go take care of my new girlfriend over there. The tow truck should be here soon. And I hope she hasn't kicked the car apart by the time the route car arrives to take her away."

A half hour had passed before the tow truck arrived. The mechanic hooked up the Volvo and was ready to haul it away inside of five minutes.

The woman shouted and yelled at the top of her lungs as she watched him secure the chains to her car. Her piercing screams resounded through the glass and Laurie wondered what sort of life could lead a grown woman to behave like this. Too full of herself, or just had a bad day? Laurie shook her head and turned away.

They moved the woman, kicking and screaming, to the back of the route car. Gunnar fought an impulse to accidentally knock her head into the roof of the car and instead, guided her tousled mess of hair as carefully as he could as he forced her into the back seat of the car and closed the door. She cursed him through the glass, but Gunnar only turned away from her as the car left the lot to bring her to jail.

"Should've called the wagon for her. A few miles gettin' flopped around in the dark with the smell of puke in her nose might teach her to behave next time. Or at least it'd make me feel better, especially if I got to drive." Gunnar tenderly rubbed the side of his bruised nose.

"Come on, I'll buy you a fresh coffee. I think the other one is cold. You can go fill out your report later."

# Chapter 19

The river would be quiet, Brandon had promised. Even though this was the first day of nice weather in several weeks and another was not promised anytime soon, Labor Day had gone by and that meant the tourists were gone for the year. They would be tied up with school and work and the approaching holiday season and wouldn't return to the river until next summer. Laurie and Brandon would have the river to themselves.

Laurie rarely took days off—with some case or another always needing her attention, there was rarely time. But her caseload was quickly forgotten in the anticipation of spending a whole day alone with Brandon. She couldn't wait to be with him, away from the whole world. The whole world except for Gunnar, that is. She dreaded the prospect of meeting him on the river. There was no room in this special day for work or any reminder of it and that included her partner.

"Hungry for breakfast?" Brandon's voice drove her thoughts back into the mist and she realized that her stomach was empty.

"Starving! What do you have in mind?"

"Just this little café in Hudson. Not much to look at, but the food is fantastic!" He pulled into the right lane of the highway and took the next exit, meeting her eyes a moment as she smiled at him.

"It's a couple hours up into New Hampshire to get to where we'll drop in on the Saco. A little breakfast will hold us over. Then I've got plenty of gourmet eats packed up for the river."

"Hmmm. Sounds like you put some planning into this little excursion."

"All for you, Love." He smiled and met her eyes again before he pulled into a parking space in front of the little café. "This is it!"

"You're right. It's not much to look at, but something certainly smells wonderful!" Laurie wrinkled her nose in pleasure as she savored the aromas that wafted toward her when they entered the tiny café.

"You think it smells good. Wait'll you taste it."

They sat at a tiny table next to the window and the waitress was immediately before them, a pot of coffee and two mugs in hand.

"Coffee?" she asked, already filling the two mugs and plopping a couple plastic creamers onto the table.

"Do you need a few minutes to see the menu?" She glanced from Laurie to Brandon.

"Actually, French toast and breakfast links would be wonderful, if you have it," Laurie smiled at her.

The waitress smiled back with a curt nod and turned to Brandon, expectantly.

"Western Omelet."

"Thank you. They should be up soon since the morning rush ended a bit ago." She smiled, spun around on her heel and headed toward the kitchen, her plump, round figure gliding effortlessly across the floor.

Brandon reached across the table and tenderly took Laurie's hands in his.

"This is our first whole day together, just the two of us, do you realize?" he asked.

"Yeah," she murmured. "There's always someplace one or the other of has to be. Can you handle a whole day with me?" She smiled coyly and winked at him.

"I think the more appropriate question is, can you handle a whole day with me? There won't be anyone around on the river to save you from me, you know."

"Oh, really! Who says I need saving?" she retorted.

"I'm not even going to let you come up for air." The corner of his mouth turned up tentatively as he held her gaze.

"Well, you know air is highly overrated." She leaned forward and kissed his lips gently. "I could kiss you all day and I just might forget to breathe." She pulled away and smiled back at him as the waitress approached with their plates.

Two hours in the car passed quickly as they drove north into the mountains of New Hampshire. Brandon suggested they take a trip overseas and they discussed which countries and cities they should visit. Laurie had never traveled across the ocean and listened dreamily as he described places he had visited—London, Paris, Prague, Rome. Brandon had done his share of traveling and now, he said, he could do it all again with Laurie. She had only to arrange time away from the job to be with him. And she was sure she could make it happen.

She waited with her dreams while Brandon arranged for a canoe and a ride to the river. And now here they were, floating peacefully on the Saco River with the picnic basket full of "gourmet eats" and two expensive bottles of wine. Laurie smiled contentedly as she leaned back into Brandon's lap.

"This is so romantic. I love you for taking me out here, for everything," she crooned.

"Mmmm. I love you too, Babe. I've always loved floating on the river. My parents and I used to do this when I was really young out in California, before my father was on the road so much. We'd pick a quiet river and float along all day and then camp for the night somewhere." Brandon sighed, his mind drifting peacefully. "Those were the days, when I didn't have a care in the world. Life should always be like that—like this." He squeezed Laurie gently. She turned her face up at him and he gave her a kiss.

"Probably not another soul around here for miles. They've all gone back to work now that summer's over. We could make love out here and no one would ever know." He winked at her.

The corner of Laurie's mouth turned up in a shy little smile. "Out here, with all the birds watching?"

He squeezed her breast gently and kissed her again. "Nothing I'm sure they haven't witnessed before. We'll just have to be careful not to rock the boat."

"Hmmm. A little cold for skinny-dipping," Laurie cooed.

One by one, Brandon undid the buttons on her blouse, while he kissed her tenderly on her face, her neck, her ear. Her body quivered with excitement and anticipation as he moved his hands over her, fondling intimately.

When he had worked the last button free of its hole, she pulled herself up to kiss him, first tenderly, then passionately as the excitement welled inside her.

Despite his best efforts to step lightly, dead leaves crinkled and twigs cracked and popped beneath his feet. He parted the trees and watched them as they undressed each other and made love in the canoe. She was beautiful; her pale skin, smooth and sensual, glistened with moisture. He stood sheltered in the undergrowth beneath the maples for a long while, watching as they drifted down the river out of sight.

When they were gone, he turned back toward his car, parked alongside the road. The vision of their lovemaking burned in his mind. He wanted what the man in the canoe had; he wanted the woman.

They paddled the boat to a rocky beach along the river and Brandon jumped into the water to pull the canoe ashore.

"Would you like to relax with a little wine and a gourmet picnic lunch? Or if you're warmed up from our little workout, maybe we could do a little skinny dipping?" He smiled his charming smile and held his hand out to her. She took it and stepped carefully onto the rocky shore. With her feet both solidly on the ground, she turned and kissed his mouth.

"If I didn't know any better, I'd think you only wanted me for my body. " She smiled coyly and moved away from him.

"Oh, I'd say I want just a little more than that." He pulled her close to him. "I think I could do this with you for a very long, long time. I want you every minute, even when we're both old and gray."

Laurie gasped. "What are you saying?"

"This is what I'm saying." He took her hand in his and fitted a ring onto her third finger then lowered himself to one knee.

Tears welled up in Laurie's eyes as she stared into his. She looked at her shaking hand where a large diamond had nestled, then looked back into Brandon's eyes and smiled.

"Absolutely, I will," she cried. She pulled him up from his knee and into her arms, kissing him passionately as tears rolled down her cheek.

"So, how 'bout that skinny dipping?" he prodded.

Laurie pushed him back. "One-track mind," she teased. Then she pulled off her shirt in one fluid motion, and dropped her shorts to her feet. Brandon fell upon her and they collapsed into the water.

When they were done swimming, dry towels from the canoe warmed them as they stood shivering naked on the shore. A cool breeze had begun to stir in the trees and raised bumps on their skin. They quickly dressed and donned light jackets to fight the chill and Brandon pulled a bottle of red wine from the basket.

"Shall we celebrate?" he asked as he cut away the seal around the cork.

"We should. What other goodies did you pack in there?"

"Why don't you take a look? There's cheese and crackers, olives, grapes, finger sandwiches, strawberries. Pull it all out; there's a blanket in there too. We can sit and relax. It's nice when it's a little late in the season like this. Kids are already back in school and there's not a soul around, but the weather's still beautiful. Better than we had this summer, don't you think?" It had been a cool, wet summer with more rain than sunshine, but it seemed the approaching autumn would be dry and pleasant.

Laurie nodded agreement as she offered her glass for him to fill.

"Here's to us, to my fiancé," she smiled and held up the glass in a toast.

Brandon touched his glass to it. "And to my future wife," he added while his eyes locked on hers.

The sun reappeared from behind a cloud and drove the chill from the air and they curled up together on the blanket to enjoy its warmth.

"So, how soon should we make this official?" Laurie asked as she snuggled up to him, her cheek resting upon his chest.

"How soon would you like to do it? We could elope tomorrow if you want, but I always figured you for wanting a formal, but small, wedding."

She lifted her head and planted her chin on his breastbone as she met his eyes and smiled warmly. "But you don't have a whole lot of family do you?" she asked.

"None, actually. At least none I keep track of. But you have a pretty large family, don't you?"

"Not too large," she smiled again and rested her cheek back on his chest.

"We could have a nice, comfortable wedding."

"'Course there'll be a lot of cops there."

"How many cops?" he asked.

"Nothing you're hiding, I hope. Off the top of my head, I think at least fifteen or twenty. You'll have to keep your hands to yourself, they could try to arrest you for molesting the bride."

"Oh really? Maybe I should get all my molesting in now, then, while you have no one to defend you." He grabbed her and pulled her up to him, kissing her passionately. He reached out and grabbed her buttock, then rolled her over beneath him.

"Any last words?"

"None." She pulled his face to hers and kissed him, wrapping her legs around him.

A loud crack sounded in the woods behind them. Laurie jumped and Brandon looked up, his gaze searching the darkness beneath the trees. More rustling of undergrowth reached them, but Brandon could see nothing moving.

Laurie pulled herself out from beneath him. "Anybody there?" she called.

No answer. The rustling stopped and there was silence.

Brandon stood up, staring into the woods toward the direction of the sound. Suddenly, the undergrowth was alive with sound. Whoever or whatever it was moved quickly away from them, breaking branches as it tore its way through the brush. Finally, the sound faded and they were alone again.

"What do you think?" Laurie asked.

"Probably a deer," he replied.

"Another bottle of wine?"

"Definitely!"

Brandon pulled the cork and they sat back down on the blanket, Laurie huddling close to him as he wrapped an arm around her shoulder. The wine disappeared from the bottle while they shared dreams of the future and polished off the contents of the basket.

A small restaurant in a rugged setting lured them from their travel along New Hampshire's winding highway. They stopped for dinner, savoring the scent of the encroaching pines and the approach of autumn as they climbed out of the Mercedes. Brandon wrapped an arm around Laurie's waist and pulled her to him, kissing her tenderly.

"Have a nice day?"

"Hmmm. The best," she cooed, her lips still touching his.

"A little dinner and maybe we can find a place to sleep around here?"

"Sounds wonderful," Laurie murmured.

Inside, the restaurant was a quaint little country setting with white linen tablecloths and red and white checkered linen napkins. They chose a tiny table beside a window that looked out onto a bubbling brook, cascading into a deep pool beneath a small walking bridge, though the fading light was beginning to obscure the peaceful scene.

Brandon reached out and took her hand, angling the ring toward the light so he could admire its sparkle.

"I can't believe that I'll soon be your wife. I'm so happy and so in love with you." She squeezed his hand and covered it with her other hand, pulling him toward her across the table until he was within kissing reach.

The waitress appeared just then and they pulled back from each other. Laurie's cheeks reddened as she turned her attention to the slender, motherly woman who smiled warmly at them, her gaze falling to the glittering diamond on Laurie's finger.

"Just got engaged?" she queried.

"This afternoon," Laurie gushed. It was Brandon's cheeks that reddened this time as the woman's gentle eyes turned his way.

"Congratulations!" she beamed. "A toast of champagne is on me. Can I get you something else to drink, too?"

"Two Manhattans, extra dry," Brandon responded. His eyes met Laurie's for confirmation and she smiled.

"Be right back then." She glanced again at the two-carat rock before she spun on her heels and disappeared.

What a coincidence that they would stop here, Gunnar thought. He turned in his seat at the bar so that he could watch them through a small window between the restaurant and lounge. With their eyes locked on one another, he was unconcerned that they might notice him. The sparkle from Laurie's hand caught his eye and he frowned with jealousy as he thought of them making love on the river, thought of them together forever.

Gunnar had never found himself obsessed with any woman before. When was it he had stopped thinking of Laurie as his friend and partner and began to see her as this beautiful, sexy, and enchanting woman. Shouldn't he have been able to tell her that before she had met this man who stole her heart? He shook his head in frustration, then quickly paid his tab and left the restaurant.

After dinner, Brandon located a small hotel in the next town and checked them in for the night.

When they reached their room, he unlocked the door and let Laurie step in ahead of him. She smiled warmly and gently kissed his cheek as she brushed by. Then the romance of the tiny room flooded her eyes.

Flowers were everywhere! Vases of roses were arranged on the dresser and on the nightstand; rose petals were strewn across the bed.

Laurie gasped then spun around and locked her eyes on his. "It's beautiful! You know you'll have a tough time living up to this." She giggled playfully and threw her arms around his neck.

"But I'll sure have fun trying," he grinned as he picked her up in his arms and threw her onto the bed.

"You know, being with you has been the most wonderful time of my life." She pulled him to her and kissed him, her head swimming with the drinks they'd shared over dinner.

Brandon was alive with desire as he quickly but delicately pulled off her clothing, caressing each supple curve as it was exposed to the cool air. And when she was naked amid the velvety rose petals, he peeled off his own shirt and shorts while his eyes remained locked on hers.

"I want you so much," he said. "Think you can keep up with me all night?"

"You've already worn me out today, but I think I can take you." She reached up to kiss him and her head swam again as her eyes closed.

"Are you alright?"

She smiled and pulled him onto the bed, swinging her leg over him and pulling herself up so she was sitting astride him.

"I think you gave me a few too many Manhattans, but it doesn't mean I can't take you."

Brandon grinned then pulled her to him and rolled her over so she was once again beneath him.

"We'll see how long you last," he murmured as he thrust himself inside her.

Laurie felt his warmth as she fought the effects of her last drink. She lifted her hips to meet his again and again until they both collapsed in a heap and Brandon rolled over to lie beside her.

"A few minutes break and we go again?" he prodded as he rubbed a gentle hand on her glistening belly.

"OK," Laurie mumbled as she fell heavily into a sound sleep.

Brandon sat up on the edge of the bed, looked down at Laurie and chuckled. "Guess you won't be taking me tonight," he smiled. He stood, strode toward the bathroom, and turned on the water in the shower.

The night grew darker as the moon dipped below the horizon. Somewhere not far from the little hotel, a scared young woman found herself gagged with a red and white checkered linen napkin. Her eyes pleaded with her attacker, but he simply laughed at her as he tore her clothing from her and had his way. When he'd satisfied his urges, he plunged a large hunting knife into her heart and a camera flashed to capture the image as he stabbed her again and again.

# Chapter 20

H ey babe, chill out!" Gunnar yelled to Laurie as she tried to rock the vending machine. Once again, the machine had robbed her of the sixty cents she had dropped in the slot. The snickers bar, her breakfast, leaned tauntingly toward her, its wrapper still caught snugly in the rack. She cursed under her breath and turned her attention to her partner.

"You got a phone call. New Hampshire," he said. "Up near Conway."

Laurie shook her head slowly, and then took the phone Gunnar offered, cupping her hand over the receiver. "You still think I'm being paranoid?"

"Relax, you don't even have the details, yet," he replied.

Laurie put the receiver to her ear.

"This is Detective Marion of Lincoln," came the gruff voice at the other end. "I heard you've been keeping an ear to the ground for rape and murder victims."

"That's right," Laurie replied, absent-mindedly spinning the diamond around her finger while she focused on the knot in her stomach.

She listened intently for the next few minutes as Detective Marion described the body of a young woman found a short distance from a rural bar. The details of the murder were similar to the others Laurie had found. The woman's blood had traces of Rohypnol and she had been stripped of all her clothing, which had been left in a tattered pile nearby. The woman was found lying face up on the hood of an old abandoned car. But instead of having her throat cut like Abra Wilson, her chest had been perforated several times with a large knife.

Laurie felt a mixture of excitement and fear as she absorbed the description of this new link in her case. Then fear turned to terror and her blood ran like ice through her veins when the detective shared the final detail.

"Could you repeat that last bit?" She asked, her voice a hoarse whisper as her throat closed.

"What, the red checkered napkin? She was gagged with it. Does it mean anything to you?" The detective at the other end prodded.

"I'm not sure. When did she die?"

"Pathologist says she's been dead four or five days. Listen, whatever you can tell us would be a great help 'cause we got nothing at this end."

"I'll let you know," she muttered. "In the meantime, could you run a comparison on that napkin with the ones at the Mountainside Restaurant?"

"But she wasn't at the Mountainside, she was at the Coyote's Den last anyone saw her."

"Just the same, could you check it out?"

"Whatever you say," was the response.

"Get back to me," Laurie whispered, then added a hoarse, "Thanks," as her hand fell to her side and she slid the phone awkwardly into its cradle.

She and Brandon were on the river five days ago. Once again a woman had died in a place she had recently visited. Was it just a coincidence? Had this man simply happened along at the same restaurant, or was he taunting her? Or was it someone she knew? Worry crept across her face as her eyes met Gunnar's and looked quickly away.

"Are you alright, babe? What's wrong? Was it the same guy?"

"Yeah," was all she said. She pulled out the file she had built in conjunction with the Wilson case and flipped over page after page, looking at each detail, remembering each date and how she seemed to have been at each place within days of a murder there. Except Clarendon, she thought. But my family's there—I visit all the time!

She twisted at the ring on her finger. There had to be another explanation. Was it just a coincidence? No. Someone was following her around. "No, Laurie," a little voice echoed in her head. Someone has taken you around.

Brandon had brought her to the site of every crime a day or two before or, in the case of the New Hampshire girl, the very day that it happened. Had he slipped out while she slept and killed the girl in New Hampshire? She had had a lot to drink and had fallen asleep very early. She remembered how her head had swum with alcohol. Had he perhaps drugged her so she would not wake to discover he had gone?

"Are you alright?" Gunnar observed the fear and confusion in her eyes. He had never seen her afraid. Something had spooked her.

"I need to take some time off," she said hastily. She glanced at her partner as she hurried past him toward the door. "I'll be back in tomorrow."

"Hey, no problem, Laurie," Gunnar said with concern. "Can I help with anything?"

"No. I need to do this alone." She hurried from the room.

Laurie rushed out into the hallway, running headlong into a group of Academy trainees who were touring the station after a class. She bumped into the tallest of the group, sending him backward a few steps.

"Excuse me," she barked angrily as she wriggled in the grip of a pair of large hands that had caught her arms to keep her from carrying both her and the trainee to the floor in a heap. She looked up into the youthful blue eyes that twinkled down at her. He towered over her by a whole foot.

"You guys really shouldn't be loitering around like this. We have work to do here and this is a busy hallway." She glared at him as she shook herself free of his grasp.

"Sorry, ma'am," the tall rookie said with a slight bow of respect. He stepped quickly aside to let her pass while the six others with him flattened their backs against the wall to allow her room.

"Please, just move along." She waved them off as she rushed down the hallway.

Outside the station, Laurie pulled her keys from her pocketbook and looked toward the Camero. She fingered the little round brass key that was hooked into the ring beside her house key. Brandon had given it to her after their second date, but she had never been to his condo alone unless she was expecting him to join her. She was sure he wouldn't be there now since he was down in Florida for two days on a work assignment.

Every step toward the car was like walking in cement shoes. Each of her feet felt like a fifty-pound weight that she hefted again and again. Did she really have so little faith in the man she loved that she could believe he was this heartless killer of young women?

There could certainly be other explanations for the coincidental timing of her trips to each of the places where the girls were killed. For instance, the killer could have been busy enough to leave so many dead women that wherever she went she was bound to be near a murder scene. But the coincidence was also in Laurie's finding murders only where she had been. If the killer wasn't someone she knew, she was certain that he knew who she was.

If she didn't at least check Brandon out a little, she would never be sure that he was innocent until she caught the killer. It was because she loved him and wanted to be his wife that she had to prove to herself that he was really the man she thought him to be and not this monster.

She'd only known him for three months, but she was sure she knew him well enough to marry him. Or did she? She twisted the ring on her finger.

She fit her key into the car, opened the door, and slid in behind the wheel. The seats were warm from the heat of the sun. It would be a perfect day to have the convertible top down, but she didn't have the heart. No matter how she tried to assure herself that what she was doing was the right thing, she felt like a traitor to the man she loved. And she felt like a traitor to herself.

Laurie turned the key in the ignition and the car roared to life. The sound of the car's engine always sparked life in her, but not today. She felt dead inside. She pulled out of her parking space and drove slowly, dreading the lessening distance between herself and the truth.

When she arrived at Brandon's condo, the complex was almost deserted and Laurie sat for a few moments in the car before she finally gathered the courage to drag herself out and move her feet in the direction of the door. She turned her key in the lock and cautiously stepped inside, feeling very much like the next victim-to-be in a bad horror flick on a Saturday night.

Inside, the home where she spent so much time with Brandon was a morgue. The air was deathly silent and the usually warm neutral tones of the place were now shades of ice. The air conditioning had been left on high and with the curtains drawn the condo seemed cold and stark as though no one had been there in weeks.

Laurie instinctively wrapped her arms around herself, rubbed her shoulders, and then started her search at the desk in the kitchen. She wasn't sure what she was looking for; she just hoped she'd know if she found it.

There was nothing unusual on the kitchen desk, only a couple unopened billing statements and a computer magazine. Brandon was always so neat and tidy in everything he did. This would be the easiest search she had ever conducted, she thought, and shuddered that she could casually think of searching her lover's home as just another one of her cases. Her stomach rolled at the thought of what she was doing.

Did she really think that this kind and gentle man could be capable of such atrocities as the butchering of Abra Wilson? Brandon was the kindest, sweetest man she had ever met, and yet she had to begin investigating the coincidences somewhere and it was too odd that she and Brandon had been together at each crime scene within days of each murder.

The longer she searched the condo, the more the condo itself began to feel like a crime scene. Was her instinct telling her something? Was this actually the right direction in the Wilson case?

"There has to be another reason," she muttered aloud and searched the drawer of kitchen knives again and more diligently, comparing each knife to the mental picture the medical examiner had given her of the blade that had opened Abra Wilson's windpipe.

"But what does Brandon do in his spare time, the times he's not with me?" she mused aloud to break the silence of the dead air around her. "He travels a lot. Does he kill women in other states?" The realization that this could be true brought acid to her mouth and she fought back the nausea that threatened the breakfast she had missed.

"Come on, Laurie, you know Brandon didn't do this shit." She shook her head angrily and cleared her head.

What am I *really* doing here? Maybe I'm just afraid to get married, she thought. Maybe I'm just creating stories and bogus reasons to be afraid of him because we're moving too fast!

She flopped down on Brandon's side of the bed. He had apparently left in a hurry, because it was not made up the way it was whenever she visited. Instead, the quilt and comforter had been roughly pulled up and didn't fully cover the pillows and the sheets beneath them were crumpled. She would fix the bed before she left, she decided. Then she could tell him she was here, even if she didn't say why.

She laid her head down on his pillow, luxuriating in its softness. She folded one arm across her belly, let the other hang down beside the bed, and let her mind wander to a warm vision of her holding Brandon's hands at the alter as he slipped a gold ring onto her finger and smiled into her eyes. His eyes were moist as he leaned forward to kiss her. She really loved the way he kissed her, but she was sure that it would be even more electric than ever when he became her husband.

Laurie smiled at her dreams as she ran her hand absentmindedly along the mattress. She slipped her fingers between the mattress and box spring and let them rest there.

Soon this would be her bed, she thought. Brandon had suggested they move in together now that they were engaged. She was ready now, she thought. Like getting a jump-start on marriage. No more nights apart, except when he was traveling.

She ran her fingertips along between the mattresses and pushed her fingers deeper until nearly her whole hand was between the mattresses and something brushed up against her fingertips, like a corner of stiff paper. She fingered it absentmindedly and pulled at it, her thoughts still floating with Brandon.

A small voice nagged through her daydreams. What is that? She fingered the corner of paper a little more. It's too thick to be a tag, she thought. She worked her hand deeper between the mattresses and got her index and middle fingers on either side of the little corner of paper. It would be so much easier to just climb off the bed and lift the mattress, but her dreams of Brandon felt tied to that bed and she stubbornly refused to leave it. With just a fragile hold on the paper, she managed to work it out a bit to where she could get a better hold of it between her fingers and finally, she pulled it out.

A photograph? She turned the photograph over and her heart stopped.

The picture was dark, taken at night, but Laurie had no difficulty identifying a living Abra Wilson. She was lying as they had found her, naked upon the boulder, but her face was clearly visible, as well as her throat, and her throat had not yet been cut.

Laurie threw the photo onto the nightstand and jumped up from the bed like it was on fire. Her chest heaved and pulled for air, but she couldn't seem to get enough as her head swam and her eyes blurred out of focus. She looked at the nightstand. The photograph had landed facedown. She wanted to turn it over again to be sure of what she had seen, but she couldn't bring herself to touch it. Instead, she gathered her courage to lift the mattress and look beneath, but there were no other photos. She looked at the nightstand again.

"There's no explaining that," she said aloud, shakily. "Definitely not," she confirmed under her breath.

She stood where she was and ran her hands through her hair, hooking her fingers into the blonde curls and letting her arms hang. The pain on her scalp helped her head clear until she was able to think. She had to think.

What else would she find in Brandon's condo? He had to be guilty. There really was no other reason for him to have a photograph. And what other evidence would she find if she looked? Would there be blood? Would she find the knife or did he take it with him for the next woman he met? Where should she look? She should get a search warrant before she did anything, she knew, but she wanted to look for herself first. She wanted to know what else she had missed all this time they'd been dating. She wanted to know just how blind she had been.

Laurie went back to the kitchen, pulling all the drawers open in search of the murder weapon, but there were no other knives other than those in the utensil drawer and they were all serrated; there were no straight blades.

What else did she know about the murders? He'd never left much at any scene, but there were fibers, most likely from clothing. Would she find the clothes to match them? Would there be blood on his shoes or clothes? The killer was always neat and careful, if he did get any blood on him, he might just throw the clothes away, or send them to a cleaner. Somehow she knew it would be a fruitless search, still, she should check. She went back up to the bedroom.

Brandon didn't keep an overstuffed closet. Although he was always well dressed, he disliked owning more clothes than he absolutely needed. Laurie flipped through shirts and pants that hung in the closet, but she noticed no blood. All Brandon's clothing was nearly new. There were no stains or dirt on any of them.

Laurie checked the closet in the other bedroom, but it was empty except for a vacuum cleaner. The bureau was likewise sparsely filled, and Laurie quickly checked his socks and jockey shorts for bloodstains, but didn't see any. He changed those out frequently also. There was nothing in the bathroom; nothing in the trash—he had emptied all the receptacles before he left for Florida.

Her search methods weren't organized. She couldn't focus to conduct her usual systematic search for evidence. All Laurie could think was how Brandon had betrayed her. She looked at the ring on her finger—she wanted to throw it into Lake Quinsigamond only two hundred feet away, but she couldn't yet. She had to hide what she knew until she shared her knowledge with the district attorney and Brandon was safely in custody.

Would the photograph be enough to convict him? It should, she thought. How else would it come to be in Brandon's condo except that he put it there? Could they argue that it was planted? She had always thought the killer was following her. Would Brandon's defense attorney try to sell this as a defense and say that the killer planted the photo for her to find?

Could someone have planted it? Why would the killer, if he were someone other than Brandon, plant a photo? It's not like they would expect her to look between the mattresses to find it.

She shook her head in frustration. "The reason it seemed the killer was following you, seemed to know you, was because you were with him all along. Brandon is the killer and there has to be something else here somewhere. No one could be that careful."

In the hallway between the two bedrooms was the utility closet. Laurie haphazardly opened the empty washer and then the dryer, where she found a single pair of jeans. She pulled them out and shook them. She noticed, on the front of the left leg, just above the knee was a large faded brownish patch.

Blood? Wasn't that what blood looked like after it had gone through the washer if it had been allowed to set in? A chill rode her spine down to her toes. Was this a dead woman's blood on the pants of the man she had agreed to marry?

Laurie threw the jeans back in the dryer and slammed the door shut then ran back to the bedroom and took the photo off the nightstand. She had to get a search warrant, or none of this would hold up. But what would be her reason for getting the warrant. She had the photo, but how could she say she happened to find it? What was she doing here, while he was away? "Worry about that when we come to it," she mumbled. She grabbed her pocketbook and stuffed the photo into it, then hurriedly left the condo, closing the door quietly behind her.

She managed to climb into the car and turn the engine over before tears welled in her eyes and rolled down her cheeks. Laurie gripped the steering wheel and let them flow as she gasped for air between sobs. The sight of a car entering the condo complex brought her to her senses. She wiped her eyes and drove out of the lot and headed for the station. Tears continued to flow in little rivulets along her cheeks, but she ignored them.

Unlike her relationship with Jeff, Laurie had given up her last toehold on solid ground, even before Brandon had proposed. But when he had asked her to be his wife, any reservations she might have had vanished. He had taken her heart—one hundred percent.

Where did she go from here? How could she deal with the heartbreak that was waiting to take her down? She thought of calling Jessie, but she wasn't ready to tell her. She had work to do.

Brandon would be back in town tomorrow and she had to work fast to get the warrant before he returned. If he found the photo missing, he would know she had it. She wiped the tears away on her sleeve and stepped harder on the gas pedal as she approached a yellow light and barely made it to the far side of the intersection before the light turned to red.

Gunnar had left the station to interview a witness to a break-in at a home on Vernon Hill. Charlie Miller was the only detective in the office when Laurie walked in. He was attacking a stack of paperwork when she stopped in front of his desk. He looked up and noticed her red and puffy eyes.

"You look like hell, Laurie. What's wrong?" he asked. He got up, walked around his desk and put a hand on her shoulder to comfort her.

Charlie had been on the force twelve years and had been her mentor when she made the detective bureau. Laurie usually called him Uncle Charlie because he always looked out for her and treated her like a daughter. He was a good and trusted friend.

She fought to keep the tears back as she opened her pocketbook and pulled out the photo. She looked at it again to be sure it hadn't changed, and then handed it to Charlie.

He looked up at her after he had studied the picture. "This looks like the Wilson girl."

Laurie nodded.

"Where...?" he started to ask.

"In Brandon's condo." She nearly choked on the words as tears poured out over her cheeks; she couldn't stop them.

"I went there to use his hot tub," she continued. "I was a little tired, so I laid down first on the bed." She told him how her hand brushed up against the photo and she pulled it out from between the mattresses.

Charlie studied her eyes a moment. She cringed inwardly as she met his stare. Charlie always knew when she was lying and now the corner of his mouth had turned up slightly. She was caught.

"Of course we both know that's bullshit," Charlie said softly. "You didn't go out there to use the tub. Unless I read the board wrong today, you're still on duty for another couple hours. You might want to sign out sick if you want that excuse to hold up. "What tipped you off?" he asked.

Laurie told him of the correlation she had noticed between the times and locations of the crimes and her trips with Brandon. She told him she thought the killer had been following her until she got the phone call from the New Hampshire detective. She described how drunk she had felt after dinner that night although she hadn't had too much to drink and how she must have passed out because she didn't remember falling asleep and didn't wake until morning.

"I hadn't thought much of it, figured it was a combination between alcohol and all that fresh air and activity on the river. But when I got the call about the woman killed in that area, well I just knew something was wrong, especially when he said the girl was gagged with a napkin from the same restaurant Brandon and I had eaten at."

Charlie nodded silently, his lips pursed together in thought as he evaluated her story.

"Did you find anything else at his house?"

"I looked around a little—closets and bureaus and stuff. There was nothing there, but I found a pair of jeans in the dryer that looked like they had blood on them."

"Where are they?"

"I left them there. I took the photo and left as fast as I could. I figured that should be enough to get a warrant and we can find the jeans when we're there. Otherwise it might look a little weird if the only evidence we find in a whole-house search is stuff I already found on my own when I was supposed to be relaxing in the tub."

"You're right," Charlie nodded as Gunnar returned from the road. "We need to get a search warrant."

"Get a warrant for what?" Gunnar grinned with expectation of a new case, then he saw Laurie's face, her puffy eyes, and flushed cheeks.

"What's going on here?" he demanded.

Charlie handed him the photo and repeated Laurie's story as he put an arm around her shoulders to steady her.

"That bastard!" Gunnar cursed. He held his arms out and Laurie stepped into them and buried her face on his shoulder.

"I'm really sorry, Laurie. I know how much you love this guy." He patted her back gently. It felt good to hold her. He only wished the circumstances were different.

# Chapter 21

The search warrant was approved the following morning. Gunnar brought it into the station, waving it at Charlie who had come in to help with the search on his scheduled day off.

"C'mon, Charlie, time to go nail that bastard!" He quickly dropped his hand to his side as he saw Laurie emerge from Charlie's office. Her face was haggard from anguish that had tormented her while they waited on the warrant.

I can't imagine how she feels, he thought. His feelings for her were stronger than ever, though he couldn't tell her. He still played his feelings off as friendship. They were partners. But still, each day it was harder to stay away, especially now, when she needed to be saved, protected.

Laurie dropped her eyes when she saw the document in his hand.

"I want to go with you guys," she said.

"You really shouldn't," Charlie told her. "You're too close to this. Look at what it's done to you. You're a wreck! Did you even sleep last night?"

Laurie shook her head.

"That's what I thought. You should just let us go do this," Gunnar reiterated.

"I know." She whispered. "I do this stuff every day to other people. But it never happens to me. I'm supposed to know better than this." She sighed as she plopped tiredly into her chair and waved them off.

"Listen, Laurie. The guy lied to you. And he's obviously very good at it. Hell, he had us all fooled, too. It happens to the best of us." Gunnar walked over to where she sat and put a comforting hand upon her shoulder.

"It'll blow over. There are decent guys out there and you will find one soon, you'll see. In the meantime, you know we're all here for you, whatever you need." He kissed the top of her head gently and clapped her on the shoulder.

"Hang in there. We'll be back."

Charlie picked up keys from Gunnar's desk. Gunnar looked in his direction and nodded silently.

"We gotta go, Laurie. We'll keep you in the loop on this, alright?"

"Thanks, guys." She gave them a weak, half-hearted smile and watched them leave.


The Plantation Club was hopping with its late lunch crowd. Jessie found a place to park on the crowded narrow street and skillfully wedged her beat-up Nissan between two shiny new cars. She checked her makeup in the mirror and carefully removed a small glob of mascara hanging from an eyelash. I'll survive, she thought. She grabbed her pocketbook and climbed out of the car, leaving it unlocked.

Inside the door, she kissed the doorman lightly on the cheek. "How ya doin', Joe? I missed ya!"

"Hey, babe. Long time no see. Tell the bartender I still owe you a drink. I'll still bet on the Sox next time, too. What can I say, I'm a dedicated fan."

Jessie had grown up in Poughkeepsie. Her father had been a Yankees fan and had passed his loyalty on to his daughter. Jessie took any chance to bet the Yankees to win over the Red Sox.

"Hey, no hard feelings, huh?" She winked at Joe and made her way to the bar where she ordered her first drink on him.

"Don't forget: we had our day," the bartender chimed in. "And we will again." He set her drink on the bar. "So, how ya been, Jess?"

181

"I'm good, Rick. How are you? Still flirtin' with all the girls around here?"

"Only you, babe." He smiled and winked at her then turned toward a balding man in his thirties who approached the bar for a drink.

Jessie pulled out a stack of greeting cards. She liked to send out cards to various friends, especially if she didn't always get to call. She used e-mail, too, but sometimes that just seemed so impersonal. It was far more exciting to receive a card than just an e-mail, she thought. Like getting a present.

She scribbled the first one out to an old friend from college whom she hadn't talked to in six months. When she had finished her scrawl, she stuffed it in the envelope, copied an address onto it from her organizer, licked the glue strip on the flap and sealed it. A quick sip from her drink and she started on the next card.

"Hi! Jessie, right?" An unfamiliar voice greeted her and she turned her attention from her writing. A moment passed before she recognized him.

"Brandon? You're seeing my friend, Laurie, right?" She held out her hand and Brandon took and shook it gently. Laurie had kept Brandon to herself for three months. Jessie had only met him once in passing while she was out with other friends and bumped into the couple as she was leaving a restaurant they were entering.

"Can I buy you a drink?" He climbed into the empty seat beside hers.

"All set for now, thanks. Maybe later, OK? So what are you doing in a place like this?"

"I was just meeting with some clients at one of the tables over there. They had to leave early and I saw you sitting here, recognized that wild hair of yours from that time we met, and I thought I'd say hello. I wasn't really ready to head home just yet anyway. You want some company?"

"Sure, I don't mind. I'll get to pick your brain and make sure my friend is making an acceptable choice in seeing you." She gave him a coy smile and sipped her drink.

"Well, at least you're honest. And I don't mind being checked out. I've got nothing to hide about my feelings for Laurie."

The bartender stopped by and Brandon ordered a drink for himself and one for Jessie when she was ready. The bartender put a glass upside down on the bar in front of her and turned to pour Brandon's drink.

"I haven't seen Laurie yet, but she tells me you popped the big question. Is it true?"

Brandon blushed slightly. "It's true. I think she's the most wonderful woman I've ever known. And tolerant, too, if she puts up with me."

"That's not too difficult from what I hear. I mean, you guys go all sorts of places together. You don't give her much chance to get bored with you. That's a lot to live up to."

Jessie sized up Brandon. This was her first and probably only chance to get this guy alone and pick his brain. Laurie was the closest thing to a sister she had, so Brandon had better be on the level if he was going to marry her.

Laurie often jumped too high and fell too hard where men were concerned. Jessie had known her through five boyfriends and countless dates. Each time, she seemed to have given away her heart, even if she claimed not to.

At least this one is attractive, Jessie thought. She and Laurie had a major difference of opinion on what was attractive in a man. Perhaps that was why they had been friends so long. Neither would ever have anything to do with dating one of the other's ex-boyfriends. Jessie knew of many girls who had lost a good friend over a guy. No man was worth losing a friend.

Brandon was smiling at her again. She checked his look to be sure there was nothing behind it. If he would flirt with her, he would certainly flirt with a stranger. But he seemed to be sincerely friendly, just chatting about the woman he loved.

Jessie was so different from Laurie, Brandon thought. And yet they were such close friends—like sisters, Laurie always said. So why did Brandon barely know her? He wondered what it felt like to run his fingers through Jessie's thick mane of brown curls. She smelled wonderful, too! It seemed weird that he thought so. Still, he was a man and she was a woman. He tried to curb his thoughts to keep them from coming out as body language. He knew women were always sharp to pick up on that—even more so than men.

He wondered if she had seen the woman he had been sitting with earlier. He had told her he was meeting with a client. It was mostly true, except he'd slept with this client many times before he met Laurie. Not since he'd met Laurie, though. But women never believed that a man would meet with a woman in a bar unless he was planning to have sex with her.

Brandon had little interest in dating other women since he met Laurie, but he still liked to admire other women. Down the road a ways, what if sex with Laurie lost its spark? He would still love her, he knew. But sex was sex. It had to be good. He considered that his nationwide travel would allow him plenty of opportunities to spend time with other women if he ever needed to. And Laurie would never have to know.

Jessie sipped at her drink. Her painted lips gently caressed the glass before she set it back on the bar.

"So, did you guys set a date? Or was this just a casual engagement?"

"I thought you women sorted these things all out before the man ever got to know anything."

"Generally, we do. But I haven't seen Laurie since last week and haven't talked to her since the other day when she told me you two were engaged. She's been really busy on this murder case of hers. You know about that." Jessie's drink was getting to the bottom and she looked around for the bartender, but he had momentarily left his post.

"Oh, right. The girl down at the hotel? What a tragedy. There's no need for any woman to suffer that." He turned his eyes away from hers and reached for his drink.

Jessie looked away also. Funny, this was one of those conversations that made women uncomfortable around men. It wasn't as though this man would do such a thing, but the fact that he was a man at all made her cringe.

"It certainly makes a girl think twice about meeting up with anyone in a bar," she mused.

The bartender returned and she waved him over and ordered another drink. He took back the glass that he had previously turned over in front of her. Time to call in the free drink.

Jessie turned to Brandon. "I have to make a pit stop," she smiled. "I'll be right back. Thanks again for the drink." She grabbed her pocketbook and walked away from the bar.

Brandon looked around the bar, mostly inhabited by men in their mid-twenties. There were only two other women in the whole place—not very attractive women.

He thanked the bartender with a nod as he returned with Jessie's drink, and then pulled it closer to the edge of the bar where she would be sitting. He folded his arms, placing his elbows up on the bar and waited patiently for her return.

Jessie flopped her pocketbook up on the bar and retook her seat. "Thanks for waiting to keep me company through another one. It's far more interesting than drinking alone." She held up the drink.

"To you and Laurie. May you have a good life together!"

"Does that mean I pass your screening?"

Jessie grinned and winked in response then put her lips to her drink.

"Ugh!" She nearly spat out the sip she had taken. Instead, she put a napkin to her mouth and spat into that. "Rick, buddy. What are you tryin' to do to me, babe?"

"What's wrong, sweetie?"

"You put tonic instead of soda water in my vodka." Jessie made a face to show her displeasure. She pushed the glass across the bar and Rick quickly dumped it out. He threw the glass into the dishwasher and used a clean one to fix the new drink. He passed it to her and waited to be certain it was okay.

"Thanks, babe. Much better!" She gave him a big smile. "You da best. Nothin' worse than tonic water," Jessie turned to Brandon.

"I guess we should toast that again. That one wasn't legal." She held up her glass and repeated the toast, then took a nice long sip of the fresh drink. Just then, her phone rang. She pulled it from her pocketbook and hit the button. It was Laurie.

"Guess who I'm having drinks with."

Laurie had no thoughts.

"Brandon! I've been checking up on him for you. I think he passes so far." She spoke into the phone for a couple minutes while Brandon watched her intently, looking for any indication that he was part of the conversation, but Jessie maintained her composure as she listened in horror to what Laurie told her quietly from the other end. Finally she hung up.

"Well, it's been fun, but I have to run. Laurie says she'll call you later. Thanks again for the drink." She picked up her pocketbook and was gone.

No one answered the door when they knocked. Laurie had said that Brandon was out of town on business until late in the day. They didn't realize he was only a little over a mile away. Gunnar used the key she had given him and unlocked the door. The house was cold and dark with the shades all drawn tight, keeping out any light. Gunnar flipped the switch on the wall and illuminated the living room.

"Where do you want to start? Should we claim rooms?" Gunnar asked of the Sergeant.

"Sure, that works. You take the bedroom; I'll start here in the living room and the kitchen. He must have left something around here." Charlie pulled the cushions off the overstuffed sofas and dug around the seams while Gunnar headed to the bedroom.

Gunnar checked each drawer in the two dressers, but found nothing out of the ordinary. Laurie had said that she had checked those as well. He checked the corners of the rug, but didn't find that any of them came loose from the floor too easily and the rugs did not appear to have been disturbed. He looked carefully through the closets, feeling inside the pockets of each garment, but again found nothing. Next, he picked up the mattress to see if there might be anything else hidden there, but there was nothing. Then he dropped to his hands and knees and looked under the bed.

"Hey Charlie! I got something here!"

Charlie rushed to his side.

"It was under the bed, leaning up against the wall." Gunnar handed Charlie a photograph.

The picture showed portions of a naked man atop the Wilson girl as she lay on the boulder. Most of his features were obscured by

SERIAL

something, it looked like a couple leaves, that had blocked the camera lens, but Charlie could see the lower half of his face and head as well as an arm and a small section of his torso. The man's hair was blonde and it looked as though he might have a mustache. Charlie studied the photo and handed it over to Gunnar.

"You've seen Brandon a lot more than I have," he said. What do you think?

Gunnar studied the photo. "I guess it could be him. The chin looks right. Can't really tell much from the amount you can see here. To bad, too. Looks like he wanted himself in the photo. Still, it's here in his condo and we found it with a search warrant, so that should be enough."

"Exactly! Good work," Charlie said. He dropped the photo into a clean baggie and zipped it shut. "Sick bastard this guy is," he commented.

"Yeah." Gunnar agreed. "I can't imagine what he might do to Laurie if she hadn't caught onto him. He fucked up, leaving that girl dead up in New Hampshire. I guess Laurie didn't tell him that she was looking at cases around New England. I can't believe he could be in bed with her one minute and doing another girl to death the next. It's just sick. This guy deserves the chair."

"That he does. Keep looking. See what else we have here to tie him to these killings. Don't forget the jeans in the dryer. We have to get those checked out and see if it really is blood on them."

They searched the remainder of the condo carefully, but they found nothing else to link Brandon with the dead women. They took fiber and hair samples, also, to try and match them to the ones that were found at the murder scenes.

When they had exhausted all ideas on where to search, they waited outside for Brandon to return home. Laurie had said his plane would land at three o'clock and that was three hours ago. They expected him home any time.

They had waited about fifteen minutes, when Gunnar's cell phone rang.

"Detective Hincks." He paused. "Hi Laurie, are you feeling any better?"

Charlie pulled out a cigarette while he listened to Gunnar's side of the conversation. He had been on the force since long before new

187

hires were required to be non-smokers. He was a grandfathered smoker and liked it that way. Charlie's only vice was an occasional cigarette and he didn't want to have to trade up to a new vice.

"What?" Gunnar's change in tone from soothing to shock, made Charlie forget his smoke. He hooked his thumbs over his belt buckle, the cigarette still dangling from between his index and middle fingers, and tried to hear the other side of the conversation coming through on the phone, but the words were garbled.

Gunnar listened for a moment, said goodbye and hung up then, turned to Charlie.

"You might need another drag on that cancer stick. Laurie says she thinks Brandon just tried to pick up her friend, Jessie. You know the one?"

"Who doesn't who knows Laurie? Those two are like sisters. Did Brandon know who she was?"

"Oh yeah. They were talking about Laurie, she says. I find it hard to believe that this guy is that bold. First he leaves Laurie's bed to go kill another girl and returns before Laurie even knows he's gone, then he tries to stick her best friend." Gunnar ran a hand across the short stubble of hair on his head and continued.

"I'm glad she pushed to make all those phone calls looking for bodies, cause I'm pretty sure Brandon was planning to take Jessie out and I don't mean on a date."

"You could be right. That or he wanted more control over Laurie by killing her friends," Charlie added.

"Anyway, Laurie thinks he's headed this way, so we shouldn't have too much longer to wait."

Gunnar no sooner spoke the words, then Brandon's blue Mercedes pulled into the visitor's lot of the complex and rolled towards them. He turned into his driveway and got out of the car, smiling broadly as he recognized the two detectives.

"Hey guys, what are you doing hanging around here?" he grinned and held out his hand first to Charlie, but Charlie's hands remained at his sides while he coldly met Brandon's eyes.

Brandon's grin faded. He looked from Charlie to Gunnar and met the same cold expression. "What's wrong?"

"You are," Gunnar replied. He held up a pair of handcuffs. "Turn around and put your hands on your head."

"What?" Brandon's shocked expression suddenly broke into a grin. "Oh God, you guys got me. You're busting on me, right?"

"No." Charlie replied. "We're *busting* you. Now do as Gunnar says and put your hands on your head."

Brandon's grin faded again and slowly he turned his back to Gunnar and did as they asked.

Charlie read the Miranda off a small card he carried as Gunnar slapped the bracelets over each wrist and locked Brandon's hands behind his back. He could recite Miranda backward if he wanted, but telling the court he was certain he hadn't missed anything because he had read them left no room for some sleazy lawyer to slip through a loophole.

"You want to at least tell me what this is about?" Brandon asked.

"I think you know, but in case you want specifics on what we've got evidence for, we've got you for the murder of Abra Wilson here in Worcester."

Brandon pulled away and turned around to face them. "What?"

"Don't even try to deny it," Charlie replied. "We've got photos of the Wilson girl."

"Deny it, I don't have a clue what you're talking about! And how, where would you have gotten this photo from?"

"Your condo," Gunnar replied. "But we can discuss all this down at the station." Gunnar guided him into the back of the cruiser while Brandon continued to protest.

"What do you mean you have photos from my condo? What're you even doing in my condo?"

"Well, see, that's another story. And we can discuss it all when we get to the station."

# Chapter 22

Laurie made certain she wasn't in Brandon's path when they brought him into the station. She wasn't ready to meet him face to face; wasn't certain she could maintain her composure and keep from falling to tears; wasn't certain her mind could overrule her heart and keep her from pulling him into her arms.

It was difficult for a heart to stop loving—as difficult as it was to go from sixty to zero in 10 feet on a sheet of ice. And although in her mind, Laurie was able to hate this demon, her heart was still bound to him.

She stood with Charlie, watching through one-way glass as Gunnar entered the interrogation room to talk to Brandon. The microphone was turned on so that they could hear what was being said.

"So, you know why you're here. This isn't a social call." Gunnar circled the table like a wolf sizing up its prey before attacking. "You've been found out! You weren't as careful as you thought and we now know just what your extracurricular activities are." He threw the two photographs down under Brandon's nose and leaned on the table with his face close to his quarry.

"What we want to know now isn't so much whether you've been killing these women, because this is pretty damning evidence even if you are disguised here. What we really want to know is how many and where?"

Brandon was silent. He kept his eyes on the mirrored wall. He knew Laurie was on the other side of that glass. They wouldn't have him here without telling her.

"Help us out here," Gunnar continued. "How many cases have you left hanging open around New England, or is it around the country? Give the families of those women some peace, at least."

"Look, I have no idea what you're talking about and I don't know who is in that picture, but it's not me. I haven't killed anyone."

"We also have the bloodstained jeans from your dryer. When we get the results back from the lab, whose blood will it turn out to be? Is it from the girl you killed in New Hampshire? We know you killed her." Gunnar stood up straight and continued his circling.

"I don't have a clue what you're talking about." He paused. "Wait a minute. This is about Laurie, isn't it? You're looking to put me out of the picture," Brandon accused. "I've noticed the way you look at her even if she doesn't. I know you've always been jealous of the relationship we have. You wish it was you loving her instead of me at night, don't you? And yet, still I've been your friend, even though I know you want to take Laurie away from me." He looked up and met Gunnar's eyes with an angry stare. I want my lawyer here. I have nothing to say to you."

On the other side of the glass, Laurie was taken aback. Not that she believed Gunnar was to blame for the evidence in Brandon's condo, but was Brandon right? Was Gunnar jealous? She looked back at the past few months. Gunnar had acted strangely since she had met Brandon, hadn't he? Had he been hoping their relationship would become something more after she had broken up with Jeff? There hadn't been much time between her breakup with Jeff and the beginning of her relationship with Brandon. No. Brandon was probably just trying to cloud the issue; to infuriate Gunnar and gain control of the interrogation. She felt Charlie's eyes upon her, probing, and she forced herself to look ahead through the glass.

The wolf was not daunted. Gunnar paused momentarily in his interrogation and met Brandon's stare. "Nice try. You know Laurie and I have been partners and friends for a long time. I won't let you tarnish our professional relationship for the sake of your own sorry ass. We'll talk more when your lawyer arrives, not that he'll be able to help you out of this one." He turned and left the room, slamming the door behind him.

"Don't let what he says get to you," Laurie soothed. "He's just trying to rattle you, and me, too. I'm sure he knows I'm standing here watching him." She wanted to speak first and quickly to avoid any awkwardness that the accusation created. She could tell by the guilt on Gunnar's face that Brandon was right. Gunnar did wish for more between them, but she wasn't ready or willing for their relationship to move in that direction.

"I'm gonna grab some coffee from the machine. Either of you want one?" Gunnar asked.

"Nah." Charlie looked at his watch. "I gotta go talk to the Chief for a minute. I'll be back."

Charlie headed for the door while Gunnar retrieved two coffees from the temperamental coffee machine by the door. He was surprised that the machine produced both cups as it was intended rather than failing to produce a cup and pouring coffee down the drain.

"Are you alright?" He pulled a chair around from another desk to sit beside Laurie and placed one of the steaming cups in her hand. His seat was so close that their knees touched slightly. He watched her intently, but she did not look up.

Laurie had been with Brandon for only a few months, but she had quickly learned to love and trust him. She couldn't believe that those things women fear most from men had been inflicted by him. He was always gentle with her and had told her so many times that he loved her. How could she have known? But everything she had learned about the killer pointed to Brandon.

"I think I just need a few minutes to myself," she said meekly. She rolled her eyes up to meet Gunnar's, but only briefly. He had helped her to bring in the man she loved and his presence beside her only compounded the guilt she felt.

"I understand," he comforted. "I'll go start the paperwork. You already told me your story, so I can just fit that in." He squeezed her hand before he walked away.

"Thanks for understanding." She smiled tiredly and a sad sigh escaped her.

Gunnar glanced at her from his desk as she buried her face in her hands. Yeah, I understand how you feel, he thought—like you want to tear him apart. I'd like a moment or two with him myself. He could see her trembling and wanted so much to hold and comfort her.

The phone rang. Brandon's lawyer had arrived and Gunnar left to meet him in the lobby.

Joe Polumbo was a short stocky man with a shiny, bald patch on the crown of his head surrounded by a monk's ring of equally shiny black hair. He shifted his briefcase abruptly to his left hand and held out a chubby right for Gunnar to shake. The broad smile that was painted on his face did not reflect in his eyes. He was a snake, Gunnar could see. He would be a barrier to his sending Brandon away forever.

Brandon's eyes met his lawyer's when Attorney Polumbo entered the room. Joe had been a friend for many years and they each had used their respective skills to help the other out whenever possible. But Brandon never thought he would need Joe's help for anything of this magnitude.

"You wanna removed those cuffs first, before we talk about anything," Joe commanded Gunnar.

"You're not going anywhere, anyway," he grumbled at Brandon as Gunnar removed the cuffs and Brandon rubbed his wrists.

"Now, what could you possibly have that would suggest Brandon killed anyone?"

"Oh he's guilty alright. These pictures say it all." Gunnar handed him the two photos from Brandon's condo.

"Who's this?" Joe asked as he held up the photos for Gunnar to see.

"They were in Brandon's home and though you can't positively identify him, they were in his condo, in his bed."

"Doesn't even look like him," Joe countered. "I see a blonde man here. My client isn't blonde. And what's that, a mustache?" He threw the photos down on the table. "That's not my client"

They were in his home along with a pair of bloody jeans.

"Blood from what?"

"We don't know yet, they're at the lab for testing."

"Then you got nothing but the possibility that the man in these photos is someone who my client knows or let into his home at some point. You say the photos were not in a place that my client would usually look?"

"Between the mattresses and under the bed."

Joe chuckled. "Well, I don't know about you, detective, but I only see what's between my mattresses once every six months and I never look under my bed."

"Who else would leave the photos in such a personal space?"

"Well, that's your job to find out, but it wasn't my client. Now if you'll excuse us, I'd like a word in private with my client." He glared at Gunnar until he had left the room and closed the door behind him.

He watched the conversation through the one-way glass and Charlie joined him after a few moments.

"His lawyer is in there with him now."

"Is that Polumbo?" Charlie asked. "I'm not surprised to see him, he only represents the worst scum."

"Actually, I think they've been friends for a while."

"Really?" Charlie huffed.

"Who knows what Brandon's telling him in there. Probably giving him the gory details. I don't know how lawyers can live with themselves, knowing what someone has done and how they did it, that they're not even sorry for it, yet they still defend them and try to get them back out on the street where they can do more harm. The system sucks!" Charlie complained.

Sergeant Charlie Miller had transferred to Worcester from a small department in Pennsylvania when his wife's mother had died. He had been a cop for twenty years, but he had never gotten used to the idea that another human being could so easily take the life of another. This bastard just tore them apart like they were animals. Just cut them apart, he thought. The world was full of injustice, but he would find justice for this man. Justice would chew him up and spit him out. If only Massachusetts had a death penalty on the books. But that would be too good for him. Let him rot!

With the intercom off, this being a privileged conversation between the attorney and his charge, Gunnar and Charlie did their best to determine the content of the conversation.

Attorney Polumbo sat with his back to the one-way glass, while he talked to his friend. Brandon shook his head a few times in response to his questions, but said little. Finally, his attorney was finished. He snapped his briefcase shut and stood up, resting a comforting hand on Brandon's shoulder before he turned to the door and left the room.

"You charging my client today with what little you've got?"
Charlie nodded.

"Well then. We'll see you tomorrow morning at the arraignment," he addressed Charlie. "Don't be late." He turned abruptly and headed for the door.

"Sorry bastard! Has his friend believing his BS story of innocence, but we got him now and he's going to pay for what he's done." Charlie turned away from the glass and went to bring the prisoner to his cell.

Gunnar approached Laurie.

"Come on. You need a break from this place and from this thing with Brandon. If you're not going to go home, how about joining me?" Gunnar positioned himself in front of Laurie's desk willing her to look up.

Her eyes were red.

"Let's go hit the road. We can slide up to the summit and follow up on some leads I got on a case over there."

Laurie nodded tiredly. It would do her good to get her mind off Brandon.

A green Taurus sat with its engine idling on a small street in Greendale around the corner from the Massachusetts Cooperative Bank.

"We didn't do enough planning this time. I'm not too sure about this, guys," the tall guy warned as he donned a black shirt over his white T-shirt. The gloves felt tight over his clammy fingers. He was nervous.

"Quit worrying so much!" his partner argued. "If we don't do this today, we won't be able to do it for another two weeks. They got us on a full schedule for a while and we won't even have time for lunch let alone an extended break like this one. The next day off we'll have is a holiday and you know the banks aren't open then. So, this is it. Let's go!" He pulled a black nylon down over his face. They were just around the corner from the bank.

The girl put on a Whoopi Goldberg mask as her disguise. She wouldn't have enough time to clean off black makeup this time before they had to return to class. She had picked up the mask as an alternative, but she didn't like the way it obstructed her vision.

Slowly, she brought the car around the block and pulled into the bank. She parked where she would not be visible from the windows and the two men jumped from the car and ran inside with their guns drawn.

The tall man fired a single shot directly at the teller in the center; it blistered the bulletproof glass and she screamed and ducked down behind the counter with her hands in the air.

"Everybody stay calm and do exactly as we say!" he ordered. "We're not here to hurt anyone. We just want the money."

The bank manager started to approach them from the side and the tall one swung in his direction, his pistol pointed directly at his head. He was a superb shot and if he wanted to, he could put a bullet right between the manager's eyes. He just wanted the money. The bank manager saw the threat and stared directly at it as he backed away from the gunman.

"Move over toward the tellers," he ordered. "I want to keep an eye on you." He followed the bank manager and shoved him up against the wall as he approached the window and threw an empty bag at the girl there. The short robber kept his mouth shut as he tossed a bag to another teller.

"Everything in the bags," the tall robber ordered them. He waved the gun back and forth. "But I want to see you fan every handful of bills," he added. "No dye packs. Now, do it!" he shouted when the teller in front of him didn't take the bag. The teller did as she was told while tears of fright streamed down her crimson cheeks. She emptied the drawer and tried to shove the bag under the window.

"Open the window, you stupid bitch! Don't try to push it under. Come on!" He kept his gun pointed at the manager who cowered against the wall.

The short robber stood beside his partner. He had already gotten money from the other two tellers.

The tall one checked his watch. "Damn!" he cursed. "It's been more than two minutes. We gotta get outa here!" He waved his gun at the tellers and the two of them turned and bolted toward the door. They plowed past a woman entering the bank as they left. She screamed and jumped back against the wall when she saw the guns.

Whoopi was waiting in the stolen green Taurus when they emerged. They jumped in and she stepped on the gas before they had even closed the door. She tried not to start too quickly because that just created more witnesses who could point out the direction they had taken. She drove north toward the traffic light. There were two cars in front of her. She needed to make that right turn to get out of sight of the bank. The light for the other direction was now yellow. She looked in her mirror. She could see no flashing lights. The traffic signal changed and the cars in front of her moved slowly across the intersection. Whoopi took her turn and a wide grin of relief spread across her face beneath the mask. They had made it!

Gunnar turned right out of the station and scraped through the intersection before the light turned red and pulled to a stop at the next intersection.

"You know, I'm here for you if you need anything," he offered.

"Thanks," was all Laurie said.

"You know, Brandon and I got along real well. He and I did a lot of fishing and stuff." Laurie simply stared straight ahead at the road. Gunnar continued, "What I mean is, he fooled me too. I actually *liked* the guy. So, you shouldn't beat yourself up about this."

"I'm not beating myself up for being fooled. He just broke my heart. I just can't believe he did the things he did; he wasn't like that. He's the sweetest, most vulnerable man I've ever known. I just don't get it."

"I thought I was the nicest guy you ever knew," Gunnar joked.

Laurie looked at him sadly and allowed the corner of her mouth to turn up slightly at the intended joke. "Thanks for letting me drop the tough routine around you."

"Hey, that's what partners are for. I know you're still tough." He smiled and put a comforting hand upon her shoulder.

They headed up Gold Star Boulevard and crested the summit where the street's identity changed to West Boylston.

The radio crackled to life. "All cars in the vicinity, head toward Massachusetts Cooperative Bank on West Boylston Street for an armed robbery. The suspects fled moments ago in a green Ford Taurus."

Laurie squinted her eyes at the road ahead and saw a green sedan slowly turn right toward the residential streets of Greendale. She pointed. "Look at that! You think...?"

"I'd say that could be." Gunnar hit the lights and sirens to warn traffic as he pressed his foot hard on the accelerator. The car was less than a quarter mile away.

Laurie picked up the microphone. "Dispatcher, Detectives Sharpe and Hincks. We are in pursuit of a green sedan turned right onto Alarie Street from West Boylston. We believe these are the suspects from the bank robbery. They're headed up toward Burncoat. Please send a cruiser to intercept."

The tires screeched loudly as Gunnar took the right at the light. The rear of the car swung hard to the left and Gunnar stepped heavily on the gas to bring it straight. He pushed the pedal to the floor and sped quickly up the narrow street.

Laurie searched the side streets as they flew past, looking for a flash of green. Then she saw it. "To the left," she shouted. But Gunnar was already past the street. He turned sharply at the next intersection and headed the wrong way on a one-way street. At the next corner he was close enough to see them. They drove quickly, but not too fast until they saw him. Then the Taurus shot away with newfound haste.

"What the fuck!" the driver shouted when she saw the flashing lights in her mirror. She had removed her mask. "Where the hell did they come from?" She kicked the accelerator to the floor and the automatic transmission downshifted with a roar. The houses whizzed by as they climbed the hill to the red light, which they flew through, narrowly missing a pickup that was crossing the intersection.

Gunnar slowed at the intersection, inching his way out as Laurie flipped the switches on the dash, sounding the air horn. They crossed quickly when they were sure it was safe. The green Taurus was already gone. Gunnar stomped on the gas pedal and the car quickly gained speed. Laurie again searched the side streets as they passed. Nothing. Suddenly, on the right, she caught a glimpse of green as it disappeared from sight in an apartment complex.

"There! Right!" She shouted.

Gunnar pulled the emergency brake and turned the wheel right. The rear end of the car spun around behind him and they stopped, facing the opposite direction. He released the brake, stomped on the gas and the tires squealed loudly as the car flew up into the complex.

Laurie was back on the radio. "Suspects have turned into Sutton Apartments on Clark Street. We are in pursuit. Have a car block the entrance. They may be changing cars in here, their usual MO."

The street branched off into several side streets and lots. Laurie scanned each one as they passed. They drove more slowly now. Would the suspects still switch cars or would they take off on foot?

The car was in the last lot at the end. Both doors were left hanging open.

"Appears suspects out on foot. We'll be in pursuit." Laurie shouted into the microphone and left it hanging as she and Gunnar jumped out of the car.

They looked around the lot, but saw no one. Then the sound of crackling branches and heavy footfalls reached their ears from the woods. Together, they broke into a run.

They could see two figures in black pushing their way down the hill. The suspects had removed the disguises from their heads and the detectives guessed from the shoulder-length hair and slender figure that one was a woman. She stumbled behind the man who did not look back as he left her in the brush.

Laurie caught up to her and Gunnar kept on after the other suspect.

"Don't even try to run again," she said to the girl on the ground. "Put your hands behind your head."

The girl did as she was told and Laurie grabbed her wrists one by one and pulled them behind her, locking metal rings around each one. Then she pulled her to her feet and turned her around.

The girl looked at her feet, her face obscured by her hair, and Laurie put a hand under her chin to lift her head. "I know you," she said.

Tears welled in the girl's eyes and trickled down her cheeks as her eyes met Laurie's. Her lips trembled as though she wanted to say something, but the words would not come out.

"It usually takes years of frustration to turn a cop dirty. You guys aren't even out of training yet. Who're your friends?"

The girl dropped her chin and said nothing.

Just then, a gunshot rang out. Laurie grabbed the girl by the arm and released one of the rings from her wrist. She pulled the girl to a nearby tree and looped the empty cuff around a sturdy branch, hoping her prisoner didn't carry a handcuff key. Then she tore off into the woods in the direction of the gunshot.

She found Gunnar standing above the suspect. He was face down in the brush with his hands cuffed securely behind him. Blood oozed from a wound on his leg.

"Stupid bastard tried to shoot me," he panted. "Lucky I got a hold of him. He shot himself with his own gun."

"Do you recognize them?" Laurie asked.

"No. Should I?"

"They're in the Academy. They've been around the station here and there."

Gunnar shook his head. "You're shittin' me. What a waste! And there's a third one. I wonder who that'll turn out to be."

"I don't know, but I have a good idea," Laurie mused as she remembered the tall trainee who had grabbed her in the hallway.

"Well, I guess we better call an ambulance. This guy's not walking out of here on that leg."

Laurie pulled a hand radio from her waist and gave the dispatcher the details of their situation. The ambulance was on its way. They could hear movement in the woods coming toward them and soon two patrolmen appeared, breathing heavily from the run downhill. A third had stayed behind with the girl cuffed to the tree.

"Well, this makes for a better day," Gunnar grinned at Laurie.

"It certainly helps. Never got that cup of coffee, though."

"Don't worry, it's on me as soon as we get these two wrapped up and on their way to the station."

They saw red lights flashing up in the parking lot. One of the patrolmen had gone up to meet the ambulance when it arrived and now Laurie could hear them talking as they worked their way down through the brush.

"Looks like the cavalry is here," she said.

"Looks like they brought a backboard so we can carry this guy outta here," Gunnar grumbled. Wheels would never be useful in the thick undergrowth. They would have to carry him out.

Laurie interrogated the girl in one room while Gunnar had gone to the hospital with the other robber. The paramedics had said the bullet had made a clean pass through his leg, so she didn't expect they would be too long before they returned to the station.

"So, you want to tell me who your other partner was? Make things a little easier on yourself. I could tell the DA that you cooperated that much anyway."

The girl said nothing. She kept her eyes trained on the scratches in the table before her. She knew of Laurie Sharpe and had always looked up to and envied her. Now here she sat, knowing that her idol thought of her as nothing more than a cowardly, thieving scum, who had betrayed the department and all those who believed in her potential as an officer.

"Nothing to say? Maybe you want to tell me what your part was in all this? Were you in on the planning of these little heists or did they just recruit you as their driver?"

Still, she was silent.

"I can't help you if you won't talk to me." Laurie waited a moment for a response, then turned and left the room.

"Gunnar's back with the other one," Charlie informed her when she had closed the door.

"That was quicker than I expected."

"Yeah. Slow day at the emergency room. They took him right in and patched him up. The bullet didn't hit any arteries or anything. All they had to do was stitch him up and send him packing. He wasn't too happy either, from what Gunnar said. He was hoping to be tied up there for awhile, put off coming back here."

"Just not his lucky day," Laurie chuckled.

She went to the interrogation room where Gunnar was questioning the boy and watched through the one-way glass. Charlie joined her.

"If you give us the name of your accomplice, we'll see if they can go a little easier on you. Your girlfriend's probably giving him up right now anyway."

"She's not my girlfriend," he replied. "She's Mike's. It was all Mike's idea to do this," he grumbled, angry that his partner had gotten away and they'd been caught.

"Mike who?"

"Stephens, Mike Stephens. He's probably gone back to training."

"At the academy?"

The boy nodded.

All eyes turned as the classroom door opened and Laurie walked in, followed by Gunnar.

"Hi, Lenny," Laurie greeted the teacher, a nine-year veteran route cop who liked vacationing from the streets while he passed on endless stories to excited recruits.

Mike glanced at Laurie, but his eyes sought and focused on Gunnar who stopped just inside the door to scan the room. The gnawing acid in his gut accompanied by a prickling sensation as the chill of fear rose to his scalp told him they were here for him. His partners had turned him in. He should have followed his instincts and gotten out after the last job, but he had stayed because he knew they would continue without him and they needed someone to keep them from doing something stupid that would get them caught. He knew his partners had wasted no time in telling detectives that it was he, Mike Stephens, who had conceived these robberies; had determined that the best time to hit a bank was in the last hour of the afternoon shift when all cops ending their shift were either at the station finishing up paperwork or tied up on other business that kept them away from the station and final paperwork.

Mike knew that it was in this hour that the city was most unprotected, that response time was longest. He had determined how much time it took for an officer to get down the stairs to his car and back out on the road and how long it would take to travel from the station to the bank being hit. Mike always got them out before time was up. Just not today.

Mike tried to hold his eyes away from Gunnar's, but he could feel them boring into him. There was no place for him to run to, no place to hide. They had him so, he finally, reluctantly, looked up.

Gunnar calmly motioned him to the front of the room and folded his arms across his chest.

Laurie paused in her conversation with Lenny and followed Mike's progress toward the front of the room. All eyes were trained on him.

"Detective Sharpe will do the honors." Gunnar nodded in Laurie's direction.

Laurie gave Gunnar a small, appreciative smile before she proceeded with the arrest. He knew the satisfaction of an arrest would go a long way in diminishing her personal troubles, if only for a few moments.

"For all of you, this should serve as a reminder that you are here to learn how to uphold the law, not how to break it," she addressed the class of uncertain students. Some had caught on to what was happening, but were too stunned to share the truth with others who were looking uncertainly from Laurie to Gunnar to Mike.

"Michael Stephens," she continued, "you are under arrest for armed robbery and assault with a deadly weapon." She read him the Miranda warnings, locked his hands behind his back, and turned him toward the door that Gunnar held open for them.

She paused at the door to again address the class. "If any of you have shared involvement in the string of bank robberies around Worcester, it would be to your benefit to speak up now. It took less than five minutes to get Mike's name from his accomplices, so don't think they won't be just as eager to give us yours if you've been involved."

"None of them were involved," Mike uttered hoarsely. "Can we just get out of here?"

Laurie hid a small smile as she replied. "Believe me, Mike—embarrassment is the least of your worries at the moment." She guided him toward the door and it closed behind them as enquiring eyes turned upon Lenny.

# Chapter 23

Gunnar found Laurie hunched over her desk, cheerily filling out paperwork in the wake of the arrest. "Sometimes it takes a great bust like that to get your mind off your troubles, don't you think?"

Laurie looked up at him and smiled. Her eyes twinkled for a moment before she plunged back into her paperwork to avoid thoughts of Brandon that threatened to crash in on her again.

"The day's over," she said. "I could use a drink after this, couldn't you?"

"Definitely," he agreed. "I have a few things to do first, though. Should I meet you?"

"Yeah. How about down on Shrewsbury Street? I'll be finished up here in about half an hour. I'll see you there in about an hour?" She looked up quickly to see him nod and returned to writing up her report.

Gunnar was late.

Laurie sat at the empty bar, swirling the ice cubes around in her half empty glass. The day had been long and harsh and she needed a friend. Someone to sit with, no conversation was necessary. But here she was at the bar, alone.

The minutes ticked by as the bartender wandered over to ask how she was doing. Her silence and sad expression disturbed him and, being an experienced bartender, he always offered his shoulder to cry on when he had the chance. It was good for tips. Plus Laurie was a regular customer with her partner, Gunnar, so they always took good monetary care of him.

"You look like you've had a rough day," he commented. "Want to talk about it?"

Laurie looked up from her drink and offered him a sad smile.

"Not anything I can or really want to talk about, but thanks for the ear, Scott."

"No problem, Laurie. Let me know if you need anything."

Laurie wallowed in her sadness as he walked back toward the far end of the bar. How do you discuss the imprisonment of a man you loved, especially when he was in jail for rape and murder? Crimes like these meant immediate annulment of any relationship. She liked Scott, but she couldn't talk to him about this. She needed Gunnar's ear. He already knew the story, so she wouldn't need to spin it out, he would just drink with her and change the subject.

Finally, he arrived and strutted cockily up to the bar. "Well, we're three for three," he said. "We took down three bad guys and lost three cops in the process."

The bartender perked up when he heard Gunnar's comment. "Did someone get shot?" he asked.

"Hey, Scott. Nah, we just took some guys down. Long story and they're still getting answers. You'll probably get to read it in the paper tomorrow." He ordered a beer, then sat down, putting his hand on Laurie's knee. It was meant to be a comforting gesture, but her stomach knotted as Brandon's accusation resounded in her thoughts. She didn't pull away.

"Sorry, I guess I've been sitting here moping. I'm still having a hard time dealing with this. I really appreciate your being here for me. I don't know what I would do without you." She smiled sadly and looked down, away from his eyes.

Gunnar squeezed her knee gently and removed his hand to his beer.

Laurie sighed inwardly with relief.

"You know, if there's anything at all that you need to help you get through this, you just have to say it. I am here for you for anything." He desperately hoped she would ask, but knew she wouldn't.

He and Laurie had been close for two years now. They worked cases together and had become good, trusting friends, but he had fallen for her, he was sure. He just hadn't realized it until too late—Brandon had come and he had missed his chance. What would happen now that Brandon had fallen from grace? He craved Laurie so badly and yet she still only viewed him as a friend. Maybe she just needed more time. Or maybe he just needed to let her know his feelings for her. Brandon had already sparked the thought in her mind, was she considering his observation? Did Laurie feel the same for him, too afraid of spoiling a friendship to let it show? Maybe it was no coincidence that she had fallen for a man who looked so much like him. Maybe it was a subconscious attraction meant for Gunnar. *Maybe.*

"We could go grab a late dinner? Or even a movie to help you get your mind off this."

"I think I just need some company for now." She rubbed her temples and sighed. "I don't think I could eat anything." Sounds too much like a date—dinner and a movie, she thought. She liked Gunnar, but never considered him to be her type. He was sexy enough to be sure, and he'd proven he could charm most girls, just not her. In fact, she had felt secure with him as her friend because he was always chasing skirts, looking for a one-night stand. She was certain he was not interested in her that way. No way Brandon could have been right about that, could he? No. Gunnar was just being kind, trying to help her forget her troubles. Dinner shared between two friends is just dinner. So is a movie. But dinner and a movie?

"So, what are we gonna do for fun, now that we're not chasing bank robbers?" she asked. She rubbed her head again and she hailed the bartender to get her another drink. He was busy mixing for someone at the far end of the counter. She rubbed her head again. She needed an aspirin.

"I'll be back," she said. "I've had a couple already and a few cups of coffee before you got here. You know how it is." She pushed her stool away from the bar and slid to the floor. The bathroom was to the left, around the corner, in a room behind the bar. Gunnar watched her grab her pocketbook off the bar and walk away.

"She's not looking too happy," the bartender commented.

Gunnar agreed. "She's had a rough couple of days, Scott. Maybe you could get her another of whatever she's drinking."

The bartender nodded and pulled down a couple bottles from which he mixed up another concoction in a glass with ice. He put the glass on the bar and turned to attend to another customer who had just walked in. There were many other patrons now, and the bartender was keeping busy. Gunnar took the glass and pulled it closer into the area in front of Laurie's seat as a middle-aged man sat down in the next seat, spreading a newspaper out before him.

Laurie returned, appearing refreshed, and retook her seat beside Gunnar. "And another round begins, I see. Thanks." She sighed and smiled weakly at Gunnar and he tipped his drink to her.

"You did the right thing, following your instincts like that."

Laurie met his eyes with a questioning look.

"Going to check out his place when you heard about the girl in New Hampshire. I mean, if he was doing girls that close to you, he might have gotten around to planning to kill you, too."

"I just can't imagine that he would ever hurt me. You've seen us together. He's really just the nicest guy."

"Nice until you do something he doesn't like. Did you guys ever have a fight?"

"No. We never disagreed enough about anything that we couldn't come to a compromise."

"Are you sure he wasn't just holding back and giving in to you? And what do you think happens when he holds back once too often? The psychopath in him is going to lash out at you."

Laurie shook her head. "You're probably right. But can we not talk about this anymore right now? You're supposed to be trying to keep my mind off of my troubles, remember?"

"You're right, I'm sorry. Drink up." He motioned to the untouched drink.

Laurie took a long sip.

"So, how are your parents doing? You call them lately?"

"Only to tell them I got engaged."

"Oh. OK. Next topic," Gunnar mumbled and lifted his drink, looking away from Laurie like a guilty dog.

Laurie chuckled.

"What could possibly be funny?"

"Your miserable failure at trying to cheer me up by trying to find a safe topic."

"Some friend, huh?"

"I appreciate the effort. He has just dominated my life lately. It's not going to be easy."

"I could tell you about my life, it's been pretty drab lately. I haven't gotten any in a whole week." Gunnar grinned.

"Wow! A whole week. That must be a record for you."

"Lately. But I was thinking of getting you drunk and trying to take advantage of you."

"Oh, really," Laurie retorted. She didn't doubt that he might be telling the truth, though he made it sound like a joke.

"Yeah. Wanna another drink?"

"No. I'm good. I think this one put me over the edge."

Laurie felt her cheeks. They were flushed and her face felt warm. Either she had reached her limit, or it was just too hot in here.

"I think I'm going to head out. My face is a little hot and I think I may have had more than I should. You going?"

"Sure. I'll get the tab."

"Thanks." She watched Gunnar pay the tab, then led the way to the door.

Gunnar noticed she was tottering and he put a hand upon her shoulder to steady her. In the light breeze that blew, he caught a gentle whiff of her perfume. It aroused his senses.

He had tried to play off hitting on her as a joke, but they had been friends for too long. He definitely wanted more with her and he was sure they could be closer if only he could get her mind off Brandon. With what Brandon had done, she couldn't still love him. She was moping for the loss of the relationship, not because she wanted to be with him.

"Are you alright?" he asked as she tripped on the pavement.

"Yeah, just a little bit tipsy, I guess I had too many on an empty stomach." She held her hand to her forehead. It was blazing hot.

"I can take you home. You don't look like you should be driving." He put a supporting arm around her and she leaned on him.

"You're probably right. My car will be fine here. Where are you parked?"

"Right over here." He led the way to his Monte Carlo.

Laurie swayed a little getting into the car. "I can't believe how fast this hit me. I wasn't drinking very fast. It just snuck up on me." She tucked her legs into the car and Gunnar closed the door.

He put a comforting hand on her knee as he settled in behind the wheel. "Are you feeling alright? You're not going to be sick or anything are you?"

"No. I'm just really lightheaded."

"Good. Cause you know there's a no puking rule in the Monte."

"I'll try to remember." Her head swam. "You remember how to get to my house?"

"Of course. I've been there how many times to help you fix stuff?" He smiled comfortingly at her.

They drove on in silence. Laurie felt too ill to speak. She leaned her head back on the headrest and closed her eyes.

Gunnar drove out of the city. He knew his way around the area like the back of his hand. He snaked his way along in the direction of Laurie's house sticking to the back roads to avoid traffic. He glanced over at her from time to time, watching her breasts rise and fall with each breath. He wanted to touch her so badly he ached with tension. Brandon had already placed the bug, maybe now was the time to tell her how he felt.

Laurie opened her eyes when she felt the car stop. She looked around. "Where are we?" she asked groggily.

"You're looking pretty ill. I thought we'd stop for a minute so you could get some fresh air. How about we take a little walk."

"You're probably right," she half-heartedly agreed. "If I go to sleep now, I'll be so hung over in the morning, I won't be able to work tomorrow."

"Let me help you out." Gunnar quickly jumped out of the car and came over to her side. He held out his hand to take hers and pulled her up out of the car.

"Thanks." She steadied herself on her feet and leaned back against the car, taking in a deep breath of the chilly night air. Her head cleared somewhat and she realized she had no idea where they were. Gunnar had pulled off the road onto a small dirt road that Laurie didn't recognize.

"Where are we?"

"I'm not sure the name of the road. We're off Route 20."

"Oh." She felt Gunnar's eyes on her and her stomach fluttered uncomfortably.

He put a hand on her shoulder to steady her as she leaned against the car. He studied the way her blonde locks reflected the moonlight—she had such beautiful hair. Her perfume tantalized his senses as he leaned in closer to her. He put a hand under her chin and gently lifted her face, so he could see her eyes. They had a glazed look.

"What are you doing?" she asked listlessly.

"Just this," he responded as he leaned forward quickly and gently kissed her lips. Her eyes focused on him, but her expression was blank. She was stunned that he had actually made a move on her.

"What was that for?" she asked.

"Because you're so beautiful. I've wanted to kiss you for a very long time." And before she could respond, he leaned over and kissed her again, this time she felt his tongue brush her lips gently and she pulled away.

"I'm sorry, Gunnar, I had no idea you felt this way. You have been my most trusted friend. You know that. Why didn't you ever tell me you wanted to go out with me?" she asked gently as she put a hand to his chest to hold him away. She didn't want him to kiss her again. The sensation of his lips touching hers was awkward.

"I never had a chance. When I figured it out, you were with Jeff and then right after you two broke up, you met Brandon and I could see how you felt about him. I couldn't tell you how I felt, knowing you were in love with someone else." He put an arm around her waist and pulled her closer to him. "I don't want to miss another chance to tell you how I feel before someone else beats me to it." He put his free hand on her belly.

Laurie felt a chill slide down her spine. Was that fear?

"Please, Gunnar. Don't touch me like that. I'm not ready for this and I don't know if I could ever feel this way about you." She tried to wriggle free but he held her tight.

Her head swam with alcohol and her stomach clenched in fear as she reviewed how many drinks she'd had—only four in two hours. Why did she feel like this? And suddenly, her heart began to beat like the wings of a hummingbird.

"I didn't have that much to drink. Tell me you didn't slip me something to make me feel better or help me sleep?"

Her head took a deep dive toward murky waters and she fought her way back toward the surface. Thoughts were speeding through her mind so fast she could barely make sense of them.

Gunnar had spent time with Brandon. They had become good friends.

Wasn't it odd that Brandon would hide photos of a murder he had committed between the mattresses of a bed that a detective would sleep in? True, psychopathic murderers sometimes demonstrated stupidity, but Brandon had given her a key—wasn't it reasonable that he would make certain there was never any evidence around that she would find?

So what did it all mean? What was she thinking? Could Gunnar have planted the photos and the jeans in Brandon's condo so she would find them? Was Brandon right that Gunnar just wanted him out of the picture? Her eyes opened wide. Her thoughts horrified and frightened her and her heart raced faster as her head grew lighter.

"Are you OK?" Gunnar asked.

Laurie shook her head and blurted out her thoughts in one long jumble.

"You went to New Hampshire the same time we did. You said you were going fishing on the Saco, right near where we would be. So, you were there, too, when that girl was killed. Did you kill her?"

Gunnar put his other hand on her shoulder and steadied her against the car. "What are you talking about? Brandon killed that girl. You found the evidence at his condo."

"Why would he leave anything in his condo when he knows I have a key and could stop by anytime? You killed that girl didn't you? Then you planted evidence in Brandon's condo just like he said. Brandon could never hurt anyone. He's too sweet for that."

"Come on, Laurie. Get a hold of yourself. You're talking crazy." Gunnar shook her.

She tried to pull away from him, but her back was against the car. "No! I won't calm down. You knew all the places Brandon and I had been because I told you about them. You know where my family is in Vermont. You killed those women! And then you set Brandon up. And now he hates me!"

Laurie felt her head swim again and she tried to push Gunnar away from her, but his grip was too tight.

"What did you slip me? I can feel it! I know it was you!" She was becoming hysterical as her fear mounted. She was here alone with a man who had killed uncounted women.

Brandon was innocent. She knew it! Would he ever forgive her for thinking he was capable of such horrible things?

She knew Gunnar had always been uncouth with women; was always in short relationships that often ended with a woman hating him. Did he just give up dating and decide to start raping and killing? Or had he planned the whole scenario to get her away from Brandon? But Abra Wilson had died before Laurie met Brandon. So for how long before had Gunnar been killing women? He never did share too many date details with her, only that he had scored.

She had to get away from him! Laurie thrust her knee upward, hard and fast, catching him solidly in the groin. He doubled over, losing his hold on her. She clasped her hands together and brought them down heavily on the back of his neck and he fell to one knee, cursing. "Fuck it!" he mumbled painfully.

Laurie's senses focused instantly and she turned and ran. She dodged through brush and trees; branches scratched at her and hanging boughs threatened to topple her. The moonlight didn't reach through the trees and the way was dark. She ducked her head and ran.

She could hear him in the woods behind her, tearing through the trees like a madman, coming after her.

"Laurie! Don't run from me! Laurie!" he called after her, but she continued running.

She should have her gun. Why didn't she have her gun with her? But she had left it in her car, locked in the glove box like she always did when she went into a bar. Guns and alcohol don't mix, she always said. But she wished now that for once she had not listened to her own reason and had brought a piece with her. Then she wouldn't be running. Gunnar wouldn't be chasing her, she would have him in cuffs.

She broke into a small clearing. Rays of silver moonlight broke through the trees and illuminated a pile of broken bottles and beer cans—a high school drinking hangout. The cops wouldn't bother them way out here in the woods. She grabbed a broken bottle as she passed through the clearing—not much of a weapon, but better than nothing.

She could hear Gunnar's thrashing through the brush drawing nearer with each terrifying moment. She broke into a run again, diving back into the brush as Gunnar broke into the clearing.

"Laurie! Wait! We need to talk!" Gunnar called out hoarsely.

Laurie's head swam and she stumbled. A leafy branch caught the uneven edges of the broken bottle and ripped it out of her grasp. She didn't have time to stop and look for it. Gunnar was closing in.

Tears streamed back across her cheeks from the corners of her eyes and Laurie realized they weren't just from the wind or the branches swatting her face. A lump had formed in her throat and she was sobbing as she ran. She forced the fear and desperation out of her mind. Fear and desperation sapped the will to live. She needed every ounce of that will she could muster right now if she was to survive.

"Come on, Laurie. What are you running from?"

"Leave me alone!" She tore on through the woods, twisting her ankle, but gritting her teeth through the pain.

Suddenly, the trees and brush ended and she found herself on a cleared path—a railroad track! She turned right and ran with every ounce of energy she had. She hadn't much left.

Her legs felt sluggish, like she wore twenty pound ankle weights on each foot, but they did not slow her. Fear gave her strength she would not otherwise have had. She ran along between the two rails with Gunnar close behind.

The way before her was brighter now. She could see better and run faster, but so could Gunnar. She could hear his footfalls drawing closer.

"Laurie," he called. He was right behind her. Her legs were failing her as she caught her toe on one of the ties and stumbled, catching herself before she could fall.

She glanced over her shoulder at her pursuer as she steadied her feet. Gunnar was not five feet behind and looked as though he could run forever. Though he was in full stride, he breathed steadily. Gunnar had always been in good shape. She would have cursed at this, but immediately behind him, she saw what he could not.

Laurie had heard stories that trains are silent when they approach from behind. She never believed that this could be possible until now.

She dove to the right just as the diesel engine struck Gunnar and she rolled out of its path and down into the trees. She heard the wheels shriek, metal upon metal, as the engineer applied the brake. The sound bored into her eardrums and she winced in pain.

The screeching continued as the train slowed and finally stopped a hundred feet down the track.

Laurie let out a long sigh and let her head drop to the ground. She was spent. She couldn't have run another hundred steps. Gunnar had her. She was dead. She looked up at her savior, in all its glorious tons of steel.

What had happened to Gunnar?

The engineer jumped down from the engine and ran back to see what he had hit. Was it really what he thought? Had he really hit a man? He aimed a flashlight at the front of the train. Nothing.

The engineer crouched and looked up under the train, expecting the worst, but there was nothing to see. Slowly, for his back was weary with age, he straightened. Puzzled, he looked around both sides of the train. Perhaps the man had been pulled to the side. He could be lying way down beside the train. He started back down the line to the left of the cars.

Laurie still lay on the ground almost buried by shrubs and grass that grew around her. Her head ached badly and she put a hand to her forehead. She felt in one piece. She drew her legs up under her and pulled herself to her feet then stood shakily for a moment and looked around.

The shadow of the engineer was moving slowly along the side of the train. The light from the flashlight bobbed up and down. He was looking for what he had hit. Did he know he had hit a man?

Of course he does, she thought. He wouldn't stop if he thought he hit a deer.

She looked around from where she stood, wondering if Gunnar was nearby or if the train had cut him to pieces.

Then, in the silence, she heard stirring in the brush beside her. Her heart jumped into her throat.

"Gunnar?" She shouted his name out in a whisper. There was no response.

Surely, he couldn't be a danger to her now. She had seen the train bear down on him. She was certain he'd been hit. No one walked away after being hit by a train.

Slowly, she made her way shakily toward the sound of branches crackling. A pine bough slapped at her face and she jumped, and then brushed it aside. She heard a loud thump on the other side of a leafy bush. She pushed her way around and through the branches, listening as she neared the source of the noises, frightened of what she might see.

The sight that met her eyes horrified her.

Gunnar had been thrown twenty feet by the force of the train. He was fifteen feet farther down the track than where Laurie had landed when she jumped.

He had come to rest with his head and shoulders in a small bush. His legs, twisted and broken, were propped up on a rotting stump. One leg had been broken above the knee, jagged bone shining silver with black mottling in the moonlight; the other leg was horribly mangled and twisted with the lower half folded at a ninety-degree angle about mid-way down his shin.

At first sight, Laurie thought those were his only injuries, but then her eyes rested on the darkening patch in his abdomen. Part of his shirt had been torn away and Laurie could see soft tissue poking out through a gash that crossed his belly from one side to the other.

Laurie winced at the sight.

Gunnar's glassy eyes looked up at her as she approached. He tried to speak, but lacked the air in his lungs to give sound to his words.

Laurie reached for him and took his hand.

"Don't try to say anything. Just hang on." She could see the fear as she looked into his eyes, then his head lolled to the side as his body went limp.

"Oh no! You don't get off that easily. Whatever you've done you've got to face the music." She felt for a pulse in the soft, fleshy part of his

215

neck. A faint beat satisfied her touch. Gunnar was holding on. But for how long?

She heard the crunch of gravel nearby and looked toward the hulking shadow of the train. A darker shadow moved in front of it.

"Help! Help me!" she shouted. The shadow hesitated, and then bounded in her direction, accompanied by the crunch, crunch of the gravel.

"Are you...?" The engineer's eyes flickered from Laurie to Gunnar's limp form twisted in the undergrowth. "My God! Is he...?"

"He's still alive," Laurie announced. "Help me get him to the train. You can drive us to the street...."

"Drive you to the street? This ain't no ambulance, lady. Ain't no...."

"An ambulance could never reach us in time. If we don't move him to somewhere accessible, he'll die. Do you have something on that train to help carry him? A blanket maybe?"

The engineer hesitated a moment before answering. "A fire blanket."

"Great! Go!" Laurie commanded.

The engineer paused a moment, shock still upon his face, then spun around and ran for the engine. Laurie watched his shadow fade into blackness as he ran ahead down the track to where the engine had stopped and disappeared within.

She felt again for a pulse. It was the same as it had been five minutes before. Precious time was being lost, but at least his pulse was steady, if weak.

"Hang on, Gunnar," she encouraged softly. "Hang on."

The engineer returned, unfolding the dark mass of blanket as he ran back along the track. He shook the blanket out as he reached Laurie's side. She grabbed two corners and helped spread the blanket on the ground beside Gunnar's twisted form.

"You grab his legs around his thighs—above the break here." She pointed to the jagged bone. "I'll grab his shoulders and when I count to three, we'll lift him together and move him quickly to the blanket. Alright?"

The engineer nodded. He was middle-aged, but appeared strong. His bare arms bulged with muscle as he cupped rugged hands around Gunnar's thighs and waited for word from Laurie.

On Laurie's count, they lifted him and quickly slid him squarely onto the blanket.

Gunnar made no sound. He was unconscious — Laurie felt a pulse.

"Alright. Ready? We need to carry him with the blanket to the engine."

The engineer nodded and moved toward Gunnar's head. "No offense, little lady, but I oughta lift his upper half, being as my arms're a bit bigger than yourn."

Laurie observed the bulging biceps and nodded agreement, moving to Gunnar's feet. She grabbed two corners of the blanket and lifted in unison with the engineer. Gunnar was cradled in a cocoon as they half walked, half ran up the tracks toward the engine. They slid him carefully on to the floor of the engine compartment, and then Laurie climbed in and stood near his feet.

"Get this thing started. I'll call an ambulance."

The engineer nodded and got the diesel engine rolling slowly as Laurie punched numbers and held the phone to her ear.

"I have an emergency," she shouted into the phone, hoping to be heard over the roar of the engine.

"I have an officer struck by a train. Compound fracture to the left femur, and a tib-fib fracture in the right leg. Bringing him to Elm Street in the engine. Meet us there at the intersection of Elm and Stone Streets at the railroad tracks.

"Ten minutes? Make it five." Laurie disconnected the call and checked the pulse in Gunnar's neck — still steady, but faint.

"Hang on, Gunnar. I need an explanation and you're not leaving without giving me one."

The ambulance arrived in seven minutes and three paramedics swarmed toward the engine compartment. A police cruiser arrived a moment later, its blue strobes creating eerie movement as the paramedics collared Gunnar, rolled him onto a backboard and lifted him to a gurney where they went to work on evaluating him.

Another police cruiser arrived. Auburn had less than a dozen cars on the road, but Laurie suspected they would all arrive unless they were otherwise occupied. By the time the paramedics had Gunnar packed into the back of the ambulance and tied to an oxygen tank, Laurie was correct. The night was alive with flashes of blue and red.

She watched wordlessly as the ambulance doors closed and the red lights pulled away, and then she collapsed against one of the police cruisers.

# Chapter 24

S o, tell me what happened," Charlie put a hand on Laurie's shoulder to comfort her as he encouraged her out of the stupor she had been in since he picked her up from the Auburn Police Department nearly two hours ago. He had brought her home where she could be more comfortable to recall the details of her ordeal with Gunnar in the woods.

It was now one o'clock in the morning. Laurie had watched as the doctors had stabilized Gunnar at the hospital. His fit condition had saved his life, but they were unsure whether he would ever walk again. Both legs had suffered multiple fractures and they had said it was too early to know the extent of damage to his spinal cord. He was still unconscious.

Laurie had been unable to relate any details of what had happened between her and Gunnar. After the paramedics had driven away with Gunnar, she had gone into shock, and with her head still revolving from the effects of the alcohol and drug, she had curled herself up into a ball beside one of the police cruisers. The cold of the metal had been soothing and she'd stayed there until two officers lifted her by her arms and half-dragged, half-carried her to one of eight cars where they lifted her into the back seat and belted her in. She sat in a stupor as the car followed the path the ambulance had taken to the hospital. Then she asked to call Charlie.

"Laurie?" Charlie prodded her to speak.

Finally, awareness flickered in her eyes and she turned her face up to Charlie. He handed her a cup of coffee, which she took in both hands, comforted by its warmth.

"I know it sounds weird, but it was Gunnar. Gunnar is the killer."

"Laurie, are you sure? That's a nasty accusation if it's false. And Gunnar isn't able to defend himself right now; may never be able to defend himself."

Laurie stared at him as a tear rolled from the corner of each eye. She nodded.

"We went for drinks after the arrest of the academy robbers. He said he wanted to help get my mind off of Brandon." She paused and gingerly sipped her coffee. "Charlie, I only had four drinks in two hours and my head was spinning like I'd had three times that. I remembered that Gunnar had ordered me a drink while I was in the bathroom. Charlie, he must have slipped something into my drink."

Charlie kept his hand on her shoulder as he pulled a chair around and sat down beside her and gently pulled her head to his shoulder. He said nothing, but let her continue at her own pace.

She was crying now. "Why would he slip something into my drink unless he wanted to hurt me? And he stopped in the middle of nowhere and starts making moves on me. Why would he drug me and start moving on me like that? I told him to stop. I tried to push him away, but he held onto me, pushed me against the car. Charlie, he just wasn't the Gunnar I know. It was like he was suddenly someone else."

She sobbed and her coffee shook in her hands. Charlie gently took the mug from her and set it on the end table beside him.

"We all know how Gunnar is with women. He's a real womanizer—always looking for a new woman, a new thrill. Maybe he just decided to take it a step further. The point is you're safe now.

"Come on. Let me take you home." He stood and pulled her to her feet. "Can I call anyone to come stay with you? Should I call Jessie?"

Laurie shook her head and slipped away from him. She tried a smile, but it wouldn't happen.

"I think I'm going to just get some sleep. A ride home would be great. I'll be fine when my head stops spinning and I can focus on all this.

"I have to speak to Brandon in the morning. He's innocent, Charlie. We've got to cut him loose."

Charlie nodded and led her toward the door.

"You want me to call you in the morning?"

Laurie hesitated, and then looked up into his eyes.

"Right then," Charlie replied to her silent response. "I'll call you at seven. Make sure you're awake. If you need me to, I'll come around and pick you up, OK?"

She nodded. "My car's still back at the bar. If it's not too much trouble, could you give me a ride back to it?"

"In the morning, sure. Not now."

"No. Not now." Laurie climbed into Charlie's car and he closed the door. She laid her head back and closed her eyes as visions of Gunnar, twisted and bleeding appeared like a movie on the back of her lids.

It seemed a short ride to her house as she relived the night's events. She opened her eyes as the car came to a stop in her driveway.

"You alright?" Charlie asked ask he turned off the engine.

Laurie nodded and opened the door, stumbling out of the car. Charlie hurried around the car to help her.

"Come on. Let me help you inside." He put an arm around her waist to steady her. Inside, he led her to the bedroom, pulled the blankets back and helped her to lie down. He removed her shoes, pulled the blankets over her, and gently kissed her forehead like she was his daughter.

"See you in the morning."

He hit the light switches as he made his way to the door and left her house.

She was asleep before the last light was extinguished.

Brandon met Laurie's eyes with a cold and stony stare as she explained the incident with Gunnar. He was out of his cell, his cuffs removed. They sat across from each other at her desk where they had first met three months ago. There was no magic between them now.

"So, I guess you have your killer now. You don't need me anymore." Brandon spoke without emotion. His voice was an even monotone like he had studied lines and was now reciting them. "So, why do you still have me sitting here? Am I not free to go, or do you have some other crimes you'd like to throw my way?"

Laurie fought back tears that threatened to brim over her lids.

"I'm really sorry." What else could she say? It was obvious he no longer loved her; that he actually hated her. And he had every reason to after the things she had accused him of.

"I know you won't believe me, but I still love you. Even when I thought you had committed those crimes, I still loved you."

She met his eyes timidly.

He looked at her for a long moment before he said anything.

"How can you even say that to me?" he seethed. "I gave you every piece of my heart and you believed that I was a murdering rapist; a monster who took pleasure in cutting women to shreds. How can you now sit before me and tell me you love me? And how can you dare even consider that I might still love you? That is why we're sitting here, right? You're thinking I still love you?"

Laurie's nod was barely perceptible and her face flushed.

"I asked you to be my wife because I thought you were special, that you cared for and trusted me. I asked you to marry me because I loved and trusted you with every part of me. But I was wrong, wasn't I. You played me these last three months, then as soon as I ask for a real commitment, you look for any possible way out. Now that you've safely chased me away, you want me to think you love me. You need help, Laurie." His face flushed red as he fought to keep control of his anger.

Two detectives on the far side of the room looked in their direction, but made no move to intervene. The situation was heated, but under control.

"I-I-I'm sorry," Laurie stammered. "All the murders were happening in places where you and I had just been together or in my home town after I'd told you where I was from. I knew it had to be someone who knew me or was following me around. Then when the girl was killed in New Hampshire.... Well the napkin that was used to gag her came from the restaurant where we'd eaten. I remembered how drunk I felt and how fast I fell asleep. You could have danced on the bed for all I knew, I was dead until morning."

"Come on Laurie, you'd had a lot to drink that night. So did I. I passed out right after you did. How do you think I managed to drag myself out and pick up a girl in the condition I was in, much less have the strength to overpower and kill her? It makes no sense, Laurie. What it basically boils down to is that you didn't want to marry me. Even if it was only subconscious, you didn't believe in me. I can't believe you would think that I could propose marriage in one moment and turn around and take the life of that woman a few hours later. That's just sick."

"But what about the photos? What was I supposed to think about those photos?"

"Right. There's a thought. How did you even come to find a photo between my mattresses unless you were looking for it?"

"I told you how. I was laying on the bed."

"Right. That pathetic story again. You went there specifically to find something on me and Gunnar obliged you."

Laurie was silent. Brandon was right. She had looked for some fault in him and where there was none she made one. Granted it took a little unsolicited help from her partner, but if it hadn't been this, she would have found some other reason to push him away. He was right.

She twisted the diamond around on her finger, then slid it off and handed it to him. He took it sullenly and stood up from his seat.

"If there's nothing more, I'd like to go now."

Laurie nodded. She stood up without looking at him and led him toward the door. Her heart was breaking with each step, but she held her tears.

"Do you need a ride home?" she asked hoarsely.

"Spencer is in town. He flew out for a little support. I do have friends who have faith in me. I called him when they processed me. He should be waiting out back."

Laurie was silent, feeling the sting from his lashing. She did have faith in him, but it was too late for that now.

"You all right?" One of the detectives called out to her. "You want me to take him downstairs for you?"

Laurie shook her head. "Thanks, Jack, but I can handle this," she replied hoarsely. Jack nodded and went back to his work.

Laurie and Brandon rode the elevator together in silence. She couldn't bring herself to look up at him and she could feel that he likewise kept himself turned away from her. The car opened at the bottom floor and Brandon got off without looking back. Laurie punched the button and returned upstairs. There was still work to be done where Gunnar was concerned.

She pulled out the paperwork to write up a search warrant for Gunnar's apartment. She wasn't certain what they would find there, but she hoped there would be something to explain his actions.

She tried desperately not to think of Brandon as she filled out the paperwork, but her eyes filled uncontrollably and she laid her head down on her arms and let the tears flow.

Jack came to her side and laid a hand on her shoulder. He knew the whole story; everyone in the station did. He didn't understand how she could still be working on this case.

"Let me take care of this stuff," he insisted. "You go home and get some rest. Take a couple days. I'll explain it to the captain."

Laurie nodded and thanked him as quickly as she could. Then she wiped her eyes, gathered her things and left the station.

Jessie arrived in front of the little blue Cape and parked behind the lonely Camero in the driveway. The blue paint peeling from the aging clapboards seemed fitting somehow. Jessie was certain that she would find Laurie curled up on the sofa in front of the TV with an empty cup of hot chocolate watching reruns of *ER* or something equally pathetic.

She couldn't imagine how Laurie must feel. Brandon had seemed such an up-front, nice guy and totally in love with her right from the start. But all the evidence had pointed to him. A girl had to look out for herself, right? He couldn't be all that great if he didn't understand that, right? But Laurie would never go for that line of reasoning.

The best medicine would be to just let her cry and be supportive.

Jessie opened the door without knocking. She had her own key. Laurie was, as expected, dressed in sweatpants and a T-shirt lounging on the couch with the comforter from her bed. Reruns of the *Brady Bunch* played on the television, but Laurie wasn't really watching them. Jessie followed her empty gaze out the window. Worse than she had thought.

She closed the door quietly. "Hey, girl. How ya doin'?" she whispered.

Laurie jumped. She hadn't heard the door. She turned a tear-reddened face to greet her friend. Her voice crackled out a short greeting and she pulled the comforter tighter to her chin.

Jessie settled herself into the chair across from where she lay and leaned forward with her elbows upon her knees and her chin in the cup of her palms.

"It's not your fault, ya know."

Laurie said nothing for a moment. Her gaze was downcast. She could not look up into her friend's eyes.

"I could've believed in him. Isn't that what love is about?" She paused and continued to look down at the floor. I mean, I never even asked him if he was innocent. I just locked him up. I don't blame him for not ever wanting to see me again." She looked up at Jessie then. Her eyes were pleading for forgiveness, but Jessie knew there was nothing to forgive. How much would it take to convince Laurie of that?

"You had to look out for yourself. If he loved you at all, he would have to understand that. Look how many girls that lunatic, Gunnar, killed. Then he plants evidence in Brandon's condo? You've got to admit he was pretty smooth about it. How could you possibly know it was Gunnar? I mean, you've known Gunnar for years. You trusted him probably more than anyone, even me. Right? He was your partner. You worked with him just about every day. How could you not trust him?"

Laurie nodded. A fresh tear ran down her cheek. "That makes me feel worse. Knowing that one of the people I trusted most could be such a horrible person. I just don't get it. Am I that bad at judging character?"

"Nah. You've just had a bit of bad luck with guys. It really is an okay world out there. People are generally good; you just hafta keep your distance a little. Sometimes I think people are more comfortable with a little less trust. It's less pressure on them. They get weirder the more pressure you add. You and Brandon moved kinda fast to really get to know one another. I mean, do you really think it was smart to get engaged after only three months? You would probably have been married after less than a year of knowing each other. You know that's not enough time to really get to know someone. You'd probably be divorced before five years were up. You should probably *thank* Gunnar for saving you from that."

Laurie turned up a weak smile. "You're probably right, but it doesn't soften the heartache. It'll take some time for me to get over him."

"Who knows," Jessie added. "Maybe he'll come to his senses and call you to get back together." She shrugged her shoulders.

Laurie shook her head. "It wouldn't work the second time around. I think we would both have a difficult time believing in the other. It's over."

"You know the honest truth? I think I miss Gunnar even more than I miss Brandon," Laurie mused. It's funny, I never had a clue he even thought that way about me; not until Brandon and I started seeing each other. His attitude toward me seemed to change then. A lot of times I thought he was flirting with me, not just joking like he used to. It was really weird. But I still miss him, even if he did do all those horrible things. That's not the Gunnar I know. I almost hope they don't find anything else in his apartment. It'll just reinforce that side of him."

"Any word on his condition? Any improvements?"

Laurie shook her head. "He's in a coma. They're not sure how long it'll be before he wakes up."

"Will he wake up?"

"Not sure. He lost a lot of blood and had a lot of internal injuries. Amazing they were able to fix everything. They say his body will heal up alright. They're just not sure about his mind. Something about blood loss combined with the trauma."

"But he has a chance?"

"Yeah. He does." The corners of Laurie's mouth turned upward just a little. She looked up at Jessie and the pain in her eyes seemed to soften. "I think maybe I've had enough hot chocolate for now. Will you have a drink with me? I'd like to drink to Gunnar's recovery; even if I have to lock him up later." She sat up and tucked her feet under her.

Jessie's face brightened. "That's my girl. To Gunnar's recovery. What'll ya have?"

Laurie was only a social drinker and if she decided that she wanted a drink, it was because she had decided to be social again and join the world of the living. Three cheers to that!

The next morning, Charlie and Captain Rich Craig arrived at Gunnar's empty apartment. Of course they knew no one was home—Gunnar lived alone—but they had their search warrant in hand and a key from Gunnar's key ring he'd left in his car's ignition to let themselves in.

Gunnar's place was not large. It was the first-floor of a small duplex with two comfortably sized bedrooms, one of which Gunnar used as his office, a small living room, and a kitchen with enough room for a small table against the wall.

"I'll work the kitchen if you'll take the bedroom," Captain Craig suggested.

"Works for me," Charlie replied, pulling on a pair of latex gloves to keep from leaving his fingerprints in the apartment.

The bedroom was neat and tidy. The bed was properly made, or at least appeared to be. Charlie pulled open the dresser drawers and felt through items of clothing in each, but found nothing. Next, he turned to the closet. There were three pairs of shoes on the floor. Charlie lifted each pair and tipped them upside down to see if anything would fall out, but there was nothing.

He pulled down a couple shoeboxes from the closet shelf. Inside one were a couple belts neatly coiled. In the other, he found a hunting knife, a handgun, and box of ammunition. The knife resembled the description of the murder weapon as determined by the medical examiner. He took a plastic bag, collected the knife from the box and dropped it in, then replaced the box on the shelf.

Charlie felt between the sweaters stacked on the top shelf, but found nothing. He flipped through the hanging shirts, but still nothing. He closed the closet door and turned his attention to the rest of the room.

Laurie had found a photo between Brandon's mattresses. Charlie considered it was possible Gunnar was regular about his hiding places. He went to the bed and lifted the top mattress.

Several photos were spread across the box spring. Charlie threw the top mattress onto the floor and collected the photos.

"Hey Captain! I got something here!" he yelled.

Captain Craig came in from the kitchen and Charlie handed him a stack of photos. Each depicted a naked woman laying on her back, or a dead woman, butchered and bloodied. One photo included a section of the killer's abdomen as he stood over the woman, but it wasn't enough detail to clearly identify the killer other than that his abdomen was well-muscled and appeared hairless.

"Shit!" Captain Craig exclaimed. "I don't think I really believed Laurie's story that Gunnar attacked her until now."

"Yeah, sure looks like our boy is a psycho."

"Tragedy. He was a good cop."

# Chapter 25

Laurie's spirits didn't match the bright sunshine—another day without Brandon. Fellow officers looked at her differently than they had before all this. Almost like she was guilty too. But that was understandable. Gunnar was her partner. Cops knew their partners as well as they knew themselves. A partner was like an extension of oneself. A cop didn't simply overlook the fact that her partner was a murdering rapist. But Laurie might never know what drove Gunnar to the crimes he'd committed. Maybe the job had sent him over the edge, but whatever it was, Laurie should have known and now her fellow officers eyed her suspiciously. She was less of a cop to them; less of a detective. She'd failed to detect a lethal flaw in someone that close to her.

But there were others who were still in disbelief that Gunnar was even capable of such crimes. Some would never believe it was true despite the evidence they had uncovered at his apartment. Laurie wondered who thought she was a bad detective and who still held to Gunnar's innocence.

No one approached her about Gunnar's condition. She felt enormous guilt over his injuries. Regardless of the circumstances, Gunnar had been her friend. She had trusted him with her life and he had trusted her with his. But he had shattered that trust and now he was in a coma from which he might never awaken.

She couldn't understand how the partner she had known could have killed all those women, but the evidence was clear. The photos found in his apartment clearly pictured the dead women. And though the photos didn't clearly define the killer, those features that could be seen looked like Gunnar's. In one photo, the shutter had clicked just as he plunged the knife into his victim's chest. There was no question that the girl had died by his hand. The look of shock on her face as she experienced the pain of the blade was horrible to see.

Laurie shuddered to think what torture Gunnar might have put her through had the train not saved her from him. She remembered his face as he looked into her eyes, feeling he was about to die. She wondered what it was he'd wanted to say to her. He'd tried to speak, but blood in his throat and lungs prevented it. Now she might never know.

Maybe she needed to go see him. She hadn't been to the hospital since she followed the ambulance. Even if he couldn't hear her, she needed to speak to him. Needed to ask him why. She left the station and the accusing stares of the other officers and headed for the hospital. As she climbed into her car, her cell phone rang.

"Laurie Sharpe."

"It's Jessie. How're you feeling?"

"Guilty. Angry. I'm heading to the hospital. I need to see Gunnar."

"He won't hear anything you have to say."

"I don't care. I still need to say it."

"I know. I'll meet you there?"

"Alright." Laurie ended the call and put the car in gear.

Jessie joined her as she sat silently beside Gunnar's bed. Laurie looked up and returned her stare to Gunnar.

"It's not you're fault."

"Isn't it? Did I have to run that night?" A hoarse whisper was all that she could manage. "Would he really have hurt me? We worked so close together. I never knew him to hurt anyone." She shook her head again in disbelief.

"You can't keep beating yourself up like this. He was chasing you. You ran. End of story. You didn't put the train there." Jessie rubbed Laurie's shoulders to comfort her but it didn't help.

"You have the audacity to visit my son's bedside after the accusations you've made?"

Laurie and Jessie looked up as an angry-faced Mrs. Hincks stood in the doorway. Laurie had met Gunnar's mother only once before at a gathering of family and friends celebrating Gunnar's 30th birthday. She had impressed Laurie then as a strong woman who would let nothing and no one harm any member of her family.

Mrs. Hincks glared at her wordlessly, but then her expression weakened and she began to tremble visibly. Laurie guessed that this was as much as Mrs. Hincks would allow herself to weep, particularly in the company of near strangers, practically enemies. Her eyes remained dry as if no tears could possibly express her pain. Her soft round face seemed sculpted in polished white marble with no color in her cheeks or anywhere—fear and sorrow had drained it all away.

Finally, she spoke. "You know my son did not kill those women." Her voice cracked with age and emotion. "Gunnar didn't have a mean bone in his body. You knew him! How could you think that he could?" Her voice rose in a crescendo of warbling notes.

"I-I-I'm so sorry. I can't imagine how you must feel. I've always cared very much for Gunnar, but he attacked me. What else can I think? And the pictures. I'm sorry, but…" Laurie didn't know what else to say and her voice trailed off pitifully.

"They told me the man in that picture was mostly hidden. How could you be sure it was my son?" She wagged a threatening finger in Laurie's face. "Gunnar was framed. By who, I can't imagine. But, if you ever have cared for and trusted him as you say, you'll find out who really did this. Gunnar is a good man. Don't let his name be tarnished like this—not while he can't defend himself." The old woman's crackling voice finally turned into sobbing and she began to cry uncontrollably. The stone pillar had crumbled.

Laurie put a comforting hand on her shoulder and then pulled her into her arms. Gunnar's mother wept and shook until her tears once again ran dry. She pulled away from Laurie and looked her in the eye for a long moment.

"I don't know where to start, Mrs. Hincks, but I will do all I can to find out what really happened here. Gunnar is a good friend and my partner, and I would like nothing more than to know that he is innocent of all this."

"Then find who really killed those women!" She forced the words out angrily through a throat choked with emotion.

Laurie was desperate for her to understand. "But, Mrs. Hincks, they found pictures of the dying women in Gunnar's clutches. Why would he have those if he wasn't the man who committed those crimes? There were two dozen photos hidden in his apartment along with the murder weapon."

Laurie didn't know how she could be any gentler in reiterating the evidence she knew had already been explained to Mrs. Hincks, and Gunnar's mother became increasingly angry and hurt.

"If you have pictures, I want to see them," she nearly shouted. She looked Laurie squarely in the eye and Laurie's gaze faltered.

"They're horrible to see," she said softly. "Are you sure you really want to do that?"

The woman nodded. "I'll be by the station tomorrow morning to see you. I need time to be with my family today. They'll be by shortly to sit with Gunnar. I'd prefer it if you weren't here." She turned away from them and took a seat beside Gunnar's bed. Laurie and Jessie left without another word.

Mrs. Hincks was at the station promptly at 7:00 am. Laurie had arrived before her and was waiting with two steaming cups of coffee. The old woman graciously accepted hers with trembling hands. She sipped gingerly at the hot liquid for a moment, unable to speak. Laurie gazed sympathetically at her but could think of nothing to say.

"Thank you for taking the time to do this for me. I know everyone here has condemned my son, but I'm sorry, I just can't let that happen. He's a good boy and I know he was a good cop. I just can't let him lie in disgrace. He may never wake up and I don't want this hanging over him."

Laurie nodded silently. Gunnar was a good cop; she couldn't dispute that.

"As I said, these photos we have are extremely graphic. Perhaps you want to take a few moments before you see them."

Gunnar's mother took a long drink from the cooling cup. "I don't think I will get any more ready. I'm an old woman, but I've seen plenty in my day. I played nurse in Vietnam. It doesn't get any more graphic than that. That's where I met Gunnar's father, you know. He came to me with a bullet in his leg. Told me I was the most beautiful thing he'd seen in four months. Course that wasn't saying much considering he'd been out in the jungle fighting for his life. He told me some of what he had experienced in those four months. It would make your stomach turn."

She sipped again at her coffee and looked for a place to sit. Laurie led her to her own desk and pulled out a weary old chair that seemed to emulate the old woman.

"Anyway," she continued, "Mr. Hincks was the kindest, warmest man I'd ever met. He saw me shaking at the sight of his leg all torn apart—I'd only been there two days—and he started cracking jokes to make me laugh. Here was this boy in so much pain and he was worried about making me laugh. He was much younger than I was, by a full ten years. But he was far older than I was for all he'd seen. He got me laughing so hard I forgot where I was.

"He went home after a couple weeks, but he left me his address and phone number. I wrote to him for the next year and then, when I returned to the states, I came to see him here in Massachusetts; I lived in Ohio at the time; and we got married.

"Mark was a good man and a good husband and father. I lost the best part of my life when he died. A heart attack took him in his sleep about twelve years ago. Gunnar was nineteen." Mrs. Hincks sighed heavily.

"My boys are everything to me. Now all I have is Peter." She looked painfully into Laurie's eyes. "Help me prove Gunnar's innocence," she pleaded.

Laurie nodded sympathetically. It was all she could do. What could she ever find to counter the damning evidence they already had against Gunnar? She reached into her desk drawer and pulled out an envelope. It was thick with photographs. Laurie handed it to the old woman, who opened it and, setting her jaw, began leafing through the photos one by one.

Laurie could see tears welling in the old woman's eyes as she laid each picture on the desk. She also could see Gunnar through the disguise. Then, suddenly, halfway through the stack, she stopped. She set the remaining photos on the desk and held one solitary picture in her hand.

The photo depicted the killer atop the New Hampshire victim as she was gagged with the red and white-checkered napkin. The camera was very close here. The details of the killer and his victim were very clear. Mrs. Hincks tapped the killer's abdomen where it was exposed to the camera's flash. Her hand shook and she looked up at Laurie, a tiny smile on her shriveled lips.

"When Gunnar was five," she began, "he was a regular little monkey. He was always out climbing trees in the back yard and everywhere else. One day, I looked out my window just as a limb he was climbing out on snapped. He fell down through the limbs below and eventually landed feet-first, just like a cat, on the ground. I dropped what I was doing and ran out to him. His shirt was covered with blood by the time I reached him. One of the branches had caught him in the ribs and ripped a hole in him. It took forty stitches to put him back together at the hospital. Left him a nasty scar. Didn't stop him climbing trees, though." She smiled at the memory.

She held the photo out to Laurie, pointing to the man's chest. "That scar was right here. It's faded over the years, but I know right where it is and there's nothing on this man like that. This is not a photo of Gunnar." Her thin smile widened a little and a tear formed in the corner of her eye.

Laurie studied the photo. The detail was so vivid that she could discern freckles on the man's abdomen, but there certainly was no scar.

"Are you sure the scar didn't fade completely?"

Gunnar's mother nodded. "See for yourself when you visit his bedside next. You'll see this is not him. Gunnar is innocent."

"I will, though I don't think it's necessary."

Laurie accompanied Mrs. Hincks out of the station. Her mind was reeling. If Gunnar was not the man in the photographs, then it *had* to be Brandon since she had found the original photos in his condo.

The two men looked so much alike. The few features that were visible on the killer in the photos could easily belong to either man. Why didn't she think of it before? When they'd released him from custody, Brandon must have broken in and planted the photos and knife in Gunnar's apartment to cement the case against him and clear away any other suspicions of his own guilt.

It had worked, too. Most of the officers at the department had been unwilling to believe Laurie's story that Gunnar had attacked her; was chasing her. Hell, she had hardly believed it herself. But when the photos, the hunting knife and all the other evidence turned up in his apartment, everyone was convinced and Gunnar was convicted since he was not able to defend himself.

Only the presence of the bloodstained jeans in the dryer was never fully explained. When he was interrogated, Brandon had insisted they were not his and wasn't sure where they had come from. Later, before they released him, Charlie asked him again about the jeans and he had suggested maybe Gunnar had left them in there.

The day after he and Laurie returned from New Hampshire, Gunnar had come out to his condo to cast a line or two into the water while they sipped on a few beers and he had accidentally knocked his pole into the water as it was leaning against one of the dock's pilings. Gunnar removed his shoes, rolled up his jeans as well as he could, and waded in to retrieve the pole, but the water was up over his knees.

Gunnar happened to have clean clothes in his car, having been to the Laundromat, and changed his pants. Brandon had offered for Gunnar to put the wet jeans in the dryer while they finished another beer on the balcony, but he wasn't certain if Gunnar had done so, since he was already out on the balcony when Gunnar had finished changing. If he did dry them, it's possible he had forgotten to take them with him.

The photos he'd said were anyone's guess. Maybe Gunnar had put them between the mattresses temporarily while the pants were in the dryer. Brandon said he had no idea how they got there, and after she thought Gunnar had drugged her and he had taken her out to the woods, Laurie believed Brandon's explanations and was eager to release him.

Now how could she prove that Brandon was really the killer? What did she really know about him? He had told her very little about himself. All she knew was his work. He had told her very little about his childhood or his family. She only knew that he had grown up in northern California. His father was rarely home and both parents had died in a car accident when he was twenty. He inherited everything they owned, having been an only child. Now he was well off with his own consulting company and a condo at either end of the country.

Laurie decided to start with Brandon's hometown. She picked up the phone and called the police department there.

The dispatcher who answered the phone sounded young and inexperienced, so Laurie asked for the most senior detective. The line was transferred and a man with an aging voice answered at the other end.

Detective Jones had been on the Susanville police force since he was twenty-one. He was now fifty-one. He had seen the small town through many years and he had a long memory, despite his age. Even though his voice failed him at times, his mind was sharp.

"Detective Jones, have you ever heard of Brandon Doyle or his parents, John and Sara Doyle?"

There was a pause at the other end.

"I remember Sara was on our bowling league. She was the only woman at that time. Took a lot of guts for her to push her way in like she did. She was better than most of us too, and I'm glad she was always on my team. Real nice lady." He paused and Laurie could hear coughing at the other end of the line.

The detective continued. "John was never around much. He was a salesman for a local company. I forget the name. He was always on the road. Their boy, Brandon, could have used a bit of fatherly discipline. Would have kept him out of trouble."

Laurie's ears burned at this. "Was Brandon a delinquent?" she asked.

"He got himself into a fair bit of scrapes. Turned punk in high school. Before that, Sara swears he was always a good boy. But in high school, he turned into a real little hellion." There was a pause at the other end as Detective Jones pulled out an old file with the name Doyle on it. Laurie could hear the shuffling of papers.

"Lookin' at Brandon's file here, we have files on everyone we've had come through here, we had him in for shopliftin' at a convenience store, joyriding a bunch o' times, several instances of fighting in a public place. Lotsa little stuff. Oh, and here's a really old note here. We questioned him in the murder of a girl he dated, Karen Callahan. Just questioned him, though. He seemed pretty broken up to hear about it, and we never found any evidence to implicate him."

The detective droned on, but Laurie's heart had stopped dead. She felt her breathing fail her for a moment, and then she forced herself to speak, interrupting the detective as he continued on through Brandon's file.

"C-C-Could you describe the details of the murder?" The detective stopped talking for a moment. The silence was deafening as Laurie waited for his answer.

"Well, now that's one I don't even need to pull up a file on," he drawled out slowly. "We don't have many crimes of that sort in this here town. And I have never seen anything like it since." He paused again as he collected his thoughts and turned his mind back in time toward the grisly scene at the pond.

Detective Jones had been the patrolman who discovered Karen's slashed and bloodied, lifeless body laid out on the diving rock at the pond. The age disappeared from his voice as he described the horror of the scene still fresh in his mind.

"They weren't able to pull enough physical evidence from the body to make a solid case and since they had no witnesses, they were never able to find the killer, though they did interview several boys who had dated her, including Brandon. She was quite a beauty; usually had more than one boy around her little finger at a time. We figured one of 'em got jealous. Terrible way for someone so young to die.

"Anyway, the Callahan family was so broken up over her death that they moved out of town the following year and no one had heard from them since. I do have information on their whereabouts should there ever be any further progress if you need to contact them."

"No, thanks. I don't think I'll be needing that." Laurie already knew who had killed Karen Callahan.

"Could you send me copies of the files on Karen and on Brandon?"

"Sure, glad to help. I'll send 'em out to you in the overnight mail."

"You wanna share some detail of what you're working on that involves Brandon?"

"I'd love to, Detective Jones, but I can't just yet. But I promise, as soon as I know any more of Brandon's involvement in things out here, I'll give you all the details. I'm sure Karen's parents would like some closure."

"This has something to do with Karen?"

"I'm not sure, but I think it might."

"Well, then, Detective. I will certainly be waiting on your call. Don't forget about me."

"Oh, I won't. Thanks for your help. I'll look for that file tomorrow." Laurie replaced the receiver in its cradle and sat back in her chair.

The room around her was empty and she felt a cold chill pass through her bones. She had been in love with a killer. She had promised herself to a man who tortured, raped, and killed women for a thrill. Or was it a thrill? What could possibly drive such a seemingly wonderful man to commit such heinous and grisly crimes?

The weight of what she had learned crashed down upon her and crushed what remained of her belief in human goodness and in love. She wondered if she could ever again believe in any man. Dating had not gone well for her in the past, but this shattered her beyond comprehension. She fought with emotions that were suddenly seeking to tear her apart and her body began to shake uncontrollably.

Laurie stood and walked toward the vending machine, fishing for change in her pocket. A sugar fix might make her feel better. She threw the coins down the slot and pushed the appropriate button. The Snickers bar moved toward her and stopped as it always did, with one corner pinned in the rack. Laurie cursed and kicked the machine. Then she pulled it over as casually as if it were an empty cardboard box and stormed out of the room, leaving the machine where it lay.

Laurie called Jessie to share the story Gunnar's mother had told her about her son's scar. She also relayed her suspicions about Brandon, which Detective Jones had renewed when he told her about Brandon's murdered girlfriend.

"Are you sure you're not just looking for a way to get back at him for breaking your heart?"

"Yes, I'm sure. You met them both. Maybe you never saw them together, but think about it. Didn't they look alike?"

"I suppose, but I think you're grasping at straws. I know Gunnar is your partner and all, but how would all that stuff have gotten into his apartment?"

"I don't know how, but I think somehow, Brandon planted it after Gunnar got hit. I mean there was a whole day between Brandon's release and the search of Gunnar's apartment. It's not unlikely that he could have broken in and planted the stuff there since he knew that we all suspected Gunnar anyway after what happened. Seeing that stuff there would just cement the case against him and clear Brandon."

"But you said Gunnar tried to rape you that night. How can you overlook that?"

"Jess," Laurie paused, afraid to tell anyone, even her best friend, why she suspected she felt drugged that night.

"What is it, Laurie?"

"Well, the thing is, I don't really know what Gunnar's intentions were that night."

"What do you mean you don't know?" Jessie interrupted. "Laurie, the man attacked you and chased you through the woods. He almost had you, too. What sort of man brings a woman to the woods, makes a move, and then chases her when she turns him down? And you said he drugged you too."

"I'm just not sure anymore, Jessie. I mean Gunnar made a pass at me, sure. He brought me someplace other than home, true. But it was on the way to my house, after all. Maybe he thought that if he took me somewhere that I couldn't just shut him off and run inside, he might have a chance in making a move on me and getting me to feel the same way about him. Still a little twisted, I guess. I don't know. I guess what he did was poor judgment, but I'm not so sure he meant to hurt me."

"But what about the drugs? Did he drug you or did you have more to drink than you thought?"

"Jess, I haven't said this to anyone, and I'm not sure if I could, really, but I had a headache that night and I think maybe I took a sleeping pill instead of ibuprofen at the bar."

Jessie's silence at the other end of the line told Laurie she was stunned so she continued, desperate to explain.

"I always keep a sleeping pill in my pocketbook for when I stay the night away from home and can't sleep. I sometimes had trouble sleeping at Brandon's. Anyway, last night I went to get it because the bottle in the house was empty. With all that's been happening lately, I guess I've needed help sleeping just about every night. Anyway, I was pretty sure I had one in my pocketbook, but it was gone. Jess, I'm worried I might have jumped to conclusions about Gunnar. I'm worried that I put him in that coma by running away. I'm worried that he didn't deserve to get hurt that night."

"Laurie, do you know what you're saying?"

"Yes, and you can't repeat it to anyone.

"I think I was still in love with Brandon and was hoping there was someone else responsible for those awful crimes. When Gunnar interrogated him, Brandon accused Gunnar of framing him because Gunnar was jealous over me. Then when Gunnar started hitting on me while I was feeling groggy after only a few drinks with him, well, I thought..." Laurie couldn't finish. The realization that she had precipitated her friend and partner's coma for no reason was too harsh to bear.

"So, he never attacked you?" Jessie asked, horrified.

"I think it was all just a matter of coincidence and poor timing. Maybe Gunnar just didn't want to lose the chance to tell me he had feelings for me. After all, I had been going to marry Brandon—that would have been it for him. But after we found the evidence against Brandon, I was suddenly free and he wanted to tell me before someone else came into my life. Some guys don't realize they love someone until their chance to tell them is gone. Maybe that was Gunnar."

"But why would he chase you into the woods?"

"I don't know. He made a pass at me, I accused him of being the murderer and asked if he drugged me, then I took off and he came after me." Laurie ran a shaky hand through her hair. "It sounds pretty lame, doesn't it? I mean, he would come after me in the middle of the woods, wouldn't he? He wouldn't just leave me there in the dark. I don't know what I was thinking." Tears formed and threatened to spill over onto her cheek.

"Gunnar's in a coma because I was looking for any way to believe Brandon was innocent. I killed him," she sobbed.

Jessie soothed across the telephone line. "It's not your fault. You don't know what he was thinking. Like you just said, it was poor judgment on his part. He should have taken you home."

Laurie shook her head. "The only way I can make this right is to bring Brandon in. No one would believe at this point that it wasn't Gunnar. They'd think we were just protecting one of our own."

"What are you gonna do?" Jessie asked anxiously.

"I'm not sure, but I'll let you know." She hung up the phone and buried her face in her hands.

# Chapter 26

Brandon's file arrived along with the file on the murder of Karen Callahan. Laurie tore open the express package and threw the wrapping into the trash then set aside Brandon's folder and opened the murder file first. An eight by ten photograph of the living girl was the very first item inside the cover. Laurie froze when she saw it and her hands began to shake uncontrollably.

"You alright?" Charlie saw the blood drain from her lips and thought she looked ready to pass out. He walked over and put a hand on her shoulder to steady her.

He saw the photograph, but said nothing then took the file from her trembling hands, and set it on a nearby desk.

"Looks a lot like you," he commented as he pulled a chair over and gently guided her into it.

He was troubled by the similarity though he didn't know what Laurie was working on that would have a photo on file of someone who resembled her. Still, Charlie kept concern from showing on his face. Laurie looked frightened enough for both of them.

She nodded fearfully before she could find her voice to explain the photo and answer the question she knew was in Charlie's mind.

Finally, she nervously began the story that Detective Jones had shared with her yesterday.

"This was Brandon's girlfriend back in high school. Her name was Karen Callahan." She paused, clearing her throat. Charlie looked at her with the best calming expression he could muster. He knew Laurie did not frighten easily and he could see she was scared to death.

"Was?" he asked.

Laurie nodded and continued. "They found her body naked and butchered with several stab wounds and her throat cut."

Charlie winced.

"One other important detail, Charlie. They found her lying on her back, with her limbs all spread out."

"Same MO as Wilson and the other girls you found around here?"

Laurie nodded. "Exactly the same, including the lack of damning physical evidence like semen, though she was definitely raped."

"So how does Brandon come into all this, other than that his girlfriend looks like you?"

"Since he was her boyfriend at the time, they questioned him along with a few other boys she had dated. They could never get enough evidence on any of them to suggest that one was her killer. But now it seems pretty certain that it was Brandon."

"My God!" Charlie exclaimed in a hoarse whisper. "You know what this means?"

Laurie nodded slowly, a tear making its way down her cheek as she responded, "It means Gunnar is in a coma for no reason and we've set the real killer free to continue his game."

"We've got to stop him, Laurie, but we need evidence. Everything we have could point to either Gunnar or Brandon equally, since evidence was found in both their homes. We know now that it was planted in Gunnar's place, but just knowing would never hold up in court. If we brought Brandon in now and charged him, he would walk, and then he'd be immune from further prosecution because of double jeopardy rules. But of course you know all that. So, you got any ideas?" Charlie asked.

"Follow him around?"

"Now that's harassment. You know you can't just follow him around. Not to mention, since you two were dating, he could say it's stalking if he sees you."

"I mean, we keep him under surveillance. Maybe we can even bait him. I mean, do you think he'd recognize me if I was disguised? I could get him to pick me up in a bar. Try to be his next victim."

"Yes, he would recognize you. And even if he didn't, you know that could be really dangerous, Laurie. Not to mention, this guy's choice of venue seems to be completely random."

"I know. You're right, Charlie, but I have to do something to clear Gunnar's name. I promised his mother. I'm responsible for his situation, I'm responsible for making things right or at least as right as they can be. Will you help me?"

"Of course I will, but this should really go through the proper channels. Let me talk to the Captain about it. He'll determine if it warrants additional manpower, which would be nice since we can't sit on him twenty-four, seven just the two of us. Captain Craig isn't Gunnar's biggest fan, but I'm sure he'll do the right thing and give me a few guys to help with surveillance.

"I'll fill him in on Gunnar's scar and show him the photos that demonstrate the killer didn't have that scar. That should be enough evidence for me to convince the Captain our killer is still out there. He won't be happy to hear it, but he'll have to act."

"Just make sure I'm part of this." Laurie stated forcefully. She could tell by the references to what he planned to do, with nothing about what her role would be, meant Charlie was trying to shoulder her out. He undoubtedly thought it was for her own good, but she wouldn't let it happen. Gunnar's good name was her responsibility.

"Don't push me out," she warned, "because I need to do this."

Charlie was taller than her by a few inches, but she stood up to him, her face close enough to his that she could feel his steady breaths as he met her determined gaze with a stony expression.

He knew he'd have a fight on his hands getting her to sit on the bench for this one. But she'd been through so much in the past few weeks; he had to look out for her. How much more could she take?

"Laurie," he began.

"Charlie, don't push me out." She set her jaw. "I mean it. I'll work this with you or on my own, but I'm not sitting out for this one. You can't make me."

Charlie tried to stare her down, but her gaze did not waver. Finally, he sighed, stepped back out of her face, and held out his hand. Laurie smiled relief and grasped it, giving it a firm shake.

"Thanks, Charlie."

Charlie nodded. "But let me talk to the Captain, will ya? If you bring this to him, he's gonna attack you for telling everyone Gunnar was our guy. It'll be better if I tell him what Mrs. Hincks said. Alright?"

"Sure." Laurie knew he was right. Her credibility was on thin ice right now. After this, everyone would be second-guessing any conclusions she made for a long time. And she didn't think she would make it worse by sharing her suspicions about having accidentally taken a sleeping pill that evening. That information she would keep between herself and Jessie. And she knew she could trust her friend.

"You wait here. I think I saw Captain Craig around his office. I'll go see if I can catch him." Charlie hurried out of the room.

Laurie sat at her desk while she waited for Charlie to work out the details. She opened the Callahan file once more and picked up Karen's photo, gazing into the two-dimensional eyes as she remembered back to the day she had first met Brandon less than a week after Abra Wilson's body was left on display.

How had Brandon just happened to call her line that day? Was it just coincidence? What about Abra Wilson? Was that also coincidence that he would commit a murder in her jurisdiction less than a week before he called her? Was he trying to get her attention even before they met?

Raised voices drifted to her from the direction of Captain Craig's office. She could distinguish the voices, but not the words. She wanted to go stand right outside, but Captain Craig was known for throwing his door open during arguments to order the person he was angry with to leave. Laurie didn't want to be caught listening at the door like a child. Charlie was right—she needed to stay under the Captain's radar for a while.

Finally, Charlie emerged from the bullfight, his face red and beads of perspiration on his forehead. He closed the door softly behind him, as if afraid to break the new silence, breathed a sigh of relief, and gave Laurie a winning smile.

Laurie smiled back.

"Before you get all excited, I gotta warn ya—he's not happy with you, but he did agree to at least allow you to be involved in this case—I think I lost a couple strips of hide winning that argument. You're in the background, though. You're not running things. It was enough just to keep you from being suspended."

"Thanks." Laurie looked shamefully at the floor.

"We got two guys 'round the clock for surveillance. We have to keep 'em out of sight. If Brandon sees us following him, he could claim harassment and we could face suit, press, or at the very least, get busted back to traffic duty."

Laurie nodded.

"Surveillance starts with you and me tonight. He'll have Jack and Paul relieve us at eleven if there's nothing going on."

"Do we get a car? Something he won't recognize?"

"Yeah. We're heading out in the Mustang. You ready?"

"Let's go." She closed the Callahan file on her desk and joined him heading toward the door.

The Mustang, an inconspicuous silver color, was a year old and devoid of any indications that it was a police vehicle, save for the tip of antenna that poked up through the fiberboard and fabric that covered the gap between the back seat and rear window. The car was used regularly for undercover and surveillance operations and both Charlie and Laurie knew its capabilities as well as its shortcomings.

"Mind if I drive?" Charlie asked.

"Not at all. I think he'll be less likely to spot me if I'm not in the driver's seat and he's only seen you a couple times."

"Right."

It was after three o'clock so they stopped at Boston Market to grab a couple sandwiches before they tied themselves down into a surveillance that might keep them away from anything resembling food until they were relieved at eleven.

Brandon's car was outside his condo, so Laurie and Charlie pulled onto a small side street that offered them a clear view of the entrance to the parking lot and waited.

"So how are you holding up with all this weight you've got on you?" Charlie asked, unwrapping his turkey sandwich.

"You trying to say I'm fat, Charlie? I'm not giving up this sandwich to you." Laurie joked to postpone the conversation she really didn't want to have. She wanted to forget about Brandon and to forgive herself for Gunnar's coma.

Charlie grinned. "Laurie, I don't think you've ever had a single ounce of useless flesh on you. No come on, you know what I'm referring to, so out with it."

Laurie sighed—Charlie would never back down from this.

"Truth is, I think I'm going to need some time off when this is all over to pull my head back together.

"Charlie, why do I have so much trouble with men?"

Charlie looked at her silently for a moment, unsure how to respond. Laurie certainly didn't deserve all that had happened to her recently and he really didn't want to speculate on a reason why bad times kept coming her way.

"You've had more than you share of bad luck lately," he soothed. "I'm sure you're due for something good to happen."

"Thanks, Charlie, but that doesn't really answer my question."

"Sorry, Laurie, I don't really have an answer for you. But it's not because you deserve the worst luck if that's what you're wondering. I mean, if I was a bit younger and hadn't met my wife, I'd jump on you in a heartbeat."

Laurie giggled then rolled her eyes. "Having men who want to jump on me isn't exactly the problem, Charlie."

"I know, but I got you to laugh."

Laurie smiled.

"You know the right guy is out there. Just don't be afraid to keep your eyes open."

Laurie nodded and looked toward the condos.

"Talk about keeping your eyes open," she pointed out the windshield. "There goes Brandon."

She checked her watch and marked the time on a small notepad.

"Well, let's get to work."

Charlie started the engine and put the car in gear. He pulled out a couple hundred feet behind Brandon's Mercedes and followed at a casual distance. Traffic was light, so he didn't think there was much chance of Brandon shaking the tail unless he noticed them.

Their target headed east on Route 9 towards Boston.

"You think he's going out to Boston?" Charlie asked.

"Maybe, although he once said that before he met me, he never got out to Boston much. He's probably headed out to eat, considering it's about seven o'clock."

"He eats alone?"

"Hates to cook for one. Brandon almost never had anything in the refrigerator unless he knew I was coming over."

"Maybe he's meeting someone?" Charlie asked.

"Could be. I don't know what his dating habits were before he met me. It wasn't something we talked that much about. Maybe I've been replaced."

"Honey, you know you're irreplaceable."

"Thanks, Charlie. I wish that were true, but I'm a realist."

"Well, don't be too disappointed. He's not anyone you want to drop your guard around, remember?"

"Right."

They traveled away from Worcester a few miles, to Westborough where the blue Mercedes turned right into a Chinese Restaurant and pulled in to park near the rear of the building. It was the same restaurant he had taken Laurie to on their first date.

"I hope this isn't a sign he's made us. Drive past the restaurant," Laurie commanded.

"What's up? I thought you said he likes to eat alone."

"That's where we went on our first date. It just seems a little too nostalgic, ya know?"

"Relax. He's not even paying any attention to us. He hasn't even looked back at traffic."

Charlie pulled into a lot a few stores beyond the restaurant and turned the car around so they could look back to where Brandon had stopped. He had already disappeared inside.

"Alright. Let's sit here and wait for him. He can't go anywhere we can't follow because there's no passage to nine west between there and here, so he's got to pass us."

"Sounds like a safe plan," Laurie agreed.

An hour passed and then two before they began to worry. Brandon had gone inside alone. It was unlikely he would take two hours to eat by himself.

"You think he came here to meet someone?" Charlie asked; his eyes focused on the restaurant.

"Maybe. The man's not without friends. He often used to go out to meet up with friends here or there when we were dating. He even hung out with Gunnar a few times. Maybe he stayed to listen to the band that starts playing at nine o'clock."

"What do you think we should do?" Charlie turned toward her, awaiting a response.

Laurie met his gaze uncertainly. "One of us could go in there and see what he's up to."

"I could do it, he'll see you," Charlie suggested.

"Charlie, he knows you too, remember? I think he might be suspicious of your showing up alone for a few drinks, since he knows you're not really the type. If he sees me, though, I can just tell him I'm waiting for Jessie. You get to watch the door in case he slips out."

"The Captain was probably right. We know this guy too well to tail him."

"That could be, but on the other hand, his seeing me might anger him into action. I don't think it's good to stay out here, not knowing what he's up to in there. I don't want him killing anyone else, especially right under our noses."

"Alright, you can go."

"Thanks, Dad," Laurie chided.

"If I'm not out in an hour and I haven't called to check with you, come find me. I can only claim I'm waiting on Jessie for so long before he gets suspicious."

Charlie nodded.

Laurie pulled open the heavy, green door and stepped inside. The restaurant was nearly empty, but the lounge had gathered an assorted crowd. Men were dressed for construction work, or in suits, or wearing jeans and casual clothing, and women were in skirts or dresses or jeans with dressy blouses. Laurie was glad for the blazer she'd worn with her jeans. At least she looked like she'd planned a night out.

She weaved her way through the crowd, ignoring the stares of leering men, to a point where she could see the bar and most of the lounge. She scanned the large wooden bar that spanned the entire left wall and had, over the years, been covered in several coats of glossy polyurethane. The right side of the lounge was set up with tiny tables where couples could sit with their drinks and snacks or appetizers—the kitchen still served those until midnight.

She didn't see Brandon, but she saw an unlikely empty seat at the bar and made her way toward it, weaving and muscling her way through the throng.

About halfway to her destination, her legs went weak and her stomach quivered. Sitting at the bar beside the empty seat was Brandon.

She hesitated in her approach, not wanting to take the seat immediately beside her quarry, but he'd already spotted her and their eyes met in the mirror behind the bar so it was too late to slip back into the crowd. Laurie paused a moment, regained her composure, and proceeded to the bar, sitting down confidently beside the man she'd once loved.

Brandon turned his head in her direction, and then casually, unimpressed with her presence, he looked away.

"What are you doing here?" he asked, facing the back wall of the bar, avoiding her gaze in the mirror. "I told you I didn't want to see you again. We really are through and there's nothing more to say about it. I'm thinking of selling my condo in Worcester and leaving the state. The farther I am from you, the better."

Laurie said nothing for a moment. She hadn't really thought of anything she might say to him when and if she saw him again.

"I didn't come here looking for you, and in fact I'm really surprised to run into you like this. I didn't see your car out front or I probably wouldn't have come in. Well, unless I wasn't able to get a hold of Jessie. I'm supposed to be meeting her here."

"Oh, cut the bullshit, Laurie," Brandon blasted. "My car's toward the back but it's pretty easy to spot it from the front."

"Get over yourself, it's not like I would know to look for you here even if I was looking for you. We were only here once, on our first date. You never brought me here after that."

"A little nostalgic then?" he taunted. "Look, Laurie. I loved you and you let me down. You didn't have any faith in my innocence. You should have known I wasn't capable of the things your partner did."

Laurie wanted to lash out in response; wanted to defend Gunnar, but she knew she couldn't. If she did, Brandon would know she still suspected him and they would never catch him on anything.

"What would you have done in my shoes? If you found lots of reasons mounting on each other that suggested the next time you went to sleep beside me, you might not wake up. Do you really think you'd still have had me sleep over? Do you really think you'd even bother to call me again? You'd probably run and hide."

"I would have come to you face to face if I had any doubts about you at all. That's what you do when you love someone. You don't go behind their back and start digging through their things. Did Gunnar put you up to that? Did he send you over to my house to snoop? Or maybe he was with you helping; making sure you found the photos he left?"

"Don't kid yourself, Brandon. If you can't understand that the evidence painted you as a killer and I had to protect myself as well as do my job, then you never really did love me. There are a lot of nuts and whackos out there. What if you were one of them?" And you are one of those whackos, you son of a bitch, Laurie thought. "Should I just let you slit my throat while I'm sleeping because you said you loved me? How could I be sure if it had been you who killed those women that you wouldn't just cut me up like one of them? I had to protect myself," she repeated.

She ordered herself a beer as the bartender passed by, interested by their heated words. He noted Laurie's good looks and hoped she might be available later for a little comforting by him after she dumped this guy.

"But as we all know now, I didn't kill anyone. You broke my heart over a false assumption and didn't even care that I got hurt. And now you're chasing me around like a lost puppy looking for another chance to do it again." Brandon sipped his drink and faced forward. It hurt to have her so close beside him yet be unable to touch her. He so desperately wanted to touch her, but he refused to allow himself. He could never let her back into his heart.

"Maybe I should find myself a different place to drink my beer," Laurie snapped. She slid off her stool, angry with herself for wanting Brandon to stop her from leaving. He didn't.

She abandoned her nearly full beer on a table near the door and left the lounge, eager for the door and fresh air, and filled her lungs with its sweetness as the darkness wrapped her in comfort. Then, feeling Charlie's questioning eyes upon her, she turned and walked toward the car.

Laurie said nothing as she climbed into the Mustang and Charlie stared at her silently for a moment.

"So he spotted ya, huh?"

"Worse," Laurie replied sullenly.

"Came over and spoke to ya?"

"Even worse."

Charlie was speechless.

"I spotted an empty seat at the bar so I was on my way over there when I realized Brandon was in the seat next to it. I was about to turn and run when he spotted me in the mirror. What could I do? I had to sit and make up a bogus story about why I was there before I could leave."

"He didn't go for it, did he?"

"He thinks I'm chasing him like a lost puppy. Like I would even stoop to something so childish."

"Well, not unless your Captain ordered ya to."

There was a heavy silence before Laurie broke into giggling. It felt good to laugh at something that was otherwise tearing her heart to pieces.

"Well it's Captain's orders that we stay til we're relieved at eleven, so you also get to see if he picks up another woman. Can you handle it?"

"Yeah, Charlie." She turned and smiled tentatively at him. "I think I can handle it."

Another hour passed before patrons began to trickle out of the restaurant a few at a time. Finally, at ten-thirty, Brandon emerged beside a young woman.

She appeared to be about twenty-five; attractive, businesslike, with wavy, dark hair and wire-framed glasses that gave her a distinguished, snobbish look. She had her arm through his and staggered as she walked with him toward his car.

Laurie's heart was in her throat.

"You alright?" Charlie asked as he saw the color drain from her cheeks.

Laurie didn't hear him—her ears buzzed with anger.

"Come on, Laurie." He nudged her shoulder. "You alright?"

Finally, she nodded. "I'm fine. I'm just frightened for that girl. She has no idea what she's dealing with. And I guess I was hoping nothing would happen while it's our shift. Now I might have to witness first-hand what he can do."

"We're not there yet. Hang on." Charlie threw the transmission into reverse and backed up between the buildings to wait, unseen, until they drove past.

Five minutes passed, then ten. Still Brandon's car had not come by.

The two-way radio sputtered to life. "Laurie, Charlie. Where are you stationed?"

"Our target is at the Yellow Lion in Westborough," Laurie responded. "We're two doors beyond keeping an eye on them."

"On our way." The radio sputtered into silence.

"Should we give 'em a few minutes longer? Whattaya think?" Charlie asked. He was growing nervous that Brandon had not yet driven by with the woman. There was no other way for them to go — Route 9 at this point was a divided highway and there was no turnaround for another mile, but he could be hurting the woman at this moment, where they couldn't see them.

"I'm going to see what's keeping them," Laurie stated. Charlie put a hand on her arm and she pushed the door open.

"Sorry, Laurie, but I should do this. Close the door and sit tight. I'll be right back."

Laurie nodded reluctantly. She knew he was right. If Brandon was looking for a woman to kill at this moment, he might try to attack her and she wasn't entirely certain she could pull the trigger if it came to that.

Charlie returned in less that a minute and quietly slipped into his seat and closed the door.

"Well?"

Charlie's face reddened as he replied reluctantly, "They're kissing and such."

"Oh. Where?"

"They're in his car. Maybe you spooked him, I don't know, but I don't think he's looking to cut this one up."

Laurie shook her head in agreement. "Every one of his victims was walked from the bar to the murder scene. It's doubtful he would attack her in his car since that would leave evidence unless she passes out and he drives her somewhere, but that wouldn't be his usual MO."

"I agree. We'll wait for Jack and Paul to show up. They should be here any minute."

Relief arrived in a blue Ford Taurus a few minutes later. They pulled into the lot and turned around so they were facing out. Jack rolled down the window on the driver's side and Laurie rolled down hers.

"Anything?" he asked.

"No. He's with a woman right now. We were waiting for the two of you before we got our eyes over there. Charlie checked on them a few minutes ago, but they were just kissing." She turned to Charlie. You want to go stick your neck out and keep and eye on them?"

"Yep. I got a cap here and a cigarette. Make it look like I've got a reason to be there if they see me." He put on the cap, climbed out of the car, and disappeared around the corner toward the restaurant.

A few minutes later, he returned.

"What's up?" Laurie asked.

"He's just put her in her car and sent her on her way. She should be passing by. There she is." He pointed to a red BMW as it drove past.

"And there he goes," Laurie added. "Well, boys, I guess he's all yours. You need us to hang in for a few?"

"Naw. Go ahead back to the station. We'll call you with the status when he goes to ground."

"Thanks."

They gave the Taurus a five-minute lead before they pulled out onto Route 9.

"You sure you're alright?"

"Yeah, just a little stirred…but not shaken," she added.

Charlie chuckled. "Hardy har."

# Chapter 27

The hunter scouted the car from a distance. It was early morning and he knew the car would be there at least a few hours. Would anyone notice if he just slipped under it to do a little work—a little damage?

Unlikely. There wasn't a lot of travel through this lot and the car was parked away from the exit and the lane of travel. No. He didn't think anyone would see him. Besides, what he needed to do would only take a moment.

He would see to it that there was justice for people who betrayed him. Loyalty was not something to be given and then ripped away. There had to be consequences and he would see that there were.

Sunlight glinted off the freshly waxed blue paint and off the windshield, threatening to blind him. A beautiful car, Hunter thought. It's a shame it would have to be destroyed.

He drove over slowly, parked behind the car, and shut off the engine. Cautiously, he climbed out of his car, crouched down near his rear tire, then slowly lowered himself to the ground and slid beneath the betrayer's car to do his work.

Laurie and Charlie relieved Jack and Paul outside Brandon's condo.

"Did we miss anything?" Charlie asked.

"Not a thing. Lights were out ten minutes after he got home last night and we haven't seen him yet this morning. There've been a few other cars in and out, of course, but nothing unusual."

"He works out of his home office. It's normal for him to be home at this hour."

"Well, we're starved. It's been a long night. Gonna go get some lunch, then some sleep. See ya later tonight."

"Thanks guys," Laurie replied and waved them off.

"So you recuperated after that little shakeup last night?"

"Charlie, seeing him with another woman last night just helped me get it through to my stubborn heart that Brandon and I are no more. I'm just glad he didn't hurt that girl. Maybe he just didn't feel like getting all up in disguise."

"Maybe."

"Look," Laurie pointed. "Looks like we got here just in time."

Brandon stepped out of his condo in jeans and a golf shirt and strolled quickly to his Mercedes. He didn't waste time warming the engine. He quickly threw the car in gear and sped toward the lot's exit then headed north.

They followed him, keeping plenty of distance between them, and hiding behind the rise and fall of the hills on the road.

Brandon turned right at the end of the street and onto the ramp for Route 290 East. He goosed the Mercedes quickly up to seventy-five miles an hour and sped away.

Charlie put the pedal down on the Mustang and followed. He could see blue metal a quarter mile ahead—a comfortable distance.

When Route 290 ended a few miles out, Brandon picked up Route 495 South and eventually got onto the Massachusetts Turnpike headed east towards Boston.

Hank Brodeur climbed up into his tractor, lunch in hand, and threw the truck into gear. He didn't have time to sit and eat if he was going to keep his delivery schedule. He dropped the sixty-four ounce Coke into the giant-sized cup-holder and urged the heavy rig out through the rest area toward the highway.

Traffic was light on the Massachusetts Turnpike at this hour. Everyone was at work and hadn't yet decided to go for lunch yet.

Even when they did take lunch, they didn't usually travel the Pike. This highway was city to city with few exits in between. He wouldn't see an exit ramp now for another ten miles.

Hank carefully unwrapped his Big Mac, keeping a couple fingers attached to the wheel while he used his thumb and index to assist his free hand with the unwrapping.

The paper folded back, Hank cradled the mess of burger and toppings in his right hand while steering with his left. He didn't really like to eat while driving, but he definitely had to keep his schedule. He'd already been chewed out twice this week and that was on top of the two times last week. The new boss really was a bastard when it came to time. His last boss, Jimmy, never cared as long as the customers didn't complain and they never complained unless they were encouraged to complain. Ronny, the new boss, loved to encourage them.

So what did it all mean to Hank? Ulcers, that's what. Ulcers from the stress of getting chewed in front of the guys, and ulcers from trying to inhale fast food while driving seventy miles an hour. He put the burger down on the seat and took a ten-ounce sip of the monster-sized drink then picked up the burger and tore into it again.

He eased into the second lane as he approached the exit for Auburn to bypass traffic that had slowed to get off the highway, took the last of six bites of the burger, he could usually put it away in five, then drank another eight ounces before he dug into the bag for French fries. He pulled out several at a time, shoving them into his mouth, and adjusted the radio to a new station that was broadcasting out of Boston. The other one had gone to static. More fries and another drink as he passed Grafton.

The traffic got a little heavier as he traveled further east, but it was still pretty light. He stayed in the second lane, passing a car or truck here and there that poked along in the right lane.

Hank finished the fries and checked his watch. Twelve o'clock. He was going to be late again. He was due in Somerville for one o'clock. It would be close, but he would definitely be late. He eased the pedal a little closer to the floor and pushed the tractor up to seventy-five.

The tractor-trailer flew past Framingham as he finished the last of the sixty-four ounces. He was becoming aware of his bladder as he checked his watch again. Maybe he had time to stop in the Natick rest area to use the toilet; maybe he could make it all the way to Somerville. He was making good time. Hank decided to judge whether he needed to stop by how fast the pressure built but when the sign appeared to signal the last mile before the rest area, he still hadn't decided. If he had no trouble sliding into the right lane, he might just stop.

There was a line of traffic to his right. Hank switched on his directional but the cars stayed glued to his side, leaving no room for a lane change. He kept one eye on the mirror and one on the road in front of him. With the prospects of a rest looking bleak, the pressure in his bladder had suddenly increased.

Suddenly, from the corner of his eye, Hank saw a flash of blue and a loud crash thundered in his ears as his tractor bucked with impact. His bladder forgotten, Hank grabbed the wheel in a death grip. A heap of twisted metal screamed along the pavement in front of him. His foot went to the brake, just as the tractor slammed into the car again. Horrified, he watched the car flip over, still in his path. He worked the brakes and tried to steer away, but there was nowhere to go. He gritted his teeth as the tractor approached the car for a third strike, then realized with relief that all movement had stopped.


Charlie punched the gas up to eighty to keep pace with Brandon on the Massachusetts Turnpike.

The Mercedes cruised along steadily, keeping to the left lane though traffic was light.

"I hope he doesn't go anywhere too snazzy in Boston," Charlie commented. "I don't think either of us is really dressed for it." He pointed out his own faded kakis and wrinkled shirt and Laurie's jeans and white cotton blouse.

"Speak for yourself, old timer. I'm stylish."

"You're in jeans."

"But I've got a body to fill them out."

Charlie laughed out loud. "No dispute from me about that."

"Look out, Charlie!" Laurie shouted.

Up ahead, Brandon's car had suddenly swerved right, slamming into a gray sedan in the next lane.

Charlie eased up on the gas and applied the brake to avoid the accident. They didn't want to stop unless they had to. If Brandon saw them, they would not easily be able to re-establish a tail anytime soon without suspicion.

They slowed to forty and watched as the Mercedes stayed in contact a moment with the sedan, then cut sharply left into the guardrail, bounce off, and swerve again to the right. The gray sedan had already moved ahead and Brandon's car shot across the empty lane directly into the path of an oncoming tractor-trailer.

The driver had no time to respond. The fully loaded, fifty-foot trailer he was towing pushed the tractor forward into the Mercedes, caving in the passenger's side before flipping the car over onto its roof. The car skidded sideways down the highway, showering sparks back into the windshield of the truck and once again, despite the driver's best efforts to bring the truck to a stop, the tractor slammed into the driver's side of the Mercedes, giving the car an hourglass shape. The impact once again threw the car out ahead of the truck as the driver was finally able to slow down. The third and final contact with the Mercedes was only a tap as the scarred metal skidded to a stop.

Traffic across all four lanes stopped. The truck driver jumped out and ran to the car, crouching to peer inside for any signs of life.

Charlie threw a revolving light onto the roof and pulled the Mustang across the second and third lanes of the highway.

Laurie was out of the car before it had come to a full stop and pushed her way in front of the truck driver, falling down onto the pavement to look inside the car from the passenger's side. The driver's side of the car was up against the grill of the truck.

"You don't want to look in there, miss," the trucker cautioned, but Laurie didn't hear.

It took only one glance for her to know Brandon was gone. His seatbelt had held; the airbag was deployed, but Brandon's eyes stared ahead lifelessly. A pool of blood had already formed on the ceiling of the car and was growing rapidly. Laurie could see fragments of white skull in the red.

She shut her eyes instantly, but it was already too late. The sight shook her to the core and she clambered to her feet and turned away, losing the contents of her stomach onto the highway.

Brandon's life had ended so quickly he probably hadn't time for memories and highpoints, but the last three months flashed through Laurie's mind like a haunting movie—their first date; the rose he'd given her that she'd nearly inhaled because she was so nervous. She remembered their hours of lovemaking, the sweetness of every minute, their trip down the river and his romantic proposal.

Then suddenly, the vision of Abra Wilson's butchered body filled her mind and was all she could see.

"Are you alright, Laurie?" Charlie stood beside her, holding her hand. She could feel the softness of cushions beneath her and opened her eyes.

"Where am I?"

"Still at the scene. You fainted. Been out over an hour."

"Brandon?"

Charlie shook his head and Laurie looked away. Tears welled in her eyes.

"Don't cry for him, Laurie," he soothed. "He was a bad guy, remember? He doesn't deserve anyone's tears."

"I know, but I can't help but remember how good he was to me and how much fun we had. We were great together."

Charlie squeezed her hand. "I know. It'll take some time to heal, but you'll get through this. I know you—you're tough. You want to go to the hospital and get checked out?"

Laurie rolled her head side to side on the gurney. "There's nothing wrong with me, Charlie, except that I seem to have lost my ability to stand the sight of blood. Not very cop-like of me, is it?"

Charlie smiled tenderly. "I don't think anyone can handle the sight of blood from someone they love. And I know part of you still loved him."

"I guess I can't lie about that. Despite all the evidence, part of me was still holding on to hope that he didn't really do it. Is he still here or did they take him away?"

"They took him about ten minutes ago. You don't want to know how he looked."

Laurie paused, remembering the pool of blood forming on the ceiling of Brandon's car, and fought back a wave of emotion.

"Could you take me home?"

"You bet," Charlie nodded. He loosened the ties that held her safely on the gurney and helped her to the pavement.

"You all right over there?" one of the paramedics yelled over when he saw her stand up.

Charlie waved him off. "She's fine. I'm gonna take her home," he hollered back.

He helped Laurie into the Mustang and they headed east to the next exit, away from the twisted metal on the highway. They would see the wreckage from a different perspective if they turned around onto the Turnpike headed west back towards Worcester. Charlie decided Route 9, though populated with frequent traffic lights, would be a much better, less traumatic road to travel. He held Laurie's hand for support, but neither said a word as Charlie watched the road ahead and Laurie stared, unfocused, at the windshield throughout the drive to her house.

It was after six o'clock when they pulled into the empty driveway—the Camero was still parked in Worcester at the police station. Charlie offered to walk her inside the house, but Laurie waved him off.

"I'll be fine," she insisted. "I just need some time to myself."

"Do you need a ride to your car in the morning?"

"I'm not sure. I think I'll be fine, but could I call you if I do?"

"Yeah. No problem. Just get some rest, OK?"

Laurie nodded. "Thanks, Charlie."

Once inside, safe from the world, she poured herself a glass of coconut rum and tossed in a couple cubes of ice, curled up on the couch, and clicked on the television with the remote.

Emeril was cooking up something scrumptious as usual on the Food Network and the sight of gourmet pasta made Laurie suddenly very hungry. She realized she hadn't eaten anything since lunch and it was now past six o'clock.

She walked to the kitchen and opened the refrigerator, knowing it was nearly empty. She hated grocery shopping, so her choices for dinner were few. A half head of lettuce, a couple of tomatoes, some sliced turkey a few days old. She smelled it timidly—still good, but not what she wanted. She put it back into the deli drawer. There was a quart of milk on the top shelf. Laurie took it down and checked the expiry date. Just what she felt like—milk and cereal was always good for curling up in front of the television.

The phone rang and she set the milk on the counter and closed the refrigerator door. Jessie greeted her from the other end of the line when she lifted the receiver.

"What's new?" Jessie asked her friend.

Laurie wasn't sure she was ready to talk about Brandon's death.

"Nothing much," she lied. She nestled the phone upon her shoulder and took down the cereal box from the cupboard. She poured herself a bowl and covered the little rings of oats with a healthy serving of milk.

"I know that sound. You're pouring yourself cereal for dinner. So, out with it. What's wrong? Your not still upset about Brandon, are you? Do I have to come over and haul you out of the house?"

Laurie winced. She had forgotten that her friend knew her bad weather indicators better than she herself did. A lump started to form in her throat before she could respond and when she spoke, her words were broken.

"Brandon's dead," she managed a hoarse reply as emotion choked her voice.

"What? You're…. What happened?"

"Car accident this afternoon. Jessie, it was horrible! I think it was the worst experience of my life," Laurie sobbed into the phone.

"You went to the scene? You saw him?"

"Worse, Jess. I saw it happen—I saw the truck slam into him."

"How?"

"Charlie and I were tailing him. The Captain agreed to round-the-clock surveillance—Charlie and I were on the afternoon shift." Laurie put the milk away in the refrigerator and left the bowl of cereal on the counter while she headed for the living room, holding the phone to her ear.

"My God, Laurie. How are you holding up? Do you need me to come over? You need company?"

"I'm alright, I guess. I think I need time alone tonight. The strangest thing, though—I actually feel relieved. I think maybe because I know he won't be out there killing more women. That and I've got a day off tomorrow and I can finally relax for a change."

"Hmmm. She's eating cereal, but she sounds like she's got a sense of humor and she definitely knows the value of time off. Maybe you're not as bad off as I thought."

"I really miss him, Jess, but I'm glad the nightmare's over and I think I'm going to be all right. Just don't expect me to go out scouting for guys anytime soon."

"I promise, Sweetie, I won't. But don't think I'm dieting with you."

Laurie chuckled. "Would you ever take guys off the menu?"

"Never. But, if you don't need company tonight and you're going to bed early, do you maybe want to grab an early cup of coffee tomorrow?"

Laurie paused a moment. Sleeping in would be nice, but sometimes it was also nice to get up early just to relax.

"You know, that doesn't sound like a bad idea. You'll need to pick me up though. Charlie dropped me off. My car's still at the station."

"You got it. Six o'clock I'll be by. You better be up and ready."

"Yes ma'am."

# Chapter 28

The bright sunshine through the windows somehow made the world feel brand new as Laurie warmed her hands on the mug of coffee in front of her. Jessie had been talking non-stop since they sat down, but Laurie had not felt like tuning in. She voiced a few "Mmmhmmms" and a couple "Ahahs" at strategic places, but her mind was gloriously blank—free of all the worry that the last three months had brought her.

"And to think, I had a drink with that guy," Jessie was saying as she stirred cream into her coffee before discarding the spoon onto her napkin. She hadn't seen Laurie since meeting Gunnar's mother at the hospital, and she was thrilled to meet her for a cup of coffee at this early hour before everyone else hit the streets. Jessie slept little—she was up late every night, and awake at the first hint of light in the morning sky. She loved the sunrise, but the last shades of pink had already faded and the sky was now a brilliant blue as she looked out at the empty street.

"What's wrong?" Jessie asked when she realized Laurie's shocked expression.

Jessie's last comment had pulled Laurie out of her morning stupor.

"You drank with Brandon? When?" Laurie's forehead wrinkled with concern.

"Don't you remember? You called me when I was at the Plantation Club and he was there buying me drinks. I told you on the phone."

Laurie hesitated a moment before recollection illuminated her mind.

"I remember. It was just before we arrested him."

"Yes. Anyway, I guess he wasn't my type or he figured it best not to mess with me." Jessie sipped delicately at her coffee, checking the rim for lipstick before setting it back on the table. Suddenly, her face paled and she raised her eyes to Laurie's.

"Jessie, what's wrong? Did you get a sour creamer?"

"Oh my gosh, Laurie. I just remembered! That day, I left my drink on the bar to make a bathroom run. When I got back, Brandon acted kinda weird when I threw it out—like I'd insulted him personally."

Laurie was puzzled. "Why'd you throw out the drink?"

"Rick slipped me tonic water instead of soda water. You know how I love tonic."

"Yeah, like cats and water. You don't think Brandon really put something in your drink?" Laurie had cooled her coffee with a cube of ice from her glass, eager for it to be drinkable so she could pour the warmth into her belly. She took a long drink from her mug now while her ears were tuned for Jessie's next words.

"I don't know, Laurie. But I guess Rick was really lookin' out for my ass—more so than usual—that day. And here's to you, Rick. I owe ya one." She raised her mug in a toast to her favorite bartender.

"I can't imagine what I'd have done if anything happened to you. You're the only sister I have." A shiver raised Laurie's hair and shot down her back to her toes as she pictured Jessie in Abra Wilson's place.

"You know, you never did tell me how you figured out it was Brandon that was killing those women. So, what tipped you off?"

Laurie sipped more coffee before she began. "I met Brandon shortly after Abra Wilson was murdered here in Worcester. I drove up to Vermont to visit with my parents and I saw an article about a girl that was murdered in my hometown. The crime scene was so much like the Wilson girl's, that I was sure it was the same guy. I just knew it, ya know?"

Jessie nodded, but said nothing.

"Anyway, when the bodies started piling up, I started noticing that Brandon and I or even me alone had just been to the places where I was finding victims." Laurie's hand shook violently as she quickly took another sip of coffee. "The final clue was a checkered napkin he used to gag one of the girls. She died the night Brandon proposed. I remember that I was so tired or so drunk that I just passed out, dead asleep. It was easy for him to slip out that night without waking me. She was killed less than a mile from the motel where we slept."

"Ouch!" Jessie exclaimed. "Sounds to me like he wanted you to find out. Did he know you were on to his trail—or the killer's trail?"

"I don't see how he could know. Unless he mentioned something that was in the Worcester paper, we never talked about my work. I mean, it's not very romantic, now is it?"

"No. Guess not. I'm really glad you're thorough about your work. I can't imagine if Brandon had hurt you."

Laurie smiled a moment as a thought crossed her mind.

"What is it?" Jessie asked.

"I was just thinking. There really is such a thing as fate."

"What do you mean?"

"Well, if Jeff and I hadn't broken up when we did and Brandon hadn't walked into my life when he did, we might not have dated. If we hadn't dated, I never would have put together the evidence and conclusions I did and he might still be out there killing women."

Jessie smiled. "I guess timing *is* everything."

Laurie's cell phone rang and she set her coffee down to answer it.

"Laurie Sharpe."

Charlie Miller responded from the other end of the line.

"Charlie, I got the day off, remember? Oh and Jessie's going to give me a ride to pick up my car."

"Forget about the car. You're not gonna like what I've got to tell you," he said grimly through the wireless connection.

"Come on, Charlie. It can't be as bad as anything I've just been through can it?"

"Worse," Charlie responded after some hesitation.

What could be worse than watching your innocent partner drift into a coma or seeing a man you had loved crushed to death by a tractor-trailer?" She waited in fear of the details. Charlie delivered them.

"They found a woman dead on the shore of Lake Quinsigamond, behind White City. She was killed last night."

White City was on the Shrewsbury side of the lake that divided the two municipalities. In earlier years, it had been an amusement park that was kept flooded with light at night, earning it the name White City. Laurie was glad that the murder was out of her jurisdiction. She had seen enough murders for a while. But why would Charlie take the time to call her about it at this hour of the morning?

"That's Shrewsbury's turf," she reminded him.

"It is, but the MO is the same as that for Abra Wilson and the other women. Laurie, our murderer is still out there."

# Chapter 29

Spencer smiled as Laurie approached the naked woman lying on the bridge abutment. He was glad to see the pain he had caused her. He could almost taste the tears rolling down Laurie's cheeks as she examined the murder scene he had left for her. He knew her partner, Gunnar, was in a coma because of fear he himself had built up in her. Brandon had confided in him that he thought Gunnar was hot for Laurie. It was enough that he had one man between him and Karen, he didn't need another.

Getting rid of Brandon had been easy, but Spencer had never guessed that Laurie would get to witness his death. He didn't know she had cleared Gunnar and put Brandon under surveillance. And now that Brandon was gone, was forever out of the picture, Spencer wanted Laurie to know that the hunter was still alive, that all her hard work had not brought him down but had instead left an open gash in her soul like the one Karen had inflicted upon him all those years ago.

Fifteen years ago, Karen had cast Spencer aside. Brandon had known that Spencer was dating Karen and, although he hadn't known that he was really in love with her, he still shouldn't have taken her away from him. Brandon had deserved to die then, but

Spencer had let him live, had tried to forgive him. Karen was already dead and Spencer couldn't bring himself to kill his only friend, too.

When Brandon introduced him to Laurie, Spencer was in love with her instantly. He wondered if Brandon even noticed that she resembled Karen. That he never mentioned it angered Spence— Brandon had scarred their friendship over a girl whose face he couldn't even remember. He tried to think of some way that he could get close to Laurie; some way that he could get Brandon away from her.

He never expected that Laurie would come to suspect Brandon of the murders he himself was committing, but it was certainly an added benefit to his work. It had been Brandon's fault, really. Spencer had forgotten about the jeans and photographs he had left at Brandon's condo.

After he had pleasured himself with the woman in New Hampshire, Spencer had noticed Brandon's Mercedes parked at the motel. He knew that Brandon was there with Laurie; he had watched the two of them on the river earlier that day.

He parked next to the car, wanting to take a baseball bat to it, to destroy it. He couldn't bear the thought of Brandon with Karen again. He sat there beside the car until gray streaks of dawn appeared in the eastern sky. Then he grudgingly drove back to Worcester where Brandon had let him use his condo while he and Laurie were away.

The stores were closed; he couldn't get a new pair of pants, so he washed the ones he had, put them in the clothes dryer, and borrowed a pair of Brandon's while they were drying.

He was looking at the photographs of the girl he had killed just before he met Laurie when he heard Brandon arrive home. Between the mattresses was the quickest place he could think to hide them.

When Brandon walked in, he greeted Spence, then found that a friend had left a message needing him urgently for a couple days of damage control—someone had hacked into their company network and destroyed files.

Brandon booked the next flight and needed a quick ride to the airport since he had no time to spare if he was to catch the flight. Since Spencer himself was flying out a little later that day, Brandon had asked if he might just head out at that moment and drop Brandon at the airport.

In his rush to leave, Spencer had forgotten his jeans and photos at Brandon's condo where Laurie later found them.

Spencer had jumped on a plane back to Worcester when he heard of Brandon's arrest a couple days later. He couldn't tell the police why he knew Brandon was innocent, but when his friend told him how Gunnar had been injured, Spencer knew he could fix things for Brandon. He couldn't have his only friend rotting behind bars, though it gave him satisfaction that he was paying a price for taunting him with Karen again. He hid the remaining photos and his favorite knife at Gunnar's place where they could easily be found.

If Spencer had known the joy he would feel at Brandon's death, he would have done the deed fifteen years earlier.

Now what would he need to do to get close to Laurie, to get her to love him?

"Laurie, this isn't good," Charlie declared. "How could this guy still be out there? Who else could it possibly be?"

Laurie shook her head as she observed the death before her.

"Whoever he is, he's here watching. I can feel him." She looked suspiciously around the parking lot, but the lot was filled with cars. She looked across the street at other parking lots, across the bridge to the Worcester side of the lake.

"He could be anywhere," Charlie mumbled. Laurie nodded agreement.

"But I think I might know who it could be," she looked away from the bloody corpse and met Charlie's inquiring eyes.

"Come on, Laurie. You sure you want to make any more suppositions?"

"Not really, but think about this. Brandon had a friend who stayed with him a few times. Gunnar has met him, too. The three of them have hung out together several times."

"But you can't tell me this guy looks like Brandon? Because even disguised, I'd say that photo of the killer was Brandon."

"Actually, Charlie, that's exactly what I'm saying. Spencer looks as much like Brandon. Brandon had said they grew up together and used to like to hang out together because everyone thought they looked like brothers. Brandon always felt that Spencer really was his brother. Brandon was an only child, so understood how he would hang with someone who seemed so much like a brother. That's kinda why they liked to hang with Gunnar, too—he was like another one of the family. I always thought it was a little weird that three unrelated guys could be so much alike."

"It is a bit weird. So where is this friend?"

"Well, if he is the killer, he's somewhere near, watching us right now."

"Where? Do you see his car?"

"He always has a rental when he's in town, so I wouldn't know what he's driving."

"I don't know, Laurie. This is just too convenient," Charlie mused.

"I know. But wouldn't it make sense? I mean, Brandon has known Spencer since they were kids. They're really good friends and Spencer is in town quite a bit. I'm sure Brandon would have discussed the time he and I have spent together with his best friend, don't you?"

"I guess that could be how he would know where your parents live, where you've been with Brandon."

"And he used to stay at Brandon's place when he was in town. In fact, I remember he used the condo while Brandon and I were up in New Hampshire." Laurie was getting excited as the puzzle pieces began to fit together.

"That would give him opportunity to leave his jeans in the dryer and the photos under the mattress," Charlie added.

Laurie nodded.

"Do you think Spencer was trying to frame him?"

"I don't know," Laurie replied. "I guess maybe if Spencer told him he was going to propose on our trip, maybe Spencer got jealous and decided to end it."

"But why would he be jealous?"

"Think about it. The detective in Susanville said Karen Callahan used to date several guys at a time. Maybe she was playing both Brandon and Spencer at the same time and Spencer found out about it."

"Could be," Charlie agreed. "But it's still a stretch."

"Maybe, but I think we should look into it."

"Where does this guy live? Full-time, I mean?"

"He lives in the San Francisco area; I'm not sure where. But if he did this," she motioned toward the dead girl as the medical examiner placed her body into a black bag and zipped it shut, "he's still around here somewhere. Brandon did say that he usually stays at the Marriott if he's not staying with Brandon and the job he's working on is in Worcester. But I don't know where he would stay if his job is out of town."

"Let's talk to Craig, then. Get some feelers out to find this guy. You OK?" Charlie asked as he saw a flash of sorrow cross Laurie's face.

Laurie nodded. "Let's get on this."

"You have got to be kidding, Sharpe!" Captain Craig bellowed as Charlie and Laurie finished sharing Laurie's suspicions.

"Come on, Captain," Charlie reasoned, "think about it. This makes sense. Sure this case has wrongly focused on innocent men, but this would make sense of why Hincks and Doyle would have evidence in their homes. Especially Doyle since there was no real reason to suspect him before evidence was found at his condo."

Laurie stayed silent while Charlie sold the theory to Captain Craig. She knew anything she might say would only spark anger from him. She watched as Craig absorbed the details as Charlie rolled them out.

"God help you Sharpe if you're wrong this time. OK, Charlie. If this all makes sense to you, get out on the horn and issue a BOLO for this guy anywhere you think he might be around here. And keep Sharpe here on a tight leash. I'm holding you equally responsible if anything happens to another innocent man."

"Yes, Sir," Charlie replied. He turned on his heel and pulled Laurie with him as he left the room.

"You sure you're on board with this, Charlie?" Laurie didn't like the idea that Charlie could suffer a reprimand for her theories and suspicions. She'd been so wrong about this case. Was she really on the right track now?

Charlie issued the lookout for Spencer Kinney to all towns from Springfield to Boston. Meanwhile, Laurie got on the phone to Spencer's employer, Ernst & Young, one of the big five accounting firms in the U.S., to get information on where he might be working. After being directed to several different offices around the country,

Laurie was finally on the line with a woman who worked directly with Spencer.

"Mister Kinney is on a two-week vacation," she informed a frustrated Laurie. Two weeks would give him time to kill a lot of women.

"Did he say anything about where he might be staying? Do you have a number where he can be reached? A cell phone?"

"He didn't say, but I do have his cell number here. It's 415-555-8928. I think he's out there in Massachusetts, if that helps. What do the police want with him?"

"We think he may have some information that could help us in an investigation that's ongoing out here."

"Oh." She paused for a long moment and Laurie could almost hear her thoughts. "He's not in any trouble, is he?" she finally asked.

"We're just looking to ask him a few questions," she feinted. "I can't really discuss the case at this time, but I do appreciate your help very much. Could I ask you to call me if you do hear from him or find out more about where he might be?"

"Certainly," The woman at the other end of the line promised. Laurie gave out her cell number and ended the call.

"Well, here goes nothing," she said to Charlie as he stood over her shoulder. She took a deep breath and dialed Spencer's cell number. After several rings, the line finally clicked open at the other end.

"Hello?"

"Spence? It's Laurie Sharpe."

"Laurie! How are you?" He hesitated a moment. "I didn't realize you had my number."

"I got it from Brandon," she lied.

"Well, it's good to hear from you," he replied.

"I'm afraid I'm calling with bad news, though." Her tone softened. "Did you hear what happened yesterday?"

"Yeah, I heard. I'm in town and it's been all over the local news. Is that how you found out?"

"I was there at the scene yesterday." There was silence for a moment. "Spence?" she checked to see he was still on the line.

"You mean after the crash?" he finally asked.

Laurie hesitated. Would he have followed Brandon and seen the crash? Was it safe to conceal that she and Charlie had been following him? She took the chance. "Yes. I got a call from a friend who was first on the scene. He knew about Brandon and me, had met Brandon, in fact. He called me as soon as he identified him. He also called Charlie and insisted that he go with me to the scene."

"You knew yesterday?" He suddenly sounded angry." If you knew yesterday, how is it you're just telling me now when you had my cell number all this time? Why didn't you call me when it happened? Why did I have to hear about it on the news?"

Spencer's genuine tone made Laurie suddenly uncertain about her suspicions of him. Did he really just hear this horrible news on television?

"I'm really sorry," she said, her throat growing tight. "There was a lot going on yesterday regarding his death. And I didn't always have your cell number, I actually got it from Brandon's cell phone so I could call you, but it's been so crazy here since it happened that I couldn't really get a call out to you until now." Brandon's cell phone had been destroyed beyond use in the crash. She could never retrieve any phone numbers from it.

"Brandon was practically my brother, you know." Some of Spencer's anger seemed to subside as he continued. "Before you two started dating, I was the only family he'd had since his parents died." He paused a moment. "Actually, he was really my only family, too. I don't see much of my parents since they divorced."

"I know. Brandon told me. I'm sorry for you that he's gone." Laurie fought off emotions that crept in on her and made her voice crackle. "You know, despite everything, I miss him."

Spencer's tone softened. "I know you probably do. How are you holding up?"

She struggled hard to keep from crying and to keep her voice smooth and even. "Not too well," she sighed. She was silent a few moments as she pondered her next statements.

"Everything alright?" Spencer asked.

"It's just that, well, we found new evidence to suggest we were wrong about Brandon's innocence." Laurie wasn't sure how much she should say to him, but she needed a plan to get him into the station as quickly as possible. There was no need to identify Brandon's body, so that would not help them. But requesting his help to clear Brandon might bring him in.

"What do you mean new evidence. I thought you found he was innocent. So, now you're saying he was guilty?" Spencer demanded. "That's ridiculous! What did you find?"

"His high school girlfriend was murdered in the same manner as Abra Wilson," she replied.

"What! That's crazy! I vaguely remember a girl was killed in high school. Was that his girlfriend? I didn't even know. That's tapped!" He sounded stunned.

We're a long way from being sure he's guilty," she said. "In fact, I was hoping you might have information to help prove he was innocent once and for all. I just don't believe that he did all those things, you know.

"Why are you even defending him now? You arrested him and dumped him."

Laurie was close to tears now. "I-I guess part of me still loves him," she stammered. Actually, she still loved him with all her heart and she knew it. Healing would take a long time and she knew she would never find another man like Brandon. He was everything she had ever hoped for and now he was gone forever. She covered the phone as she sniffled back the tears.

"Sorry to hear that. That makes it tough on you," Spencer continued. "But why do you think he's innocent?"

Laurie was silent as she pondered her answer. Finally, she replied, "We found another body this morning."

"What! Another body? Where?" Spencer sounded shocked.

"Lake Quinsigamond. I mean, it's not necessarily the same killer, but the MO certainly fits. Though with all the press that Abra Wilson's murder has received, it could just as easily be a copycat. I really want to make sure that this guy isn't still out there.

"But you found photos in Brandon's condo and now this murder of his girlfriend. If he's not guilty, who do you think it is?"

"It's weird, but I think it's someone with an axe to grind on me.

"Now you're being paranoid," he challenged.

"Not really. He killed a girl on my turf and framed the two men I care most about. What else can I think? That's just too many coincidences for me."

"That is a lot of coincidence, but maybe there's another explanation. Maybe it's someone with an axe to grind with Brandon or with Gunnar," Spencer mused.

"Maybe, but Brandon and Gunnar didn't know each other when Abra Wilson was killed. They became friends because of me."

"True," he agreed.

"I have some items of Brandon's, including his computer that I want you to look at and I also have a few questions I want to ask you about Brandon. Since you're in the area, I was wondering if you would be able to come take a look and see if there's anything that might clear him. Could you make it in here tomorrow morning? I'd really appreciate any help you can give me with this."

Spencer hesitated a moment, then asked softly. "Laurie, why did you lie and tell me you got my number from Brandon."

"Huh?" she asked.

"When I first answered the phone, you said Brandon gave you my number."

Charlie watched her intently as Laurie's face blanched. She quickly composed herself and replied, "I did get it from Brandon; I got it from his phone. It just seemed awkward to say it that way, especially when I hadn't shared the news about him yet. Are you OK, Spence?" Shit! Did he know she suspected him?

He hesitated. "Yeah. I guess I'm still just shaken about Brandon's death. I can't believe he's gone."

"I know. I just doesn't seem real, does it?" she asked, silently breathing a sigh of relief that he had accepted her explanation.

"I guess I'll see you tomorrow. Ten o'clock alright?" he asked.

"Ten is good, "she agreed. "I'll see you tomorrow." She hung up the phone.

"Sounds like you've got a date," Charlie grinned. "Well done. I thought you were going to lose it there for a moment."

"I thought he had me. I thought he knew." She looked up at him. "I know he was there watching us at the crime scene this morning."

Charlie placed a tender hand upon her shoulder. "He may well have been watching you this morning. But that doesn't mean he knows you suspect him. Don't worry. We'll nail his ass tomorrow. Then you'll feel much better about all of this."

"I guess."

Charlie looked at his watch. "Look, it's getting late. We haven't had much sleep in the last few days. The ball is rolling and we don't have any other leads to chase on this case today. Let's relay your conversation with Spencer to Craig, then let's go catch some sleep."

"I suppose you're right. Six o'clock tomorrow morning?"

"I'll be around," he replied.

# Chapter 30

All lights were off on Laurie's street when she pulled up in front of her little Cape. Most of her neighbors were working folks and those who weren't were elderly. Either way, it was lights out all around by ten o'clock. It was now eleven.

Laurie climbed out of the Camero and shuffled her way to the door. It took her a few moments to fit her key into the lock and she pushed the door open and stumbled inside. She closed the door and felt something heavy crash down on the back of her head.

When she awoke, she found herself lying on her bed, her hands and feet bound to the head and footboards. Her clothing was gone except for her undergarments. She was instantly awake, her head aching violently. A twinge of panic ran through her, but she doused it instantly when she saw her captor.

"So how do you feel? Head hurt a bit?" Spencer stood over her, glowering.

"What do you want?" she asked calmly while her insides twisted into knots. If she lost her cool, Laurie knew it was over for her.

"A second chance, of course."

"I know you got my message this morning, Laurie. I watched you. I wanted you to know it was me, and you did. You didn't fool me on the phone yesterday, acting all nice and cool. Tell me, what did it feel like to have the one you love ripped away from you?"

"Are you gloating aver his death? I thought you and Brandon were friends. Brothers, even."

"Brothers, friends: they're just words. Friends don't steal their friends' girlfriends." He slowly traced a finger up Laurie's midline, from her pelvic to her breast bone. Laurie fought her revulsion. "Brandon did that to me once, took my girlfriend. Did you know?"

"Karen Callahan?" she replied coldly.

"Ah hah," he smiled. "You've done your homework. I toyed with Brandon for a while after that, but when he met you and didn't even mention how much you look like Karen…well that was just adding insult to injury. He stole the girl I loved and he couldn't even remember her face. He didn't deserve to live. I was done playing with him."

Laurie was incredulous as she realized his implication. "Are you telling me you're responsible for his death?"

Silence.

"What did you do?" she demanded.

Spencer glared at her, then smiled triumphantly. "Just a little cutting on his tie rods."

"What!" Laurie struggled against her bonds.

"I didn't actually think it would let go on the highway and kill him. Not that I'm disappointed with the outcome. I'm quite happy to be rid of that traitorous jackass. But I really just thought he'd get banged up a little in a minor fender bender. Maybe fuck up that pretty face of his. But it's just as good he's gone now. Now I can get my girl back." He smiled at Laurie.

Laurie's terror was mounting as she listened to his insanity. "Spencer, I'm not Karen. That was a long time ago for Brandon. It's understandable that he wouldn't remember her face. He's not the one who imprinted her face in his mind by killing her. How many other girls' faces are etched there?"

"Guess you haven't done all your homework. Not to worry. It's nothing that you really need to know and pretty soon you won't care either," he replied cheerfully.

"Spence, I'm not Karen. Karen is dead, remember? You killed her years ago."

He chuckled. "Don't you know it was all about Karen's face? I didn't care about the person she was. It was just her face. Her eyes; her lips all drew me to her. You have her same eyes, her lips, her whole face really. I just want a second chance, Karen."

"Spencer, I'm not Karen. I'm Laurie."

Spencer reached for her face, touching her lips a moment and letting his hand slide down her chin and neck.

"You're not afraid of me, are you?" I was a stated observation. He raised a long curving blade that he'd been concealing behind him in his other hand.

Laurie shook her head. She recognized the knife as one of her own from the kitchen. At least he didn't plan this in his usual way. Maybe the outcome would be different. She struggled to maintain her composure as she pulled her eyes from the blade and raised them again to meet Spencer's stare.

"Good. Because I don't want to hurt you. I just want a second chance now that Brandon's not around to interfere."

A knock on the door jarred them both. Laurie looked around and noticed light cutting through the curtains that were drawn across the windows. It was morning. She opened her mouth to scream, but Spencer's hand clamped down hard over her mouth. She struggled.

"Stop it!" he hissed. "Who is that at six o'clock in the morning? Did you replace Brandon already, you slut?"

Laurie ground her teeth into the tender place at the base of his fingers and Spencer jerked his hand back in response.

"Charlie, help!" she screamed. Spencer backhanded her hard across the face. But despite the punishment, Laurie's scream was rewarded, too, as she heard the front door kicked in. Spencer ran toward the noise, knife held high, ready to strike. As he disappeared out the bedroom door, Laurie heard a gunshot. Spencer staggered backward through the door, holding his abdomen.

"Charlie! In here!" she called.

Spencer looked over at her, pain contorting his face, and staggered to her side. He placed the sharp edge of the blade against her throat and focused his eyes on the bedroom door.

"I'll kill her if you don't throw me the gun."

"You won't kill her. You love her. That's why you're here," Charlie replied calmly.

"Yes, I love her. If I die, I'm taking her with me so we'll be together."

"You know that's not how it works, Spencer." Charlie retorted. "You kill her and she's gone. That's it. There's no happily ever after beyond this. And if there is a heaven and a hell, you're not both going to the same place.

"Shut up!" Spencer bellowed. "Throw me your gun or I'll kill her, I swear I will."

"Laurie, you OK?" Charlie asked as he poked his head around the edge of the bedroom door.

"I'm fine, Charlie. Just shoot him. Don't worry about me. We've got to get him off the street. That's all I care about."

"I'm going to enjoy killing you, slut," he grumbled at her. He started to pull the knife slowly across her throat while he glared at Charlie. A thin trail of red appeared behind the tip of the knife. Laurie winced.

"Shoot him, Charlie!"

"OK. Stop it! Here you are." He tossed his gun into the room. "Just let her go."

"Charlie, No!" Laurie pleaded.

Spencer smiled dryly and moved away from Laurie a bit as he hedged his way toward the gun. "Come inside the room where I can see you," he demanded.

Charlie stepped partway into the room. "You sure you're OK?" he asked Laurie.

"Yeah."

"Shut up!" Spencer waived the knife in the air as he moved toward the gun on the floor.

"Spence," Charlie said.

"What!"

"Didn't you know cops generally carry a backup?" He lifted a second gun and pointed it at Spencer's head.

Spencer looked at the gun, at Laurie, at the gun on the floor. He dove toward Laurie, the knife raised overhead. The blast caught him in the back of the head and he fell dead onto Laurie. She rolled her head to the side to avoid the blade as it came down toward her.

Charlie was at her side in an instant. He grabbed the blade and cut Laurie's bonds. Laurie pushed Spencer's lifeless body off of her, onto the floor.

Charlie helped her to her feet and pulled a blanket from the bed to wrap around her. "Thank God you're in one piece," he smiled.

"Just a little nicked," she smiled back, pressing her fingers against the wound on her neck.

"Had me worried for a minute when I saw the blood," he replied.

"No, I'm fine. It's a good thing we decided to start from my house today." She smiled with relief as the tension melted from her. "Whose idea was that anyway?"

"Think it was mine." Charlie smiled back. "Remember? You argued; I won."

# Chapter 31

Mrs. Hincks smiled as Laurie walked into the hospital room. She stood from her seat beside the bed and wrapped her arms around Laurie. "Thank you for clearing his name."

Laurie squeezed back, then pulled away and met her eye. "Thank you for showing me the truth."

Mrs. Hincks smiled, nodded toward Gunnar, and left the room.

"So, I hear you're feeling better."

Gunnar smiled weakly; his purple and swollen lips barely turned upward. "I hear you got the guy."

Laurie smiled. "Yeah."

"Shame it had to be Spencer. I thought he was a friend."

"Yeah. He took us all by surprise."

"Close call for you. Remind me to thank Charlie for keeping you around for me to harass.

She chuckled, "I thought I was done for sure. I completely forgot Charlie was even coming to the house. I was so relieved when I heard him knock on the door. But of course he's not letting me forget that he's now seen me in my underwear."

"Of course he wouldn't. And I'm sure he's broadcast a detailed description of what you were wearing to everyone in the station."

"At least it was lacy and somewhat respectable, otherwise I'd have had to bribe him to say that it was." Sadness crept into her voice and she laughed to hide it, but not before Gunnar recognized it.

"Hey, I also heard about Brandon. I'm really sorry." His tone turned solemn.

Laurie averted her eyes in a moment of reflection. So much had happened in only a few months. She'd found and lost the love of her life, and almost lost the only man she'd ever trusted. But thankfully he was now safe and back in her life. Could that trust and friendship become something more? Was all that had happened a means to push her closer to her friend and partner? He'd given her so much to think about, though she knew she wouldn't be thinking clearly anytime soon.

"You OK?" he asked as he studied her face.

"Now that you're awake, I am." She reached out to squeeze his hand and the warmth of his touch surprised her like sunshine from behind a cloud. "Maybe sometime I can stop thinking of you like a brother, huh?"

He smiled. "Maybe."

3/P

9 781604 741193